AFRICA

A Novel

By

WF Waldrip

WF Waldrip

AFRICA

WF Waldrip, attorney, adventurer, and big-game hunter is the author of six previous novels, all available at your local bookseller or online: *The Man With Two Last Names, The Guards Themselves, Honor Among Thieves, Shadowland, Gaslight* and *The Float.*

Waldrip eschews prescribed literary conventions, his wide-ranging novels reflecting his varied life experiences. His favorite novelist is Henry James.

BOOKS BY WF WALDRIP

Africa

Gaslight

Shadowland

The Man with Two Last Names

The Float

Honor Among Thieves

The Guards Themselves

Africa

WF Waldrip

FIRST PHARAOH Paperback EDITION

July 2023

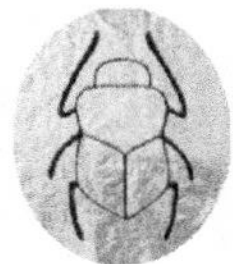

Africa is a work of fiction. Names, characters, places, and incidents are either the product of the author's imagination or are used fictitiously. Any resemblance to actual persons, living or dead, events, or locales is entirely coincidental.

The Cataloging-in-Publication Data is on file at Library of Congress.

ISBN 978-1-7374774-0-2

Cover design by Maurice Azurdia

For Attorney Douglas Meiklejohn, a good man and an inspiration

But at my back I always hear
Time's winged chariot hurrying near.
And yonder all before us lie
Deserts of vast eternity.

Andrew Marvel
Upon Appleton House,
to my Lord Fairfax

There is no need to tell lies about hunting, for so many curious things happen within the knowledge of a man whose business is to hunt; but this is by the way.

H. Rider Haggard
King Solomon's Mines

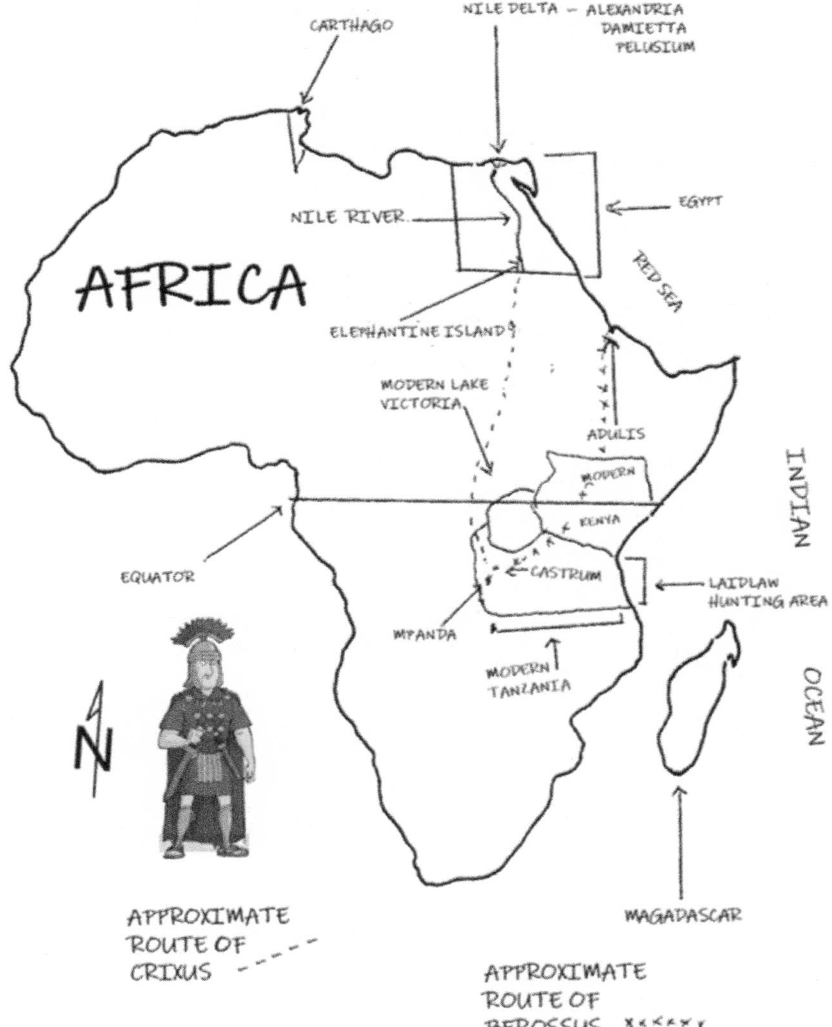
NILE DELTA – ALEXANDRIA
DAMIETTA
PELUSIUM
CARTHAGO
NILE RIVER
EGYPT
RED SEA
AFRICA
ELEPHANTINE ISLAND
MODERN LAKE VICTORIA
ADULIS
MODERN
KENYA
INDIAN
EQUATOR
CASTRUM
LAIDLAW HUNTING AREA
MPANDA
MODERN TANZANIA
OCEAN
N
APPROXIMATE ROUTE OF CRIXUS
MAGADASCAR
APPROXIMATE ROUTE OF BEROSSUS

ONE

"I DIDN'T WANT TO come, you know."

They were sitting in fading light on the right bank of the Rufiji River. Less than 75 yards away, a pod of hippos noisily splashed, grunted, and quarreled in the main channel.

Alexander Laidlaw was nursing his second Scotch, neat, staring contemplatively into the guttering flames. Somewhere in the darkness beyond the palisade of their boma a lone lion moaned lugubriously. The faraway shriek of a hyena broke Laidlaw's reverie.

"I'm sorry? What?" He looked at her, blankly, across the dying fire pit. He'd forgotten she was even there.

"I didn't want to come," she repeated. "I thought you should know."

Laidlaw drained his Scotch and leaned slightly forward to place the empty glass on the earth next to his chair. One of the camp staff would police the area after everyone had gone to bed, restoring everything to immaculate order. Along with several other Masai boys, he would be up all night, gathering firewood, hand-washing and ironing clothing and linens, tidying up the boma, washing dishes, preparing tomorrow's meals. Just before dawn, he would stand smartly outside each tent and softly announce that breakfast was served. Rather than conventional tents, the lodgings utilized by Laidlaw's hunting clients resembled compact, one-room cabins with canvas walls and roof, wooden floors, two cots, a toilet, and showers with hot water. A gasoline generator provided electricity. Even at that early hour he would be formally attired, wearing white gloves and holding a stainless-steel tray. As each hunter pushed aside the flap and groggily emerged into the semi-darkness, he would wish them a good morning as he handed them a glass of fresh orange juice.

"No, I was unaware, Mrs. Pyper." It was not the first time a wife had confided to him her reluctance to accompany her husband on his dream safari. Now, as every time before, he found the subject awkward.

"I think George must've read every Capstick book at least a dozen times," she continued, unbidden. "Even after all the rumors that Capstick probably made most of the stuff up, George didn't care. He used to read sections of them aloud to me, even. I tried to act interested at first, but…" her voice trailed off.

Though sunset had occurred only a half-hour previously, darkness descends quickly in East Africa. The area immediately beyond the fading glow of their dwindling fire was already shrouded in blackness.

"Well, my father always maintained that facts have no business getting in the way of a good story," Laidlaw observed.

"And you believed him?

"Of course, I believed him. He was my father." Somewhere in the darkness the lion softly chuffed. "I hope you don't find the experience to be completely unrewarding, Mrs. Pyper," he continued. "The staff and I have enjoyed having you in camp and I have no doubt that your husband is glad you're here. There's a lot more to safari than just hunting." His standard rejoinder whenever an unhappy tagalong complained about getting roped into safari. "I daresay you have never seen such a profusion of wildlife, for example. Africa is truly a paradise for animal lovers."

Although unable to clearly see her face in the growing murk, he heard her quietly cluck her tongue.

"You're an animal lover, Mr. Laidlaw? Really? I'd be interested to learn how you're able to reconcile your purported love for animals with your occupation."

Although couched as a question, it was a veiled accusation.

"Sportsmen like your husband pay significant amounts of money for the opportunity to hunt African big game and I have the privilege of guiding them, Mrs.

Pyper. Those animals possess concrete, quantifiable economic value. They are worth far more alive than dead, which they would otherwise be in the absence sportsmen like Mr. Pyper: unlamented casualties to man's ineluctable march toward progress. Think of the passenger pigeon and the American bison. The first was obliterated through indiscriminate slaughter, the latter nearly so."

"So, it's preferable just to let a bunch of rich white men randomly shoot them?" she sardonically responded.

"Without regulated hunting, most of Africa's wildlife would have been swept from the entire continent centuries ago, the victims of wholesale butchery. 'Rich white men' aren't to blame for the elimination of entire species, Mrs. Pyper. On the contrary, they're responsible for preserving them. The reality is that, 'if it pays, it stays'. Without the millions of dollars generated through hunting, land that currently supports wildlife populations will simply be plowed under and converted to other uses. Their habitat destroyed, the animals living there won't be far behind. In the context of the American bison, a biologist, Dr. Harold Danz, said that, 'to continue the bison's continuance as a species, the best thing we can do as custodians of this resource is to eat the surplus products.' It's no different with Africa's game animals. I didn't make the rules." Laidlaw paused to let his words sink in. He'd made the same speech more times than he could remember, for all the good it did.

"What about Cecil?" she countered.

"'Cecil' who?"

"Cecil. You know...the lion."

"What about him?"

"He was shot illegally."

Laidlaw sighed. "Nonsense. An American dentist paid a pile of money to legally hunt a lion in Zimbabwe with a bow and arrow. The lion he bagged happened to be Cecil...the guy didn't specifically target him and, at the time, didn't know 'Cecil the Lion' from the backside of the moon. The Zimbabwean authorities confirmed that the guy's hunting permits were in order, invited him to return to their country in the future, and wished him Godspeed. The whole 'Cecil' brouhaha was nothing but a propaganda campaign orchestrated by the hysterical anti-hunting Western media. In Africa, Cecil's death was a gigantic non-event. Know what Zimbabwe's Information Minister said when Western reporters fell all over themselves to ask about poor Cecil, hoping for a heart-wrenching sound-bite?"

"I couldn't begin to guess."

"'What lion'? I'm not joking, that was his literal response. Hoping for better luck with South Africa's president at the time, Jacob Zuma, they also asked him about it. His assessment was equally disappointing, at least from the reporters' perspective. Zuma said that, as far as he knew, a hunter just saw a lion, killed it, and the lion turned out to be Cecil. He described the whole thing as 'just an incident'. It was the Western media that whipped the whole thing up into something vile and illegal, which it wasn't, and intentionally destroyed that hunter's livelihood and reputation in the process. In the end, it was much ado about nothing."

"I had no idea," she confessed.

"That was the whole idea. Like my old man said, facts have no business getting in the way of a good story."

He paused, listening again for the hyena. The fire had become reduced to a collapsing heap of glimmering embers. The familiar, comforting scent of charred Makobokobo wood lingered in the air. He was getting sleepy. A cinder popped from the ashes and landed in the soil near Laidlaw's feet, where it glowed momentarily before winking out.

"Do you know why there are no bears in Africa, Mrs. Pyper?" he softly asked. "The Atlas Mountains used to teem with them. Barbary lions, too."

"I didn't know there weren't any," she yawned. "Hunters?"

"Roman hunters. There are no longer any bears in Africa because the ancient Romans slaughtered 'em all. That's also why elephants, leopards, hippos, crocodiles, and lions no longer exist in the Maghrib."

"What's that?"

"The Maghrib? Basically, all of North Africa. The Romans created an entire system for rounding up millions of animals, large and small, and shipping 'em across the Mediterranean from what are now Algeria, Tunisia, Morocco, Egypt, and Libya," Laidlaw said. "In fact, one of best-preserved Roman cities on earth, Leptis Magna, is located in Libya. The capture and transportation of wild animals was a huge part of the Roman economy and required tens of thousands of people. Most of the animals came from the African interior and were transported to the various ports of the Maghrib for shipment to Rome and more distant parts of the Empire. It was a huge undertaking but the Romans did it for centuries."

Her interest was piqued. "What did the Romans want with all those animals?"

"The *venationes.*

"Speak English, please," she chuckled.

"A hunt. What the Romans called their mass destruction of animals in the arena."

She frowned. "I don't understand."

"Because of movies and TV, the first things that usually come to mind when we think of, say, the Roman Coliseum are gladiators...gladiators and burning Christians, anyway. But no Christians were ever executed in the Coliseum and wild animal *venationes* were at least as popular as gladiator exhibitions. The Romans would pit various animals against one another: bears against bulls, wolves against lions, elephants against rhinos. When they got bored with that, they'd use animals to execute condemned prisoners; they called it *"damnatio ad bestias."* There was even a type of gladiator who specialized in killing wild animals in arena."

"Guess there just weren't enough rich white men around to protect 'em, huh?" she scoffed.

Laidlaw ignored the jibe. "No, the Romans finally just ran out of animals." He paused. "Ever read Barbara Tuchman's history of 14th century France, *A Distant Mirror*?

"'Fraid not. Are you literary man, Mr. Laidlaw?"

"If, by 'literary' you mean I can read, then, yes, I guess I'm 'literary'," he laughed.

"So, tell me about that book."

"Tuchman titled it that because, as she says in her Forward, people in those days may as well have been from a completely different planet because the physical, moral, and psychological circumstances they lived under were vastly different from our own. Their motivations, even their thought processes, are elusive and puzzling to us. The philosopher Ludwig Wittgenstein once said that, even if lions could speak, we wouldn't understand them. I think the same could be said of the 14th Century French, the Romans, or any past civilization. They will always seem alien because, irrespective of how similar to us they appear, they viewed the world from an entirely different perspective. Xerxes, the 'Great King' of Persia, for example, ordered that the waters of the Hellespont be flogged because a storm there prevented him from invading Greece. Although we rightfully dismiss flogging the ocean as childish, it evidently seemed the most logical thing in the world to Xerxes. Our brains obviously work differently from those who lived long ago."

"I fear such abstruse musings are far beyond me," she said. "Especially after three gin-and-tonics." She changed the subject. "You're an American, Mr. Laidlaw? Was your father also a hunter?"

"Yes, an American. My father was a doctor."

"A doctor? How did you end up here?"

"Africa?"

She nodded in the darkness.

"My old man got an appointment teaching at the national university. When his contract ended he and my mom returned to the States. I stayed...it seemed like the thing to do at the time."

"And now?"

He shrugged.

"Brothers and sisters?"

"Nope. I was an only child."

"Your parents still living?"

"Mom is, but she's ailing. Dad died a while back."

"You miss her?"

"Who doesn't miss their mom?" he softly countered.

"What is your first name, if I may ask?"

"Alex."

"May I call you that?"

"Of course."

She smiled in the darkness. "Thank you, Alex."

They sat in silence for a few minutes, listening to the restive hippos brawl.

"Do you have a family here in Africa?"

"'A man with wife and children leaves hostages to fortune.' That's what Bacon said, anyway."

"Again, you surprise me, Mr. Laidlaw," she smiled. "Quoting Francis Bacon in the wilds of Africa."

"There's a lot of dead time between safaris," he responded without elaboration.

"So, what prompted you to become a professional hunter?"

He shrugged in the darkness. "It seemed like the thing to do at the time."

"And now?"

Laidlaw stood and grasped the heavy bolt-action rifle that leaned against an adjacent chair. It was suicidal to walk, unarmed, anywhere in the bush. Although only wood and steel, his rifle breathed more life than all of his collective clients over his nearly three decades of guiding them.

"And now I think I will retire for the evening. Good night, Mrs. Pyper. I hope you sleep well. Your husband will be hunting Nyasa Wildebeest tomorrow. One of the boys will be along in a moment to see you to your tent. Please don't wander about during the night, unescorted, as those guys," he nodded toward the river, "are getting ready to head out for their grazing area about a half-mile from here. They'll amble through the boma en route and you don't want to get between a two-ton hippo and dinner. I'll see you at breakfast."

With that, he melted into the night, accompanied by the mocking whoop of the distant hyena.

In Primis Anno Regnantibus Imperator Caesar Titus Vespasianus (78 CE)

"BY THE TWIN GODS, I wish the old man hadn't shat himself to death," Crixus remarked. "Vespasian was no genius, but he was better than any of the fools who preceded him. I doubt whether his son will be as good...Rome just got lucky with the old man."

"Except for the deified Augustus," Junius corrected him, a little too quickly, as he coiled a rope.

"The divine Titus is said to be a fearsome soldier...just ask the Jews," Neocles interjected. He grinned. "Well, you could ask if there are any left alive to ask. The bastards forced four legions to besiege their capital for two entire years before they finally capitulated. By that time, most of the Jews inside its walls had already starved to death. It is said the city was polluted with over a million bloated corpses by the time the legions breached its walls! Even so, Titus leveled what remained of Jerusalem, crucified some Jews that were still alive, sent some to the arena, and sold the remainder into slavery. By the time he was finished, Jewish blood rose to the bellies of the legion's horses. It is beyond dispute that the war between the Romans and the Jews was the greatest of our time, perhaps greater than any war in history," he proudly concluded.

"Those ungrateful cockroaches got what they deserved," opined Junius. "Rome should consider itself fortunate that Vespasian chose as his heir a man possessing such *virtus*, rather than his other halfwit son, Domitian."

Crixus stood and stretched his back luxuriously. "Jerusalem wasn't *my* victory, though I was there. And if Titus wants to celebrate his victory over a bunch of half-starved Jews, why doesn't he capture his own beasts? On top of that, Vespasian's dead; it's the worms who should be celebrating."

Neocles prudently changed the subject. "You were a soldier, Crixus?"

Crixus swatted a fly away from his sweaty face. "*Legio VIII Augusta*, in Gaul. I enlisted to fight barbarians but was instead assigned to capture bears for the *venationes*. Other than the scum hanging around our camp, begging for handouts, I never even saw a barbarian."

"I have never seen one, either," Junius affirmed, "but would like to. I heard they are hairy giants!"

Crixus shrugged. "I was led to believe that the barbarians were tall of body, with rippling muscles and pale skin. Their hair was said to be uniformly blond. But the layabouts I saw, though taller and hairier than us, were not especially impressive. They clothe themselves in the skins of animals and reek of woodsmoke. I cannot speak to the color of the barbarians' hair or skin because they were always caked in filth. They live in trackless forests and swamps, where the rivers are always frozen, so they never bathe. Agriculture is unknown to them, and most of their food consists of milk, cheese, and the flesh of wild beasts, which abound in their native land."

"I heard the barbarians of *Germania* and Gaul are recruited for our own legions," Neocles interjected. "Those surely cannot be as wretched as the ones you encountered, Crixus. Varus and his legions learned that the hard way and Julius Caesar, himself, considered Vercingetorix a formidable adversary."

"Varus was an incompetent fool and Caesar was as canny a politician as he was a general," Crixus shrewdly observed. "He wrote of his campaigns in Gaul for the consumption of the plebians in order to magnify his military achievements against the barbarians...Caesar would have written the identical words had his opponents been *andabatae*. Equal blowhards were Terentius Varro, whose legions were annihilated at Cannae, and Claudius Glaber, who was routed at Mount Vesuvio by a shabby collection of escaped gladiators, runaway slaves, and riff-raff. The only difference between them and Caesar is that Caesar actually won battles.

Junius began laughing. "By the gods, Crixus, I have never encountered such irreverence for our deified leaders! It is good that you are here, rather than in Rome, where your seditious words would likely earn you a one-way trip to the arena."

“If I never see Rome again, it will be too soon,” Crixus responded.

“How, in the name of the gods, did you end up here?” Neocles swept his arm around, indicating the surrounding area.

“I got tired of the cold of Gaul and heard that Numidia was warmer, so I left,” Crixus shrugged. “I did not like Numidia, either, though.”

“You ‘left’? Were you not concerned that your desertion would subject your comrades to decimation?”

Decimatio, a brutal practice utilized by Roman commanders following catastrophic military defeats or for other infractions deemed equally shameful, including desertion, was intended to punish legions for their perceived, or actual, cowardice in battle, and to set an example for the future. Five hundred soldiers were divided into fifty groups of ten. By lot, one man from each group was chosen to be clubbed to death by his comrades. The survivors were considered disgraced, reconstituted into new legions, and banished to remote posts on the fringes of the Empire.

“That is true,” Crixus nodded. “But when one’s job is to capture beasts instead of killing barbarians and you don’t return after several days, the centurion simply assumes that you had fell prey to animals or accident. This fiction spared my comrades decimation and my commander additional paperwork.”

Junius laughed again and pointed north. “You’re a long way from Numidia, my friend. Numidia lies in that direction!”

"No matter," Crixus shrugged. "I did not linger in Numidia but went thence to Libya, which was no better. After that, Alexandria, which I found more to my liking. But I disliked the Egyptians, who consider themselves superior to all other men. They are convinced that the antiquity of their country entitles them to their pretensions."

"Egypt is indeed old. But their arrogance is misplaced, for not even Egypt dares defy the fist of Rome," Junius snorted.

"I have not been to Egypt but travelers tell me it is filled with wonders," Neocles remarked.

Crixus shrugged. "If you consider huge stone blocks stacked one upon another a 'wonder,' I suppose that is true. Like the effeminate Greeks, the Egyptians are ignorant of the arch. Nor do they have any trees in Egypt, so everything is built of stone and needlessly massive."

"Still," said Neocles, "I would like to see such things."

"I rapidly had my fill of the smug Egyptians," Crixus continued. "Knowing that Titus was at that time besieging Jerusalem, I resolved to make my way to the Province of Judea, thinking I could avail myself of the plunder that would certainly flow from the ruination of the Jews' capital. I traversed the *Via Maris*, through Pelusium and Rhinocorura, to Gaza and Ashkelon, thence to Jerusalem. Titus and, before him, Vespasian, had already reduced most of Judea to a barren field of charred boulders. I eventually enlisted in *Legio V Macedonica*, which Vespasian had previously transferred from Moesia, and participated in the annihilation of the Jews and the destruction of their capital."

"Wait!" Junius blurted. "Did you not just say that you were already enlisted in *Legio VIII Augusta*, in Gaul?"

"I did, but Titus' recruiters did not know that," Crixus chuckled. "His legions were having a hot time of it with the Jews and desperate for soldiers to replace those killed in battle. *Macedonica* was only too happy to welcome me into its ranks, no questions asked."

"The Jews were good fighters?"

"Never have I witnessed such reckless fury as displayed by those Jews!" Crixus declared.

"They were fighting for their lives and their hearths."

"Indeed, though Caesar sought peace following every Roman victory, personally inviting the Jews to make terms. I personally observed how, with tears in his eyes, Titus begged them to save their city, reminding the Jews that they, alone, would bear ultimate responsibility for the utter destruction of their Holy House and repeatedly entreating them to prevent its defilement. Titus promised in good faith to respect their laws and pardon the rebels, if they would but throw down their arms. The Jews' Temple would remain inviolate and they would enjoy perfect freedom to practice the rites of their fathers unhindered. No Roman would enter their holy places, let alone profane them."

“Why did the Jews reject Caesar’s overtures? Were they so blind that they not see that their doom was inevitable?”

“They did not care. The Zealots who had seized control of the city were mad with hatred, both for Romans and for their fellow Jews. They despised the Romans as cowards and rejected Titus’ demands for unconditional surrender because they claimed their oath forbade them from yielding to any earthly power, however desperate their circumstances. One of them shouted from Jerusalem’s battlements that their ancient forebears swore they would never serve the Romans, nor any master but their own god. In order to enforce that vow, the Zealots executed any Jew that attempted to flee the city or who was suspected of aiding the Romans. That was their excuse, anyway. If you ask me, it was just a pretext and they killed their countrymen only for their money, because most of the Jews menaced by the Zealots were wealthy aristocrats of the highest dignity. Moreover, because of the countless outrages and deceptions they had committed against the Romans during the course of the war, the Zealots knew that flaying and crucifixion would be their fate if they fell into Roman hands. Accordingly, they vowed to fight to the death despite their certainty of Jerusalem’s calamitous destiny.”

“You were present when Jerusalem's walls finally toppled?”

Crixus nodded. “I think you are right, Neocles, when you say that the war between the Romans and the Jews is the greatest in history. Though it took many weeks, their walls, which the Jews foolishly believed impregnable, finally yielded to Titus' siege works. When the legions finally poured into the city, no quarter was shown the survivors because of the wanton misery and death caused by the Jews' obstinate refusal to surrender. All were indiscriminately put to the sword, armed and unarmed alike: old women, men, children, infants suckling at their mother's breast, Jews that pledged their unshaken fidelity to Rome and begged to be spared...all were killed without exception. No pity was shown; no distinction made between rich and poor, guilty and innocent, sick and healthy. You could not find a single patch of earth anywhere in Jerusalem that was not thickly strewn with corpses. Legionnaires roamed the city, forced to clamber over mounds of bodies in order to reach additional victims. The Romans' thirst for vengeance was not slaked for three days, during which time patrician ladies, toothless grandmothers, and children were raped before having their throats slit...others, they crucified. Titus' anger, and that of his legions, was a raging fire impossible to quench."

"Mercy in war is a ruinous thing," Neocles sagely observed.

Junius clucked his tongue. "And was there also plunder to be had?" he inquired.

"Legionnaires convinced themselves that wealthy Jews attempted to conceal valuables by swallowing them, so sliced open their bodies to search for gold and silver. They did this even to reeking corpses that had perished from starvation, injury, or disease during the course of the siege, but which the surviving Jews, weakened by war and starvation, lacked the energy or time to burn or bury. Everywhere was death."

"The Jews' temple...it must certainly have been filled with marvels."

"Mountains of purple cloth woven with gold and silver thread; a great table for shewbread, of gold several hundred-weight; golden candlesticks as tall as a man; heaps of gold and silver coins, in numbers, numberless; chains of electrum, the links of which exceeded in size a man's clenched fist; golden and inlaid furniture; crystal drinking vessels; olive wood, cedar, ebony, agathis, myrrh, kyphi, cassia, cinnamon, and other sweet spices; jewels; ivory; and exotic hides beyond counting," Crixus confirmed. "The Jews' treasures beggar both calculation and description."

"What became of it all?"

"Titus rightfully seized it. Some he distributed among those legionnaires who had most distinguished themselves during the fighting. The rest he sent back to Rome for display in his triumph."

"And, pray, Crixus, what spoils did you find yourself in possession of?"

He smiled, cannily. "I was fortunate to uncover a hoard of silver tetradrachm, as well as gold dinars, in an abandoned house. In another, I found a store of copper prutot. The terrified, starving old Jew who lived there begged me to spare his life and gave me this knife in exchange for it." He indicated the Damascus steel blade hanging at this hip. "I later had it engraved with my name."

"Did you honor your bargain?" Neocles probed.

"Of course. I gave the old Jew some food and cautioned him to remain concealed within the ruins of his house, lest one of Titus' men find and kill him."

"What became of him?"

Crixus shrugged. "I know not, though I *do* know the fate of Jerusalem." Both Neocles and Junius arched their eyebrows, expectantly. "As Scipio chastened Hannibal by devastating his homeland so, also, did Titus chasten the Jews by razing their capital. All of Jerusalem, not excluding its walls, temple, sanctuary, and even the Jews' Holy of Holies, was leveled to its foundations on Caesar's order. Two squared stones, resting one upon another, could not thereafter be found in that place. Nothing remained to suggest the existence of a metropolis that once rivaled Rome in magnificence. The Jews, alone, must bear the infamy for the wanton destruction of Jerusalem, mother city of their nation where God, himself, was said to have dwelt. Nor will the passage of a thousand generations be enough to efface the blood from their hands."

His two companions reflected in silence. Junius finally spoke.

"Jerusalem was destroyed nearly a decade ago, yet you only now arrive here," he said. "Where did you travel in the interim?"

"Although Jerusalem was erased from the earth, the war with the Jews did not end," Crixus responded.

"The surviving Jews scattered, burrowing themselves like ticks into a number of redoubts scattered across Judea, three principally: Herodium, Machaerus, and Masada. Titus returned to Rome to celebrate his triumph, leaving instructions with the governor, Lucilius Bassus, to destroy these remaining holdouts, once and for all. I remained with *Legio V Macedonica* during those final mopping-up campaigns. Bassus died while besieging Machaerus, leaving the new governor, Lucius Flavius Silva, to complete the task. The last entrenchment of Jews, at Masada, was finally eliminated three years after the destruction of Jerusalem, though I was not present when it fell. A Parthian from *Legio X Fretensis*, who participated, told me that when Masada's defenses were finally breached, Silva found over a thousand Jews, dead by their own hand. Thus, their revolt ended in ignominy, the Jews finding it a more desirable thing to kill themselves wholesale than to acknowledge Rome's suzerainty."

"And, afterward, what?"

"Afterward, I made my way to Syria, where I took a wife and had a son. A fever took them both. Having no reason to remain, I departed Syria and traveled throughout the East. Finally resolving to return West, I wished to remain as far from Roman corruption as possible. In Alexandria, I finagled passage aboard a boat traveling up the *Nilus*, through Nubia and Punt. Negotiating the Great Cataract proved a ticklish business; more than once I was convinced that it was the end of me! But I now find myself here." He paused and looked about. "Wherever here is."

"This place has no name," Junius asserted. "But the gods must favor you, Crixus, because they led you to *Legio XVI Bestia.* Without the gods' intervention, you would undoubtedly have perished in this wasteland long before finding your way to us."

"Your entire legion is stationed here?"

"It is a legion in name only," Neocles sheepishly clarified. "*Bestia* is not even a cohort."

In the Roman army, a cohort was a military unit comprised of roughly five hundred soldiers, one-tenth the size of a legion, commanded by a *tribunus militum.*

"How many men?"

Neocles glanced at Junius as he furrowed his brow in thought. "Less than two *centuriae.* No more than that." He arched his eyebrows, as though seeking confirmation from his companion.

"Two *centuriae* less three," Junius grunted. "We lost some last week, though that is unusual," he hastily added.

"Who is the *tribunus*?"

"Pompeius Cornelius Corvo."

Crixus frowned. "He appears to be aptly named, though I do not know that name or that house."

"Why would you?" Junius scoffed. "No one has heard of them! I think Corvo hails from a long line of nobodies in one of Rome's shit-provinces. If he came from a better house, he would certainly have been able to secure a more desirable posting than this *cloaca.*

He, or one of his relatives, obviously managed to antagonize some fucking senator."

Neocles nodded in silent agreement.

Crixus laughed. "It appears that I have finally succeeded in reaching the *ultima thule*. Having done so, I unintentionally reduce myself to beggary, though one cannot long survive on nothing but air and water."

"That is easily remedied, Crixus," Neocles replied. "Join us. As Junius just said, we are presently short three men. We will simply explain that you are a traveler whose comrades died by misadventure. By your own admission, you already have experience capturing wild beasts in Gaul."

TWO

GEORGE PYPER SHONE LIKE a new penny.

Like many first-time clients, he appeared to have outfitted himself primary by watching old Jungle Jim movies and "reality" hunting programs on television, which led him to purchase a multitude of items of dubious utility for the low-end "plains game" package he'd purchased at a recent hunting-and-fishing expo. Scarcer, more desirable species sharing the same habitat...kudu, sable, eland, zebra...were reserved for higher-paying, more discriminating clients. But Pyper paid for the sizzle, not the steak and, largely indifferent to what particular animals he would be hunting, could boast to his drinking buddies down at the union hall/Elks Club/VFW/American

Legion/Lions Club/Moose Lodge that he'd been on an actual, by-God, African safari.

Pyper and his wife arrived in camp the previous day, for a five-day safari, with a dozen suitcases stuffed with superfluous clothing. They were clearly unacquainted with the fundamental rule of packing: when going on a trip, any trip, make two piles on your living room floor, one pile of clothing and a second pile of money. Cut the clothing pile in half and double the money pile. You are now ready to depart.

Notwithstanding that the most powerful rifle Pyper had ever fired was a diminutive .243 and the largest animal he'd ever shot was a white tail deer, which seldom exceed 150 pounds in weight, the first thing he purchased for his safari was a genuine elephant rifle, despite the fact that he wasn't hunting elephants. Pyper's license restricted him to quintessential African fauna: impala, wildebeest, warthog, and blesbok. With the exception of the wildebeest, the remaining animals "on license" were roughly the same weight as a garden-variety white tail. The traditional "Big Five" of Africa...elephant, lion, Cape buffalo, leopard, and rhino...were only pursued by well-heeled clients with at least one safari already under their belts. First-timers like Pyper contented themselves with the more abundant throwaway species, which suited Laidlaw. Their ubiquity rendered them easier to hunt and, unlike the Big Five, plains game was less likely to kill you. The only exception to the proverbial lethality of the Big Five is the rhino. Looking like a refugee from the Miocene

Era, which is exactly what it is, the myopic, hapless rhino can't get out of its own way.

No matter. When traveling to the Dark Continent, it is *de rigueur* to arm oneself with nothing less than a .416 Rigby or .458 Winchester. After all, this is Africa! Pyper had even upped the ante by ordering a custom bolt-action rifle chambered in the formidable .460 Weatherby Magnum for his plains game safari. Only once in his career had Laidlaw encountered anyone who could handle the ferocious recoil of a .460, and that was another professional hunter who used a Weatherby when trailing rogue elephants through heavy brush. Used .460's are occasionally encountered on the used racks in gun shops in like-new condition; people buy them, shoot them once or twice, then promptly dump them for rifles in more benign calibers.

Like most newbies, it was clear in Pyper's case that he was more-or-less afraid of his own rifle. At the obligatory sighting-in session the day he arrived in camp, Laidlaw was able to assess his client's marksmanship by having him shoot a paper target 100 yards away.

Pyper lifted the lustrous new Weatherby from its case. Swaying perceptibly, he pointed the heavy rifle in the general direction of the target, closed both eyes, gritted his teeth, and yanked the trigger.

Downrange, the massive 500-grain bullet plowed into the ground four feet left of the target. Pyper was knocked backward on his heels because of the Weatherby's substantial recoil.

"Good shooting," Laidlaw assured him. It was obvious that he'd end up bagging most of Pyper's trophies for him. Pyper grinned and gave him a thumbs-up. He was surprised, and relieved, that he'd done so well. He didn't relish having to shoot the .460 a second time.

When guiding clients, Laidlaw used a plain-Jane Remington Model 700, chambered in .375 Holland and Holland. He considered the Remington his "Goldilocks" rifle: neither too big, nor too small. Just right. Probably a little on the light side for stopping an enraged 1,500-pound Cape buff or a five-ton elephant, but it would do in a pinch...hopefully, he'd never have to find out. Hell, Harry Manners bagged countless elephant and buff with a .375 H&H and never suffered a scratch, Bell shot over 1,000 elephants using only a 7mm Mauser, and Lake used nothing but a surplus .303, a relic from the British army, everywhere in Africa! If those guys could do it, so could he. The exquisite Austrian scope atop Pyper's Weatherby, by itself, cost more than twice as much as Laidlaw's rifle and scope!

Laidlaw heard the approach of Pyper's clumping footsteps and looked up from the breakfast table as his client entered the rondovel. He was wearing matching khaki shorts and shirt, a bush jacket, gaiters, and heavy hiking boots. A wide leather "culling belt" encircled his waist and an Aussie-style wide-brimmed hat, with one side snapped to the crown and a fake leopard-skin hat band, completed the look. Multiple nickel-plated cartridges, as big as cigars, glinted from loops in his new belt. Pyper's rifle was slung over his shoulder.

He looked ridiculous.

Pyper slipped the cumbersome Weatherby from his shoulder and handed it to one of the kitchen staff before flopping into one of the chairs that ringed the circular table. The staff member carefully leaned the rifle against a wall before retrieving another mug, filling it with coffee, and placing it in front of Pyper.

"Good morning," Laidlaw greeted him. "I hope you slept well...the hippos were raising hell most of the night. Will Mrs. Pyper be joining us this morning?"

"Hippos? I guess I must've slept through the brutes! Nothing like Africa to guarantee a good night's sleep, aye?" he added. Pyper slurped his coffee and grimaced. "Margaret wanted to sleep in today. She said that she'd just hang around the boma today while we hunted."

Their server, Winston, materialized and wordlessly placed a plate of hot breakfast in front of Pyper: filet of impala, scrambled eggs, fried potatoes, thick slices of fresh-baked bread with butter churned in the kitchen, and a slice of peach pie. Pyper dug in as Winston silently topped his coffee mug and stepped away.

"You're not eating?" he asked Laidlaw around a mouthful of food.

"I ate earlier." Laidlaw sipped his coffee. He learned earlier that morning from Moses, his head tracker, that a small herd of Nyasa wildebeest were grazing about a half-hour away. "You ready for some action after breakfast? Moses tells me there's a herd of wildebeests not too far away. We'll hop in the bakkie after breakfast and head in their direction."

"Bakkie!" Pyper guffawed. I love how you Brits have names for everything!" Margaret Pyper obviously failed to inform her husband of Laidlaw's nationality. He wondered whether they ever talked.

Pyper held his empty coffee mug aloft and waved it around.

"Actually, I'm an American," Laidlaw patiently explained. "But the British were the first Europeans to invade this part of Africa and they introduced their colloquialisms into the language. Trucks are called 'bakkies"' because that's what the British call 'em and the name stuck."

Pyper distractedly nodded. His attention was focused on Winston, who was hustling toward the table with the carafe of hot coffee.

"Well, like I said, I like it," he reiterated. "Unlike you Brits, we Yanks have no imagination." He nodded toward Laidlaw's unpretentious Remington, which rested against the table. "I think my Weatherby may be better medicine against those wildebeests."

"Yeah, it's a nice rifle," Laidlaw replied, because that's what you're supposed to say when somebody brings an expensive Weatherby rifle on safari.

"It should be!" Pyper snorted. "I could have gotten something smaller," a not-so-subtle jab at Laidlaw's .375, "and the beast cost an arm-and-a-leg, but one never knows what one might encounter in the bush...don't want to be under-gunned if we blunder into an angry jumbo! Am I right?"

What good is a rifle against "jumbo," angry or otherwise, if you can't hit a barn from the inside with it? Laidlaw thought. Besides, ammunition for the Weatherby was around $15 per round. Pyper clearly possessed more money than good sense.

"As Ruark advised, 'Use enough gun'," Pyper solemnly intoned. He awarded Laidlaw another thumbs-up.

THEY PARKED BENEATH A FEVER tree. The only wildlife they saw en route were a couple of distant impala ewes, which bounded away the moment they spotted the bakkie.

"Don't want to spook the herd," Laidlaw explained. "We'll walk from here." He stepped from the doorless vehicle and grabbed the Remington. "Sling your rifle but don't chamber a cartridge," he instructed Pyper.

Moses and Smoke, his cousin, hopped from the rear of the bakkie. Although Moses was Laidlaw's primary tracker, both men invariably went afield together. Laidlaw also used Smoke as his backup if he had multiple clients or Moses was unavailable. Though neither of the trackers carried firearms, both were armed with machetes, a tool far more useful than a rifle because it could be used to dispatch venomous snakes, unearth tubers and roots, hew firewood, butcher game animals, cut through thick brush, dig for water, and chop fruit from trees. Moses also carried "shooting sticks," three slender, lightweight, wooden shafts five feet in length, bound together a foot from the top with a strip of rubber inner tube. The resulting tripod would be used as a stable shooting platform in the field, its height adjustable simply by spreading the legs farther apart.

The two trackers instinctively began crisscrossing the area around the bakkie, intently scanning the ground for animal tracks. After a moment, Moses looked at Laidlaw and grinned. He said something in Kiswahili and pointed south.

"The herd was here about an hour ago. Three mature bulls, a young bull, and a couple dozen cows," Laidlaw said. "They're nervous 'cause a pack of jackals has been harassing them all morning."

"He can tell all that just by lookin' at the ground?" Pyper marveled, indicating Moses.

Laidlaw laughed. "Hell, either one of 'em can tell you which cow any particular bull screwed last night and what they had for breakfast a week ago!"

"Amazing!" Pyper exclaimed.

For once, Laidlaw agreed with him.

"We'd better get after 'em," Laidlaw urged. "If the herd gets overly agitated 'cause of the jackals, they'll bolt and won't stop runnin' 'till next week. That's the problem with wildebeest. They're skittish by nature and if one of 'em gets a wild hair up his ass and starts runnin', the rest of the herd will panic and automatically follow him, even if none of them have the slightest idea what they're running from...a leopard, a lion, a strange noise, or a blowing leaf. Doesn't matter. Their instinct is to run."

Pyper shifted the heavy Weatherby to his other shoulder. His stiff new clothes were already beginning to chafe and he was sweating. "How far away do you think they are?" he asked, uneasily.

Laidlaw gazed in a southerly direction before answering. "Not too far, I don't think. Probably no more than three-quarters of a mile." He looked at Moses for confirmation, who smiled and nodded. "Don't chamber a round until I tell you to," he said again. Although it had never happened to one of his clients, Laidlaw was well aware that first-time hunters are often struck with "buck fever" when they get within shooting distance of their quarry. When that occurs, their brains abruptly stop working and, in their bumbling haste to bag the animal, they can end up shooting the bakkie, one of the trackers, their professional hunter, or themselves.

"Yeah, I understand," Pyper testily responded. He transferred his rifle back to his other shoulder and wiped his brow on the sleeve of his safari jacket.

"Let's go," Laidlaw directed, heading into the bush. Moses and Smoke fanned out on either side.

IT IS A TRUISM THAT THE blue wildebeest, so named because of the blue/gray hue of its coat, is a creature that 'looks like it was designed by a committee'. Also known as the 'brindled gnu,' these common antelope look like a cross between a horse and a cow and bear little resemblance to their smaller, rarer, and even more bizarre-looking cousins, the black wildebeest. Notwithstanding their inelegant appearance, however, blue wildebeests are among the fleetest of antelope species, which undoubtedly explains their profusion across the savannas of much of sub-Saharan Africa. Who hasn't seen innumerable nature documentaries on television, showing immense herds of blue wildebeests streaming across the Serengeti, only to be dragged by the nose, struggling, into rivers teeming with crocodiles? The abundance of wildebeests explains why they are invariably included among the handful of African species on the inexpensive, cookie-cutter safaris like the one purchased by George Pyper.

The Nyasa wildebeest is one of four recognized sub-species of blue wildebeest. It is slightly smaller than the blue, occupies a more limited range, and its pelage is more brownish in color. The most arresting feature of the Nyasa is, however, the striking blaze of white hair running laterally across its black face.

“I gotta rest,” Pyper wheezed. “Gimme a minute.” He slid his Weatherby off his shoulder and leaned it against a waist-high termite mound that was as hard as concrete. Leaning forward, he placed his hands on his knees and began gulping air. His sweat-soaked hat tumbled to the ground and perspiration dripped from his face. His bare legs were scraped and sunburned.

Laidlaw paused and glanced rearward. "You okay?

Pyper nodded without looking up. "Yeah," he panted. "Just a little out of shape, I guess. How close do you think we are?"

Moses and Smoke were nowhere in sight, having loped ahead to scope-out the herd.

"Well, we've only gone about a quarter-mile," Laidlaw replied. "Shouldn't be much longer, though. You sure you can make it?"

"Yeah, I'm okay." Pyper reached down to retrieve his hat before straightening. He managed a weak smile. "Just a little light-headed from the heat…gimme a minute." He donned his hat and removed a sodden pack of cigarettes from one of the multiple pockets of his safari jacket.

Laidlaw sighed and slouched against another termite mound. He removed his baseball cap and used it to mop his brow. "No hurry. Just let me know when you're ready." He unhooked a canteen from his belt at the small of his back, unscrewed the cap, and handed it to Pyper.

"I didn't expect it to be this hot," Pyper said after nosily guzzling water from the canteen and handing it back to Laidlaw. He wiped his mouth with the back of his hand, lit a cigarette, and inhaled it deeply.

Heat waves shimmered in the stagnant air.

Laidlaw sipped water from the canteen. "Yeah, it can get pretty warm out here," he acknowledged. Out of habit, he confirmed that his Remington had a cartridge in the chamber and that its safety was engaged.

“That thing is damned heavy!” declared Pyper, indicating his .460.

Laidlaw shrugged. “Yeah, Weatherbys are hell for stout and get heavier the longer you carry ‘em. That’s one reason I prefer a .375: a lot slimmer and there’s not much .460 can do that a .375 can’t, for a lot less weight and recoil.”

“Do many of your clients use Mark V’s,” Pyper probed, referring to the Weatherby’s model number. He was hoping that Laidlaw would validate his extravagant purchase.

“A few. Usually not much need for the stuff we’re hunting.” Not even an ‘angry jumbo,’ he was tempted to add.

Pyper ground his cigarette out underfoot and hoisted his rifle back onto his shoulder. “Whenever you’re ready.”

“The boys should be back any minute with an update on the herd,” Laidlaw said as he grasped his rifle. Even while he was speaking, Moses and Smoke silently materialized from behind a thicket, seemingly out of thin air. “What did I tell you...like clockwork,” he grinned at Pyper.

Laidlaw listened intently as Moses spoke rapidly in Kiswahili. He turned to Smoke, who swiftly confirmed his cousin’s recitation.

“Excellent news. The herd apparently managed to drive the jackals away and has settled down.

They've moved back toward us a little and are grazing about a quarter-mile from here." He looked expectantly at Pyper.

"Good," the latter grunted. "Which way?"

Laidlaw pointed and began walking in that direction. "Don't forget your rifle," he called over his shoulder.

Moses and Smoke melted back into the brush as abruptly as they'd arrived.

THEY WERE CONCEALED IN A COPSE of stunted trees upwind of the skittish herd.

Through binoculars, Laidlaw scanned the animals in silence as they snorted and cropped dry grass, 200 yards distant. Pyper squinted at them through the dusty haze. Neither Moses nor Smoke were anywhere to be seen.

Laidlaw lowered the binoculars to his chest and turned to his perspiring client. "There's a shootable bull in there," he whispered. "Not record book, but respectable. You can either take him or we can keep looking...your call."

"Which one?" Pyper hissed. Not that he could distinguish one wildebeest from another if his life depended on it.

Laidlaw looked through his binoculars again before slipping the strap from his neck and handing them to Pyper. "Second from the left. He's behind a cow, so you'll have to wait until one of 'em moves to get a clear shot."

Pyper took the heavy Leicas in his sweaty hands and, after reversing them twice, finally jammed them against his face. He could discern nothing but blinding sunlight. Laidlaw reached over and adjusted the focus ring. The grazing herd sprang into view. Pyper's heart thumped in his chest and he almost felt giddy...he couldn't believe that he was actually in Africa, hunting big game! He fumbled with the binoculars before handing them back to Laidlaw.

All the wildebeest looked exactly alike.

"Well, what do you figure?" Laidlaw asked, matter-of-factly.

"I think I should shoot him," Pyper mouthed.

"Okay, get your rifle ready but don't chamber a cartridge until I tell you," Laidlaw reiterated. "Steady your rifle on that limb," he gestured, "but don't lay it directly on it. Cushion it with your off hand." A shot from a rifle resting directly on a branch will, as often as not, go wild.

Pyper nervously slipped the Weatherby from his shoulder and, in exaggerated slow motion, carefully laid it across the designated limb. He was almost afraid to breathe. Pyper cast an expectant glance toward Laidlaw, who ignored him and resumed evaluating the herd through the binoculars.

"Yeah, he's a pretty nice bull," Laidlaw muttered, more to himself than to his client. Pyper wondered how he was apparently able to remain so unflappable.

"What do you want me to do?" he whispered.

"Square up and slide your left hand under your rifle. Put your scope on the lowest power and look through it to see if you can isolate the bull I'm talking about...the one with big horns. He's moved closer to the center of the herd."

Pyper wanted an animal with big horns but, as far as he could tell, they all had big horns. He turned his attention back to the grazing wildebeests and, using only his naked eye, attempted to identify the designated target.

Preoccupied with eating, the herd had wandered slightly closer to the concealed men. To Pyper's untrained eye, however, they appeared to be a mile away.

Two hundred yards, a mere 600 feet, doesn't sound very far. But, in graphic terms, it's the length of two American football fields, placed end-to-end. From that perspective, two hundred yards is a long way. Pyper was unable to distinguish one animal from the next at that distance and was even lucky to ascertain that he was, in fact, looking at wildebeests. He wiped his forehead on his sleeve, fiddled with the magnification ring on his scope with a sweaty hand, then leaned forward to peer through it.

The herd continued to crop the sparse grass as it edged closer. Still, Pyper was unable to identify the specified animal because they all looked the same. He lifted his head from the scope and looked at Laidlaw.

"Should I shoot?"

The guide continued to placidly watch the herd through binoculars.

"Do you see the bull I'm talking about?" Laidlaw asked.

"Yeah," Pyper lied.

"Do you think you can make a clean shot from here?"

"Uh, yeah, I think so."

Laidlaw lowered his binoculars and looked calmly at his client. "Chamber a round, get your feet set, find him in your scope, and take him." He grasped his Remington and flicked the safety off. "I'll back your shot."

"Uh, ok," Pyper stammered.

He slid his left hand beneath the Weatherby and closed his fingers around its polished wooden forearm. Trembling, he hunkered behind the scope, slowly retracted the bolt to feed a live round into the chamber, slid the bolt forward until it locked into position, and flicked the safety off. Sliding his finger through the polished trigger guard, it rested against the trigger.

"See him?" Laidlaw idly inquired. His Remington was trained on the shoulder of the clueless bull.

"Yeah, I think so," Pyper assured him.

"Take him," Laidlaw ordered.

Pyper's Weatherby boomed.

In Primis Anno Regnantibus Imperator Caesar Titus Vespasianus (78 CE)

"THE DIVINE TITUS EXPECTS to destroy no fewer than 9,000 beasts to mark the opening of his father's amphitheater on the Palatine, his gift to the people of Rome," Junius remarked. The three men crowded together in the uneven shade of a scraggy thorn bush.

"9,000!" Neocles snorted in disgust. "I heartily wish that Titus and Vespasian would go fuck each other...by the gods, I'd even pay to watch them! Caesar slew but a fraction of that number to commemorate four triumphs and Augustus, of venerated memory, sacrificed only 260 lions and 36 crocodiles to honor his own grandsons! I also heard that even that half-wit, Nero, was only able to butcher 400 bears and 300 lions at his *venatione!* Titus presumes to strip the entire world of beasts in order to gratify his arrogance!"

"His amphitheater is said to hold tens of thousands and beggars even the prodigies of Egypt," noted Junius, by way of explanation.

"Of course, the emperor boasts of his new amphitheater," Crixus opined. "How could it possibly profit him to admit that any of his achievements is inferior to those of Rome's conquered enemies?"

"Besides, the Circus Maximus holds *hundreds* of thousands," Neocles snorted. "But I don't remember any such bloodbath as Titus proposes as ever having occurred in the Circus. And it will take months, maybe years, to capture and transport such a vast quantity of an animals to Rome. When is the inauguration supposed to occur?"

Junius shrugged. "Whenever the 9,000 beasts are ready, I suppose."

Crixus listened thoughtfully. "Whenever it is, it won't be anytime soon," he remarked. "As Neocles said, it is likely to require months or even years to assemble all the beasts that Titus apparently requires."

"To say nothing of feeding and transporting them," Neocles added. "For every animal that reaches Rome alive, five or more will have died of starvation, disease, or accident...it is not 9,000, but 45,000, beasts that will have to be collected in order to magnify Titus' victory over a handful of starving Jews!"

Crixus furrowed his brow. "Some will certainly be *Africanae bestia* but others will undoubtedly come from other parts of the Empire: bears from *Germania*, bulls from *Hispania*, stags from *Britannia*. The burden will not, therefore, fall entirely to us. Nor will all the animals necessarily be ferocious, or even wild. Though the emperor desires only beasts of distant origin as tangible evidence of Rome's might, he will have no choice but to supplement them with domestic herbivores like sheep and asses. The drunken fools in the stands won't care; all they wish is to see blood spilt, whatever its source."

Junius laughed. "Perhaps, Crixus, you will be reunited with your former comrades in *Legio VIII Augusta* after all!"

"I should hope not," Crixus responded, "as they believe me to be dead!"

"Bears, bulls, stags, sheep, asses...they are all one to me," grumbled Neocles. "The only creatures that Titus will succeed in gathering in such numbers will be hares and mice."

"The emperor also expects to slaughter fifty hippos and an equal number of elephants," Junius revealed. "In addition to all the hares and mice you speak of."

"Hippos and elephants! How do you know this?" Neocles demanded.

"Berossus told me." Berossus was the sub-commander of *Legio XVI Bestia.*

"Where in almighty Jupiter's name did he get that information?" Neocles challenged. "Berossus does not have brains enough to pour piss from a shoe! No messenger from Rome bearing such tidings could possibly have found his way here. And I was unaware that a *haruspex* traveled with the legion," he dryly added.

"Berossus must have divined it by observing the behavior of birds. Everyone knows that the gods manifest their will by such signs. I, myself, have witnessed this," Junius gravely asserted.

"So, it is the gods who want hippos and elephants?" Crixus interjected. "If that's the case, why do they not just create them out of nothing and save us the trouble of capturing them?"

"No, no," Neocles laughed. "I want to hear more about Junius' ability to determine Jupiter's fancies. If there is anything to it, I will know whether to back the reds, the greens, the whites, or the blues in the chariot races, and which gladiator to wager on in the *munera*." He and Crixus looked at Junius expectantly.

Their companion was pleased to have such an attentive audience. "The augurs tell us that the gods use birds to communicate their wishes," he solemnly began. "In order to interpret what the gods are trying to tell us, one must be attentive to several things. What kind of birds are they? Are they common or rare? What color are they? Are they many or few? What do their cries sound like? Do they fly or perch? If they fly, in what manner and in what direction?"

Neocles playfully nudged Crixus. "If I had knowledge of letters I would make a record of all this, as it is much to remember!"

"And you believe Berossus to be skilled in this art?" asked a dubious Crixus. "In what manner did birds manage to enlighten him regarding the gods' sudden desire for elephants and hippos?"

"Maybe Berossus saw some elephants flying overhead and simply mistook them for birds," Neocles innocently suggested.

Junius looked at him sourly. "I am not in Berossus' confidence and know not what explicit signs he relied upon, Crixus. But he surely would not have proposed, of his own accord, that we undertake the capture of great beasts unless directed by the gods."

"Why would he not do so?" Neocles scoffed. "What does Berossus care? He is not the one risking life and limb to capture them! No god instructed Berossus to include hippos or elephants on the list of beasts we are already charged with ensnaring. What will be next? Centaurs? The Ethiopian Pegasus? A cyclops? The gods be damned!"

Crixus laughed. "If not the gods, who? Both Berossus and Corvo have been as sober as Bacchus since my arrival here. Neither are in any condition to issue orders about anything."

"The gods, birds, Corvo, Berossus...it makes not a straw's worth of difference to me," Neocles sulked. "What is certain is that all the ass-lickers in Rome are tripping over one another trying to impress the new emperor with proofs of their loyalty. The beasts Junius speaks of will not be the last of it. Next thing you know, the gods will demand that we lasso the moon and transport it to Rome in a chariot pulled by harpies because the Divine Titus wants to use it to light his villa on the *Mons Palatinus*! Believe me when I tell you that both Corvo and Berossus would happily send their wives and children to the *ludi* if they thought they would profit by it."

"By the gods, your words could have been spoken by Sancus, himself," Junius affirmed.

"In only one respect do you misspeak, Neocles," Crixus suggested. "It is not Titus who stands most in need of the radiance provided by the moon. His father, Vespasian, requires its light for his residence in Tartarus...he and his brother emperors, as well as all the pigs from the senate."

"They, the Equestrians, and all the other aristocratic scum who nurse at Rome's tit," Junius added.

"Tit?" Crixus responded in mock surprise. "I thought they all suckled at Rome's cock!"

"Methinks none of them is likely to know the difference!" Neocles derided. "Even if they did, every one of those *cinaedi* would happily choose cock!"

"Well, brothers," Crixus said, changing the subject, "There are war elephants enough in *Carthago* that can be shipped to Rome. And if there is a legion in India, it can provide additional elephants to slaughter for Titus' amusement. That is not our concern. But Junius's news about the hippos requires confirming, as capturing that number will be a formidable task. If he is sufficiently sober, let us ask Berossus."

The other two men grunted and stood. With Crixus in the lead, they headed back toward their *castrum*.

"**AS DEMONSTRATION OF HIS FIDELITY** to the gods and his love and esteem for the senate and people of Rome, the emperor has ordered 50 elephants, and as many hippos, to be dedicated with thanks to Fortuna and slaughtered at the inauguration of his amphitheater in Rome," Berossus stiffly informed them.

'Ass-licker' Neocles furtively mouthed to Crixus.

"A sufficient number of war elephants may be had in *Carthago*," Crixus coolly responded. "They can be transported to Ostia on a simple *navis oneraria*. There is no need to capture more of them."

Berossus narrowed his eyes and looked at Crixus with suspicion. "Perhaps, but the Carthaginians long ago eliminated what few hippos once existed there. Do you none-the-less intend to make them responsible for providing those, also?"

"We do not have enclosures large enough to hold half-a-hundred behemoths," Junius interjected, "nor forage, nor people to look after and transport them! We are already too few!"

"Then, build more enclosures. That is not my concern," Berossus snapped. "Rather than bitching about your orders, your time would be better spent complying with them. If you lack adequate *virtus*, use the Aethiops...they are expendable and there is no shortage of them. Unless you would find it more to your liking to accompany the elephants and hippos into the arena," he disparagingly concluded.

"As you order, Commander," Crixus interjected to prevent his companions from impetuously blurting something that would result in the reduction of their already-meager rations. Berossus flicked his fingers, dismissing the three men.

“I am cursed by the gods if I know the biggest bunghole, Berossus or Corvo,” Neocles said, once they were out of earshot.

“Berossus,” Junius immediately declared.

“It is about as broad as it is long,” remarked Crixus. “If you put both of them in a sack, shook it up, and turned it wrong-side up, neither would fall out first.”

“Ha! I would like to put them in a sack...along with a starving *cinaede simiae*!” Neocles laughed, “then throw the whole fucking shiteree into the Tiber.”

“We need to talk to Jugurtha,” Neocles proposed, referring to the local tribal leader. “His people are undoubtedly more skilled at trapping hippos than we are. And, if some of them get crushed in the process, it will be no great loss,”

“Jugurtha and his people are ignorant savages,” Junius scowled.

“I do not ask that you marry him,” responded Neocles. “Or would you find it preferable that one of us, rather than Jugurtha, gets killed while trying to capture 50 hippos?”

THREE

LIKE DEATH AND TAXES Newton's Third Law is inescapable.

Neglecting to firmly grip his Weatherby and forgetting its violent recoil, Pyper's rifle lunged rearward at the moment of discharge. The Swarovski scope atop the heavy firearm inflicted an ugly crescent-shaped gash on Pyper's forehead. He dropped his rifle and stumbled backward, tripping over his own feet, blood streaming from the laceration. The herd of wildebeests instantly bolted as if collectively shot from a cannon.

"Oh, my God!" Pyper shrieked as he frantically pawed at his face.

Throughout, Laidlaw kept his Remington trained on the bull he'd identified to Pyper. Because he possessed zero confidence in his client's marksmanship, Laidlaw didn't wait for the telltale 'thump' of bullet striking flesh signaling, at a minimum, that Pyper had at least managed to actually hit an animal. Laidlaw's follow-up shot was, accordingly, virtually indistinguishable from Pyper's.

Because the herd was already in full flight when he fired, Laidlaw's bullet entered the bull slightly farther back than he would have liked. Even so, the 300-grain bullet penetrated its chest cavity and would prove fatal. After a mad dash of less than 100 yards, the animal would automatically collapse after running out of adrenaline.

The lungs of mammals are sealed inside the chest cavity, a chamber where the internal air pressure is lower than that of the external atmosphere. When the animal inhales, its lungs are inflated by higher-pressure air rushing into its lungs, filling them. By contracting its chest muscles, the animal pushes its diaphragm toward its lungs, increasing pressure on them and expelling air via the windpipe. This regular process of inspiration and expiration is called "tidal breathing." If an object like a bullet penetrates the animal's chest cavity, however, high-pressure external air immediately floods the chamber, equalizing the two pressure levels. Tidal breathing is thereby rendered impossible. It is irrelevant whether the lungs, themselves, are punctured because the sealed chest cavity has been irreparably breached, rendering death inevitable.

"Did I get him?" Pyper babbled as he squinted toward the cloud of dust raised by the vanishing herd. He looked with dismay at his bloody hands and gingerly touched his forehead.

"Yeah, you got him," Laidlaw responded. He pulled a bandana from his shirt pocket and handed it to Pyper, who pressed it to his forehead. "But we gotta go after him. Get your rifle." He nodded toward Pyper's Weatherby, which lay in the dirt at his feet.

"Yeah, I thought I did," Pyper hopefully stated. "I heard the bullet hit home." He bent to retrieve the Weatherby with one hand, his other hand still pressing the bandana against his bloody forehead. He straightened and looked sheepishly at Laidlaw. "This bad boy bites from both ends," he said with forced bravado. "Surprised that wildebeest didn't go down in a heap!"

"Yeah, wildebeest are like that," Laidlaw noncommittally replied as he walked toward the area where, moments before, the herd grazed. An abundance of frothy blood on the ground would confirm a lung shot. He had no idea where Pyper's wild shot ended up, but hoped that his client hadn't executed a "Texas heart shot"...shooting an animal in the ass. If that was the case, they had a long day ahead of them, tracking the wounded antelope, and Laidlaw knew that Pyper was not physically up to the task. His client trailed him wordlessly, though Laidlaw could hear him huffing and puffing as Pyper continued to dab his injured brow with the bandana. Although he hadn't seen either of them since their conversation nearly an hour ago, Laidlaw knew Moses and Smoke were hot-footing it after the fleeing herd. As he hoped, the churned-up earth revealed large splotches of dark, oxygenated blood. Unfortunately, it also contained a diffuse smattering of random droplets.

Laidlaw straightened and peered in the direction of the now-vanished herd. "He's hit pretty hard...I don't expect he'll get too far."

Pyper awkwardly shifted his rifle to his other shoulder and grinned nervously. "Yep, that's what I figured. I hit him pretty good." He patted the stock of his Weatherby.

"Yeah, well, I think you hit another animal but only wounded him. Do you remember where you shot him?"

Pyper looked nonplussed. "I hit him right in the boiler room," he declared.

"If you hit him 'right in the boiler room' he'd be layin' on the ground in front of us," Laidlaw said. "I think you just winged him."

"No way. My shot was right on the money." Pyper's voice trailed off.

Laidlaw sighed. "Well, it's easy to find out." He began striding after the herd.

"Why don't we just use the truck to follow 'em?" Pyper suggested, without moving.

Laidlaw stopped and turned toward his client. "Whatever you like, Mr. Pyper, though I think the bull I shot probably dropped only a hundred yards or so from here, if that. There's no telling where the one you shot is, but we have to find him."

"The one I shot?" Pyper sputtered.

"Yeah, I can tell from the blood trail that we shot two animals. I know where mine was hit...he's laying right out there somewhere," Laidlaw pointed. "It's yours I'm worried about. We have an ethical duty to put it out of its suffering if you only wounded it."

"How do you know we shot two animals?"

"Like I said, the blood spoor," Laidlaw repeated. "I shot the bull I told *you* to shoot. I have no idea which one you shot, or where, but we gotta find him. If we're lucky, he'll bleed out and die, sooner rather than later. If that happens, the vultures will spot him before we do and we can find where he dropped by watching to see where they're circling. It all depends on where you hit him. Hopefully, Moses and Smoke have been trailing the herd and have already spotted the wounded one."

"I have no idea what you're talking about," Pyper pouted. "I guarantee that I shot the one you told me to." His face was smeared with blood and the cut on his forehead was swollen and inflamed.

"We'll soon find out," Laidlaw said, turning on his heel.

HE'D GUESSED WRONG. They found the wildebeest bull crumpled in a small depression only 75 yards away.

Laidlaw squatted to examine the solitary .375 diameter hole in the antelope's rib cage.

Pyper leaned his rifle against the body of the glassy-eyed antelope and leaned over to squint at the prostrate animal, hands on his bare knees. "Yep, that's exactly where I put my cross-hairs," he announced, straightening. "Looks like the Weatherby took care of business, just like I expected."

Laidlaw stood. "You can tell by lookin' that's from a .375, not a .460. A bullet hole made by a .460 would be half again as big. The wildebeest you shot is still out there." He removed his baseball cap and ran his hand through his hair. "One of us should head back to retrieve the bakkie so we can load him in the back. The other person needs to stay here to keep lions and hyenas away from the carcass. Which job you want?"

"There are lions out here?" Pyper gulped.

"A few. I don't think there's any in the immediate area, but I don't want to run the risk of finding one here when we return with the bakkie."

"Fuck that!" Pyper spat. "It sounds like a damned catch-22! I don't think I could even find my way back to the truck! And what am I supposed to do if a lion shows up while you're gone? Why can't one of your boys just bring the truck here while we wait together?"

Laidlaw struggled not to laugh out loud at his client's consternation. "They're tracking the other, wounded wildebeest. Besides, neither of them knows how to drive. If a lion or hyena is lured-in by the scent of the blood while I'm gone, try to scare it away. If worse comes to worse, you've got your Weatherby." He arched his eyebrows and looked at Pyper, expectantly.

The likelihood of a lion or hyena wandering past was basically nil. Laidlaw simply wanted to hasten to retrieve the bakkie without having to stop every few minutes to wait for the lumpish Pyper to catch up or take a cigarette break. It was critical that they locate Pyper's crippled wildebeest as rapidly as possible.

"Where the hell am I supposed to sit while I'm waitin'?" Pyper complained as he peered about. "It's hotter than a bitch out here and there's no place to get out of the fuckin' sun!"

"Head back to that little stand of trees where we just were," Laidlaw instructed. "Sit on the ground in the shade and you'll still be close enough to keep an eye out 'till I get back...shouldn't take me more than an hour to hike back to the bakkie and drive it here."

"You remember where it's parked?"

"It's in my GPS. I'll walk right to it." Laidlaw paused. "You good?"

Pyper was clearly annoyed. "I guess...what choice do I have?"

Laidlaw ignored the question. "Want me to leave the canteen with you?"

"Yeah. God only knows how long you'll be gone while I'm out here sweatin' my balls off."

Laidlaw unhooked the canteen from his belt and passed it to his client. "I'll be back before you know it. We'll load this guy into the bakkie then head out to find the other wildebeest. With any luck, he's already piled up somewhere."

"How we gonna find your trackers?

"We won't have to. They'll find us," Laidlaw said. He extended his hand, which Pyper anemically shook. "See you in an hour."

Pyper heaved his Weatherby to his shoulder and began trudging back toward the clump of trees.

LAIDLAW SPOTTED MOSES and Smoke lounging in the shade, chatting, as the bakkie bumped across the corrugated veldt. Pyper sat nearby on the ground smoking a cigarette, ignoring them.

"Habari!" Laidlaw greeted as the truck, in a swirl of dust, bounded to a stop at the trees.

"Salam aleikum," Moses grinned.

Laidlaw stepped from the bakkie and walked toward the men. He extended a canteen of water to Moses and nodded toward Pyper, who cast him a sullen glance but didn't get up.

"How's he doin'?" he asked Moses in Kiswahili.

The tracker took a drink of cold water and shrugged. "He is not very friendly." Moses passed the canteen to Smoke.

"You noticed, huh?" Laidlaw chuckled.

"He has nice clothes and a big rifle that he is afraid of, but he does not like safari, mabwana."

"Yeah, I know. Did you find his wildebeest?"

"It is about a half-mile from here," Smoke informed him. "He shot a cow with a broken horn in the rump and it could not keep up with the herd. They left her to die. "

Laidlaw nodded. "I'll let him know." He turned to Pyper and switched back to English. "Good news, Mr. Pyper. Moses and Smoke found your antelope only about a half-mile from here. That'll save us a great deal of tracking. Would you like something cold to drink before we retrieve it? We've got tea, sodas, and a coupla beers."

Pyper flicked his cigarette away and used his Weatherby as a staff to struggle to his feet. "Yeah, I could use a beer."

Laidlaw returned to the bakkie, removed two icy cans of beer from an insulated cooler, and returned to the shelter of the trees. He handed one can to his client and popped the tab on the other can.

"They're not drinkin'?" Pyper asked, indicating the two trackers, who'd resumed chatting in low tones.

Laidlaw shook his head. "Moses and Smoke are Muslims."

His client absently nodded as he guzzled his beer. "Where was it hit?" he asked when he'd finished drinking.

Laidlaw took Pyper's empty beer can. "The wildebeest? Smoke said it was a cow that'd been shot in the rump."

"The rump!" Pyper scowled. "Well, it wasn't my shot, you can damn-well bet that!"

"We'll know when we examine the carcass," Laidlaw said. "But we'd better get movin' so we can get back to camp and let the boys start skinning 'em."

He turned on his heel and returned to the bakkie, trailed by Pyper. He tossed Pyper's empty, and his nearly full, beer cans into the back of the vehicle before sliding into the driver's seat. He cranked the engine as his client climbed laboriously into the passenger's seat.

They bumped out to the wildebeest bull, Moses and Smoke having already disappeared.

USING THEIR MACHETES, THE two trackers had already gutted the antelope and carted its entrails away. Using sticks, they'd propped the animal's body cavity open in order to encourage air circulation and keep the meat relatively cool until the carcass could be properly skinned and butchered once they returned to the boma. With the aid of the bakkie's come-along, Laidlaw winched the bull up the vehicle's tail gate and into its bed.

"Moses will meet us en route to the other wildebeest and lead us right to her," he informed Pyper as he started the engine.

"How do you know which direction to go?"

Laidlaw pointed. "Look." In the distance, a column of vultures wheeled in the updraft. He cranked the steering wheel and headed south.

LAIDLAW SPOTTED THE SAUNTERING trackers after only a few minutes of driving. He slowed and they bounded over and jumped into the rear of the vehicle, where they settled onto the body of the lifeless wildebeest. Moses and Smoke commenced an animated conversation as the bakkie accelerated.

The rough terrain necessitated a circuitous route to the second antelope.

"So, how are we gonna determine who shot which one?" Pyper shouted over the engine noise.

"Doesn't matter," Laidlaw replied. With a thud, the bakkie momentarily bottomed-out in a shallow hole and he gritted his teeth. "Both animals are yours, though you're gonna have to pay for the cow, too, because you accidentally shot her. Her hide will make a pretty rug and you can turn the bull into a nice shoulder mount."

"I shouldn't have to pay for two wildebeests since you shot the other one," Pyper protested.

Laidlaw glanced over at him. "Okay, if that's what you think is fair. You can keep the cow, because she's the one you shot. But cows are smaller and she also has a broken horn. But if that's what you want..."

"How do you know that *you* didn't shoot the cow?"

"Because I shot the bull," Laidlaw replied, matter-of-factly.

Pyper turned away without responding.

"Mabwana." Moses pointed through the windshield and Laidlaw steered the bakkie in the direction indicated.

The rawboned wildebeest cow was lying on her side, facing them.

Moses and Smoke jumped from the vehicle as it slowed. Laidlaw put the bakkie into reverse and slowly backed in an arc until its rear faced the prostrate animal. Once it had come to a stop, Pyper lumbered out.

"We'll put her on top of the bull," Laidlaw said as he grabbed the come-along.

As they'd done with the other wildebeest, the trackers had already gutted the cow and propped open the body cavity with sticks. Pyper was bent over, scrutinizing the bullet hole in her flank, as Laidlaw approached. He squatted and briefly examined the wound.

"That's a hole from a .460," he pointed. "See the difference?" Without waiting for Pyper's answer, he cinched the come-along's cable to the animal's one intact horn, her other horn having been broken sometime in the past, probably while battling Cape hunting dogs or lions.

Pyper lit a cigarette and watched in silence as Laidlaw slowly winched the antelope up the bakkie's tailgate. Moses and Smoke stepped forward and, between them, muscled the heavy carcass so that it rested securely atop the larger bull already in the truck bed. Smoke removed the come-along and Laidlaw replaced it behind the driver's seat.

Laidlaw walked over to his client. "Looks like your .460 busted her hips," he observed. "She's pretty gaunt but her hide's still in pretty good shape and she'll be good eatin' for dinner tonight." He looked directly at Pyper. "So, what'd you decided about the bull?"

Pyper looked at him coldly. "I ain't happy about it, but I guess I'll pay for the cow, too."

Laidlaw nodded. "Accidents happen, Mr. Pyper. She'll be an extra $350, over what you already paid for the bull. Like I said, you'll get a nice rug out of her." He returned to the bakkie without saying more.

THE REMAINING DAYS OF PYPER'S SAFARI were uneventful.

In addition to the two wildebeests, he ended up wounding a pair of small impala rams, a blesbok, and a diminutive warthog. More accurately, Laidlaw ended up shooting his client's disabled trophies for him but, as long as they dropped immediately and didn't require additional tracking, Pyper appeared satisfied. He didn't seem troubled by the fact that it was Laidlaw who actually bagged most of them. Once their taxidermied heads were hung in his man-cave, the gang in Pyper's bowling league wouldn't know or care, one way or the other, who rendered the killing shot and Pyper had no incentive to clarify matters. Displaying no apparent interest in her husband's safari, Margaret Pyper stayed in camp the entire time, drinking wine and reading paperback novels.

"You should have seen the way I rolled him like a pumpkin...ass over tea kettle!" Pyper chortled as they dined on the warthog that Laidlaw shot earlier that afternoon. "I tell you, Mags, that Weatherby is a thumper!" He drained his glass of wine and looked at Laidlaw. "Am I right?"

Winston stepped briskly forward and refilled Pyper's glass.

"Yeah, it's a helluva rifle," Laidlaw blandly acknowledged. "There's not many people who can handle it like you did."

Margaret Pyper cast him a quizzical look before taking another sip of wine.

"I'm thinking of a Euro mount for the warty," Pyper continued after another drink. "What do you think, Laidlaw?"

"Warthogs make handsome European mounts," their host acknowledged. "More impressive than traditional shoulder mounts, in my opinion."

"See, Mags? I told you he would agree with me. This man knows his stuff! A Euro mount will really accentuate the brute's tusks!"

"Your trophies are all drying down at the skinning shed, Mr. Pyper," Laidlaw informed him. "The boys will get them salted and ready to ship to your taxidermist in a couple of days. Until then, you and Mrs. Pyper can just take it easy around camp or

I'll be happy to take you on a photo safari tomorrow, or the next day, if you like."

"Sounds good," Pyper enthused. "What do you think, Mags?"

"If that's what you'd like," she indifferently responded as she idly pushed food around on her plate.

Laidlaw looked at her with curiosity. "Dinner isn't to your liking, Mrs. Pyper? We grow our own vegetables here in camp and the bread and pasties are baked on site. Of course, the main dish is the game our clients, themselves, bag...your husband's warthog, for example."

Pyper grinned and elevated his wine glass in a mock toast.

"No, it's fine," she listlessly assured him. "I'm just a little tired, I think."

Her husband reached over and solicitously patted her arm. "Well, we'll be back in Phoenix soon enough, Mags. Why don't we just take it easy and go take some pictures tomorrow? Hell, I don't think you've left the boma since we got here! Lord knows I could use some down-time after all the hard hunting we've been doing. Aye, Laidlaw?"

Laidlaw gave him a thin smile as Winston wordlessly refilled Pyper's wine glass.

"If you'll excuse me, I think I'll take an aspirin and just go to bed," she said.

"Of course." Laidlaw stood. "Winston will see you to your tent."

“Women,” Pyper grunted after they left. “They’re always sick but they never die.”

“The heat, the remoteness, the bugs, the idleness...it’s understandable,” Laidlaw shrugged.

“Mags wasn’t keen on coming in the first place,” Pyper confided. “I basically had to strong-arm her into it.” Laidlaw sipped a cup of coffee but said nothing.

“In my experience, it’s an unusual wife who fully shares her husband’s passion for hunting,” he observed. Laidlaw’s vocation required that he wear multiple hats: professional hunter, zoologist, physician, historian, psychologist, marriage counselor. And, no matter how much he may have personally enjoyed a particular client, Laidlaw was always glad when they finally departed camp.

Especially poseurs like George Pyper.

“Would you like a cup of coffee, Mr. Pyper?”

“Yeah, I think I might. I’m afraid all that wine may have given me a little headache.”

Laidlaw gestured to Winston, who’d returned from his errand. Filling a coffee cup from an urn, he gently placed it on the table in front of Pyper.

“There’s no hurry to leave camp early,” Laidlaw assured him. “Mrs. Pyper will be able to sleep-in and take her time because there will be plenty of wildlife to photograph, no matter what time we finally make it into the field. I’ll have the boys pack a picnic lunch for us.”

“Will I need my rifle?” Pyper was dismayed at the prospect of having to lug, to say nothing of actually shoot, his Weatherby again.

Laidlaw shook his head. "No. I'll have mine and I doubt we'll encounter anything dangerous since most predators are nocturnal." Excepting angry jumbos, he thought. "The only thing you and Mrs. Pyper will have to bring are your cameras."

"Splendid," Pyper beamed. "Assuming she isn't already asleep, I'll let Mags know."

"In that case, I'll bid you goodnight." Laidlaw slid his chair from beneath the wooden table and stood. "I look forward to seeing you and Mrs. Pyper in the morning."

"Yeah, goodnight, Laidlaw." Ignoring the cup of coffee before him, Pyper looked at Winston and tapped the rim of his wine glass.

LAIDLAW HAD JUST FINISHED cleaning and oiling his rifle when he heard cautious footfalls approach his tent. None of the camp staff would have reason to be there at that hour and would, in any case, have announced themselves.

He leaned the Remington against his cot, stood, and stepped quietly to the doorway to listen. The footsteps paused only inches away. He flung aside the entrance flap.

Margaret Pyper stood immediately outside, clad in a robe and slippers.

Laidlaw maintained his sangfroid. "Can I help you, Mrs. Pyper?"

"We'll be leaving soon and I couldn't sleep," she bumbled. "I thought you might like some company. I know *I* would."

"Your husband?" he began.

She scoffed. "Asleep. With his CPAP running, George wouldn't hear an earthquake if it was right on top of him." She awkwardly paused. "May I come in?"

Laidlaw remained immobile. "I don't think that's a good idea, Mrs. Pyper."

"You misunderstand, Alex," she quickly interposed. "I wish for nothing more than to talk."

He hesitated before finally moving to one side,. He held tent flap open with one hand. "Come in," he sighed.

Margaret Pyper stepped across the threshold into Laidlaw's tent. "May I?" she smiled.

"Sure."

She eased into a collapsible "campaign" chair constructed of heavy canvas and teak adjacent to Laidlaw's cot. "You keep a tidy house."

"Habit," he shrugged as he sat on his cot, facing her.

She leaned back in the chair and demurely crossed her bare ankles. "I hope I'm not interrupting anything."

"No, just cleaning my rifle." He paused. "Your husband had a good hunting day today, Mrs. Pyper."

She smiled, impishly. "I hope you'll forgive my bluntness, Alex, but that's bullshit. George previously told me about the wildebeests and it doesn't take a genius to figure out that he shot the wrong animal.

You and I both know that George couldn't hit the ground with his hat if his life depended on it."

Laidlaw couldn't help but smile. "I don't comment on a client's marksmanship."

"You didn't. I did." She glanced about the interior of Laidlaw's tent before settling her gaze on him again. "So, what does a professional hunter do to occupy his time in the middle of Africa? Aside from cleaning his rifle and reading Francis Bacon, I mean."

"Not much," he chuckled. "But I manage to stay pretty busy just making sure that things are running the way their supposed to. It's important that my clients feel like they're getting their money's worth."

"Well, you don't have to worry about George. He thinks he died and went to heaven."

"Thank you for sharing that with me, Mrs. Pyper. I sincerely appreciate it."

"It's 'Maggie' and you're welcome." She uncrossed her ankles and leaned slightly forward, closer to Laidlaw. Her robe opened slightly, revealing a trace of cleavage. "Be honest, Alex. Don't you get lonely out here in the middle of nowhere? There's no Internet, so you can't even get PornHub or Xhamster! I mean, what do you do?"

"Like I said, I manage to stay busy," Laidlaw noncommittally replied. He didn't like the direction their conversation was headed.

Never taking her eyes off him, Maggie reached up with one hand and tugged her robe open, partially exposing one breast. "I thought perhaps you'd like a break from rifle-cleaning and Bacon."

It wasn't the first time a client's wife had come on to him. Allan Quatermain Syndrome.

"I would like that very much, Mrs. Pyper," he sighed. "But I'm sure you can appreciate the necessity of avoiding even the appearance of impropriety...Caesar's wife and all that."

"Of course. As I said, though, I can't sleep and no one need know I was even here tonight."

"I would know, Mrs. Pyper." Laidlaw paused. "I'll have one of the kitchen staff whip up a toddy for you; it may help you relax and get to sleep," he anemically suggested.

She was surprised, and slightly nonplussed, by his rebuff.

"No, no, Alex. I'll be fine, thank you," she deferred.

"I'll grab my rifle and see you back to your tent."

Although the Pypers' tent was less than 200 feet from Laidlaw's, experience had amply demonstrated the folly of traveling anywhere in the bush unarmed. Death in Africa is always lurking just out of sight. He stood and picked up the Remington. Margaret Pyper rose from her chair and awkwardly retied her robe.

"Please," he said, holding the flap of his tent aside.

She turned wordlessly and headed back to her tent.

Goddammit, Laidlaw thought.

ON THE LAST DAY OF THEIR safari, George and Margaret Pyper sat with their luggage in the large rondavel that served as the camp's kitchen and dining area. They had already eaten breakfast comprised of fresh biscuits with homemade butter and plum preserves, scrambled eggs, slab bacon, and fresh-baked chocolate eclairs, with coffee, chilled milk, and a variety of fresh juices. Laidlaw sat at the table opposite the couple, drinking a cup of black coffee. Due to its remoteness, the camp was accessible only via light plane and the couple waited for the scheduled arrival of the single-engine Cessna that would ferry them back to civilization.

"I had a terrific time, Laidlaw," Pyper blathered. "I'm delighted that I was able to wring out my Weatherby...it's a beast!"

"That it is," Laidlaw concurred. "I'm pleased that you and Mrs. Pyper enjoyed your safari, Mr. Pyper. It was a pleasure having you both in camp." He deliberately avoided eye contact with Margaret, though he thought he could sense her gaze boring into him.

"What does next year look like?" Pyper inquired. "Mags and I were thinking about coming back."

"Honestly, I don't know how many safaris have already booked for next year," Laidlaw lied. "Your best bet is to send me an email once you return home. That will give me time to see whether I still have slots open for next year."

"Done," Pyper burped. "I think Mags may have enjoyed being here even more than I did! Right, Mags?"

Laidlaw finally glanced at her. She wordlessly arched her eyebrows and Laidlaw quickly looked back at Pyper. "Well, we do everything we can to exceed our clients' expectations," he blandly asserted.

"You do that in spades old boy!" Pyper assured him. "You Brits have the safari business down to a science! We Yanks could learn a thing or two from you guys!"

The distant drone of an airplane engine interrupted their conversation.

"Sounds like your plane is close," Laidlaw said. "I'll have a couple of the boys carry your bags out to the airstrip." He stood and extended his hand. "Thank you again for being my guests. I hope to see you both on safari in the near future."

Pyper enthusiastically grabbed his hand and began to vigorously pump it. "Oh, I'm sure you will! "

Laidlaw finally pulled his hand away and extended it to Margaret, who anemically shook it.

"Thank you," he said, softly.

"Of course," she wanly smiled. "There's always next year."

George Pyper hooked a meaty arm around his wife's waist and began propelling her in the direction of the camp's dirt airstrip.

In Primis Anno Regnantibus Imperator Caesar Titus Vespasianus (78 CE)

HIPPOS DESTINED FOR THE *venationes* are invariably yearlings because they are appreciably smaller and, consequently, easier to capture and control than fully mature animals. They are also generally less aggressive. Once in captivity, the yearling hippos are placed in holding pens, where they are fed with the intention of conditioning them to the foods they will eat until being slain in one of several amphitheaters scattered across Roman Europe. After several weeks of captivity, the hippos are caged and transported overland to the Nile, where they are floated downriver on barges to Alexandria, Pelusium, or Damietta and placed aboard a waiting *navis oneraria* for transit to Rome or other ports of the Empire.

Their sheer size and surly disposition render adult hippos invulnerable to natural enemies, though a foolhardy crocodile may occasionally attempt to make a meal of a hippo calf. Should this occur, the calf's enraged mother simply bites the crocodile in half. Given this propensity, the actual capture of hippos and other dangerous animals was usually entrusted to local natives rather than being undertaken by Romans. Notwithstanding that they weigh approximately four tons, even adult bull hippos were regularly captured singlehandedly by lone hunters.

Because their bald, pinkish skin is extremely sensitive to the sun, hippos spend virtually all day partly or fully submerged in rivers deep enough to accommodate their enormous bulk. Surprisingly, however, hippos do not feed in this aquatic habitat. Instead, they depart their riverine sanctuaries every evening to trek inland, sometimes many miles, to graze all night on ordinary grass. At dawn, before the sun grows too intense, they make their way homeward, back to the river. Hippos consistently use the same paths, year after year, to access their nocturnal feeding grounds. Hunters use this predictability against them.

A three-foot-deep cone-shaped pit is dug in the center of a well-trodden path. Covered with branches and reeds, a hippo will inevitably drop into it. The sloping walls of the pit force the hippo's front feet together, completely immobilizing it. The hunter then loops a noose over the helpless animal's snout and ties a bandage around its bulging eyes. After cinching a rope around the hippo's enormous belly and working it backward until arrested by its hind legs, the sides of the pit are cleared away. After hobbling the front legs with cords, the belly-rope is tightened until the hippo yields to the pressure. The now-compliant animal is then led away to a holding pen.

CRIXUS, NEOCLES AND THEIR Roman interpreter, Aulus, were accosted the moment they entered Jugurtha's kraal.

"We talk Jugurtha." Through the interpreter whose linguistic prowess was disputable, Crixus addressed the shriveled tribesman who barred their ingress. He had but one eye and an iridescent fly on his grizzled cheek crawled in-and-out of the vacant, encrusted socket. Crixus found this distracting.

The man leaned on a stick and squinted leerily at them through his remaining, good eye, the sclera of which was creamy yellow. A circle of his apparent relatives, barefoot and draped in filthy djellabas, began to drift over. Although Romans were irregular visitors to their village, Arabian merchants from what is now Yemen were frequent callers. Sailing their dhows across the Red Sea and around the Horn to the Indian Ocean, these peripatetic tradesmen bargained with the various tribes they encountered throughout sub-Saharan Africa: cheap cotton cloth and copper implements in exchange for ivory, gold, ostrich feathers, animal skins, and other exotic merchandise from the interior of the continent. Even the legionnaires occasionally traded with the Arabs. As a consequence of this regular commercial intercourse, a number of native Africans, as well as some Romans, spoke a smattering of Arabic in addition to their native languages. Indeed, Jugurtha was reputed to be a veritable prodigy of learning, purportedly being accomplished in both Arabic and Latin.

A handful of the village's remaining inhabitants warily followed the confrontation from the doorways of huts loosely constructed of sticks, mud, and animal dung. Hundreds of elephant tusks were stacked along the periphery of the kraal. Some tusks were sunk vertically into ground to create arched walkways that were shielded from the sun with ostrich feather fans. Mountains of hippo ivory and the skins of lions, giraffes, leopards, zebras, kudus, impalas, bongos, cheetahs, crocodiles, and a multitude of other species were piled indiscriminately, everything destined to be bartered with Arabian traders for manufactured goods.

"Jugurtha?" the interpreter repeated as he swung his arm around to encompass the kraal.

The man blinked. "Jugurtha?" he grimaced, revealing black gums devoid of teeth.

"Yes, by the gods, *Jugurtha*!" Aulus shouted in frustration. The gathering crowd began to murmur uneasily.

Aulus turned to Crixus. "The old bastard has no idea what I'm trying to say." He placed his hand on the pommel of the bronze dagger sheathed at the waist of his tunic and glanced apprehensively about.

"How to you say 'king' in their tongue?" Crixus asked.

"'*Mfalme*', I think."

Crixus turned to the tribesman and smiled reassuringly. "Mfalme?"

The old man grinned and nodded. "Mfalme. Upesi."

"What did he say?" Crixus asked the interpreter.

"'Soon.'"

Crixus turned to Neocles. "I think it prudent to await Jugurtha's return. The curs will not attempt to harm us because they are starving wretches."

"They may be starving wretches, but they have spears and clubs," Aulus uneasily remarked.

"We are Romans," Crixus reminded him. "We wait."

He and Neocles turned, strode to the nearest hut, and eased themselves onto the packed earth in its marginal shade. Their interpreter wordlessly trailed them, never taking his hand from the hilt of his knife.

AS THE SUN SLOWLY ARCED across the sky, Crixus, Neocles, and Aulus were repeatedly forced to move to different areas within the dusty kraal to escape its searing rays. Still, there was no sign of Jugurth. His impoverished subjects largely ignored the three Romans.

"I could use a drink," Aulus sulked.

"These savages drink cow's piss and eat cow's shit," Neocles grunted. "You speak their language...why don't you ask for some?"

Aulus looked at him peevishly. "Is it not plain that these rascals are playing us for fools? They *have* no king! We will still be awaiting his arrival when it gets dark, whereupon they will cut our throats and eat us. Let us return to the *castrum* rather than waste more time among them."

Crixus began laughing and placed his hand on Aulus's shoulder. "We have already waited this long...how would it profit us to leave now? If Jugurtha does not appear before the setting of the sun, we will go."

Even as he was speaking, their attention was arrested by commotion in the vicinity of one of the larger huts. Milling about the entrance, which was blocked by an animal skin tacked to its exterior, a large group of tribespeople comprised of both sexes congregated. Spontaneously, the females burst into a shrill ululation, while the men undertook rhythmic clapping.

The Romans rose to their feet, their interest piqued.

The howls of the women grew in intensity as the entire assembly began an extemporaneous dance.

"What in the name of Jupiter..." Aulus muttered.

"Methinks Jugurtha has arrived," Neocles opined.

As they watched, the hide covering the door of the hut was pushed aside and a tall, impressive man with exceptionally dark skin emerged. A leopard skin was slung over his shoulders and he stepped arrogantly into the ring of his ebullient subjects.

"That him?" Crixus asked.

Neocles nodded.

"What now?" asked the latter.

"We talk," Crixus replied as he began walking in the direction of the hubbub.

The Romans crossed the packed-earth square at the center of the kraal.

"Hail, Jugurtha!" Crixus cried in Latin over the din of the fawning crowd.

Jugurtha gestured for his acolytes to part, thereby enabling the Romans to draw nearer. He motioned for silence.

"Romans!" he contemptuously spat in passable Latin. "I was informed that you were polluting my kraal."

Aulus shouldered his way to the fore. "Polluting? You knew we sought an audience, yet kept us waiting all day?"

"A warrior and a king is not at the beck and call of everyone who desires an audience, nor does he serve at their pleasure," Jugurtha tutored. "Who are you?"

Crixus stepped forward. "I am Crixus, of *Legio XVI Bestia*, Excellency."

Jugurtha looked at him, superciliously. He pointed at Neocles. "Him, I know. You and the other one are unknown to me."

"I am Aulus, also of *Legio XVI Bestia* and am skilled in your language."

One of the king's subjects discretely slid a carved acacia wood throne forward. Before easing himself down, Jugurtha carefully used a fly whisk fashioned from a gembuck's tail to dust the seat.

"I know your tongue and do not require others to speak my words for me," Jugurtha sniffed. "Some of those in my kraal also speak Latin. Your presumptuousness exceeds that of your betters, Roman. You do not possess a monopoly on intelligence and boast the manners of a pig." He crossed his legs and leaned back in his throne. "For what reason do you disturb me?"

His ragged subjects crowded near the colloquy, watching and listening intently to the exotic Romans, though it was unclear whether any of them actually understood the conversation.

Crixus was half-tempted to simply let Aulus use his dagger on the arrogant monarch. Unfortunately, the Romans needed him, at least in the short run.

"We wish to discuss business," Crixus informed him.

"Business? What business might the invincible legionnaires of Rome have with me?" Jugurtha taunted. "And what do they offer in return?"

Crixus smiled. "Your life, as well as continued dominion over what passes for a kingdom."

Jugurtha was visibly taken aback by the brusque response. Quickly recovering his poise, he leaned slightly forward and grasped the arms of his throne.

"You dare threaten me?" he menacingly challenged.

"I have no need to threaten," Crixus replied. "You asked a question; I answered it."

Jugurtha's expression grew hard. "I could easily send your heads back to your commander on the point of a spear."

"Admittedly," Crixus acknowledged, "if you want your kraal burned and your people slaughtered by this hour tomorrow. Mark me: you will be the first to be crucified." He casually rested the palm of his hand on the hilt of the Damascened blade that hung at his side, obtained from the old Jew following Jerusalem's bloody capitulation to Titus.

Damascus steel, a rarity so named from its reputed origin in Damascus, Syria, and characterized by a beautiful swirling pattern formed in the metal during the forging process, was highly prized. Similar to the technique employed to create Samurai swords, Damascus steel is fashioned by alternately heating a billet of iron before plunging it into an oil bath to cool it. Flexible, strong, and easily sharpened, vastly superior to its bronze and iron counterparts, Damascus steel was, and remains, highly valued for knives and swords.

Outplayed, Jugurtha visibly slumped in his throne. "What do you want?" he asked after a pause.

"Hippos. Perhaps additional creatures later."

"For what reason?"

"Our emperor and senate desire them. That is reason enough."

The king narrowed his eyes. "Why don't the Romans hunt the animals themselves?"

"Your people are more skilled."

Jugurtha sighed and surveyed the uncomprehending faces of the pressing throng. “If the only thing the Romans desire is a few hippos, I am prepared to provide them. That is easily enough done. My people tie heavy stones to ropes and harpoon the beasts. They quickly drown.”

Crixus shook his head. “That will not do. The hippos must be captured alive and transported to our *castrum*.”

Jugurtha bolted upright. “Alive? You ask too much, Roman. Their size renders that impossible.”

“That is untrue,” Neocles interjected. “I have personally witnessed your people capture hippos merely by digging a hole in the ground.”

The king waved his hands dismissively. “If it is as simple as that, you Romans have no need of me. I invite you to capture your hippos yourselves.”

“It is unwise to reject the opportunity to display one’s goodwill,” Crixus cautioned. “You will find Rome generous toward her friends.”

“I desire neither Rome’s friendship nor her generosity,” Jugurtha retorted.

Crixus thoughtfully nodded. “Perhaps not. But, while you may not desire Rome as your friend, you most assuredly do not want her as your enemy.”

Their host surveyed the matter-of-fact Romans in silence.

“How many hippos are required?” he finally asked.

“Fifteen, promptly. Additional hippos, as well as additional creatures, in due course.”

Crixus realized that requiring Jugurtha to straightaway produce 50 hippos would be certain to alienate the chieftain. Although *Legio XVI Bestia* lacked the immediate ability to accommodate and feed the huge animals, Crixus was confident such facilities could be constructed before the tribespeople actually delivered the hippos.

Jugurtha frowned as he surveyed the Romans with suspicion. "What 'additional creatures'?"

"Our commander has not yet informed us," Neocles replied. "However, you must begin immediately with the hippos."

"They are savage beasts and there are too few men in my kraal to undertake their capture," Jugurtha protested. "It is impossible to produce such a large number of animals."

"There are additional kraals with additional men."

"Many are likely to be hurt or killed," the monarch insisted.

"That is possible," Crixus conceded. "You must ensure that such injuries are kept to a minimum. Make no mistake: Rome is mindful that, if too many perish before your task is complete, it will reflect poorly on your stature among your people."

"So, Rome now presumes to superintend me?" Jugurtha snarled.

Neocles looked directly at the king. "Rome superintends the entire world. Even backwaters such as this."

It was clear that the intractable Romans would not be cowed, leaving Jugurtha no choice but to capitulate.

"I must consult with the headmen of my tribe regarding this matter," he said at last, in a feckless display of authority.

"Consult whoever you wish," Crixus said, "provided the hippos are swiftly delivered to us."

THE THREE MEN RETURNED to their *castra stativa*, which lay about five Roman miles north of Jugurtha's kraal, by following a game trail that paralleled the Mara River.

"What is the likelihood the barbarians will honor their promise?" Aulus mused as they tramped.

"Although they are savages, Jugurtha has never deceived me," Neocles replied.

"Or at least you've not yet caught him," Crixus clarified.

Aulus chuckled at Crixus's sarcastic rejoinder while Neocles cast him a waspish look.

"By the gods, I daresay that Jugurtha hates you, Crixus," Aulus declared.

"Let him hate," Crixus shrugged, "provided he also fears."

FROM THE DAWN OF THEIR CIVILIZATION and continuing without deviation through monarchy, republic, and empire, the Romans were relentless colonizers, their legions the emissaries of Rome's bellicose foreign policy. As a corollary, the Latins became resolute fort-builders, the designs of which varied depending on their intended use.

While on campaign, Roman commanders relied on *castra aestiva*, temporary, movable encampments that served as staging areas and supply depots for their mobile legions. Following the inevitable subjugation of defiant nations, commanders erected *castra stativa*, permanent, impregnable fortresses, tangible representations of Roman power designed to dissuade conquered states from rebelling against their uninvited overlords.

While differing in individual features, primarily a reflection of the local building materials, all *castra stativa* conformed to more-or-less standardized designs. They were invariably rectangular, their walls constructed of timber or stone above a sloping earth rampart. A double row of parallel defensive ditches surrounded the perimeter of the fort, the soil from which was utilized to construct the rampart itself. The interior was accessed via one, sometimes two, gates secured from the inside with cross-bars and surmounted by adjacent towers of wood or stone. Within these fortifications various structures were erected: barracks, stables, storehouses, workshops, an armory, a kitchen, a mess hall, and an infirmary. These buildings were set away from the interior wall of the fort, separated from it by a firebreak intended to shield them from missiles launched over the walls by besieging enemies. Once completed, *castra stativa* were continuously occupied by cohorts of Roman troops and their auxiliaries, rotating over periods of months or years.

In contrast to the permanent *castra stativa*, *castra aestiva* were, essentially, impromptu shelters constructed on an as-needed basis, often daily, while a legion was on the move. Although frequently erected while under enemy fire, they generally reflected the rectangular aspect of their more robust counterparts, with a simple wooden palisade enclosing leather tents instead of wooden or stone buildings. If permitted by the circumstances, legionnaires sometimes piled rocks against the tents for added protection against the weather or enemy assaults.

The *castra stativa* of *Legio XVI Bestia* was one of Rome's most formidable, attributable less to potential threats to its occupying garrison than to the fact that the legionnaires who were marooned there had little else to occupy their time but to fortify their dwelling-place. Constructed largely of rammed earth and stone because of the region's lack of timber, it was situated on a small island in the center of the Mara River, which provided a natural fosse to shield the fortress from assault. Narrow causeways, ingeniously designed to collapse beneath their own weight when a series of chocks were removed, linked the structure to either bank of the river and provided additional security by further isolating the *castrum*. Despite the redoubt's unconventional location in the middle of a river, it none-the-less embraced the general configuration of its counterparts located in the Empire's more northerly climes.

IT WAS NIGHTFALL BY the time they ultimately arrived at the *castrum*. Crossing the near causeway, they stood before the barricaded gate.

"Hail, friends!" called the guard from a towering stone turret.

"Hail, Lothar!" returned Neocles.

"Unbar the entry!" hollered Lothar to someone on the ground. "Your mission to the savages was successful?" he amiably inquired as the heavy wooden beam that secured the entrance was noisily withdrawn.

"We were not boiled and eaten, if that is what you are asking," Aulus muttered.

"I am certain of Jugurtha's help," Crixus answered, more diplomatically. "It was only necessary to remind him of Rome's continued friendship."

In the center of the tall wooden gate was a modest door, used to admit individuals, rather than cumbrous wagons, animals, or entire legions to the *castrum*. It was through this portal that the trio finally stepped.

They were immediately confronted by Berossus.

"You three were gone long enough!" the centurion growled.

"Jugurtha's kraal is distant and we were kept waiting," Neocles explained.

"Waiting? Since when does an Aethiop keep the legionnaires of *Legio XVI Bestia* waiting?"

"Since this afternoon," Crixus pointed out.

Berossus looked at him irascibly. "Other than pissing away the day, did you *feminae* accomplish anything while at the Aethiops?"

"Although they are ignorant barbarians, you may rest assured of their unwavering fidelity," Aulus pledged. "My skills as interpreter enabled me to impress upon the Aethiops the grave folly of trifling with Romans."

Aulus' unexpected brazenness prompted Neocles and Crixus to exchange puzzled glances.

"What does that mean?" Berossus snapped. "I care less than nothing for the Aethiops 'fidelity'. I am a soldier, not a politician. My only job is to make certain that Corvo remains drunk and happy, which can only be accomplished if you do your jobs by providing the animals demanded by the senate, with or without the assistance of the 'faithful' Aethiops."

"Yes, that is what I meant, Centurion," Aulus hastily stammered.

"I don't give your grandmother's cunt about what you meant. I care only for what you *do*!"

"Understood," Aulus acknowledged, chastened.

Berossus turned to Neocles. "I have given thought to what he," indicating Crixus, "said about transporting elephants from *Carthago* to Rome, and am in agreement. You will begin to capture the other beasts at once. I will have enclosures constructed and fodder laid up. Requisition as many men as you require but take him, as well." Berossus pointed at Aulus.

Neocles glanced at Crixus, who nodded almost imperceptibly.

"We begin on the morrow," Neocles said.

Berossus nodded. "See to it." He stomped off to resume a round of drinking.

FOUR

AFRICA IS A CONTINENT OF improbable animals.

The predictable, unvarying subject matter of virtually all television documentaries on African wildlife is either "magnificent" lions or "noble" elephants. Specific animals are invariably highlighted by the sonorous narrator, assigned pseudo-exotic, anthropomorphic names that are heavy on vowels, and filmed stalking various herbivores or patiently trekking through a waterless moonscape with baby 'Imfoozi', or some other contrived name, struggling to keep up with a ponderous elephant herd. Uninformed viewers may be forgiven for concluding that the only animals that exist on the African continent are lions, elephants, crocodiles, wildebeests, zebras, and an occasional cheetah. In a similar vein, marine wildlife documentaries would suggest that sharks, along with an occasional whale, are the only creatures to inhabit the world's oceans.

Yet, Africa abounds in extraordinary fauna that goes completely unheralded.

Laidlaw read somewhere that Africa is home to seventy per-cent of the world's antelope species, many of them among the most striking and beautiful animals on earth. The eland, for example, by far the largest antelope species on the planet, is as large as a Brahma bull, which it strongly resembles. Despite its huge size, the eland is a pacific creature that has been semi-domesticated by many African tribes, which utilize its milk as they would that of an ordinary cow. Indeed, elands have successfully bred with cattle, though their offspring are invariably sterile.

There is also the regal-looking sable antelope, its long, curving, anthracite horns resembling scimitars. Fearless and powerful, neither lions nor hyenas will attempt to bring down a healthy sable bull. The stately kudu looks like a chimera from the Arabian Nights: fawn-colored and banded with pale striations, its spectacular spiral horns can approach six feet in length, yet kudus bound over eight-foot fences with ease. Even the prosaic impala, with delicate lyrate horns, is sublime.

Of quintessential African wildlife, however, Laidlaw's favorite was the zebra: a black-and-white striped horse. Who'd a thunk it?

A noisy and gregarious animal typically found grazing among herds of wildebeest, or in smaller family units led by a dominant stallion, the plains zebra is often depicted in popular media as charming and gentle, little removed from a child's pony. In reality, zebras are high-strung, fractious creatures. Mature stallions constantly battle one another over breeding rights, leaving them gashed and scarred from the bites and kicks of competing males. And, although they are a favorite prey of lions, imprudent predators are routinely crippled or killed by the well-placed kick of a zebra. The impeccable zebra rugs sold at airport gift shops in Jo'burg, Nairobi, and Lusaka, as well as over the internet, are from farm-raised mares, bred for their hides.

Zebra hunting is a challenge because of the creature's inherent edginess. Compounding matters is the fact that there are always multiple eyes, ears, and nostrils on alert for the slightest peril. Should any member of the group sense danger, real or imagined, zebras characteristically emit a distinct bark, sounding nothing like a domestic horse, thereby sending the entire herd into headlong flight. If the threat is sufficiently close, zebra stallions instinctively go into attack-mode, violently biting, kicking, stomping, and battering the assailant with their muscular necks and chests.

Because the zebras' senses are uniformly acute, it is essential to stalk them from upwind, taking full advantage of all available cover. The hunter must also be prepared to aim and fire his rifle in an instant, before the fleeing herd disappears over the hill in a cloud of dust.

Like George Pyper, first-timers to Africa typically purchase prepackaged, *prix fixe,* hunting packages from vendors at "outdoor" or hunting-and-fishing expos. Such safaris offer a limited assortment of generic species, usually antelope, which Africa possesses in abundance. By contrast, experienced hunters are more selective. They eschew such prosaic offerings and typically confine themselves to one or two varieties of more exotic game, hoping to bag an exceptional trophy. Tyros like Pyper consider themselves lucky to shoot *anything.*

Laidlaw's current client was a discriminating huntsman.

Grigori Rostov made his fortune in telecommunications in the aftermath of the collapse of the Soviet Union. He currently owned a home on the Black Sea, flats in Paris and Rome, and properties in Costa Rica, Ireland, Argentina, and San Francisco, and was the veteran of multiple African safaris. Laidlaw guided Rostov on most of them.

And, as it happened, his passion was zebras.

"The big stallion is pretty banged up," Laidlaw whispered as he and Rostov watched a small herd through binoculars. The two men hunkered 400 yards away, behind a large mopane tree.

"Yeah, he's missing part of one ear," Rostov confirmed. "One toward the back has a better hide."

Laidlaw focused his binoculars on the subject animal. "But, I think that one's a mare...not that it makes much difference." Zebras of either gender are generally as plump as sausages and sexes can be difficult to distinguish.

"I can't tell from this distance, though I don't see an udder or a penis."

"It's hard to tell, but her neck is thinner and her muzzle not as broad. That big male probably got in a fight with another stallion. Could've also lost his ear to a lion, I guess, 'cause it looks like he's got some pretty deep scars on his flank, too."

"Yeah, I see 'em."

They continued to observe the grazing animals in silence.

Laidlaw lowered his binoculars and looked at his client. "Well, what do you think, Greg? You interested in any of those or ya wanna keep lookin'?"

"I think I want the fucked-up one. He's big and has a lot of character. He'll make a nice pedestal mount." Grigori was about to add an additional comment when Laidlaw softly hissed and placed his hand on his client's forearm. The old stallion had ceased grazing and was gazing in their direction.

"They're gonna bolt," Laidlaw cautioned. "Get ready."

In a single fluid motion, his client brought his rifle, a CZ in .300 mag, to his shoulder.

"If they run, the mares will lead and the stallion will bring up the rear," Laidlaw rapidly reminded him. "But, at some point, he'll stop and look back to see if the coast is clear. When he does, bang him!"

Grigori nodded and, at that moment, the zebra herd exploded in a tumult of crashing hooves and loud barking.

From previous safaris, Laidlaw knew his client to be an excellent marksman. Even so, he automatically whipped his rifle to his shoulder in case Rostov's shot went awry. If a cloud passes over the sun the moment the trigger is pulled, for example, the shot will go high. Though Laidlaw had no explanation for this phenomenon, he had personally witnessed it more than once. Also, small twigs, even a blade of grass, interposed between the hunter and his quarry, invisible even through a high-powered rifle scope, can deflect the bullet in mid-flight, resulting in a clean miss.

Through his scope, Rostov calmly watched the zebra herd crash forward, pell-mell, the stallion trailing exactly as Laidlaw predicted. After dashing fifty yards, the stallion momentarily hesitated to look over his shoulder, rearward, in the direction of the mopane tree that shielded the two hunters.

Because the stallion was facing away from the men, its rump basically dead-center to them, Rostov was presented with only three practicable aiming points: straight through the stallion's anus, which would result in catastrophic organ destruction and rapid death; the root of the tail; or the zebra's neck, the lower part of which was partially blocked by the animal's shoulder and rotund body. Either of the latter two shots would sever the zebra's spinal cord and produce instantaneous death. Irrespective, all three shots demanded absolutely precise bullet placement in order to ensure a humane kill. While a brain shot was also a possibility, Rostov did not favor them because it was not unknown for bullets to ricochet off an animal's skull when fired at an oblique angle. Although partially obscured, the animal's neck provided a larger target area and, at least theoretically, slightly more room for error.

Successfully hitting a mark the size of a tennis ball at a distance exceeding 400 yards requires exceptional shooting ability particularly where, as here, the target is not completely stationary. A miss of even a couple of inches, while inflicting a painful wound, would prove catastrophic, as it would neither ensure the animal's immediate death nor arrest its panicked flight.

Rostov was able to process the foregoing matters in an instant and determine that a neck shot represented his best option.

His shot rang out.

Because of the intervening distance, Laidlaw was unable to hear the distinctive, satisfying thump of a bullet striking flesh though, through his rifle scope, he discerned the blossom of red that erupted on the zebra's neck. A follow-up "insurance" shot was unnecessary, as Rostov's aim was faultless.

The stallion took two stumbling steps forward before collapsing. The remaining members of the stampeding herd had already vanished into the vast emptiness of the veldt.

“Good shooting, Greg,” Laidlaw softly remarked as he engaged the safety on his Remington and lowered it. He removed his baseball cap and used it to mop his perspiring brow.

Rostov ejected the empty brass casing from his rifle, flicked its safety on, and leaned it against the trunk of the mopane tree. “Thank you. The angle wasn’t ideal and I was fortunate.”

“You didn’t have the luxury of time. Had you not fired when you did, he’d have been off like a prom dress and you’d have forfeited the shot. Let’s go check him out.” Laidlaw placed his cap back on his head and stepped away from the tree. He began ambling in the direction of the prostrate zebra, his rifle cradled in the crook of his arm. Rostov grabbed his rifle and followed.

“Right on the money,” Laidlaw remarked when they finally drew abreast of the fallen animal.

The zebra was sprawled on its left side. Rostov’s expanding bullet entered the stallion’s neck three inches behind the temporomandibular joint, where it nicked both the spinal cord and the primary artery in that region. Death ensued one and one-half seconds later.

As was their practice, Moses and Smoke materialized, seemingly out of nowhere. They grinned as they enthusiastically pumped Rostov’s hand.

“Let’s get a coupla pictures before I head back for the bakkie,” Laidlaw said. “Help me roll him into a better position.”

Zebras are large, heavy animals. In Kiswahili, Laidlaw delivered some cursory instructions to his two trackers. He and Rostov laid their rifles aside and, between the four men, managed to wrestle the stallion into a more aesthetic pose. Having done so, Laidlaw removed a small point-and-shoot camera from his breast pocket and squatted.

"You'll have to kneel, Greg," Laidlaw instructed.

"I want Moses and Smoke in the photo, too," Rostov insisted.

"'Course." Laidlaw motioned with his head and the trackers joined Rostov next to the zebra. The three men put their arms around one another's shoulders and beamed as Laidlaw snapped a few photos.

"Shall I wait here while you bring the bakkie?" Rostov asked after standing.

"Yeah, I should be back in less than an hour 'cause it ain't too far . You okay with that? The boys will hang around and keep you company, if ya want."

Rostov smiled. "Of course, Alex. I don't need a babysitter but, if they want to wait here until you get back, they're welcome to do so."

"Fair enough. I'll let 'em know."

Laidlaw conveyed the essence of his conversation with Rostov to Moses and Smoke before turning back to his client.

"It's getting pretty late in the day and they said they'll hitch a ride to camp in the bakkie, rather than hike back. So, it looks like you'll have some company whether you want it or not!" Laidlaw grinned.

"I welcome it. I'll work on my Kiswahili while you're gone."

"You got enough water 'till I get back?"

Rostov patted the canteen suspended from his belt. "No worries."

Laidlaw nodded and retrieved his rifle. Placing it horizontally across his shoulders and hooking his wrists over it, he began tramping back to the bakkie, parked a mile away.

AFTER WINCHING THE ZEBRA into the bed of the bakkie they headed back to the boma, where they would offload their cargo at the adjacent skinning shed. There, expert skinners would "cape" the stallion and preserve its hide by coating the flesh-side with a layer of coarse salt until it could be transported to Rostov's taxidermist for tanning. After skinning, the kitchen staff would then butcher the animal; some of the meat would be broiled for dinner at camp that night, the rest divided among the staff, trackers, and skinners. The zebra's bones and entrails were used to make soup; its tail fashioned into a fly whisk, individual strands utilized as sewing thread to mend clothing; the collagen in its hooves boiled into glue, the hooves, themselves, carved into spoons.

In Africa, nothing is wasted.

Moses and Smoke comfortably plopped atop the body of the zebra as the bakkie bumped homeward across the veldt. The former leaned forward, close to Laidlaw's ear.

"Mabwana, I want to tell you something," he confided, as Laidlaw abruptly torqued the steering wheel to avoid a rut.

Laidlaw glanced at him

"What are you talking about?"

"A place I have not told you of."

Given that Moses and Smoke had been African trackers for twenty years, half of them for Laidlaw, and were intimately acquainted with the region's geography, fauna, and flora, Laidlaw was puzzled.

"I don't know what you mean, Moses," he said.

"A big building, mabwana. It is very old."

"A 'big building'? What kind of building?"

Moses shrugged. "I do not know."

"Where is it?"

"The Mara. No one goes there because it is bewitched. Giants live there, mabwana."

A belief in magic and witchcraft, considered by unenlightened Westerners to be a foolish anachronism, remains pervasive in native communities throughout Africa. One manifestation of this phenomenon is the number of ill-omened sites scattered across the continent, the reputed abode of jinns and other malevolent entities. Zanzibar's former slave markets and multiple sanguinary locations in the former Belgian Congo, Idi Amin's Uganda, and Rwanda are such inauspicious places. These, however, represent merely the tip of the iceberg. Innumerable other localities, most obscure and unnamed, share this infelicitous distinction. Pondoro Taylor's mysterious 'Ghost Bushman Hill' is but one such site.

The Mara River, once a substantial watercourse dotted with numerous islands, reduced over the centuries to little more than a swamp because of erosion and shifting rainfall patterns, lay many miles distant. Laidlaw had never been inclined to travel there due to its inaccessibility, though its reputation among the locals as unpropitious was widely acknowledged.

"What were you and Smoke doing at the Mara?"

Moses scowled. "He wanted to go. He said we would find lots of animals there because they have not been hunted before." He paused. "I did not want to go."

"And you found a big building there?"

"Yes, mabwana," Moses confirmed.

"Were there people there, too?"

"Only spirits, mabwana. I don't think people have been there for a long time."

"Animals?"

Moses solemnly nodded. "Many animals: 150-pound elephant, waterbuck, sable, buffalo."

As he drove, Laidlaw pondered Moses' revelations. A "150-pound" elephant meant that at least one of its tusks weighed a minimum of 150 pounds, an astonishing colossus. Hell, Laidlaw had never even *seen* an elephant that big, but he'd never hunted the Mara, either. Nor did he know anyone who had. The inherent remoteness of the area was sufficiently off-putting to discourage such forays, especially since there was no shortage of huntable animals much closer to home. But, as far as he knew, there hadn't been a 150-pound elephant in Africa for well over a century. If what Moses claimed he and Smoke encountered was true, the Mara apparently contained a treasure-trove of game, all of it unmolested by hunters.

"What was the building you saw there?" he pressed Moses.

"We did not go inside because it was falling down and we were afraid. But it was made of stone, like a white man's fort."

"And no people were there?" Laidlaw asked again.

"No one," Moses affirmed. "Not for a long time, mabwana."

THEY DEPOSITED ROSTOV'S stallion at the skinning shack after finally arriving back at the boma.

"I'm gonna clean up while the boys prepare dinner...zebra fillets," Laidlaw told his client as they unloaded their gear from the bakkie. There's something I wanna talk to you about, too."

"Yeah, a shower sounds good," Rostov replied. "We'll have a coupla drinks before dinner. I'll have a smoke and see you in an hour or so."

Laidlaw nodded as he slung his rifle over his shoulder and began carting the rest of his equipment to his tent. He knew Rostov had hunted all over Africa and wanted to pick his brain about what Moses told him during the ride back.

"YOU EVER HUNTED THE Mara?" Laidlaw asked. It was sunset and they were sitting around the fire pit, drinking rum and Coke. The scent of broiling zebra steaks wafted toward them from the kitchen.

"River?" Rostov responded.

"Yeah, the Mara River." Laidlaw took a sip of his cocktail and watched Rostov over the rim of his glass. "You ever hunted around there?"

Rostov furrowed his brow. "I don't think so," he finally said. "If I have, I don't remember. Is it nearby?"

"Not really. Probably about a half-day." Laidlaw drained his glass and placed it on the ground next to his folding canvas chair.

"Why do you ask, Alex?"

"On the way back to camp this afternoon, Moses told me that he and Smoke hoofed it out to the Mara because they heard there was a lot of game there."

"You've not hunted there before?" Rostov asked, somewhat surprised.

Laidlaw shook his head. "Never had any reason to. Might have to now, though."

"How so?"

Laidlaw quickly related the substance of his conversation with Moses.

"What the hell kind of 'building' would be out there if the Mara is as remote as you say?" Rostov asked when Laidlaw finished his recitation.

"Beats me. But 150-pound tuskers are about as common as Egyptian leprechauns."

Rostov finished his cocktail and cupped his hands around his glass while he reflected.

"You think the building they saw may be some kind of secret government installation?" he ventured.

Laidlaw laughed. "Greg, we're not in the States or the USSR. The government in this country is so inept and corrupt that it couldn't arrange a decent backyard bar-b-que, much less plan, organize, and build anything elaborate out in the middle of nowhere. Besides, Moses said it was old and falling down. Even if it was some top-secret government, Area 51, UFO installation, which it ain't, whoever built it must've abandoned it a long time ago."

"So, what do you think it is? Something akin to Great Zimbabwe?"

"I have no idea," Laidlaw admitted. "But, if you're up to it, I'd like to jump in the bakkie tomorrow and head out there. No matter what sort of buildings may, or may not, be there, I think it's probably worth checking out. Hell, I'd like to see a 150-pound elephant just to say I did, irrespective of all the other game that Moses says is out there. We might even run across another herd of zebra on the way."

“We’re out in the middle of fucking Africa, Alex,” Rostov grinned. “What else do we have to do? It isn’t as though there’s a beautiful woman waiting in bed for me!”

“I’ll have the kitchen staff pack a big lunch,” Laidlaw said. “I want Moses and Smoke to come too, since they know exactly where we’re going.”

Rostov nodded. “Of course. That will also give me a chance to work on my Kiswahili.”

“Good, good.” Laidlaw stood. “Well, I think it’s approaching dinner time. You about ready to eat?”

“We have an expression in Russia for meat that is very tough. We say that it is ‘as tough as old boots’,” Rostov said. “I think the stallion I shot today is going to be as tough as old boots.”

Laidlaw started laughing as they headed for the dining palapa. “I hate to tell you, Greg, but that expression is used pretty much everywhere, not just Russia.”

“That may be so,” Rostov conceded, “but we were the first to use it!”

IT TOOK NEARLY SIX hours of torturous driving to reach the Mara.

Laidlaw’s shoulders and arms ached from wrestling the bakkie’s steering wheel back-and-forth over the trackless route. Twice, they got mired in choking sand and had to use shovels to dig out; once, the vehicle high-centered and it took over twenty minutes and all four of them to finally rock the bakkie free. Laidlaw ruefully concluded that it probably took Moses and Smoke only half as long to travel to the Mara on foot.

"I hope you told the kitchen to pack lunch, dinner, *and* breakfast," Rostov said through gritted teeth as they bottomed-out in yet another crater.

"Yeah, it don't look like we're gonna make it back to camp tonight," Laidlaw concurred, torquing the bakkie hard to the left in an effort to minimize the pummeling. In the back, Moses and Smoke clutched the vehicle's roll bar as it bucked and swayed, both of them grinning broadly. Although they encountered a small band of zebra, a few topi, and a herd of impala en route, they elected not to pursue them because of their eagerness to reach their destination.

"How much longer you figure?" Rostov shouted over the laboring engine.

Without taking his eyes off the course, Laidlaw half-turned his head toward the trackers to relay the question. He nodded as Moses replied.

"He says we're gettin' close...only a few more clicks."

"Who the fuck would want to build anything way out here?" Rostov rhetorically marveled as the bakkie shuddered and bounced. "More to the point, why?"

"Before the British, but especially the Dutch, Belgians, and Portuguese, arrived and started shooting everything in sight, this entire region was divided into a bunch of fiefdoms that constantly fought with each other," Laidlaw informed him. "Although Cecil Rhodes and his buds pretty much drove the last nail into their collective coffin, I'm thinkin' that one of the tribes may have built whatever it is that that Moses and Smoke found out here…like you said, kinda like Great Zimbabwe. The locals have probably known about it forever, but don't talk about it because they consider it haunted, taboo, or whatever. And Anglos don't know about it because they've never had any reason to come out this far."

"If that's true, it would really be something, Alex."

Laidlaw whipped the bakkie's steering wheel to the right to avoid a large rock. "Yep."

THEY ARRIVED MID-AFTERNOON.

The fortress, if that's what it indeed was, appeared to be little more than an extensive heap of ruins. It vaguely reminded Laidlaw of El Castillo, concealed in the jungles of southern Nicaragua on the bank of the San Juan River. At some point during its existence, the Mara edifice must have been an imposing one because it occupied a significant area in the middle of a bog that was, at least nominally, the Mara River. It was apparent that the site had once been higher and drier, for no one would have erected any sort of structure on such a sodden, insubstantial foundation. Its spatial orientation as derived from surviving sections of its stone walls suggested that the Mara once flowed on either side of the structure which, for reasons of defense, was probably isolated on a small island near the center of the river.

Rostov swung his legs out as Moses and Smoke sprang from the rear of the bakkie.

"This it?" He looked inquiringly at Moses, who nodded. "Well, you were right about one thing, Alex. It looks older than my grandmother's mustache! I wonder why archaeologists aren't all over it!"

His curiosity piqued, Laidlaw began picking his way through the marsh toward what appeared to be the remains of a circular tower. He was eager to see whether any inscriptions, carvings, or ostraca could be found to assist in identifying or dating the structure. Rostov followed; Moses and Smoke loitered around the bakkie.

"It kinda looks like Great Zimbabwe, I guess," Laidlaw mused. "At least what's left of that tower does."

"You think native Africans built this?"

Laidlaw paused and surveyed the area. "Well, for decades European historians insisted that Great Zimbabwe had to have been built by Arab traders who traveled inland from the coastal areas...either Arabs or unidentified Anglos from somewhere to the south. The thinking was that native Africans were simply too primitive to build anything as elaborate as Great Zimbabwe. Turns out, local tribes did build it, so there's no reason to think they couldn't have built this place, too."

Rostov drew abreast of him. "All the way out here? Why?"

"This place wasn't always 'all the way out here'," Laidlaw laughed. "The Mara used to be a substantial riverine system. For whatever reason, somebody obviously figured that it made sense to build something like this out here. Maybe to protect boat traffic that used the river at one time...who the hell knows?"

"How long since the Mara has been navigable, do you think?"

"A long time...generations." Laidlaw swiveled toward the bakkie and relayed the question to Moses, who shrugged his response. "He says the Mara has been a swamp since before his grandfather's grandfather," Laidlaw reported.

"Does he know what it was? A fort? An entrepot of some sort? A palace?"

Laidlaw shook his head. "They don't have a clue. Like I said, they consider it taboo and shun it."

"Wouldn't it be cool if we were the first to explore this place?" excitedly responded. "Who hasn't dreamed of discovering a lost city."

"Well, 'lost city' might be something of an overstatement," Laidlaw chuckled.

"No matter. Who knows what might be buried here!"

Laidlaw resumed ambling toward the ruins. "Let's go have a look-see."

They had to tread carefully on the marshy soil to avoid sinking up to their ankles in muck. The two trackers remained around the bakkie and watched them with unease.

"The place is really something, Alex!" Rostov enthused as he stepped over a squared cube of masonry, half-buried in the soft earth.

Although the visible architectural elements of the abandoned structure defied precise identification, the area was broadly littered with stone blocks of various dimensions, some of them bearing the faint shadows of carved, but badly eroded, characters. Here and there Laidlaw thought he recognized ashlars, fragments of long-collapsed columns, and carved entablatures. He bent to closely examine a shattered plinth tilting from the soil, exploring its once-polished surface with his fingertips.

"This feels rough, like sandstone," he called to Rostov.

His client paused his exploration and looked back at Laidlaw. "Sandstone? That makes sense 'cause I suspect this entire region used to be at the bottom of some huge lake in prehistoric times. But why would anyone go to all the trouble of hauling, carving, and fitting stone blocks to build this place, rather than just using what the locals used: soil, mud, and sticks?"

Laidlaw straightened. "The Mara was navigable at one time, so floating stone blocks downriver on rafts from where they were quarried wouldn't have been a big deal. Hell, the Egyptians built the pyramids that way, except they had to wrestle with gigantic blocks of granite and limestone. Besides, just because they used stone in part of the construction didn't preclude their use other materials. Depending on how old this place is, everything but the stonework could just have rotted away or disappeared into the swamp when the river dried up."

"How old do you think it is?"

"No idea," Laidlaw said. "But some of these stones look like they have writing on them."

"You recognize the language?"

"Hold on." Laidlaw picked his way to a large chunk of broken masonry resting on the soggy ground. "Believe it or not, it looks like Latin," he announced after a moment.

"Latin! Can you read what says?"

"I can barely read English!" Laidlaw laughed. "On top of that, it's broken all to hell and pretty much illegible."

Rostov made his way to Laidlaw's side. "Show me, please, Alex."

Laidlaw pointed to the curious inscription, which his client squatted to inspect.

"It certainly looks like Latin, but who speaks Latin around here?"

"Nobody, now," Laidlaw responded.

Rostov looked up from the stone. “Okay, who *used* to speak it?”

“Romans.”

Rostov was perplexed. “Romans came this far south?”

“If something happens, it must be possible,” Laidlaw shrugged.

THEY POKED AROUND THE site until darkness intervened, then erected a fly-camp on a dry patch of ground near the center of the ruins. After lighting a Coleman lantern for Laidlaw and Rostov, Moses and Smoke retreated to the security of the bakkie, spreading their bed rolls on the ground beside it.

Rostov cradled an enameled mug of steaming Irish coffee in his hands and leaned back in his folding canvas chair, stretching his legs before him. He nodded toward the two trackers.

“Looks like they’re spooked.”

“Yeah, native Africans are pretty superstitious,” Laidlaw responded without looking up from their small cooking fire, where impala fillets and sliced potatoes sizzled in a dented skillet. He poked the victuals with a fork before rocking back on his heels and taking a sip of Serengeti Lager.

“How long you figure they’ve known about this place?”

Laidlaw glanced toward the trackers, who sat in the rear of the bakkie, quietly chatting.

"Moses claims that he and Smoke just stumbled onto it. They obviously think it's taboo, bad medicine, or whatever." Laidlaw took another drink of Serengeti and jabbed the fillets again, which spattered energetically. "The only reason Moses told me about it was because, when he came out here with Smoke, they saw a boatload of game."

"We didn't see much today," Rostov noted as he nursed his drink.

"True, but we didn't really look for game, either. We basically hauled ass out here just to find this place. We'll get down to some serious hunting tomorrow." Laidlaw speared a filet and slid it onto a tin plate before scooping some potatoes and dumping them beside the sizzling meat. He handed it to Rostov. Moses and Smoke hopped from the bakkie and ambled toward them.

Rostov placed his mug on the ground next to his chair before taking the plate. "You think anybody else knows about these ruins?"

"Other members of their tribe, but who knows? They certainly kept it to themselves."

"What about the government? Or archaeologists?"

"Wouldn't surprise me. If so, they've been keepin' it under wraps in order to preserve 'em and prevent looting."

Laidlaw prepared plates of food for the two trackers before scraping the remainder onto a plate for himself. As the trackers wandered back to the bakkie, he dumped some water into the hissing skillet before plopping into a second canvas chair.

"You ever been to Mexico?" he asked Rostov.

The Russian shook his head.

"Southern Mexico, and pretty much all of Central America, are loaded with ruins: Mayan, Aztec, Zapotec, Toltec, Olmec...you name it. *Chicleros* looking for gum trees out in the middle of nowhere accidentally discovered most of the ruins over the last century. Unless you happen to stumble onto 'em, the ruins are harder than hell to find. You can't even see 'em from the air because the jungle is too thick. But 99 per-cent of the ruins have never even been explored. They're usually left untouched because there's not enough money to excavate them properly and museums don't want 'em destroyed through half-assed digging. Even now, you can still find unexplored ruins all over Mexico and Central America just by driving around in the sticks in a Jeep. They look like gigantic mounds of earth but are actually pyramids and temples that the jungle reclaimed over the enturies...archaeologists figure that, one day, there will be enough money, and improved technology, to explore them properly. Until then, they stay buried."

"Like that one?" Rostov gestured with his plate to a nearby tumulus of earth looming in the darkness.

Laidlaw chuckled. "I don't think the Aztecs or Mayans made it all the way to Africa."

"I had no idea you were so talented, Alex," Rostov snorted. "A professional hunter *and* a comedian!"

"Well, that pile of dirt doesn't look like a natural feature so, yeah, I guess something could be buried under it." Laidlaw speared a piece of fried potato with his fork.

"I think it's marvelous," Rostov enthused. "Sitting here at this moment reminds me of what Napoleon supposedly said to his troops when they saw the Egyptian pyramids for the first time: 'Soldiers of France, from the heights of these pyramids, forty centuries look down on us.'"

"I don't know about 'forty centuries,'" Laidlaw said, "but these ruins are obviously pretty old."

"So, assuming it knows about them, why do you think the national university hasn't properly excavated them?"

Laidlaw shrugged in the darkness. "Bureaucratic inertia, poverty, corruption, mismanagement, indifference, incompetence, other priorities." He reached into a cooler for a fresh Serengeti.

"How can we find out more about them?" Rostov excitedly asked.

"There's no Internet back at camp, so that's out. But I've been planning a little vacation to Paris, anyway. I'll see what I can dig up while I'm there." He smiled to himself in the gloom. "No pun intended."

"I adore Paris," Rostov wistfully declared. "It's the only *real* city in the entire world."

"Including Moscow?" Laidlaw innocently responded.

Rostov clucked his tongue. "Moscow isn't a city. It's a sprawling, dreary, pig farm. Now, St. Petersburg...

"'The Paris of the East'," Laidlaw finished the sentence for him.

MOSES AND SMOKE HAD already left camp to scout for game and Laidlaw was sitting by the small campfire, quietly drinking coffee, when Rostov awoke. It was not yet dawn and air was cool and damp.

"Morning, Greg," Laidlaw greeted him. "Coffee?"

"Thought you'd never ask."

Rostov dragged himself from his sleeping bag and, hopping about on one leg, awkwardly tugged his pants on.

Laidlaw scooted forward in his chair and reached down to fill a second mug from the soot-blackened coffee pot that rested on the glowing embers. He handed it to Rostov, who eased himself into a folding camp chair and began pulling on his socks and hiking boots.

"It's been a while since I've slept on the ground," Rostov chuckled as he juggled the mug of hot coffee.

"That makes two of us."

The men sipped coffee in contemplative silence.

“The boys out scouting?” Rostov finally broke the stillness.

“They left about an hour ago. Figured we’d have a light breakfast before heading out. We’ll head back here around lunch time and poke around a bit more if ya want.”

Rostov nodded. “Yeah, I’d like that. Wouldn’t mind looking for some zebra today.”

“Moses and Smoke will find us once we’re out in the field. They'll let us know if they’ve seen any.” Laidlaw reached over with the coffee pot and topped-off Rostov’s mug. “You hungry?”

“Yeah.”

“Okay, I’ll rustle up some breakfast. We should have enough food and water to last us a few days, at least if we supplement it with game.”

“Sounds good. I’m going to nose around a bit while you cook...might stumble onto something that'll help identify the place.” Rostov grinned at Laidlaw in the increasing light. “I feel like Indiana Jones!” Still clutching his coffee, he stood and ambled into the ruins.

Laidlaw drained his mug, sighed, and prepared to make breakfast.

“HEY!” ROSTOV SHOUTED from somewhere within the ruins.

Laidlaw looked up from the campfire, where he was frying bacon.

"I found something interesting!"

"Yeah? What is it?" Laidlaw idly inquired. His question eliciting no response, he began spearing slices of bacon and placing them on a steel plate. Having done so, he placed another plate atop it, clamshell style, to keep the bacon warm until Rostov wandered back.

Laidlaw just resumed his seat in a camp chair with a fresh cup of coffee when he saw Rostov trudging across the marshy soil, lugging what appeared to be a fragment of stone tablet, some eighteen inches square. His empty coffee cup dangled from one finger.

"That thing looks mighty heavy," he called to Rostov. "Too bad there's nobody here to help you carry it." He took a sip of coffee and stretched his legs out.

"You have a gift for understatement, Alex," Rostov chuffed as he slogged back toward their camp. "This thing is much heavier than it looks!"

"I don't know about that," Laidlaw chuckled as he took another drink of coffee. "That looks like a ball-buster from where I'm sitting." Rostov gave him a sour look as he lurched across the broken ground clutching the slab. Finally reaching him, he lowered it to the ground, resting it vertically against his legs. Panting, he handed his empty coffee cup to Laidlaw.

The fractured stone panel was about two inches thick and, like the broken plinth that Laidlaw found the previous day, appeared to be sandstone. Carved in low relief on its surface were the unmistakable images of humans juxtaposed with animals; various types of antelope were easily identifiable because of their distinctive horns. Before being obliterated by a large crack running laterally along the bottom of the stone, Laidlaw could also discern a partial Latin inscription: *io XVI* Bes. He instinctively leaned forward and gently ran his fingertips across the surface of the stele.

"What do you think it is? Or was," Rostov mused.

"Well, it definitely looks Roman. It's got Roman numerals, anyway. I guess that makes sense considering the Latin inscription I found yesterday." Laidlaw leaned back in his chair, folded his arms, and frowned in thought as Rostov steadied the relic against his legs. "Maybe it's some sort of decorative plaque? A part of a wall, or something?"

"That's what I was thinking, also," said the latter. "You know how, at Pompeii, the interior of some of the houses have frescoes painted on their walls? That's what this reminds me of."

Laidlaw nodded, contemplatively. "Yeah, except I can't remember whether those scenes were just painted on or whether, like this one, they were actually carved, then painted."

"I don't remember, either."

"Where'd ya find this?"

Rostov bent and gently lowered the stone until it lay flat on the ground. "I'll show you."

"You wanna eat somethin' first? More coffee?"

Rostov paused. “I’m good with coffee, but could eat something. What’s on offer?”

Laidlaw nodded toward the covered plate. “Nuthin’ special. Just some bacon.”

“I could probably gag some of it down”, Rostov laughed.

Laidlaw stood, grabbed the plate of bacon, and offered it to his client. Rostov lifted the cover and, with his fingers, removed three thick slices of bacon from the lower plate.

“Follow me,” Rostov invited, over his shoulder, as he ambled back into the ruins munching on bacon.

Laidlaw complied by grabbing additional bacon and trailing his client.

The ground on which they walked was littered with ostraca and chunks of broken masonry. Notwithstanding the intercession of daylight, however, the dolorous condition of the ruins rendered it impossible to ascertain their extent, to say nothing of their original design or orientation. Aside from the fragmented Latin inscriptions they'd found, additional carvings or inscriptions were not immediately in evidence. As he picked his way across the spongy earth, Laidlaw tried to envision what the site must have looked like in a pristine, undamaged state, but quickly abandoned the exercise as futile.

“Here,” Rostov indicated. He halted in an area that looked exactly like every other place in the ruins. “The tablet was laying on the ground right here. I just happened to blunder onto it.”

The unremarkable spot was, as far as Laidlaw could determine, on the periphery of the ruins. He surveyed the area in silence.

"Maybe that stele was placed here specifically because this was some sort of special area?" Rostov suggested.

"Or, it could have ended up here for no particular reason. Maybe, once upon a time, somebody just carted it over here so they could sit on it. Who the hell knows? It's anybody's guess how old this place is and stuff could have been moved around over time." Laidlaw half-heartedly kicked the muddy earth with the toe of his boot. "Let's see if we can find anything else."

The two men separated and began combing the area for additional artifacts.

AS THEY'D ESTABLISHED THE previous afternoon, the entire site was littered with carved stonework in various sizes. In addition, about an hour of casual poking around produced a handful of more intriguing finds. Rostov discovered, half-buried, additional chunks of engraved stone, though it was impossible to determine their association, if any, with the stele he'd found earlier that morning. Like it, they bore incised anthropoid figures interspersed with images of animals. The vestiges of Latin letters were almost discernible, obscured by dirt and eroded by time and weathering.

Laidlaw's explorations yielded an even more tantalizing artifact.

Not far from the place Rostov stumbled upon the broken stele, Laidlaw's attention was arrested by an unassuming object jutting obliquy from the surface of the damp earth. His interest piqued, he bent to examine it more closely.

The focus of his scrutiny was nearly indistinguishable from the dark soil from which it protruded. Somewhat resembling a bare tree root, Laidlaw quickly determined that its inherent symmetry mitigated against its having been fashioned by nature, without human intervention. He reached down and gingerly wiggled it; the rigid object seemed metallic.

Laidlaw grasped the object more robustly and attempted to wrench it free. It didn't budge. He straightened and gently kicked it, hoping to dislodge it. The curious object finally yielded after three well-aimed kicks.

It was a dagger.

The exposed portion of its blade was corroded almost beyond recognition. The remaining two-thirds of the weapon, until now buried in the earth, was caked with mud. Laidlaw bent and picked it up. Using his fingernail, he excitedly scraped at the accumulated grime. Overall length of the dagger was about ten inches. Wooden grip panels, formerly riveted to its hilt, had long ago rotted away. Laidlaw used his shirttail to remove as much as he could of the thick accretion of muck that covered it.

The process of carburizing and quenching iron to create steel was practiced sporadically in the Near East from about 800 BCE. However, because the process was intrinsically difficult and required extraordinarily high temperatures to achieve satisfactory results, steel-making remained spasmodic throughout the ancient world. While the Romans routinely utilized easily malleated materials like tin, copper, and bronze to make helmets, armor, weapons, jewelry, and quotidian household articles, their knowledge of iron and steel was rudimentary. The comparatively few examples of ferrous implements surviving from that era reveal them to have been fashioned almost exclusively from meteoric iron.

Damascus steel, an extraordinary rarity deriving its name from its reputed origin in Damascus, Syria, and characterized by a beautiful swirling pattern formed in the metal during the forging process, was especially prized in the ancient world. Similar to the technique employed to fashion Samurai swords, Damascus steel is created by alternately heating, hammering, and chilling a billet of iron. Flexible, strong, and easily sharpened, vastly superior to its bronze and iron counterparts, Damascus steel was, and remains, highly valued for knives and swords. Although impossible to definitively ascertain the type of metal that was used to make the dagger in Laidlaw's hand, the unmistakable glint of Damascened steel glinted in the sunlight.

"Hey, Gary! Look at this!" he shouted, holding it aloft.

"What is it?" Rostov called.

"A knife."

"What kinda knife?"

"I don't know. An old one."

"No kidding?" his client hastened across the marshy earth. Laidlaw handed him the dagger.

Rostov carefully examined it.

"How old do you think this is?" he wondered aloud as he turned it over in his hands.

Laidlaw shook his head in silence.

Rostov looked up from the knife. "Do you think it's original to this place?"

"Damned if I know," Laidlaw shrugged. "But, it looks pretty damned old."

"There's lots of swirls on the blade but, if anything's actually written on it, I can't see it," Rostov lamented as he scrutinized the relic, angling its blade first one way, then another in the sunlight. "Is it bronze?"

"I think it's probably Damascus steel but will have to wait until we get back to camp to confirm it with a magnet."

Rostov handed it back to Laidlaw. "Where'd ya find it, Alex?"

He pointed to the spot where he'd unearthed the dagger. Rostov immediately began to comb the area, hoping to duplicate his friend's success. Laidlaw turned to explore a different area of the ruins.

After an additional 45 minutes of searching, the men decided to suspend their efforts. Aside from a handful of unrecognizable of lumps of metal, they'd turned up nothing of particular interest. Rostov's initial excitement had cooled and he was eager to resume hunting.

Carrying their finds, the men threaded their way back to the fly-camp where, after additional coffee and bacon, they piled their hunting gear into the bakkie and headed into the field.

"WHERE ARE THE BOYS?" Rostov shouted over the grinding noise of the bakkie's engine.

"They'll find us." Scarcely had Laidlaw uttered the words than he spotted the two trackers sauntering in their direction, 200 yards distant. He cranked the steering wheel and accelerated toward them.

"Habari!" Laidlaw greeted as the bakkie lurched to a stop.

"Salam aleikum," Moses grinned in response.

Laidlaw switched the engine off and Rostov handed Smoke a canteen of water. In Kiswahili, Laidlaw probed for specifics regarding game animals in the vicinity: what species? How many? How large? Alternating between them, the trackers relayed the requested information.

"There's a big herd of buffalo about a mile east of here," he translated for Rostov. "Smoke said it has several bulls better than 45 inches." In other words, a buffalo whose horns measure at least 45 inches 'across the spread', from tip-to-tip. "They also found tracks of a small herd of old, bachelor bull elephants. Based on the size of the prints and the length of their gait, Moses says that at least two of them exceed 100 pounds."

"Wow! Those must be monsters! Did they see anything else?" Rostov eagerly inquired.

"A small herd of Roosevelt sable and the usual stuff: impala, hartebeest, wildebeest, some topi."

"Zebra?"

Laidlaw grinned. "Oh, yeah, I almost forgot... some nice Burchell's hanging out with the wildebeest, too."

"I wouldn't mind trying for one of them before lunch," Rostov said.

Laidlaw nodded and directed Moses and Smoke to climb into the rear of the bakkie. They complied by tossing the canteen into the vehicle, clambering over the hunting packs and rifles heaped behind the front seats, and grasping the roll bar. Once they were settled in, Smoke pointed over Laidlaw's shoulder. He started the engine.

Laidlaw goosed the bakkie and they spurted across the veldt toward the zebras.

LAIDLAW SLOWED AND MOSES and Smoke lept from the bakkie before it came to a complete stop.

"We'll hoof from here," Laidlaw said after he killed the engine. He and Rostov stepped from the vehicle and grabbed their rifles and shooting sticks.

Laidlaw turned to Moses. "Zebra?" Moses pointed west and the other man nodded. Saying nothing further, he slung his rifle over his left shoulder and began plodding in that direction.

ROSTOV SWIFTLY ERECTED THE tripod of shooting sticks. As usual, Moses and Smoke were not in evidence and, though out of sight, undoubtedly remained nearby. The other two men hunkered down and scanned the grazing zebra through binoculars.

"There's a big mare in there," Laidlaw whispered. "See her?"

Almost imperceptibly, Rostov nodded. "Yeah."

"Her hide looks pristine."

The other man nodded again. "I think I'll take her."

Although concealed 150 yards away, Rostov straightened with almost agonizing slowness to avoid spooking the herd. He inched his rifle onto the cradle formed by the crown of the shooting sticks and eased behind its scope. Laidlaw continued to watch the herd through binoculars. Isolating his intended target, Rostov paused only momentarily before pulling the trigger. Because his attention was focused entirely on Rostov's zebra, Laidlaw was utterly unconscious of his client's shot.

Except for the mare, which instantly dropped, the remaining animals in the herd bolted.

Laidlaw stood. "Good shooting." He extended his hand for a congratulatory handshake.

MOSES AND SMOKE ABRUPTLY materialized and, while the other two men headed back to retrieve the bakkie, gutted Rostov's zebra, leaving a pile of entrails for the omnipresent scavengers. After Laidlaw and Rostov returned with the vehicle, the four of them muscled the 500-pound zebra into the rear of the bakkie, taking care not to damage her unblemished hide. Like their counterparts back at the boma, the trackers at the fly camp would skin the animal and carefully apply a layer of salt to the flesh-side of the coat to perserve it. The zebra's meat would be eaten.

Laidlaw always enjoyed watching the trackers prepare an animal, exhibiting the dexterity of trained surgeons. In Africa, nothing is wasted.

Once back at camp, he grabbed a beer from the cooler and pulled up a folding chair to watch them work. He stretched his legs and allowed his thoughts to agreeably wander as he sipped his coldish beer. The coals over which the zebra steaks would be broiled were already glowing.

Rostov, meanwhile, prowled the ruins, hoping to surpass Laidlaw's discovery of the dagger earlier that morning.

THERE ARE AS MANY VARIATIONS of the Bloody Mary as there are places that lay claim to its creation. About the only fact that appears unassailable is that the cocktail made its first official appearance during the inter-war years; beyond that, the genesis of the Bloody Mary resides in the realm of myth.

Some insist that Hollywood gadabout and *bon vivant* George Jessel invented the Bloody Mary in 1929, optimistically intended as a hangover antidote after a night of boozing. Alternate sources concede that, while Jessel may have fashioned the first Bloody Mary, that event occurred sometime in the 1930's at New York's '21 Club'. Other advocates for the primacy of the 21 Club decry any association of Jessel with the Bloody Mary, attributing its discovery to bartender, Henry Zbikiewicz.

Of all the contenders for pride-of-place, however, Laidlaw considered Harry's New York Bar, located at 5 Rue Daunau, in Paris, to be the most fitting.

Established in 1911 by Harry MacElhone, the *lingua franca* inside his eponymous tavern was, and remains, English. Accordingly, it became the chief watering-hole for post-WW I's "Lost Generation," including Hemingway, Pound, Fitzgerald, Wilder, Coward, and the ubiquitous duo of Gertrude Stein and Alice B. Toklas. But Harry's also attracted a non-literati crowd: Rita Hayworth, Knute Rockne, Gene Kelly, Humphrey Bogart, and other luminaries. While rancorous disagreement may continue to dominate the problematic origins of the Bloody Mary, there is no dispute that Harry's was the birthplace of at least two other cocktails, the Sidecar and the French 75, the latter named in honor of a formidable French artillery piece.

The original Sidecar contained cognac, Cointreau, and lemon juice, though multiple variations have since evolved.

The French 75 is somewhat less well-known, the product, according to the Savoy Cocktail Book, of two-thirds gin, one-third lemon juice, and a spoonful of powdered sugar. This concoction is poured into a tall glass containing cracked ice before being filled to the brim with champagne.

Even before their discovery of the Mara ruins, Laidlaw had been planning his annual sojourn to Paris. He'd fly into Roissy and, after checking into the Hotel Britannia, hail a cab to Harry's by instructing the driver, "Sank Roo Doe Noo," in pidgin French.

He could almost taste Harry's incomparable Bloody Mary even while marooned in the middle of bloody Africa.

LAIDLAW BROUGHT THE DAGGER with him in one of his checked bags, hoping he might be able to locate an antiquarian in the French capital who would be able to provide some information about it. Failing that, he'd haul it across the Channel to London, where he'd try to button-hole somebody at the British Museum to help identify the dagger. Aside from its staggering collection of classical antiquities, pilfered or wangled from its distant colonies when Great Britain was still an empire, the experts on staff at the Museum spoke a form of English, which would facilitate Laidlaw's efforts to secure definitive information about the relic.

He'd previously determined that its hilt was probably made of bronze, like the preponderance of weapons from the ancient world, because a magnet wouldn't stick to it. Absent a formal metallurgical analysis, however, it would be impossible to definitively ascertain its composition. As far as he could tell, the hilt was a one-piece casting, though its severely corroded state rendered this surmise impossible to confirm. Laidlaw's efforts to clean the blade with an old toothbrush and rubbing alcohol proved futile.

Laidlaw initially toyed with the idea of researching the Mara ruins at the *Biblioteque Nationale de France*, but quickly dismissed the idea. He figured that, in order to gain access to its vast archives, he'd probably be required to produce some sort of academic credentials, which he obviously didn't possess. Moreover, even if he could take a peek at whatever documentation existed in *la* BNF's staggering collections, everything would probably be written in either French, Latin, Greek, or some other Continental language, none of which he spoke or read. He ultimately decided to undertake research via the new old-fashioned way: the Internet.

Sitting at the writing desk in his room at the Britannia, he fired up his laptop and immediately encountered a plethora of unhelpful monographs addressing the geological history of central Africa, such as, "Later Permian Palaeoenvironmental Evolution in the Moatize-Mara Basin," and, "The Structure and Geological History of the Congo Basin." He moved on.

Ninety minutes later, Laidlaw was still no closer to finding any information regarding the history or purpose of the Mara ruins.

He closed his laptop and stretched. A Bloody Mary from Harry's beckoned.

In Primis Anno Regnantibus Imperator Caesar Titus Vespasianus (78 CE)

ALTHOUGH HIS PUTATIVE MASTERS ordered him in no uncertain terms to provide hippos for their exhibitions, Jugurtha had no intention of kowtowing to the imperious Romans. He was confident that he could justify to his credulous overlords his failure to comply merely by explaining that he could find no hippos in the vicinity of his kraal. He'd remind the Romans that there were hippos aplenty in the river that flowed around their *castrum*; let the interlopers risk *their* lives trapping the behemoths! But, because he knew the boorish Romans were not likely to quietly depart, Jugurtha was mindful that he'd be forced to propitiate them by providing something to take their place.

Far less dangerous than hippos, zebras were plentiful and easily captured through the simple expedient of spearing mares with colts when the herd congregated around waterholes to drink. The orphaned colts would refuse to leave their mother's dead body, despite starving from lack of milk. It then proved a simple matter to throw a halter around the confused, docile colts and lead them away before they fell prey to lions, hyenas, leopards, or other scavenges. The mares would be butchered, the meat turned into biltong that would feed Jugurtha's tribe for many months, and their hides bartered to the Arab merchants who regularly called at his kraal. The colts, themselves, would be collected into large pens and reared until such time as the Romans decided to take them off Jugurtha's hands. They would likely be at least yearlings by then. After having been shipped to various venues across the Empire, the zebras would be trained to race in the Circus, pull chariots, or perform tricks in the arena.

Catering to those in the stands who flattered themselves more discriminating, some of the animals would be used to reenact noteworthy military campaigns from Republican Rome's celebrated past, the 190 BCE Battle of Magnesia, for example. In that particular recreation, dwarfs astride zebras represented Scipio's victorious Roman legions, while other dwarfs, riding ostriches, acted the part of Antiochus' defeated Seleucid forces. At the conclusion of the staged massacre, a pack of starving wild dogs was loosed upon the surviving participants, animal and human, to the delight of the crowd.

Not a few of the zebra stallions would also be trained to mount and engage in sexual intercourse with both men and women: criminals, prostitutes, prisoners of war, patricides, or defiant slaves.

Without exception, wild animals with previous exposure to humans very sensibly fear and avoid them. Despite this, the Romans trained a wide variety of creatures to fornicate on demand with humans, including dogs, mules, bulls, chimpanzees, baboons, stags, and boars. As an additional, exciting novelty, even lions and giraffes were occasionally utilized though, because of their inherently inoffensive, detached temperament, giraffes proved especially difficult to coax.

Animals' natural aversion to humans, coupled with an alien, tumultuous, noisy, confused venue filled with thousands of howling spectators, rendered the training of animals to copulate on cue highly problematic. Furthermore, the panicked object of the animal's sexual attentions, although pinioned and helpless, was understandably refractory, invariably shrieking in horror, despair, and pain, responses the audience found immensely gratifying. Given these challenges, animals reared in captivity were preferred over their undomesticated counterparts, as the former were already accustomed to human interaction and their natural repugnance for humankind more easily surmounted. Even so, enticing them to rape humans was a considerable chore. Roman trainers addressed the problem by using soft cloths to absorb the blood of female animals when they came into estrus. Once collected, the bloody rags were liberally rubbed over the bodies, and pinned to the clothing, of slaves conscripted for the purpose. Through this expedient, even the most reluctant creatures could, with patience, eventually be induced to couple with humans. That the latter never survived the ordeal was a matter of indifference to the Roman state.

But, Jugurtha realized, it would take more than a few zebras to mollify the insufferable Romans. He'd have to sweeten the pot. Fortunately, there was no shortage of exotic animals with which to beguile them.

Africa's surfeit of dazzling antelope would render it relatively painless to satisfy the Romans' craving for novelty. An embarrassment of riches, some species like the placid eland, are enormous. Others, the diminutive suni or dik-dik, scarcely larger than rabbits. Between the two poles lay such species as the impala and the reclusive bongo. Aside from myriad antelope, there were ostriches, baboons, warthogs, and a multitude of other creatures available to titillate the voracious Romans. Of course, lions and other large carnivores would satisfy them, though Jugurtha was indisposed to undertake their capture.

Contrary to their reputation for ferociousness, African lions resemble all felines generally: simultaneously indolent and jittery. Unlike leopards, their small-boned and solitary cousins, lions are social creatures, the only cat to live in groups. While both species will fight viciously if threatened and no other option is available, their initial instinct is to flee rather than confront. To the disgust of Roman audiences, terrified lions, leopards, bears, and other carnivores often had to be forced to attack and fight in the arena by a *lorarius*, an attendant who either whipped the animals into compliance or applied twists of blazing straw to goad them.

Jugurtha disdained capturing the large species of cats, not because of their savagery, but because antelope, warthogs, and ostriches were more prolific and accessible. Consequently, they required less effort to ensnare. Moreover, to prevent them from attacking each another, carnivores had to be isolated in any number of individual purpose-built cages, which was an additional vexation. Feeding them was also an issue because the substantial quantity of meat they consumed on a daily basis took food directly from the mouths of the people of his kraal.

He called a meeting of his headmen to discuss the matter.

FRAIL OF LIMB AND blunt of tooth, humans are physically outclassed by virtually every other member of earth's biological community. In terms of morphology and function, the body parts of many animals are vastly superior to those of humans. But mankind possesses an attribute without parallel in nature: extraordinary stamina. Admittedly, the caninae also display remarkable stamina; their ability to dog-trot, hour after hour without tiring, is proverbial. Certain species of antelope, such as eland, also possess great stamina. But that of human beings remains unsurpassed, enabling them to prevail over all other species while seizing possession of every continent on the planet, happily extirpating all other competing creatures possessing far superior somatic attributes, in the process.

The vast majority of earth's mammalian faunae, predator and prey alike, are typically quick out of the starting blocks but, after an initial mad dash, become rapidly fatigued. Ironically, predators are unable to fully exploit their prey's dwindling energy reserves because they, themselves, are burdened with the same limitation. A state of virtual equilibrium therefore prevails. It is a commonplace that, unless a lion succeeds in killing or disabling its prey with the first few seconds of its initial charge, its odds of success plummet and the lion will go hungry. By contrast, neither humans nor canines suffer this infirmity; their redoubtable stamina enables them to outlast even the fleetest prey. Mexico's Tarahumara Indians, for example, are renowned for their long-distance running skills, possessing even the ability to outdistance deer. Nor is the efficiency of ordinary dogs to be despised, having been utilized for millennia to tirelessly follow and capture game animals for their human masters.

Jugurtha knew from experience that antelope can easily be prompted into mindless flight merely by approaching them on foot. Skittish by nature, the herd will panic and, predictably, race at breakneck speed away from the perceived threat. Nor must the danger be genuine: a man, a leopard, a lion, a strange noise, or a blowing leaf. It is irrelevant. Their first instinct is to run. Because antelope quickly grow tired, however, even a small group of men strolling in pursuit is thereafter able to subdue and tether animals that trembled from exhaustion. Employing this method, sometimes an entire herd is driven into large nets, where the animals become hopelessly entangled in their panicked efforts to free themselves. Dogs from Jugurtha's kraal were frequently used to run down species possessing unusual stamina, such as oryx, that would otherwise outdistance their human pursuers. The dogs bring the terrified animals to bay and, by their excited barking, alert the trailing men.

In circumstances where sizeable numbers of heterogeneous animals were, for whatever reason, immediately required, Jugurtha's men simply excavated a deep pit before setting the surrounding underbrush aflame for thousands of yards in all directions. Attempting to flee the conflagration, frightened wildlife of every description...reptiles, antelope, lions, rodents, horn bills, ostriches, elephants, rhinos, giraffes...stumbled into the pit but lacked the ability to free themselves. Many perished outright, crushed by the accumulated weight of animals, or suffocated. At a minimum, most suffered broken bones. But there were invariably some uninjured survivors. These were ignored until the flames abated, and for several days thereafter, during which period dehydration and starvation weakened them into submission. After having been dug from the pit, carnivores were forced at spear-point into wooden crates for transport, while herbivores were led by ropes to holding pens. The remaining animals in the crater, young and old, injured or dead, were left for other carnivores and scavengers to feast upon.

"What sorts of beasts do the Romans want?" demanded one of Jugurtha's men.

"Hippos," Jugurtha shrugged, "though I do not intend to indulge the whoresons."

"The Romans are many and their legions powerful."

Jugurtha laughed. "Undoubtedly, but dysentery and fevers are more powerful, still. As long as we pretend to be their friends and allies, the Romans will not molest us and disease may soon claim them."

The other man frowned, skeptically. "Until that happens, how do we appease them?"

"As easily as breathing," Jugurtha assured him. "The Romans are like children. We will supply them with animals, though they will be of *our* choosing."

"The Romans will not be content unless they get what they want."

"There are many hippos near their camp," Jugurtha pointed out. "We will provide some men to instruct the Romans how to capture them. We have no place to keep hippos, anyway," he concluded.

"If not hippos, what?" interjected another.

"Impala, hartebeest...whatever may found near the kraal. Romans are keen on zebras; do not fail to include those among the beasts," Jugurtha replied, with a dismissive wave of his hand.

"How quickly do the Romans expect the animals?"

Jugurtha smiled without humor. "How quickly do you wish to rid yourselves of the stupid Romans?"

SUB-SAHARAN AFRICANS, like all cultures on earth from time immemorial, produce a potent variety of alcoholic intoxicants derived from barley, water, mint, honey, coriander, wheat, fruits, berries, coffee beans, and whatever else is at hand. Owing to its vast antiquity, knowledge of brewing and distillation is said to have derived from ancient Egypt, the supposed fountainhead of civilizations spanning the entire African continent. Aside from its intoxicating, and purported medicinal properties, alcohol is also used to incapacitate wildlife, albeit indiscriminately.

Although random in scope and slow to take effect, Jugurtha's men dumped quantities of potable alcohol into every watering hole within five miles of their kraal, effectively contaminating them. No matter. The animals had no choice but to imbibe the tainted water, thereby sealing their fates.

Smaller creatures...hares, birds, snakes, hedgehogs, monkeys...either died by the hundreds or were quickly rendered insensible after drinking from the polluted waterholes. Such inconsequential wastage excited no interest and was left for the ubiquitous scavengers. Larger quadrupeds were more problematic. Provided they ingested a sufficient quantity of the befouled water, it might require hours before they finally stumbled to the ground. Jugurtha's men would be forced to closely follow them the entire time; were they not vigilant, their quarry would rapidly be reduced to mere tufts of hair and fragments of bone by leopards, jackals, vultures, and other denizens of the veldt. Hyenas especially relish eating bones, their powerful jaws able to crush them without difficulty and their chalky dung reflecting the large quantity of calcium they consume in the process.

When the unsteady animals finally collapsed, they were either lashed to makeshift sledges and dragged back to the kraal or, once revived, placed in halters and led there. Notwithstanding the inherently uncertain, haphazard character of this technique, Jugurtha's men favored it, particularly when capturing large carnivores because, aside from tracking the impaired animals, it required little effort.

One of them stood after squatting to examine the muddy rim of a waterhole, jumbled with the tracks of wildlife.

"A herd of zebras drinks here often," he announced, "warthog and rhinoceros, too. A leopard stalks them. With any luck, we will be able to take all of them."

"How many?" a companion asked.

He scrutinized the churned-up earth again. "Ten zebras: one stallion and some mares...young, also. A big rhinoceros bull and many warthogs. Others, too.

"They will return at nightfall to drink and more men will be required to track them. We must return to the kraal and inform Jugurtha."

The other man stood and nodded. Together, they headed homeward.

EMPLOYING MULTIPLE TECHNIQUES, the men ensnared numerous animals over the succeeding weeks. Jugurtha was especially pleased with the fourteen young zebras that his men captured by concealing themselves near a natural spring. Using arrows and darts, they easily dispatched the adult members of the herd that regularly watered there, thereafter lassoing the confused juveniles that survived the slaughter and wandered among the corpses.

In addition to the zebras, their aggregate haul included impala, sprinkbok, hartebeeste, roan, sable, and four leopards.

Aside from poisoning their water holes, Jugurtha's men used torches and drums to drive the herds of antelope into waiting nets. Using stabbing spears, they immediately killed all the old or injured animals. Those remaining stayed entangled for the next several days, until they were too weak from hunger and thirst to resist being led away.

Carnivores required more elaborate preparation.

Jugurtha's men dug a deep pit with inwardly-sloping earthen walls, in the bottom of which they erected a column, fashioned from a stout tree trunk, reaching nearly to the surface. Around the pit's circumference they fabricated a wall of stones and mud, nearly four feet high. The preliminaries having been completed, a bait animal...a goat or small antelope...was tethered to the top of the column. Predators, lured to edge of the trap by the immobile animal, attempted leap across the intervening void in order to secure it. Invariably, however, they tumbled into the pit and were subsequently unable to climb out. After three or four days, a wooden crate containing scraps of meat was lowered into the chasm. The ravenous carnivore promptly entered the box, its sliding door was dropped into place, and the container lifted out of the pit to be transported back to the kraal.

The foregoing artifice was most often used to trap leopards, though an occasional lion fell victim to it, as well. The latter's far greater weight and bulk, however, militated against serious efforts by lions to reach the defenseless bait. The successful capture of lions therefore necessitated a more productive strategy.

At the threshold, Jugurtha's men had to identify the location and composition of a pride. Because lions have no natural enemies and live in large groups, they are tracked with relative ease.

A pride of lions varies in size, primary depending on the availability of game, but is generally comprised of at least eight to ten females, a couple of males, and their cubs. Much larger prides have, however, been observed. Juvenile males, as well as old males, are typically driven from the pride by larger, virile males. The exiled juveniles often form small, temporary "bachelor" groups before increasing in size and strength sufficient to interpose themselves into another pride, where they challenge the dominant male for breeding rights.

Like ordinary house cats, lions are both lazy and curious, in equal measure. Nocturnal hunters, they spend their daylight hours sleeping and lazing about. Jugurtha's men used this characteristic against them.

Having located a pride with cubs, Jugurtha's men, never less than a dozen, concealed themselves upwind in tall grass and bushes no less than 75 yards away. One of their number intentionally showed himself without fanfare to the resting lions, gently swaying from side-to-side and slowly waving his arms. Once this curious display excited the attention of the dozing pride, one of them, typically the dominant female, roused herself from her lethargy long enough to trot out in order to investigate. The remaining animals continued to sleep, unconcerned.

As the lioness drew near, the man darted into the thick grass, where his companions knelt with spears and clubs. Nonplussed by his abrupt disappearance, the lioness's instincts took over and she crouched, pressing herself to the ground, before beginning a painstaking stalk of the potential prey.

The moment she entered the vegetation, Jugurtha's men swarmed her, stabbing and clubbing while attempting to minimize any commotion that would alarm the remainder of the slumbering pride.

Destruction of an animal's brain or kidneys will result in its instantaneous, and silent, death. Accordingly, two men on either side of the lioness immediately drove fire-hardened spears into her body, aiming for her kidneys. Simultaneously, another hunter brought a spiked club down onto her skull, intending to crush it in a single blow. Other men indiscriminately slashed and stabbed the stunned animal, whose destruction required but a few seconds.

Because of their efficiency, Jugurtha's men were often able to execute animals without making a sound. In the event the lion managed utter a cry before dying, it merely had the effect of rousing another member of the pride to investigate. Languorously wandering in the direction of the disturbance, the tribesmen simply repeated their ploy. Inevitably, a single young lioness would be left to guard the prides' multiple cubs, often numbering more than a dozen. The entire hunting party then emerged from the brush to confidently approach, knowing the lioness would, under no circumstances, abandon the young ones.

The encircling men laughed at the feckless lioness as she roared, snarled, and bluff-charged them, knowing that the creature had only moments to live. Finally growing bored, they plunged spears into her, ending the affair.

The tribesmen began scooping up the defenseless cubs and shoving them into burlap sacks, which they slung over their shoulders. The adult lions would be decapitated and skinned, their skulls and hides bartered to Arab traders.

"Ten little ones," one of the men grinned. "Jugurtha will be very pleased."

"I think I shall get drunk and fuck my wife tonight," remarked another as he wiped his bloody spear on the dry grass.

"WHERE ARE MY FUCKING BEASTS?" Berossus demanded. "The dedication of Titus' asinine amphitheater is approaching and we don't have anything to put in it! You good-for-nothing cunts are as stupid as the beasts you hunt. What about that worthless Aethiop who promised to catch hippos? What the fuck is he doing?"

"Jugurtha has already captured a number of beasts for the divine emperor, including some lions and leopards," Crixus patiently informed him.

Berossus scowled. "A handful of lions will not long survive in the arena. Corvo informs me that he received recent intelligence from Rome, informing him that beasts are pouring into the capital from legions across the Empire...stags from *Britannia*, bears from *Germania*, leopards and tigers from Asia. Even independent operators elsewhere in Africa have managed to trap a wealth of animals, including hippos and elephants, for the arena's inauguration. Yet *Bestia* is content to idle away its time in the *castrum*, placing its trust in a treacherous Aethiop to do the job of legionnaires. I am of a mind to have done with the fucking animals altogether, place the entire legion in fetters, and ship every one of you bastards to the editor of the games in their stead."

"Of course, Rome boasts of the marvelous achievements of its other legions," Crixus shrugged. "Do you honestly expect Rome to admit that its remaining legions have accomplished absolutely nothing? Field commanders will tell the emperor and senate whatever they wish to hear, trusting that other legions will make good any shortfalls, and Rome will happily embrace their lies. First, because everyone in Rome is a fool and, second, in the hope that it will encourage its legions, including ours, to even greater effort. I am certain that Corvo, himself, has peddled the identical fiction to Rome."

"Except that, in *Bestia's* case, it is not a lie because the Aethiop actually has secured numerous creatures," Aulus quickly added.

"Mark me, Crixus, your easy tongue will, in due course, prove your undoing," Berossus commented. "But that is for another day. For the nonce, depart for the Aethiop's camp immediately and make an exact tally of the beasts he has there. Corvo will demand this information."

Crixus nodded, stoically.

Berossus turned to Aulus and Neocles. "You will accompany him, since both of you are clearly afraid to undertake anything more hazardous than lie about the castrum, playing at knucklebones and sucking each another's cock. I am sick of looking at all three of you! And tell the Aethiop to bring me some fucking hippos!" Berossus barked before stomping away.

"We're fucked if Jugurtha has failed to capture any animals," a worried Neocles remarked.

"That is easy enough to determine," Crixus responded. "Though he is an ignorant savage, Jugurtha knows better than to trifle with us. Come, let us hie ourselves to Jugurtha's kraal.

"I AM CONVINCED THAT YOU arrogant Romans actually believe that no others except yourselves possess sufficient daring to subdue wild beasts," Jugurtha scoffed. "Yet, my ancestors occupied this land long before Rome even existed, at a time when your timorous predecessors were living in caves, subsisting on dirt, and pissing themselves every time an aurochs wandered past. I, myself, killed my first lion using only a spear when I was but a boy. I daresay you effeminate Romans cannot boast as much."

"That is quite true, Jugurtha," Crixus acknowledged, "though the Romans' failure to match such an enviable achievement may be attributable to a want of lions in Italy, rather than to an absence of fortitude." Neocles surreptitiously elbowed him, entreating prudent silence.

Jugurtha surveyed Crixus through narrowed eyes. "You have a quick tongue," he remarked.

"No, Excellency. I hunger to praise those whose abilities so clearly exceed my own trifling accomplishments. Neocles elbowed him again, more urgently.

"Do you mock me, Roman?"

"No, indeed, Excellency," Crixus assured him. "Rome is envious of your daring."

An uncomfortable silence ensued, during which the Romans stood rigidly before Jugurtha's wooden throne. Jugurtha finally turned to one of the tribesmen near him.

"Show the Romans what gifts we have assembled," he crisply instructed in his native tongue

The underling stepped forward and bowed.

"Follow him," Jugurtha directed the Romans. They glanced at one another before trailing the subordinate.

"I think the bastards are leading us right into their cooking pots," Aulus whispered as they walked. Both Crixus and Neocles laughed.

"Put yourself at your ease, Aulus. You're far too tough for the savages to chew!" Crixus assured him.

"On top of that, you would taste like shit," Neocles added.

Aulus wrinkled his nose. "By the gods! Speaking of shit, it reeks here!"

The site resembled hundreds of identical places that spanned the known world, established for the sole purpose of supplying Rome with an endless supply of fauna for slaughter in arenas stretching across the Empire. The Romans personally operated only a handful of these entrepots; most were established, controlled, and maintained by local populations under the loose supervision of a governor and occupying legions.

Jugurtha's menagerie stretched along the river, a collection of makeshift pens and crates in which languished a multitude of animals. An emaciated, milky-eyed, leopard cub snarled and spit at them as they drew abreast of its wooden cage.

"That is probably the size of the lion that Jugurtha supposedly dispatched with a spear," Crixus dryly remarked as they walked past.

In the paddock nearest the men, a collection of sickly zebras huddled together, their heads hung low. Another enclosure contained a small herd of black-faced impalas; one animal, obviously dead, lay in the dirt, bloated, all but obscured by a thick blanket of feasting insects. Other stockades held additional species: eland, kudu, topi, bush pig, some frail wildebeest, a few jackals.

Their custodian abruptly suspended his perambulation, uttered something incomprehensible in his native language, and haphazardly swept his arms about the area.

"I do not understand how the barbarians can tolerate the stench," Aulus again complained.

"They obviously cannot," Neocles responded. "That is why they placed it here, rather than closer to their kraal." He turned to Crixus. "How many creatures do you suppose are here?"

Crixus peered up and down the river in an effort to gauge the extent of the assemblage. Their escort walked over and plopped down beneath a tree, impatient for the Romans to depart.

"It is impossible to guess. What I do not see are hippos." Crixus gestured toward their attendant, who had seemingly fallen asleep. "I would ask him, but..."

"None of the beasts appear long for this world," Aulus interjected, looking around. "The barbarians appear to have spared the emperor the necessity of killing the creatures in his new amphitheater and will probably expect to be paid more for the additional service!"

"Well, brothers, let us try to determine the number of animals that Jugurtha proposes to supply," Crixus suggested. "Berossus will have us flogged if we return to the *castrum* without such information. Hopefully, most of what is here is still alive."

"The quicker we finish, the better," Aulus grumbled. "The stink is about to make me vomit."

In Primis Anno Regnantibus Imperator Caesar Titus Vespasianus (78 CE)

ACCORDING TO GIBBON, the Roman Empire "comprehended the fairest part of the earth, and the most civilized portion of mankind. The frontiers of that extensive monarchy were guarded by ancient renown and disciplined valour." By far and away, the most visible manifestation of that "ancient renown and disciplined valour" was not Rome's formidable legions nor its dreadful engines of war: *ballistae*, mangonels, battering rams, *scorpios*, *catti*, catapults, *petrarii*. Without question, the Empire's most potent weapon was the unpretentious network of macadam roads that girded its vast territories. The *gloria exercitus* would have been rendered nothing more than a hollow slogan unless Rome's legions could be rapidly transported, wholesale, over enormous geographical distances in order to interdict foreign armies...Dacians, Germans, Parthians, Gauls, Sythians, Goths, Huns...that threatened its frontiers, or to crush nascent rebellions within its own provinces.

Aside from expediting the movement of troops, Roman roads also served as important thoroughfares for the conduct of trade across the Empire, the transportation of mail, and avenues that enabled senators, ambassadors, consuls, and other functionaries to travel to and from the capital in relative safety, speed, and comfort.

The "Queen of the Long Roads," the *Via Appia*, dated from relatively early in the Republic and connected the Roman Forum with the Adriatic port of Brundisium. Another route, the *Via Minucia*, ran roughly parallel to the *Appia,* though farther inland, and also terminated at Brundisium. The *Via Nomentana* linked the capital with its surrounding suburbs, as did the *Via Flaminia.* The *Via Salaria* traversed a distance of only 150 miles, bisecting the Italian peninsula from Rome to *Castrum Truentinum* on the Adriatic coast. Numerous additional arteries of impressive length crisscrossed the Empire. One, the *Via Egnatia*, ran from the Adriatic to the Aegean Sea, spanning Macedonia and linking Rome to Greece, serving as a gateway to more alien, and more exotic, regions beyond.

A contemporary historian of the Eastern Roman Empire, Procopius, noted in his *Secret History* that all Roman emperors were at pains to ensure that everything that occurred across their far-flung domains, "should be reported to them instantly and should be subject to no delay--such things as damage inflicted by the enemy on this country or that, trouble in the cities caused by faction-fights or by some other unexpected disaster, and the actions of the Emperor's officers and everyone else in every part of the Roman empire. Secondly, they were anxious that those who conveyed the yearly revenues to the capital should arrive there safely and without danger. With these two objects in view, they organized a speedy postal service in all directions."

Notwithstanding its prodigious expanse, however, Rome's network of imperishable roads did not fully encompass the entire breadth of the Empire and sections of it in peripheral areas were poorly maintained. Furthermore, roads were entirely lacking in many regions, including all of Africa. Having little practical value in a roadless milieu, wheeled vehicles were of dubious worth in both Africa and the Near East, where horses or camels were the primary mode of transportation for goods and people. For this reason, it required more than three months by courier for the emperor's letter to finally reach the commander of *Legio XVI Bestia*, Pompeius Cornelius Corvo.

"What does he want?" Berossus inquired as he drained a cup of dark Ethiopian wine in the commander's sparse quarters.

"Titus has no fucking clue what he's doing," Corvo scornfully replied. He gulped his wine before wiping his mouth with the back of his hand. "He wishes to preside over games inaugurating his new amphitheater on the Palatine but, having spent most of his career slaughtering Jews in Judea, has no clue how to go about it." He peered into his empty cup. "Nor does he have any friends in the senate because those swine have long memories and haven't forgotten how Titus purged his old man's political enemies while he was praetorian prefect."

"Because he feared the Jews had short memories, I heard that Titus was forced to leave *Legio X Fretensis* behind when he finally returned to Rome. I feel sorry for those unlucky fellows, as Judea may be an even greater cesspit than Africa, if that's possible. Titus should consider himself lucky to be back in Italy, even if the senate despises him."

Berossus extended his cup, which Corvo refilled before slopping more wine into his own.

"You are wrong, Berossus. I daresay that even Tartarus would be a more desirable posting than Africa."

Berossus laughed, drunkenly. "Perhaps, though I am already acquainted with many of the residents of Tartarus!" He took a gulp of wine. "Does the emperor seek your assistance, Pompeius?"

"Titus ordered me to provide him with someone competent to advise him regarding the staging of his upcoming games."

The other man narrowed his eyes. If Corvo personally departed for Rome in response to the emperor's summons, Berossus would automatically assume interim command of *Legio XVI Bestia* unless and until the senate got around to appointing a permanent replacement, which was not likely to happen quickly, if at all. An increase in rank and pay would follow, as well as the award of a plot of land in Italy upon Berossus' retirement.

"My friend," Berossus soothingly began, "is it not obvious that Titus desires your personal knowledge and assistance to ensure the success of his games, but perforce cannot explicitly say as much because his enemies in the senate will automatically oppose any such request, no matter how prudent?"

Corvo shook his head. "I, also, am not without enemies in Rome. For all its hazards, Africa is more congenial to life than is the capital." He guzzled his wine.

Berossus thoughtfully nodded. Undeterred, he tried a different tack. "Your fears are doubtlessly well-founded, for Rome is little better than a nest of vipers. However, I am unknown there and would be honored to represent *Legio XVI Bestia* before the emperor and senate," he boldly proposed.

Corvo sighed. "Would that I could spare you, Berossus. By the gods, I would recommend you to Titus' service if I could! But such is not possible because I require you here."

Berossus was unable to conceal the scowl that darkened his face, though he didn't verbally respond.

"On that subject," Corvo continued, "what progress is being made toward the capture of Titus' beasts?"

"A local chieftain has agreed to assist my men," Berossus said, after a pause.

Corvo appeared satisfied with his subordinate's non-response.

"Provide me an accounting of the beasts as soon as you have compiled one," he directed.

Berossus returned to the subject of Titus' recently-received communique. "How do you intend to respond to the emperor?" he probed.

Corvo sighed again. "Make no mistake. Whoever I send to Rome will not have an easy time of it. If the emperor's games are a success, Titus will take full credit and simply eliminate my envoy in order to silence him, thereby enhancing his prestige with the senate and people. And if the games are a failure, the envoy will also pay for that disaster with his life. Either way, he will not survive his sojourn to Rome. You should consider yourself blessed that I refuse to condemn you to such a fate, Berossus."

His subordinate unconsciously frowned as he contemplated Corvo's remarks.

"How, then, will you respond?" he cautiously repeated.

"Who among your men do you wish to be rid of? Surely, there are some who are quarrelsome or simply lazy. The gods have presented us with an opportunity that must not be squandered."

Berossus reflected as he sipped his wine. He had disliked and resented Crixus since his unexpected arrival at the *castrum*. Crixus was too clever by half and Berossus considered him a cancer, infecting the other men of *Bestia* with his uncooperative, impertinent attitude. He smiled, coldly.

"I have just the man Titus seeks," he assured Corvo.

His commander cocked an eyebrow. "You no longer require this man?"

"He is not a legionnaire and is as worthless as tits on a boar," Berossus informed him. "A parasite who will not be missed."

Corvo nodded. "Prepare this man for Rome at once. That should not prove difficult, as the fool will leap at the opportunity to depart Africa, undoubtedly believing himself favored by the gods."

"Undoubtedly," Berossus smirked.

CRIXUS, NEOCLES, AND AULUS were engaged in conversation when Berossus stomped up to them.

"If you have belongings, collect them," he barked at Crixus.

Crixus looked at him in surprise. "Why?"

"Gather your things" Berossus repeated. "Now. You are leaving *Legio XVI Bestia*."

"Leaving?" Neocles blurted. "Whither?"

Berossus smiled coldly. "The gods have blessed Crixus, for he leaves for Rome immediately."

"Rome! For what reason?"

Berossus faced Neocles. "The fancies of the emperor and senate are not your concern. Should you wish to accompany Crixus to Rome, though, I'm sure there will be room enough…you can join the other criminal trash in Titus's new arena and amuse the crowds."

Neocles glared at him but did not respond. Berossus turned back to Crixus.

"You are still here? Did I not just tell you to gather whatever belongings you wish to take with you?"

"I have nothing," Crixus indifferently shrugged, realizing the futility of resistance. By design, the unexpectedness of Berossus' announcement deprived him of the opportunity to abruptly decamp of his own accord.

Men and animals alike were transported from sub-Saharan Africa to Rome via two primary routes, depending on the circumstances. Irrespective, the initial stage required an overland journey to either the Nile or to one of several ports that stretched along the east coast of Africa, debouching into either the Indian Ocean or the Red Sea. If the Nilotic route proved most expedient, the payload would be placed aboard a ship and navigated downriver, across Lake Sudd and through the Nile's cataracts, to one of Egypt's Mediterranean harbors: Alexandria, Pelisium, Tamiathis, Canopus. There, the cargo would be transferred to one of several large Roman commercial vessels that lay at anchor and ferried across the Mediterranean to Ostia, Rome's primary port, thence to Rome, itself.

If, alternatively, an Indian Ocean or Red Sea port was chosen, the impedimenta would be placed shipboard following an overland journey from the African interior. An Indian Ocean voyage required that cargo subsequently be transported northward, around the Horn, to the Gulf of Aden and through the *Bab-el-Mandeb.* Passage across the Red Sea was considerably shorter but both routes ultimately terminated at Arsinoe, where the ships were offloaded. The freight was thereafter hauled overland, westward across the Bitter Lakes, to Egypt's Delta and a Mediterranean port, for ultimate conveyance to Italy aboard a Roman *navis oneraria.* In prehistory, the Nile Delta was, itself, a gulf of the Mediterranean Sea before being filled with silt, carried seaward from the Ethiopian Highlands by the ceaseless river.

"Picked legionnaires will escort you, just to make certain you don't lose your way," Berossus smirked.

"Neocles, Aulus, and who else?" Crixus casually responded.

Berossus smiled without humor. "You will find to your dismay that the men who conduct you to Rome will be unimpressed by your quick tongue, which is more than I can say of your friends."

"My friends have no need of my, or anyone else's tongue, for they are able to speak for themselves," Crixus shrugged, "which is more than I can say of some others." He observed a legionnaire, an obvious Gaul, draw silently drew abreast of Berossus, his hand on the hilt of his sword.

"This is Eros," Berossus said. "He will accompany you to the capital. Romo commands and Eros shall be his second."

"'Eros' is not a Gaulish name," Crixus dryly observed.

"I am a Roman, not a Gaul," Eros clipped.

"Of course, you are," Crixus sarcastically responded. "But who are the remaining legionnaires tasked with guarding me during my pilgrimage to Rome?"

"Junius and a few others," Berossus informed him, "though it is of no moment to you."

Crixus turned to Eros. “Let us depart at once, not-a-Gaul Eros, before Berossus changes his mind and begs me to remain.” He turned to his two companions. “Do not distress yourselves, brothers. If the gods will it, we will be reunited in the fullness of time.”

“And if the gods do not will it?” Berossus smirked.

“In that case, it will not matter.” Crixus removed the knife in its sheath from his waist and turned to Neocles. “There will be daggers aplenty in Rome and I am unlikely to need this one when I arrive there, as I will simply pluck one from the back of an obliging senator. You can return this to me when we are reunited.” He extended it to his friend. Unlike the workaday bronze knives issued to Rome’s legions, Crixus’ was costly, beautiful Damascened steel.

“No, Crixus, I cannot accept such a rare gift,” Neocles deferred.

Crixus pressed it into the other man’s hands. “My friend, it is not a gift. I entrust it to you for safekeeping until such time as I am able to reclaim it. Recall me whenever you use it, as I daily recall the Jew who exchanged it for his life."

The men clasped and held one another's forearms. After a moment, Neocles released his grasp and wordlessly accepted the offering.

Crixus looked coolly at Eros and gestured. “Come, not-a-Gaul, Eros. I must hie myself to Rome at once, as my presence there is evidently highly desired.” He turned and strode confidently away, Eros meekly trailing.

FIVE

ASIDE FROM FOUR GERMAN tourists sitting in a booth, boisterously sharing a bottle of Green Chartreuse, Harry's was devoid of customers. Laidlaw's favorite bartender, Anatole, was polishing the bar with a cloth and looked up when he entered.

"Mr. Alex! Always a delight to see you, sir. It is good that wild animals have not yet eaten you," he grinned.

Laidlaw slid a barstool out and plopped down. "Not yet, anyway. How's your family?" Anatole's extended family remained in Senegal while he worked in Paris.

"They are very well and a blessing to me. My oldest son is attending technical college in Dakar and I am happy that there are no wild animals there to eat him!" he laughed. "Thank you for asking about them."

“Of course. Please tell your wife that I inquired about her.”

“I will certainly do that,” Anatole smiled. “You will have your customary?”

“Naturally.”

Anatole carefully folded his cloth and laid it aside before turning to rinse his hands at a small sink at one end of the bar. After drying them on a towel, he began to make Laidlaw’s Bloody Mary. While he waited, Laidlaw swiveled on his bar stool to observe the boisterous Germans.

The four, two males and two females, were stereotypical back-packing twenty-somethings. One of the females sported florescent orange hair, the other, blue. Both males had half-assed beards, though Laidlaw suspected that it had taken them several months to achieve what thin growth they managed to flaunt. All four had various items of jewelry protruding from ears, noses, eyebrows, cheeks, and lips.

Anatole placed Laidlaw’s drink on the bar, interrupting his reverie. “Will you be in Paris long?”

Laidlaw turned from the Germans. “A week or so, probably…haven’t quite decided yet.”

“Business or pleasure?”

Laidlaw sipped his drink and a look of ineffable contentment smoothed his features. He removed the celery stalk and crunched on it. “A little of both, actually. Ever been to the *Biblioteque Nationale*?”

Anatole laughed. “Me? Mr. Alex, I am a bartender, not a scholar.”

"Yeah, well, I'm still trying to figure out exactly what *I* am," Laidlaw commented.

Anatole laughed again. "You? You are a hunter...everyone knows that."

Laidlaw smiled wanly without responding.

"Why do you ask about the *Biblioteque Nationale*?"

"I need some information about something and thought somebody there might be able to help me."

"I know nothing about the *Biblioteque* except that it is very big and one must be very smart to go there. Do you speak French, Mr. Alex?"

Laidlaw shook his head.

"If you do not speak French, I am not sure you will find anyone at the *Biblioteque* who will help you. Although many Frenchmen speak English, they often pretend otherwise."

Because he'd been engrossed in his conversation with Anatole, Laidlaw had failed to notice the departure of the four Germans. He suddenly realized how quiet the interior of Harry's had become.

"How's business been, Anatole?"

"As you see, we have Germans," the other man chuckled. "They are loud and messy and do not spend much money. But Australians are worse...although they spend money, Australians are even louder than Germans. They get very drunk and usually vomit and get into fights."

"Sounds like pretty much every redneck bar in America on Friday and Saturday nights," Laidlaw remarked as he finished his drink.

"No, no, I like Americans," Anatole gently protested. "Americans spend money and are polite, though they have mostly stopped coming."

"How come?"

"Who can say?" Anatole sighed. "Bad economy? Fear of Covid? Everyone just forgot about Harry's? Who can say?" he repeated.

"Well, I'll have another one," Laidlaw tapped the rim of his glass with his finger, "while you ponder it."

"Of course," Anatole smiled. He scooped up Laidlaw's empty glass and returned moments later with another Bloody Mary. Placing it in front of Laidlaw, he asked, "What kind of information do you hope to get at the *Biblioteque Nationale*, Mr. Alex? Perhaps there is someplace else you can go."

Laidlaw experienced a sudden epiphany as he listened to Anatole. "Wait!" he blurted. "*You're* from Africa!"

Anatole began laughing at the abruptness of Laidlaw's exclamation. "Yes, of course. I am Senegalese."

"Do you know much about the African interior?"

Anatole looked puzzled. "The African interior? I do not understand."

"Well, there's an old fort, or what looks like an old fort, out in the bush," Laidlaw said. "I'm thinking it might be Roman 'cause I found some Latin inscriptions, but I didn't know the Romans made it that far into the African interior. I also found an old knife and was hoping somebody at the *Biblioteque* could identify it, one way or the other."

Anatole frowned. "I am afraid I know little of such things, Mr. Alex. But there is a man who teaches history at the Sorbonne, I think, who often comes into Harry's, though I have not seen him for a few days. Maybe he could help you?"

"Do you know him? Can you get in touch with him?"

"I know him only because he comes in here."

"Does he speak English?"

Anatole grinned. "Mr. Alex, this is *Harry's*!"

Laidlaw reflected for a moment.

"I'll be in town for the next week or so. If I give you the number to my hotel, will you call me if the guy comes in and I'm not here? I'll race over and try to button-hole him. If I'm out just leave a message but don't let the guy leave until I get here…tell him that I'll pick up his bar tab if he sticks around."

"Of course. Let me get something to write on." Anatole paused. "Would you like another drink?"

"Naw, I'm good but am getting kinda hungry. I don't suppose you could rustle-up a hot dog?"

"It will be my pleasure. You want 'the works', of course?"

"However you do it is fine, Anatole. Surprise me."

The other man grinned as he swept Laidlaw's empty glass from the bar and headed for Harry's kitchen. Laidlaw swiveled on his stool to face the now-empty room and slouched rearward, against the bar.

The floor in the vicinity of the booth previously occupied by the Germans was littered with wadded and torn napkins. The empty liqueur bottle sprawled atop the table on its side in a puddle of Green Chartreuse, ringed by three of Harry's monogrammed glasses; the Germans had evidently pocketed the fourth glass as a souvenir.

"One 'the works' hot dog," Anatole announced as he deftly deposited a plate on the bar behind Laidlaw. "And a Bloody Mary, compliments of the house."

Laidlaw turned back toward the bar.

"That's pretty much the best-looking hot dog I've ever seen," he gravely observed.

"I told the kitchen that it was for one of our best customers." Anatole gestured toward a pad and pen adjacent to the plate. "Please write down the number of your hotel. Even if I am not here, I will leave instructions that it is vital that Mr. Alex speak with the man from the Sorbonne and that he is not to leave until you arrive here."

"Assuming he even shows up again, there won't be much you can do to stop him if he decides to split," Laidlaw shrugged.

"Do not worry, Mr. Alex," Anatole smiled. "After two or three of Harry's cocktails, he will be in no condition to go anywhere."

"Yeah, speakin' of," Laidlaw acceded, "I think you might wanna call me a cab."

FORTUNATELY, LAIDLAW WAS IN his hotel room when Anatole telephoned to inform him that "the gentleman from the Sorbonne" just walked in.

"Make sure he doesn't leave...I'm on my way." Laidlaw hung up and raced downstairs to the cabstand in front of the hotel, hurled himself into a Citroen, and shouted the address to the bewildered driver.

"*Oui, monsieur,*" the cabby acknowledged. He shoved the transmission into gear and pulled from the curb as Laidlaw slammed shut the passenger's-side door. Glancing at his watch as the taxi weaved through horrific Paris traffic, Laidlaw estimated it would take at least twenty minutes to get to Harry's. He hoped he could rely on Anatole to ensure the guy didn't split in the interim. He anxiously leaned back in his seat and glanced at his watch again.

Laidlaw began to open the passenger door even before cab drew to a complete stop. Glancing at the meter, he handed the driver some euros as he exited the vehicle. The driver grunted his approval and pulled from the curb as Laidlaw slammed shut the passenger door. He headed for the swinging-door entrance to Harry's.

Unlike his visit two days previously, the place was busy. Laidlaw immediately looked about for Anatole and was relieved to spot him behind the bar, chatting with a patron. Anatole looked up from his conversation, spotted Laidlaw, and wordlessly nodded toward the singular personage standing at the far end of the bar.

Pierre Dunn was extraordinarily tall; Laidlaw estimated no less than six feet, seven inches. Aside from his remarkable height, Dunn was distinctive because of his bushy black hair and prominent Adam's apple. He wore a bow tie and black plastic horn-rim glasses that he reflexively kept pushing up even when they hadn't slipped down the bridge of his nose. But for his prodigious height, Dunn could have been the long-lost brother of former media personality, Gene Shalit. He stood by himself, drinking one of Harry's incomparable Sidecars.

Laidlaw threaded his way toward him, unsure how to begin the conversation. He decided on a head-on approach.

"Hello," he said as he approached the guy. "Please forgive the intrusion."

Dunn glanced down at him, guardedly. "Hello," he warily responded.

"My name is Alex Laidlaw and I'm hoping you can help me."

"Sorry, I'm straight," Dunn replied.

Laidlaw started laughing. "Me, too! No, I meant help me in a professional sense. I was hoping to pick the brain of an academic, and Anatole," he pointed to the bartender, who had resumed his conversation with the customer, "informed me that you teach at the Sorbonne."

"You're an American?"

"Yes, American, though I presently live in Africa. Are you French?"

Dunn shook his head. "No, from Ottawa. And, yes, I teach at the Sorbonne...early Medieval history." He paused and narrowed his eyes. "Is that a subject you're interested in?"

"Honestly, I'm not sure," Laidlaw admitted. "You see, a friend and I recently stumbled on the remains of what appears to be a very old settlement, or some kind of fort, out in the bush. We found some Latin inscriptions, which led me to think the ruins may be Roman. But it's my understanding that the Romans never made it all the way to sub-Saharan Africa. That's why I wanted to talk to an expert."

Dunn unconsciously nodded as he listened. "How did you learn of this place?"

"One of my trackers told me about it. He said the ruins have been there for as long as anyone can remember, though his tribe avoids them because they consider them ill-omened."

"It's not impossible that they're Roman," Dunn remarked. "We're still discovering evidence of Roman penetration into areas we previously never suspected. Between the Republic and the Empire, Rome existed as a political entity for about a thousand years. Its aggressive militarism inevitably carried Rome very far afield, as evidenced by the broad distribution of modern Romance languages...Italian, French, Spanish, Portuguese, and Romanian...all of which evolved from Latin, the language of the Romans.

Laidlaw felt like he was listening to an undergrad history lecture.

"Do you speak any languages other than English?" he asked.

"I'm conversant in French, of course. I also have a reading knowledge of Latin and Greek, plus a smattering of Hebrew and Coptic."

Laidlaw was genuinely impressed. "Aside from halting English, I also speak a little Kiswahili." He caught Anatole's eye and pointed discreetly to Dunn's empty glass, then to an unoccupied booth near the window overlooking the sidewalk in front of Harry's.

Anatole nodded.

"If the ruins we found are Roman, what do you think they're doing in the middle of bloody Africa? If you have a moment, I'd sure like to pick your brain a little about them," Laidlaw resumed.

"Certainly." Dunn extended his hand. "It occurs to me that I never introduced myself. I'm Pierre Dunn."

"Okay if I call you 'Pierre', rather than 'Professor Dunn'?" Laidlaw grinned.

"Of course," Dunn laughed, provided I can call you 'Alex'."

"I don't know why not, everybody else does. If it's okay with you, why don't we sit down? More comfortable than standing at the bar." Laidlaw suggested.

"Yeah, good idea."

The two men threaded their way to the empty booth. No sooner had they seated themselves than Anatole materialized and placed fresh drinks in front of them, another Sidecar for Dunn and a Bloody Mary for Laidlaw.

"Compliments of the house, gentlemen," he smiled before retiring.

"To Paris," Laidlaw proposed, hoisting his drink.

"To Rome," Dunn responded as they touched glasses.

Laidlaw sampled his cocktail. "Pierre, you obviously know a lot about ancient Rome. I'm curious why that is, given that your specialty is, as you said, early Medieval history.

"That's a fair question. The answer lies in the peculiar composition of the Middle Ages, which arose, generally, from the confluence of three distinct cultural streams: the surviving tatters of the Western Roman Empire; the destabilizing ascendancy of a multitude of tribes whose original homeland lay east of the Rhine and north of the Upper Danube, indiscriminately lumped together by the Romans as 'barbarians'; and the Church. In order to get a grasp of the Middle Ages, it's necessary to have an understanding of all three of those disparate influences." Dunn took a sip of his Sidecar. "Not sure that answers your question, but I'm afraid that's about the best way I can explain it."

"No, it makes sense."

"And, as to Roman incursions into sub-Saharan Africa, although I'm unaware of any specific examples, that doesn't mean it didn't happen."

Laidlaw silently nodded as he listened intently.

"Along with ancient Egypt, Rome was undoubtedly one of the most successful polities in world history. Egypt and Rome were certainly among the most durable, anyway," Dunn continued. "And, although we know a great deal about ancient Egypt, we know a lot more about Rome because it's much closer to us in time and, furthermore, the history of ancient Rome is extraordinarily well documented. The works of many historians, diarists, and epistolarians from that period survive, in whole or in part: Livy, Tacitus, Caesar, Josephus, Sallust, Q. Aurelius Symmachus, Plutarch, Cassius Dio, more than a score of others."

Dunn sipped his Sidecar before continuing.

"Like virtually all ancient cultures, the economies of Greece and Rome were based on chattel slavery. Despite this, both were relatively open and free societies, as paradoxical as that may sound. Cicero said, without a hint of irony, 'that the Roman people should ever not be free is contrary to all the laws of heaven'."

"He obviously meant the freedom enjoyed by the Roman elite, not slaves," Laidlaw remarked.

"That's true," Dunn conceded. "But, as far as the xenophobic Greeks were concerned, 'freedom' meant only the freedom to continually fight among themselves. Classical Rome, on the other hand, displayed a more expansive and pragmatic attitude toward the notion of 'freedom'. For the Romans, it meant the freedom to be a Roman, whether one wanted to or not. The Romans were cultural snobs no less than the Greeks and, like every civilization in history, absolutely convinced of their cultural exceptionalism. The Romans simply couldn't imagine why anyone would *not* want to be part of the *Pax Romana*...it was, literally, inconceivable to them. They were determined to spread 'Romaness' into every corner of the globe, by force if necessary. That conviction lay at the heart of Rome's militant, imperialistic, foreign policy. "

"I always figured Greece and Rome were, basically, two sides of the same coin. At least that's what I remember from the few history classes I managed to stay awake in. They all wore togas and had beards, anyway," Laidlaw chuckled.

"Hardly. By its own admission, Rome was practical and down-to-earth, in contrast to the Greeks, who excelled at more cerebral pursuits. Although the Romans admired and copied Greek art, they basically dismissed everything else the Greeks did as effeminate and irrelevant. They were contemptuous of the Greeks and weren't shy about mocking the Greeks' pretensions to superiority." Dunn paused and faintly smiled. "At least from their perspective, the Romans may have had a point. For example, even though it was a staple element in Roman architecture, the Greeks never managed to figure out how to construct a simple arch. In both Egypt and Greece, every structure was built on right angles. The Romans were mystified, and amused, by the supposedly erudite Greeks' inability to figure out something as basic as an arch."

"I didn't see any arches in the ruins we found, but they were pretty dilapidated."

Dunn drained the remains of his Sidecar before responding. "Paradoxically, Roman society was simultaneously expansive and insular, pretty much in equal measure. Rome's ambivalence stemmed from an inherent fear of 'barbarians', having been repeatedly invaded throughout its long history. A Gaulic chieftain named 'Brennus' occupied Rome as early as 387 BCE, for example. Later, in 102 BCE, Gaius Marius barely defeated an army of Teutoni and Cimbri that came close to overrunning Italy. The *coup de grace*, of course, was Alaric's 410 sacking of Rome, even though, by that time, the Empire's political center of gravity had already shifted east, to Constantinople. In any case, the perceived threat of barbarian invasions haunted the Roman psyche and was a theme that Roman writers constantly obsessed over."

While interesting, Laidlaw failed to see how Dunn's recitation had any relevance to Africa.

"But Rome was never invaded by anyone from Africa, correct? Because they had nothing to fear from that quarter, the Romans wouldn't have had any reason to construct any sort of fortification or buffer in sub-Saharan Africa, right?"

"Maybe," Dunn commented. "But the Romans constructed settlements and fortifications for reasons other than real or imagined protection from barbarians."

"Like what?"

"In Africa? As staging areas and collection points for the millions of animals that Rome needed to exhibit and slaughter in amphitheaters across the

Empire. I seem to recall there were at least two legions assigned to Africa at different times, but I can't immediately remember exactly where they were stationed. Wherever it was, they would have built *castra stativa* to billet the legionnaires.

"What's that?"

"Forts, basically."

"So, you think it's possible the ruins we found are Roman?"

Dunn shrugged, slightly. "Sure, it's possible. I mean, I wouldn't be surprised. Like I said, archaeologists continue to turn up remnants of Roman outposts all over the place. Of course, experts specializing in that particular historical period would have to go on-site to definitively establish provenance. Did you take any pictures?"

"No," Laidlaw ruefully admitted. He playfully smiled. "But I have something else."

Dunn arched his eyebrows in anticipation.

"A knife."

"What do you mean? You found a knife in the ruins?"

"Yep. It was basically laying on the ground, in front of God and everybody."

"No kidding?"

"No kidding."

Dunn looked skeptical. "It's probably a late accretion and isn't contemporary to the ruins. It's extremely unlikely that a relic from such a remote period would just be 'laying on the ground.' Somebody visiting the ruins in the recent past simply dropped his knife."

Laidlaw shook his head. "Maybe, but I'm a professional hunter and know knives. The knife I found was not a modern hunting knife. It was actually pretty much buried in the dirt, not laying on top of it, with just part of the corroded blade protruding from the earth. The grip panels, which I'm guessing were originally wood, were rotted away. And, according to my tracker, nobody visits the ruins. I'd be surprised if any white man even knows they exist, so it's unlikely that somebody accidentally dropped his knife while picnicking. Isn't it possible that the knife could have been completely buried for millennia, and only recently exposed because of who-knows-what: a flood, an earthquake, soil erosion, an animal digging in the dirt, or just an act of God?"

"Anything's obviously possible. It's simply a question of probabilities, and the probability is that the knife you found isn't contemporaneous with the ruins you found, even assuming the structures are, in fact, ancient." Dunn paused. "Take Great Zimbabwe, for instance. Putting aside the fact that, for a long time, nobody knew who built it...native Africans, Romans, Portuguese, Arabs, the Chinese, ancient Egyptians, Myans... nobody had the slightest idea when Great Zimbabwe was built because whoever built it left no records and the site has been repeatedly occupied, and altered, over the centuries by an assortment of foreign invaders. They left behind pottery fragments, tools, spear points, coins, all kinds of confusing debris that muddied the water when it came to determining the identity of the original builders. 19th Century racial attitudes also informed the debate, as it was widely believed that native Africans weren't sufficiently intelligent to design and build complex stone structures. Accordingly, the prevailing view in the 19th Century was that Great Zimbabwe had to have been constructed by either white Europeans or, possibly, Arab traders traveling inland from ports on the Indian Ocean. However, the modern consensus is that native Africans *did* design and build Great Zimbabwe."

Laidlaw listened politely. "Okay, but native Africans don't communicate in Latin."

"True," Dunn acknowledged.

"We found Latin inscriptions at the Mara site, carvings. If Romans didn't make 'em, who did?" Laidlaw looked intently at Dunn across the table. "Who else spoke Latin?"

Dunn didn't volunteer an answer. "Do you have the knife with you? I assume you undertook some Internet research in an effort to identify it?"

"Knife's at my hotel. Came up empty, Internet-wise."

"The Louvre has quite an extensive collection of Roman artifacts. If you like, I'll accompany you there and you can compare your knife to those on display."

Laidlaw looked puzzled. "I thought the Louvre was an art museum."

"You've not been there?" Dunn responded in surprise.

"I can only take so much of looking at portraits of dead guys with spade beards, ruffed collars, and plumed hats," Laidlaw chuckled.

"Well, the Louvre certainly has those," Dunn acknowledged, "but they comprise a relatively small portion of its collections. Besides, 'art' is where you find it. Robert Burton anticipated the Food Network by 300 years when he remarked in the 17th century that even 'cookery has become an art'. You might be surprised by what you might find at the Louve."

"I never considered going there," Laidlaw confessed. "Thank you for the suggestion."

"When are you free to go to the museum?"

"Hey, I'm ready at your convenience. You'd do me a monster favor, Pierre, so just let me know what works for you."

"How about tomorrow?"

Laidlaw grinned. "I'll send a cab for you. What time?"

In Primis Anno Regnantibus Imperator Caesar Titus Vespasianus (79 CE)

ASIDE FROM ESCORTING CRIXUS to Rome, a supplementary task of Eros and Romo was to oversee the transportation of a menagerie of creatures destined for annihilation during the inaugural ceremonies of the emperor's new amphitheater: a dozen emaciated lion and leopard cubs; five giraffe calves; assorted juvenile ostriches; three rhino calves supplied by Jugurtha; bear and hyena cubs; miscellaneous lynx, antelope, monkeys, warthogs, servals, ant eaters, and zebra colts. Even, submerged in shallow tin vats, their seams sealed with tar and partially covered with wooden planks to minimize sloshing, several dozen juvenile crocodiles. Corvo had hoped to procure an extraordinarily rare cephos, a creature from Ethiopia reputed to possess the hands and feet of a man, but not even the native Africans had been able to capture a specimen. No matter. More than year remained before commencement of the games intended to commemorate Titus' new amphitheater on the Palatine, his extravagant gift to the Roman people. There remained enough time to locate a cephos, to say nothing of the thousands of other animals that would be required for the occasion. The present consignment of doomed creatures would be conveyed to the capital in a solid procession of wagons, carts, and tumbrels drawn by Sanga cattle bartered from native tribes.

Because the cargo had to be husbanded with great care, Berossus instructed Eros and Romo to travel to the capital via the relatively sedate Nile. It was late June, the peak of the Indian Ocean's violent typhoon season, and he feared a maritime crossing, even one that hugged Africa's east coast, would prove perilous.

Once the doomed animals, or at least the relative handful that managed to survive the tortuous journey, and thousands of other luckless creatures from across the Empire, reached Italy, they would be placed in holding pens and nursed back to full strength until being butchered in the arena.

"Am I to be fettered and pinioned?" Crixus needled his captors as the ponderous caravan creaked out of the *castum* on its northward journey.

He'd been confined to the compound's guardroom, incommunicado, for the past four days, until the motley armada was ready to depart for Rome. Sixteen additional legionnaires and more than 150 native Africans had been press-ganged to serve as porters, herders, scouts, cooks, animal tenders, and guards. Other Africans were forced into service as hunters and trappers. Because tons of fresh meat would be necessary to fill the bellies of the laborious convoy, human and animal, the hunters would spend their days paralleling the column, some distance away, to intercept and slaughter animals that conveniently fled from it in alarm. The herbivores in the train would be fed either barley cultivated at the *castrum*, or forage collected along the route. Trappers were expected to opportunistically ensnare such additional creatures as the cavalcade might encounter on its overland journey to the Nile. Legionnaires, porters, hunters, and trappers were collectively responsible for protecting the armada from belligerent tribes, through whose territories they traveled.

"If that is your wish, I will gladly accomodate you," Eros responded. "Though Titus may wonder why his esteemed advisor arrives trussed like a hog."

"What are you talking about?"

"Have you not heard?" Eros laughed. "You were personally selected by Corvo to school the emperor on how to conduct his bloated games."

Crixus frowned. "'School the emperor'? I know nothing of such things."

"In that case, you are certain to prove a ringing success, since none of Rome's consuls or senators know anything, either. You will fit right in with the rest of the do-nothings."

"I have no desire to school the emperor about anything."

"It is a matter of indifference to me," Eros shrugged. He vaguely gestured toward the encompassing wilderness. "If you wish to depart this very moment, I heartily invite you to do so. When we eventually arrive in Rome, I will simply inform the emperor that you perished from a fever en route." He paused. "You should know, though, that should you flee, the lives of your *Bestia* comrades will be forfeit."

"Aulus and Neocles?" Crixus blurted in alarm.

"Exactly. Know that I am charged with conducting you to the capital. If, for whatever reason, you fail to arrive there, your comrades who still remain at the *castra* will be strangled. Berossus instructed me to personally inform you of this."

Crixus reflected for a moment. "Why was I chosen?"

"I am not privy to such things. Berossus informed me only that Corvo received a message from Rome, directing him to provide Titus an 'advisor.' It appears that whoever has the emperor's ear convinced him that *Legio XVI Bestia* is overflowing with competent men, rather than the dregs and castoffs that actually fill its ranks."

"You and Romo are also such 'dregs' and 'castoffs'?" Crixus needled. He gestured casually toward the head of the column, where Romo trudged at the van.

"I do not presume to speculate about the gods' fancies." Eros sniffed. "*Bestia* is a festering sore. Though the senate accords it the status of a full legion, it lacks an adequate number of able-bodied men to muster even a mere cohort. Worse, Corvo is a drunkard and Berossus a cut-throat. Were not the gods displeased with me, my posting would not be with *Bestia*, but in the East, Gaul, even Spain, rather than in Africa. I have clearly offended the gods, even if unwittingly."

"It appears that my status with the gods may be happier than your own, Eros, since it was I who was chosen to go to Rome. It is a commonplace that nothing happens without the gods' knowledge and approval." Crixus paused. "An odd circumstance, to be sure, given that I do not even believe in the gods. Be assured, however, that if the gods did not exist, men would be forced to invent them."

"It is of no moment whether one believes in the gods, for no mortal is privy to their will. Besides, if there is any place less desirable than Africa, it is the viper's nest that is Rome. Your sojourn there may turn out to be very far from a boon."

"Still, I do not know why I was chosen."

Eros began laughing. "Are you blind as well as foolish? Is it not obvious?"

"Pray, tell me," Crixus invited.

"Berossus loathes you. Shipping you off to Rome eliminates a vexation to him."

"I have done nothing to warrant his scorn."

Eros scoffed. "I freely confess my ignorance. Perhaps Berossus simply dislikes your Gallic name...it is not for me to speculate."

"I did not name myself."

"So?"

"I am blameless for the decisions of my parents. You are a Gaul who took a Roman name. I am a Roman burdened with a Gallic one."

“Your parents did you no favor when they named you,” Eros laughed. “Everyone knows that Gauls are inferior to Romans, so very little is expected of them.”

“I agree,” Crixus concurred. “I am glad that I am Roman by birthright, rather than masquerading as a Roman simply by adopting a different name.”

Eros puzzled over Crixus' assertion while they walked.

Crixus broke the silence. “What am I expected to do when I get to Rome?”

“My only task is to convey you and these damned beasts to the capital. I expect Titus will send someone to retrieve you upon our arrival. If he does not, I suppose there is nothing to prevent you from taking to your heels, though Berossus would undoubtedly prefer that I deny you that opportunity by strangling you first.”

“That is your intention?”

The other man shrugged. “I have no particular quarrel with you, Crixus. Nor am I Berossus’ *carnifex.* If he wants you dead, he also possesses two hands.”

Crixus laughed without humor. “It would appear that my choices, such as they are, resemble a fork. No matter which tine I pick, I will always end up at the handle. If the gods exist, they clearly possess an ironic sense of humor.”

Eros merely grunted in response.

THE CARAVAN LUMBERED NORTHWARD, toward Meroe, ancient capital of the Kingdom of Kush, located in modern Sudan. Wending its way through central Africa for over two months, many creatures in the train had already succumbed to disease, starvation, or maltreatment: a third of the lion cubs, one rhinoceros calf, two of the giraffes, one bear cub, numerous antelope and warthogs. Eros and Romo were indifferent to the loss, mindful that roughly three-quarters of their consignment of animals, as well as several of the porters, were likely to perish during the arduous journey northward. The dead animals were actually a dual blessing: aside from lightening the overall load, they would be butchered and eaten. Although Eros also urged feeding the dead or dying porters to the remaining men and animals, Romo immediately overruled his suggestion.

The arid region through which they'd been traveling for the past week was basically comprised of low hills covered with stunted trees and dry elephant grass. The typography would soon begin, by increments, to flatten, becoming increasingly green and fertile, the humid air growing dark with swarms of winged insects. They were at last approaching the Nile, the Mother of Rivers, a broad, languid, watercourse that, at this latitude, provided no hint of the grueling barrier that would soon confront them.

Arising far south of the equator in the dark breast of the African continent, the Nile races unimpeded northward toward the Mediterranean Sea, carrying incalculable volumes of silt and verdure from the roof of Africa to its lowlands, until ultimately depositing them onto the broad expanse of the Nile Delta. Even among the ancients, the source of the Nile presented a tantalizing mystery. Herodotus; Alexander; Cyrus the Great and his son, Cambyses; Julius Caesar, and many others speculated on the subject. Although Ptolemy II Philadelphus authorized an abortive expedition in the third century BCE, the earliest documented attempt to identify the headwaters of the Great River occurred under Nero in 60 CE. The emperor commissioned a group of legionnaires to travel upriver in an effort to identify the Nile's source, presumed to be located somewhere in central Africa. After innumerable travails, a handful of surviving legionnaires managed to limp back to Rome where, according to Seneca, they reported their discovery of, "two rocks from which an immense quantity of water issued." The identity of these "two rocks," and their precise location, remains a matter of contentious dispute among modern historians and geographers. Nero's subsequent death put an end to further expeditions and it was not until the mid-19th century that the actual source of the Nile was definitively established.

After flowing more than a thousand miles from its headwaters, the river finally exhausts itself in a vast, stagnant, primordial morass of rotting vegetation, impenetrable thickets of papyrus reeds, and muddy shallows.

A nightmarish swamp neither fully land nor fully water, Lake Sudd, its name derived from the Arabic word for "barrier," is a labyrinthine quagmire of narrow, weed-choked runlets and marshy estuaries occupying an area larger than the British Isles. Spongy rafts of detritus, large enough to support the weight of an elephant, drift like grotesque icebergs across its shallow, fetid waters. Colliding with one another, these temporary shoals join, break apart, reform, and ultimately transform themselves into sodden hillocks before finally dissolving into glutinous mounds of stagnating ooze. Neither deep enough to sail across, nor shallow enough to traverse on foot, three primary canals meander through the Sudd, though all are likely to be blocked with rafts of tangled vegetation at any time.

Aside from fish that attempt to navigate its constricted channels, and the crocodiles and hippos that splash about in its sluggish waters, the only other inhabitants of the Sudd are an occasional elephant, a thousand varieties of birds, and swarms of mosquitoes and other insects that choke the torpid air. For men, the uninhabitable region offers only disease, starvation, and death.

The timeless pattern of creation and destruction, of building and collapse, that defines the Sudd is without beginning or end, enduring forever. Cambyses and his 50,000 did not vanish into the limitless sands of Egypt; they were simply absorbed by the pitiless waters of the Sudd.

Finally emerging from the Sudd and once again able to reassert its inherent vigor, merely dormant after nearly abandoning itself to its enervating sludge, the eternal Nile eventually succeeds in reconstituting itself into a mighty watercourse before plummeting into the cataracts, rocky outcroppings and dangerous rapids that herald Egypt's southern frontier with Nubia. Beyond the perilous cataracts, the river assumes a more placid character until finally debouching into the Mediterranean Sea, the *Mare Nostrum*, "Our Sea", of the Romans.

"Have you seen the Great River before?" Eros asked Crixus as they walked.

"I sailed it upriver until reaching *Bestia*."

"What did you think of your journey through Egypt?"

"It was hot and tiring."

"The Egyptians boast that they exceed all others in dignity and wisdom," Eros scoffed.

"All men, including Romans, claim that for themselves."

"Romans are not 'all men'," Eros huffed. "We are Romans."

"It is all one to me," Crixus shrugged. "But, if you believe in such things, the Sibylline Oracles, themselves, prophesy that, 'Not foreign invaders, but Rome's own sons will rape her, a brutal gang-rape, punishing Rome for her many depravities, leaving her prostrated, stretched out among burning ashes'." He paused to look directly at Eros. "If the Sibyl is correct, I daresay that Rome does not appear to enjoy any particular favor with the gods."

"No one can gainsay the source of the Great River, though the *incendiarius*, Claudius Nero, of accursed memory, supposedly commissioned an expedition to find it," Eros abruptly stated, disquieted and desirous of changing the subject. "I do not know whether it succeeded."

"I have no affection for Nero, nor for any emperor but, as for his being an *incendiarius*, we have only the opinion of the Flavians and their lickspittles, who desire nothing more than to blacken the reputation of their predecessor in order to magnify their own accomplishments. I was not present in Rome when the blaze sprang to life, nor when the flames fully spent themselves nine days later, and do not presume to speculate about what, or who, bears responsibility for the destruction wrought by the fire...Nero, an errant spark, an unattended cooking fire, a thunderbolt. It is unknowable," Crixus stated. "As for the source of the Great River, is it not obvious that it springs from remote massifs originating in the bowels of Africa?"

"By Hercules!" Eros guffawed, "I daresay you are the most impious man I have ever encountered!"

"I do not know whether that is a good thing or a bad thing," Crixus responded, "though what is, is."

"Did you encounter the great bog during your travels south?" Eros probed.

"It is impossible to do otherwise."

"How did you manage to cross it?"

"I fashioned a raft and poled my way through it, hacking my way as I went."

"You did so alone?"

“I had little choice. The dhow that transported me upriver declined to enter the great bog.”

“How long did your passage take?”

“Weeks, months...I do not specifically recall,” Crixus indifferently responded. “I remember only that it was difficult and I regretted undertaking it.”

“I have heard many frightful things about that crossing and am anxious about undertaking it,” Eros confessed. “My previous journeys have always been by sea. I think Berossus a fool to order us into the great bog in the company of all these creatures.”

“Berossus is a fool no matter which route you take,” Crixus affirmed. “But do not despair, Eros. The happy tidings are that, by the time we emerge from the great bog, *if* we emerge, all of the creatures, and most of your men, will be dead. The remainder of your passage to Rome will be substantially lightened.”

The other man looked at him askance without commenting.

THE SLOW-MOVING COLUMN creaked northward on a time-worn track about a quarter-mile west of the Nile. The shallow water table combined with the proximity of the approaching Sudd rendered the earth over which they traveled discernibly more pliant underfoot. Groaning beneath the weight they bore, the heavy wagons began to sink into the soft earth, further slowing their already-laborious progress. Not a few of the vehicles tipped precariously, threatening to topple their overbalanced, unstable cargoes.

"You must have traveled through Meroe on your previous journey south," Romo idly observed. He, Crixus, and Eros stood beneath a marula tree, sharing a skin of water and overseeing a group of porters struggle to free a wagon that had become mired in the peat. The panicked animals trapped in its mephitic interior lunged, bit, and kicked as they struggled to free themselves from confinement, causing the trapped wagon to violently rock and shudder.

Eros abruptly began to laugh at the struggling men.

"By the gods, these Aethiops are excessively stupid!" he hooted with mirth. "I daresay the dumb beasts possess more sense than these Africans!"

Romo and Crixus ignored Eros' latest mocking outburst directed at the men toiling to extricate the mired wagon.

Two days previously, a porter drew too near a caged leopard, which snaked out a paw and hooked its claws into the man's arm, shredding it. Although Romo and Crixus immediately undertook to bind the gruesome wound, bacteria that thrived on the decomposing meat trapped in the leopard's claws would inevitably result in sepsis. Between infection and loss of blood, a lingering death was certain.

"Death has already marked the Aethiop," Eros opined as he slouched in the shade and casually watched them attend to the injured man. "Better to allow him to die now and be done with it. Feed his corpse to the beasts...though worthless in life, he will prove of some value in death."

The injured man lay on his back, insensible, in shock from pain. His eyes rolled upward in his head, the sclera nearly luminescent.

"I fear he is right," Romo muttered through clenched teeth as they frantically attempted to bind his shredded limb. "The Aethiop has no hope of surviving; once his wounds begin to suppurate, he will be dead in no more than a few days. Better to end his suffering now, Crixus."

The other man slowly nodded, reluctantly abandoning further effort to swathe the man's wounds. Romo quietly did the same, rocked back on his heels, and wiped the sweat from his face.

"What is his name?" Crixus asked.

"I heard some of the other Aethiops call him 'Koma'," Eros indifferently replied.

Crixus kneeled next to the victim and delicately stroked his forehead. Lowering his voice, he spoke so gently that his words were nearly inaudible to Romo, who was but two feet away. As he continued to caress the man's forehead, Crixus reached to his waist with his other hand and unsheathed a bronze dagger.

Without hesitation, he swept the dagger downward and slit the African's throat.

The man's eyes instantly flew open and he issued a gasping cough as blood spurted from the wound. Moving his slackened jaw, as if straining to talk, his body tightened and he arched his back.

Crixus continued to tranquilly stroke the porter's forehead and speak softly as the man's life ebbed from him. A moment later, his lifeless body slumped to the dirt.

"It is finished," Crixus finally said, sheathing his dagger and standing.

"May the immortal gods preserve the Aethiop's soul," Romo softly intoned.

"The gods do not care a fig about Aethiops, nor any other barbarians," Eros remarked. "I'll order one of the others to prepare him for the beasts."

"No!" Crixus barked. He glared at Eros. "Leave his body intact and conceal it beneath brush. If creatures consume him after our departure, it will not be by our hand."

Scarcely believing their nominal captive's temerity, Eros stared at Romo, though the latter did not countermand Crixus' order.

"As you wish. It is nothing to me if the cursed animals starve," Eros shrugged before stalking off.

"Yes, I saw Meroe," Crixus responded to Romo's inquiry. "It lies on the east bank of the Great River and is exceedingly ancient. While I do not believe it is as old as Egypt, Meroe possesses pyramids of a similar kind, though far less imposing in size."

"Is it near?" Romo hopefully inquired.

"No, not near. Meroe lies beyond the great bog, which still lies before us. It will not be long before we encounter it."

GREAT FLOCKS OF BRILLIANT white egrets gliding in the azure sky heralded the impending Sudd. Although the caravan's wheeled vehicles became embedded in the soft earth with increasing frequency, Romo ordered the remaining wagons to continue their ponderous trek northward without halting, leaving porters behind to eventually free the immobile vehicles with a combination of levers and muscle-power.

Eros stopped and wrinkled his nose. "Immortal gods, what is that stench! It reeks of the *Cloaca Maxima*!"

Romo cast a quizzical glance at Crixus. "We are nearing the great bog," the latter stated. "The river overflows its banks, loses itself in countless lagoons and quagmires, and becomes putrid."

"Why do we not simply go around that obstacle? Our arrival in Rome has been delayed for too long already and the beasts are dying by the score," Eros groused.

"It is impossible to skirt the great bog."

"Impossible?" Eros scoffed. "You are clearly not a Roman, for whom nothing is impossible!"

Crixus thoughtfully nodded as he continued walking. "You are undoubtedly correct, for my parents were Greeks though, by a happy circumstance, I was born in Paestum. Pray, Eros, whereabouts in Italy were you born?"

"You are a fool, Crixus, exactly as Berossus warned me," Eros sneered. "Like my parents and their parents before them, I was born in Gaul."

Crixus affected not to hear his response, though Romo chuckled.

"Look." Crixus abruptly stopped and pointed into the distance.

Eros and Romo directed their attention toward Crixus' outstretched arm.

"The great bog," he softly intoned.

Extending outward from the base of the descending swale upon which they walked, and stretching from horizon to horizon, a burnished expanse of water rippled gently in the late afternoon sunlight. Kaleidoscopic swathes of verdure drifted languidly across its surface and vast flocks of birds looped, curled, and squawked in the air above the dazzling panorama that unfolded before them.

Eros turned to Crixus. "You will guide us through this."

Crixus laughed, scornfully. "Me? Have you so quickly forgotten that I am your prisoner? How would it profit me to guide you?"

"That cannot be gainsaid. But, should you refuse, do not forget that I possess an abundance of animals eager to devour you," Eros shrugged.

Romo swiftly interjected. "Indeed? I would very much like to hear you explain to the emperor your impulsive decision to feed to wild beasts his specially chosen expert, summoned all the way from Africa."

“Yes, I, also, would be most interested in hearing that,” Crixus added. Both men folded their arms and looked expectantly at Eros.

Eros’ eyes flicked back-and-forth between the two men. He smiled, coldly. “So, he has bewitched you too, Romo? As you wish! Crixus would undoubtedly have led us astray before entirely abandoning us, anyway. It is just as well that we place no trust in a Greek.” He stalked off.

Romo turned to Crixus. “Is there a path through the great bog?”

Crixus shook his head. “If one exists, I never located it. Only uncertain troughs scarcely wide enough to admit a coracle. Even then, such channels as may suddenly appear become choked with vegetation just as quickly.”

“We cannot go around it?”

“It will take weeks, if not months, to locate a route around the great bog, if one even exists. By that time, all of us, as well as the animals, will have perished from want of food.” Crixus paused. “But perhaps that is what Corvo and Berossus intended.”

Romo frowned. “If there is no land route through the great bog, it will be impossible to convey the beasts through it, for we do not possess any watercraft and there do not appear to be a sufficient number of trees with which to build any.”

Crixus reflected a moment before responding.

“Some of the animals can probably be bound and carried on the backs of porters. As for the remaining beasts, it may be possible to fashion rough skiffs on which to ferry them across the great bog."

"Neither porters nor skiffs will be able to transport the larger creatures in the train."

"Yes, as you say, it will prove impossible to convey the largest animals across the great bog," Crixus acknowledged. "If you undertake to do so, the beasts will certainly become exhausted, founder and drown, to be torn apart by crocodiles. As an alternative, if you simply abandon the creatures without first releasing them from confinement, death from starvation is a certainty." He paused and looked intently at Romo. "There remains a third choice, however."

The other man cocked an expectant eyebrow.

"Free at least the largest of the creatures, here and now. Allow them to return to the wild, where they will have the opportunity to prosper."

"And how, upon our arrival in Rome, am I to account for their absence?"

"It is far from certain that any of us will ever reach Rome," Crixus responded. "If we are fortunate enough to do so, you must be forthright about the disposition of Titus' beasts. The truth will inevitably reveal itself, anyway, whereupon any lie will be exposed and its author disgraced. Also, human nature renders it impossible to keep track of a multiplicity of lies." He paused and a tiny smile crossed his face. "Finally, if you are not completely frank, Eros will not hesitate to betray you, and enrich himself in the process, by claiming that you fattened your own purse by bartering the emperor's property during the course of our journey to Rome."

"That would be a damnable lie!" Romo snorted.

Crixus laughed. "Put yourself at your ease. As Eros counts his reward money, you will have ample leisure to proclaim your innocence while hanging from the executioner's cross."

Romo scowled.

"You need merely explain that, because none of the great beasts would have survived passage across the bog, you spared them an ignominious death by freeing them," Crixus continued. "You will be held blameless. Indeed, the emperor and senate will applaud your sound judgment and compassion. Other legions, to say nothing of ambitious traffickers eager to ingratiate themselves to Rome, will make good all the losses we have suffered during our crossing."

Romo nodded as he listened. "You speak sensibly, Crixus. We will await the arrival of the trailing wagons. When they finally reach us, we will undertake passage across the great bog with such beasts as are most likely to survive the ordeal. I will release the other animals to their fate." Saying nothing further, Romo walked away.

In silence, Crixus surveyed the vast swamp that stretched before him to the horizon.

SIX

DUNN STOOD NEAR THE window of Laidlaw's hotel room, examining the knife in the morning sunlight that streamed through the pane. He unconsciously frowned as he scrutinized it, slowly turning it over in his hands.

"I have to agree with you," he murmured. "Although traders from the Arabian Peninsula navigated the Red Sea for millennia, and established entrepots along the East African coast, I really don't know how far inland they ventured. And this certainly appears to be Roman, not Semitic."

"Any idea how old?"

Dunn peered over the rim of his glasses and shook his head as he returned the knife to Laidlaw. "I couldn't even hazard a guess. You'd have to consult an expert."

"Know any?"

The other man playfully smiled. "As it happens, Doctor Leo Hubertus, at the university, is the preeminent French authority on ancient Roman arms and weaponry. If anybody can identify your knife, it's him."

"I don't suppose I could induce you to arrange a meeting?"

"Depending on his schedule, I'd be happy to," Dunn assured him. "Professor Hubertus' English isn't too good, though, so I should also be there."

"Absolutely. I'd be completely at sea, otherwise."

"Until I can talk to him about it, let's head over to the Louvre. Its collection of ancient artifacts, though not as extensive as British Museum's, is still pretty impressive. One of the Louvre's docents may be able to provide information about your dagger."

"Let's bounce!"

"AS I SAID, THE BRITISH MUSEUM also has a collection of Roman antiquities," Dunn said as they climbed into the rear seat of a Citroen taxi. "It's larger than the Louvre's simply because the British were more adept at looting, conniving, and extorting. It's said the only reason there are still pyramids in Egypt is because they were too big for the British to cart away."

"I gather you don't care much for the English," Laidlaw dryly observed.

Dunn shrugged as he pulled the door of the cab shut. "English, French, American, Canadian, Russian, German, Albanian, Chinese...pick your poison." In French, he apprised the driver of their destination and settled into the seat as the taxi pulled from the curb. "I surmise that you've not yet taken your knife to the British Museum? At least they speak a form of the mother tongue there."

"Yeah, that may be true but they don't have a Harry's in London," Laidlaw explained. "Besides, the English can't cook worth a damn."

"Nonsense," Dunn corrected him. "That's a myth perpetuated by Luddites envious of the unparalleled ability of the British to boil food."

Laidlaw began laughing.

THEIR CAB RIDE TO THE Louvre took 45 minutes because of the horrendous Paris traffic.

"Don't we need tickets, or something?" Laidlaw idly inquired after they clambered from the cab and he paid the driver.

"Nope. I just show 'em my faculty ID from the Sorbonne and we get in free."

As always, the area in front of the museum overflowed with tourists. Bypassing the public entrance, where a long queue had already formed,

Laidlaw followed Dunn around the Pyramid to a nondescript door at the side of the building. Dunn pressed a recessed electronic button and held his ID card before the adjacent camera. After a moment, the door unlocked with an audible click. Dunn opened it and gestured Laidlaw inside.

"Rank has its privileges," he grinned.

A uniformed museum employee sat at a small desk immediately inside. Dunn greeted him and mechanically began emptying his pockets, preparatory to stepping through a metal detector. Laidlaw hesitated.

"What do we do with the dagger?" he asked Dunn *sotto voce*. He slightly lifted his briefcase, which contained the relic. "If the guy sees that I'm carrying a knife, all hell is liable to break lose."

Dunn nodded. "Good point. Let me talk to him."

Once through the metal detector, Dunn retrieved his personal effects before approaching the seated guard. He once again produced his Sorbonne ID. After scrutinizing it, the guard indicated a sign-in roster and handed Dunn a pen, who began chatting amiably in French while signing his name to the sheet; he gestured over his shoulder toward Laidlaw as he wrote.

While Laidlaw restlessly waited on the other side of the metal detector, Dunn and the guard engaged in conversation entirely in French.

"*Merci*," Dunn finally said. He shook the man's hand before turning to Laidlaw. "It's okay, c'mon through." He motioned for Laidlaw to step through the metal detector. "I explained to Christophe that we're carrying an ancient dagger that we're trying to get information on and he said, 'no problem'. Unfortunately, he also said that the Louvre's Roman expert has been out on a dig for several weeks but he doesn't know exactly where. Irrespective, we obviously won't be able to pick his brain about your dagger."

Clutching his briefcase, Laidlaw gingerly stepped through the metal detector, thereby setting off multiple blaring alarms. Christophe sprang from his desk and promptly disabled them.

"Crap," Laidlaw grumbled after joining Dunn. "Do they at least have some daggers on display that we can compare ours to?"

"Christophe thinks so, but isn't sure. Unfortunately, he said that we're prohibited from bringing your dagger into the museum proper. We'll have to leave it with him while we're on site. You can take pictures of it with your phone and use those, though."

"That'll work, if that's the best we can do," a disappointed Laidlaw responded.

As Dunn watched, Laidlaw placed his briefcase atop Christophe's desk, popped the latches, and opened it. The guard peered over the upraised lid as Laidlaw withdrew an oblong object, wrapped in an old towel, from its interior. Laidlaw closed the briefcase and pushed it aside before placing the object on top of the desk. Carefully unwrapping it, he then took a slight step back.

Christophe was singularly unimpressed with the artifact. He looked at Dunn and said something in French.

"He says that it looks like something his kids use to dig for worms in his garden," Dunn informed Laidlaw.

"Yeah, well, I wouldn't be surprised if some Roman kid used it to dig worms once-upon-a-time, either," Laidlaw muttered as he leaned over Christophe's desk and began taking pictures of the dagger with his cell phone. He rewrapped it when he'd finished and looked at Dunn. "Ready?"

"You bet!" Dunn spoke a few words to Christophe, who nodded. "The museum's Roman exhibits are in Galleries Four and Five. Hopefully, they'll have a knife on display that's similar to yours," he continued as he headed for the exit.

Laidlaw cast a final look at Christophe's desk, and his dagger, before trailing Dunn from the antechamber.

They walked down a deserted hallway illuminated by overhead neon tubes, their footsteps echoing off the polished floor. Dunn stopped in front of a prosaic beige door with a metal handle.

"Gallery Five." Dunn swung the door open and motioned Laidlaw across the threshold.

They stepped into a brilliantly-lit salon thronged with milling tourists. Various exemplars of Greek and Roman sculpture, bas reliefs, and amphorae, shielded behind thick sheets of bullet-proof glass, were spaced between rows of enormous display cases brimming with artifacts. Majestic busts of illustrious soldiers and statesmen, dead for millennia, occupied niches along the gallery's walls.

"I'm not sure whether Roman weapons are here or in Gallery Four," Dunn said. "I suggest we separate and give these displays a quick once-over to see what's here. Otherwise, we're liable to be stuck in just this one gallery all day. If we don't see anything resembling your dagger here, we'll check Gallery Four."

"Yeah, it's pretty overwhelming," Laidlaw remarked with some dismay as he gazed around the enormous room. He nodded toward the far wall. "I'll start over there and you can start on the opposite side...we'll meet in the middle. Hopefully, we'll find what we're looking for sooner, rather than later, 'cause we've still got another gallery to go through."

"Agreed," Dunn assented.

"I'll text you the pictures I just took."

The two men began to thread their way through the massed crowd.

Laidlaw shouldered his way through a pack of Japanese tourists, all talking simultaneously and taking selfies with one another, to a display of small fetishes and amulets carved from stone. He glanced into the case and moved on.

An adjacent cabinet held ostraca; another, jewelry. A fourth case contained oxidized copper cooking and storage vessels, bronze eating utensils, and small bottles of multi-colored glass, rare because of their fragility. A bronze Roman helmet encrusted with verdigris, with associated martial accouterments, occupied a fifth display case, though no knives or other edged weapons were in evidence.

Laidlaw dreaded spending the entire day jostling with the crowd, searching in vain for a knife similar to the one he'd found at Mara. He sighed and scanned the massive gallery in hopes of catching sight of Dunn. Failing to spot him in the congested throng, he pressed toward another display case.

APPROACHING THE MID-POINT of the gallery an hour later, Laidlaw was becoming bored and fatigued by the sheer number of relics on display. Even so, he'd failed to spot any knives, swords, or daggers. Laidlaw was unsure whether their absence reflected an intentional omission by the Louvre's curators, or there was simply a dearth of weaponry surviving from ancient Rome. He suspected the former. He'd managed to spot Dunn's head bobbing above the crowd a couple of times and was hopeful he'd had better luck.

"Find anything?" Dunn queried as they approached one another.

"Too much. They've got boatloads of Roman ear-wax spoons and chamber pots, but no knives. You see anything?"

Dunn shook his head. "Maybe in the next gallery."

“Yeah, maybe,” Laidlaw responded without enthusiasm. “I’m wondering if they just keep ‘em stored in a back room, or something.”

“Why would they do that?”

Laidlaw shrugged. “Because it’s the world we live in. Nowadays, people won’t let their kids roughhouse or ride a bicycle without GPS, body armor, a helmet, a first-aid kit, a heart monitor, and a parachute. Hell, they’d rather their son wear a skirt and lipstick than allow him to go hunting or fishing. Everyone’s terrified of knives, guns...even pointed sticks...despite that fact that most people have never even seen a real gun except on a cop’s hip, much less ever fired one. Locking away reminders of our brutal past is a deliberate attempt to sanitize history...out of sight, out of mind. If all anybody had to go on was the stuff on display in this room, they’d think that the amiable Romans conquered the world through nothing more than friendly diplomacy and handshakes, rather than by massacring tens of thousands of people and routinely putting entire cities to the sword before burning them to the ground.”

Dunn looked at him, dubiously. “You honestly think the Louvre is engaged in a calculated effort to manipulate history?”

“Of course, it is...you’re surrounded by the proof. But, in fairness, it’s not just the Louvre. I’ll say no more until I see what else they’ve got, though. It’s possible that I’m completely wrong.” Laidlaw paused and grinned. “But I doubt it.”

“Well, I don’t think we’re gonna find anything in here, so I guess we should head over to Four.”

Laidlaw nodded in agreement. “Lead the way.”

The two men threaded their way through the jostling crowd to a short connecting passageway and another cavernous room. Like the previous gallery, it brimmed with Roman antiquities: mosaics; sculpture; terra cotta bowls and oil lamps; figurines, carved votive objects; busts of stern-looking, dead Romans; bronze coins; ivory and wooden hair combs; dented platters fashioned from tin; decorative beads.

“I’ll start on that side, if you wanna start here,” Laidlaw proposed, pointing to the far side of the room. “Hopefully, we’ll have better luck.”

Gallery Four appeared slightly less chaotic than its counterpart down the hall. Laidlaw surmised that its relative calm was attributable to two factors: busloads of Japanese and Russian tourists hadn’t yet found their way there and, more importantly, it was approaching lunchtime. Taking advantage of the lull, he approached the first repository and surveyed its contents. Assorted brooches and rings. He moved on.

A half-hour later he finally hit paydirt.

Kind of.

In a display case containing prosaic household goods... tin cooking pots and ewers, copper spoons, and unidentified knobs of various sizes...Laidlaw finally spotted a knife. Or at least what resembled a knife.

Only about six inches in total length, the unlabeled relic resembled nothing more than a narrow, flat, dun-colored billet of lumpy metal with more-or-less parallel sides that tapered to a rounded point at one end. A rounded haft projected three inches from the opposite end. At first glance, Laidlaw mistook the object for a badly corroded file. He leaned over the case and squinted more closely at the implement through the thick glass.

It was definitely a knife, if scarcely identifiable as one.

Laidlaw looked up, excitedly, hoping to catch sight of Dunn. The taller man was looking intently into a display several rows away.

"Pierre!" Laidlaw hissed.

The other man glanced toward him.

"I found something. Check this out!"

Dunn straightened and wended his way around several display cases as he made his way across the room.

Laidlaw pointed to his find. "Look."

Dun bent and peered at the object through the glass. "Looks like a rusted lump of metal."

"It's a knife. I can't tell what it's made of, but it looks like cast bronze. If so, it's just badly corroded. But it could be iron, I suppose. Either way, it isn't like the one I found."

"Yeah, no kidding," Dunn replied. "Apples and oranges. Yours looks like it was made by Tiffany's compared to that thing.

Laidlaw fished his cell phone from his pocket and scrolled through the photos until he found the one he wanted. He placed his phone on top of the display case, adjacent to and above the corroded artifact. "The one I found is made of Damascus steel, which hardly rusts. It's also bigger and in better condition. What do you think?"

Dunn scrutinized the knife on display before comparing it with the photograph on Laidlaw's cell phone. "I don't know...maybe yours isn't Roman, after all...maybe, like I originally suggested, it's a subsequent accretion."

"Yeah, it's possible. I can't say exactly why, but my instinct is still that it's Roman, though," Laidlaw responded. "I'm thinking that it probably belonged to somebody important, though, because Damascus steel was pretty rare outside the Near East, which made it valuable. Only somebody rich, or well-traveled, would probably have owned the knife I found."

"Okay, I'll play the devil's advocate. The knife you found came from the Near East. Maybe an Arab trader dropped it while passing through the area long after the Romans. Problem solved."

"It may have originated in the Near East," Laidlaw conceded, "but I think it was actually made for, or at least owned by, a Roman. We both agree that the pattern looks Western, not Near Eastern. Also, as I understand it, the Arabs stuck more or less to the coastal areas, I think, and didn't have any incentive to penetrate inland. I'm not aware of any permanent Arab settlements anywhere in central Africa, anyway. Like you told me at Harry's, everybody thought for years that Arabs built Great Zimbabwe, but it turns out that wasn't true because the Arabs never made it that far inland. Besides, after the Romans left Africa, there'd have been no reason for Arab traders to go into the interior because there was no one left there to trade with. Why would the Arabs have bothered? And, remember, I found the knife in ruins containing Latin, not Arabic, inscriptions."

Dunn looked at him, dubiously. "Even if I give you all that, it's still a pretty thin reed to establish provenance."

"Well, it's the best I can do for now. I'm hoping your guy at Sorbonne can pinpoint exactly where the dagger I found originated but, until we talk to him, let's keep looking. At least we found a knife, which is encouraging."

"You got me beat, since I haven't seen anything remotely similar."

"I'm gonna try to take a picture of it through the glass."

"Don't let the guard catch you," Dunn warned. "They take a dim view of photos."

"I won't use the flash. It's light enough in here that I shouldn't need it."

Dunn wandered off and Laidlaw glanced around the room. No one appeared to be paying the slightest bit of attention to him so he casually placed his hand over his cell phone, which still rested atop the glass display case, and slid it directly over the corroded knife. Surreptitiously depressing the phone's shutter button, he snapped several photos before sliding it back into his pocket and moving to another display case.

AFTER 90 MORE MINUTES OF TEDIOUS SEARCHING, neither of them managed to locate any additional displays of edged artifacts.

"The Louvre is lucky to possess what is evidently the only Roman knife in existence," Laidlaw joked as they sat on the museum's patio, drinking espressos.

"I'm more than a little surprised. I assumed we'd find several examples to compare yours to."

"Well, I was hoping. I guess there's still your guy...Hubertus?"

Dunn nodded as he replaced his empty cup on its saucer. "That's right: Professor Hubertus. I'll stop by his office at the university tomorrow to see when he'll be available. In the meantime, I think you should consider a quick jaunt to London. Take the Chunnel directly from Paris or the train to Calais then hop a ferry to Dover. Either way, it's an easy overnight trip. You might have better luck with the Brits...I think they're more into the martial stuff than the French. Kind of ironic for a 'nation of shopkeepers'."

"Napoleon had his feelings hurt because nobody offered him any bubble and squeak," Laidlaw grinned. "The British Museum or the Imperial War Museum? Or both?"

"Don't bother with the Imperial War Museum. Its collections only date from the First World War."

"No kidding? I didn't know that."

“If they went any further back, they wouldn’t be able to find a building with enough floor space to accommodate all the exhibits from Britain’s innumerable wars,” Dunn chuckled. “Parliament considered contacting Airbus about leasing one of those huge hangers where they assemble commercial jet liners, but ultimately decided it wouldn’t be big enough.”

“I’m getting the impression that you don’t care much for the Brits.”

“Like I said earlier, “English, French, American, Canadian...take your pick.”

Laidlaw looked thoughtful. “I’ll take your advice and head over to the British Museum when we leave here. It’s been a while since I’ve been to London, anyway. I’ll grab an overnight bag at my hotel and snag a hotdog at Harry's on my way to the train. Wanna join me?”

“You're not gonna take the Chunnel?”

“Naw, I’m in no hurry and prefer the ferry. Aside from the fresh air, I’ll be able to take in the scenery from the deck. The Chunnel’s a cross between an ant hill and a coffin."

“I’ve never heard it described like that but, now that I think about it...”

"So, how 'bout joining me for a Harry's dog?"

"Love to, but I've got classes at the university and will have to take a rain check. Besides, I wanna talk to Professor Hubertus."

“How ‘bout another expresso?” Laidlaw proposed. “Might be the last decent one I get until I get back from London.”

“You must be psychic,” Dunn grinned. Laidlaw scooped up their empty cups and headed to the museum’s cafeteria for two refills.

DETERMINED TO END DOMINATION OF INDIA BY France's historical enemy, Great Britain, and desirious of securing control over the entire Eastern Mediterranean, Napoleon Bonaparte invaded Egypt in 1798. It was while digging the foundations of a fort in the Nile Delta at a place called *Rashid*, "Rosetta" in English, during the course of the subsequent, disastrous military campaign that a French soldier named either "Bouchard" or "Boussard" accidentally unearthed the celebrated Rosetta Stone. The relic thereafter passed to the British in 1801, following their successful siege of French-occupied Cairo. Formal transfer was officially memorialized pursuant to legal niceties embedded in Article 16 of the subsequent Treaty of Alexandria. Over the intervening two and one-quarter centuries successive Egyptian governments have attempted to pry the chunky, black Stone from the acquisitive British, with a predictable lack of success.

The last time Laidlaw visited the British Museum, the Rosetta Stone sat, in front of God and everybody, in the middle of the museum's Egyptian Gallery. Society having thereafter been commandeered by lunatics, the Stone is now shielded behind thick sheets of laminated, bullet-proof glass.

Laidlaw skirted the crowd of tourists ogling the Stone, ducked between the towering lamassu guarding the Assyrian Gallery, and hustled past the Elgin Marbles in the Duveen Gallery. Though all were imposing and majestic, he was resolved to devote his time seeking a knife like the one he'd found in Africa. He quickly ascertained that the museum's collection of ancient weapons encompassed much of the classical world: Greek, Roman, Persian, Assyrian, Parthian, Babylonian, Phoenician, even arms from the Vikings, China, and Japan. Even more fascinating was the museum's display of accouterments employed by gladiators in the hundreds of arenas, large and small, that spanned the Empire. One, a bronze helmet, bore a massive indentation that was obviously inflicted by a sword wielded by an immensely powerful opponent, its unfortunate wearer having unquestionably been rendered insensible as a result of the ferocious blow. Equally possible, his skull had been fractured and he'd simply died on the spot.

Laidlaw went from one gallery to the next, each one more engaging than the last. Although there was no shortage of edged weaponry on display, he was becoming frustrated by his inability to locate a knife like the one he'd unearthed at Mara. He nevertheless resolved to keep looking, even if multiple follow-up visits proved necessary. It also remained possible that somebody at the museum's information desk might be able to point him in the right direction.

After more than two hours of searching, he finally encountered a knife somewhat similar to the dagger back at his hotel room. A tiny label adjacent to the implement stated simply: "Roman knife, iron, Syria, circa 100 CE".

Although forged from iron, rather than Damascus steel, the artifact appeared to be about the same overall length as Laidlaw's Mara knife and was visibly thinner than its counterparts fashioned of cast bronze. Laidlaw bent over the display case to scrutinize the dagger more closely. Even through the patina of rust that coated its blade, he could clearly see the iron lacked the elaborate swirls and arabesques characteristic of Damascus steel. Despite this lacuna, the knife reflected a similar overall design to the Mara dagger, presumably a testament to their shared geographical origin. Encouraged, Laidlaw removed his phone from his pocket and discreetly snapped a few photos before moving on. He was optimistic that the remaining exhibits contained additional specimens.

Alas, it was not to be.

The single iron-bladed knife was apparently an outlier. Disappointed and hungry, Laidlaw decided to call it a day and hit the information desk on his way out.

"I AM UNAWARE OF the specific exhibit you're referring to," the matronly functionary peremptorily sniffed. Her badge identified her as a volunteer at the museum.

"It was located in Gallery Four," Laidlaw helpfully specified. "I can show you a picture of it." He began to pull his cell phone from his pocket.

"Photographs are not allowed in the museum."

"Uh, yeah. It was just a picture of one similar to it. Never mind."

"Yes, I'm sure," she clipped. "I believe the gift shop sells miniature reproductions of some of the museum's more popular pieces. You might inquire there for assistance."

"Is there a staff member, an actual human, I can talk to?"

She arched her eyebrows. "Are you suggesting that I am not human?"

Laidlaw found it hard not to laugh at her superciliousness. "No, I only meant that I'd like to speak with a staff member or docent."

"I'm sorry, but staff are not available to respond to inquiries from the general public. You may submit your question in writing by post and, circumstances permitting, a member of the museum's staff may respond. Forms for that purpose are located at each exit and postage stamps may be purchased in the museum's gift shop. The museum also sponsors regular tours and symposia; consult the schedule displayed near the main entrance."

"So, your suggestion is that I either talk to somebody in the gift shop about a souvenir toy replica or wait for a tour?" Laidlaw dryly remarked.

"The gift shop has several books devoted to the museum's various collections. I'm sure you'll find one of them satisfactory. And the museum's symposia are most informative. Good day, sir."

Hopefully, Dunn's Professor Hubertus will prove more helpful, Laidlaw thought as he turned away. It being London, he didn't even have a decent meal to look forward to until returning to Paris.

In Primis Anno Regnantibus Imperator Caesar Titus Vespasianus (79 CE)

FEW OF THE CREATURES SURVIVED the ordeal.

Romo ordered that crude rafts be assembled through the expedient of lashing together such sparse construction materials as the porters were able to scrounge in the vicinity: grasses, reeds, twigs, tree branches. Though optimistically intended to bear the aggregate weight of animals, equipment, and supplies, the improvised barges rapidly became sodden and speedily disintegrated.

The few crocodiles that had managed to stay alive during the overland trek were unceremoniously dumped into the waters of the Sudd. Romo thereafter ordered porters to carry most of the remaining smaller creatures, including the lion, leopard, and hyena cubs, in wicker baskets suspended between poles. Most were so weakened from abuse and starvation that they were scarcely conscious. Antelope, zebra, and other juvenile ungulates were conveyed by binding their legs and slinging them over the porters' shoulders. Rhinoceros and giraffe calves were half-herded, half-lured, into the bog with chunks of sugar cane, a species of tropical grass otherwise unknown in the

Roman Empire but introduced into Sub-Saharan Africa by traders from across the Indian Ocean.

Where the water proved sufficiently shallow, some of the creatures, mostly antelope, were able to lunge their way onto floating patches of detritus, where they collapsed, shivering from a combination of malnutrition and exhaustion. The majority of the animals were not as fortunate. Panicked wart hogs, zebra colts, juvenile hyenas, ostriches, buffalo calves, and a multitude of other wildlife bellowed and shrieked in terror as they were enveloped by the Sudd's murk. Many of the Africans summarily jettisoned their frightened payloads by shoving them into the opaque water, prudently choosing their own survival over that of struggling, unmanageable wildlife.

Partially submerged, the animals rapidly became pinioned between dense islands of floating vegetation and the bog's muddy bed, causing them to panic. Desperately thrashing about in the tea-colored water until utterly exhausted, they were simply allowed to drown. One porter, struggling to lasso a fleeing ostrich, was horned through his back by a panicked sable antelope. Running in a blind circle, the sable vigorously tossed its head from side to side in an attempt to fling the encumbrance from its curving, ribbed horns. It finally tumbled into the enveloping waters of the Sudd, thereby putting an end to the man's agonized screams. The terrified ostrich, the unfortunate porter's plaited rope still dangling from its neck, desperately attempted to vault a narrow channel cutting through the dense vegetation, failed, and quickly followed them in death.

Nor was it merely animals that perished in the deafening bedlam.

In a frantic effort to save themselves, several of the porters leaped into the water, hoping to distance themselves from the raucous mayhem. Terrified, convulsing animals often cartwheeled after them, crushing, drowning, or disemboweling the men with their flailing hooves.

"Your supposedly fearsome swamp is truly a boon, Crixus," Eros smirked, greatly enjoying the tumult from a safe distance. "The gods have blessed us by providing the means of getting rid of these worthless beasts. Would that we could rid ourselves of all our Africans with equal ease."

"It does not seem to me such an easy thing," Crixus sorrowfully murmured as he, too, witnessed the spectacle.

Eros turned to look directly at him. "Indeed? Your professed solicitude toward wild animals and barbarians is a curious thing, Crixus. Given your compassion, perhaps you should lend the Africans your personal assistance. I will speak to Romo of it."

"Speak to whoever you wish, though I remind you that you are charged with personally conveying me to the emperor in Rome. I daresay you will find that an impossible task if I am drowned at the bottom of the great bog. But I leave it to you to grapple with that dilemma."

"So, your cowardice in declining to fly to the barbarians' aid gives the lie to your supposed concern for their welfare," Eros replied.

It was not the cowardice that deterred Crixus. Based on Eros' previous disclosure, he knew that if, for whatever reason, he failed to arrive in Rome, the lives of Neocles and Aulus would automatically be forfeit.

Crixus shrugged. "I do not recall speaking of my 'concern', Eros. I said only that attempting to shepherd animals through the great bog does not seem an easy thing. Whether that rises to the level of 'concern' I do not pretend to know." He cast a contemptuous glance at the other man. "Like the gods, you are evidently able to see into other men's hearts."

"The gods, alone, know what lies there," Eros scowled.

"In that case, I find myself in excellent company, for it is a simple matter to see what lies in your heart, Eros: oafishness, stupidity, cupidity, and sloth. I am gratified at the ease with which I apparently managed to join the rarified company of the gods." Crixus stood. "For the nonce, however, let us find Romo."

ROMO STOOD ON A SMALL hillock overlooking the chaotic scene.

"Safeguard the beasts!" Romo barked over the cacophony developing below. "Any man who allows an animal to perish will share its fate!"

The clamor of thrashing, crazed animals and cursing men filled the air. Intent only on preserving their own lives, the flailing porters ignored Romo's threat, even assuming any of them managed to hear it above the din.

Eros watched the floundering men and animals with amusement. "I fear, Romo, that you will have little to boast of upon your arrival in Rome. In the absence of beasts, perhaps you can induce the senate to accept some of the Aethiops in their stead. Africans are little removed from mindless animals, anyway, though they exceed even dumb brutes in their stupidity." He turned and looked at Crixus, derisively. "Perhaps, though, the emperor's personal consultant can better advise us."

"Crixus did not choose to travel to Rome any more than we did," Romo coldly replied as he grimly observed the unfolding catastrophe. "Corvo and Berossus, alone, are responsible for this fiasco, and for the route they insisted we take. Your disdain should be directed at them, not Crixus, for he is as blameless as either of us. As for the Aethiops, I intend to allow most of them to return to their homes, as they obviously will no longer be needed. You, too, may return to the *castrum* if you wish, Eros. I will proceed to Rome with whatever beasts remain, where I will also deliver Crixus, as I was commanded to do."

“I think not, Romo,” Eros deferred. “No less than you, I, too, was ordered to convey Crixus and the beasts to Rome. It is plain that your invitation to return to the *castrum* is nothing more than a clumsy ruse intended to embarrass me before Corvo and Berossus, who will conclude that I failed to follow orders and slunk back in shame. You, then, will be the sole beneficiary of such credit as may yet redound from this ill-conceived misadventure.”

“I daresay you do not require Romo’s assistance to embarrass yourself,” Crixus wryly observed. “Methinks you excel at doing so without any help.”

Eros flashed an angry glance at Romo, expecting him to rebuke Crixus for the latter's impertinence. Romo ignored him. “Well, at least the crocodiles will feast today,” he finally grumbled.

“The crocodiles be damned!” Romo angrily retorted. “Hie yourselves thither and order the porters to do whatever is necessary to rescue as many beasts as possible, especially the antelopes, before more of them plunge into the bog. The inhabitants of Tartarus will rejoice and make merry before I allow the damnable crocodiles to sup better than we do! Go!”

Eros and Crixus hastened to the edge of the swamp, where they separated and raced along its periphery, shouting to the beleaguered, cursing men and flailing animals. “Stop the beasts from plunging into the great bog! Break their legs if you must!” They cried until they were hoarse.

Ignoring their entreaties, most of the porters had already abandoned the hapless creatures to their fates.

Leaping into the warm, waist-deep water, they began to slog their way toward dry land while trying to dodge the flaying hooves of their former charges. Unfortunately, the rampant commotion excited the attention of the newly-liberated crocodiles which, propelled by their powerful tails, now swarmed the area. The reptiles snapped wildly at the convulsing, twisting bodies of the drowning animals, rapidly transforming the churning water into a bloody foam as men and animals were indiscriminately seized by the rapacious saurians.

Fish comprise crocodiles' primary food source, which they swallow whole. Even so, crocodiles will attempt to eat anything that will fit into their mouths: birds, domestic stock, antelope, baby hippos, human beings, garbage. Their comparatively weak jaw muscles and jagged teeth function to securely grasp and hold prey, not chew it. Because of their inability to masticate, crocodiles are incapable of efficiently ingesting large quadrupeds. They employ two methods to surmount this anatomical limitation.

In the first, the crocodile simply clamps down on the struggling prey and executes a rapid horizontal spinning maneuver. Chunks of the victim’s flesh are thereby ripped free, which the crocodile then swallows with ease.

If, for whatever reason, the first method proves unavailing, the crocodile pulls the unwieldy prey beneath the surface of a river or lake, where it drowns. Once quiescent, the body is dragged to the bottom and buried in the mud until the carcass decomposes, at which point it is consumed at crocodile's leisure.

Crixus watched in horror as, with sinuous undulations of its powerful tail, a four-foot crocodile glided through the muddy water toward a staggering, inattentive porter. Only the crocodile's nostrils and flinty eyes were visible above the roiling surface.

"*Crococilus*!" Crixus screamed at the man, attempting to be heard above the din. He frantically gesticulated toward the rapidly moving reptile. The porter either failed to hear him or chose to ignore the alarm.

With a final explosive lash of its tail, the crocodile was upon him. Half-lifting its body from the water, the creature opened its maw and hooked its barbed teeth into the man's forearm.

The porter shrieked in a combination of surprise and pain. Simultaneously, he stumbled rearward in the muck while attempting to free himself from the reptile. For naught.

Whipping its powerful tail, the crocodile, its teeth still clamped to the man's arm, lunged forward, bowling him over. The man's screaming was silenced only when he disappeared beneath the frothing, bloody water. A group of smaller crocodiles immediately swarmed the area and began to blindly attack one another, their snapping jaws producing a distinctive hollow thud that was discernible above the frenzy. Crixus frantically surveyed the immediate area in the hope that he'd be able to rescue some of the struggling men.

To his left, an animal handler unsuccessfully attempted to rope another refractory ostrich. Darting its head one way, then another to avoid being lassoed, the agitated bird finally kicked its tormentor in the abdomen. Slicing open the man's stomach, the hooked claw on the ostrich's middle toe disemboweled him. The porter frantically attempted to push his intestines back into his body with both hands before collapsing to his knees with a groan. The desperate ostrich promptly leapt into the teeming water, where it was immediately attacked and dismembered by lurking crocodiles.

To Crixus' right, two juvenile crocodiles engaged in lethal tug-of-war with a bleating hartebeest calf. Each reptile seized an opposite leg of the helpless antelope and furiously churned the water as they vigorously tugged and spun in an effort to disjoint its splayed limbs. Had he a spear, Crixus would have launched it at heart of the forsaken hartebeest in order to put an end to its pain, though he was unarmed.

Nearby, a frantic black-backed jackal pup vaulted across a narrow channel onto a floating cluster of water lilies, unaware of the peril. Cloaked in its blooms, a waiting crocodile swallowed the pup whole.

A porter, a trembling, impala calf draped across his shoulders, attempted to slog his way through the chest-deep Sudd. Finally tiring of the twisting, writhing animal, he flung it into the teeming water in disgust. Utterly helpless, the bound animal foundered only momentarily before drowning.

Moments later, the porter stepped into a submerged depression and permanently disappeared from sight.

Crixus turned from the wrenching spectacle.

He sprinted away, along the perimeter of the Sudd, in search of Eros and men yet savable.

"LOOK AT THOSE PERFECT FOOLS." Eros gleefully gesticulated toward shrieking, desperate men attempting to fight their way to safety through the foul water. "I daresay that I have never seen such buffoonery my entire life!"

He was lounging in the shade of a tree near the edge of the Sudd.

"It amuses you to see men and animals in their death throes, Eros?" Crixus spat.

"All men are doomed," the other man indifferently responded. "Those whose deaths afford us some amusement have been favored by the gods."

"I do not find it amusing, nor am I sure that they feel themselves particularly favored."

"Your lack of discernment is not my concern. I would expect nothing more from a Greek."

"Or a Gaul," Crixus added in disgust.

THE DISTANT, WAILING LAMENTATION of those porters who, through luck or skill, managed to survive the afternoon's debacle, wafted through the cloying night air as they mourned their lost comrades.

"Listen to those childish halfwits," Eros laughed as he tossed the gnawed rib bone of an impala into the campfire. "Though the worthless Africans shamed themselves today, their follies accrued to our benefit. We acquire fresh provisions while ridding ourselves of a multitude of useless eaters. The gods have blessed us."

Romo looked across at him with repugnance. "No, the gods do not bless us. The beasts we were charged to safeguard have signally perished and we will undoubtedly have to answer for it when we finally arrive in Rome."

With another rib, Eros gestured toward Romo.

"You are truly a fool, Romo. Your anxiety regarding the fate of either the beasts or the Aethiops is *absurditas*. Berossus confided to me that it was a matter of indifference to him whether a single beast survived the journey to Rome. He wished only to rid *Bestia* of the blight that is Crixus. Neither he nor Corvo cares a fig whether the beasts, or any of us, actually arrive in Italy. Assuming that his throat hasn't already been slit by his underlings at court, the emperor has undoubtedly already forgotten his request for an expert to tutor him on his games. It is far from certain whether Titus' proposed games are, in fact, anything more than a foolish dalliance. Indeed, I have no doubt that your arrival at court, should you actually make it to Rome, will occasion only astonishment and mirth." He paused only long enough to tear a chunk of meat from the rib in his hand. "For the nonce, I suggest that you display appropriate gratitude to the gods for the gift they bestowed on us today."

"I suspect that neither the surviving beasts nor the Africans are disposed to share your cheerful assessment of the gods' generosity," Crixus volunteered from across the fire.

"Aethiops mean less than nothing to the gods," Eros informed him. "And, like the unthinking beasts, you are nothing more than cargo, Crixus. Your opinions are, therefore, of no moment."

"You do not intend to accompany us to the capital, Eros?" Romo interjected. "Why, then, did you not return to the *castrum*, as I urged you to do?"

"I told you earlier, some good may yet arise from this disaster. It is impossible to guess the will of the gods. Should that occur, I intend to claim my rightful share of the emperor's tokens of gratitude."

"The emperor's 'tokens of gratitude'?" Crixus commented. "You expect Titus to liberally shower you with gifts and praise."

"Why should he not? I have done as much as anyone to ensure the success of this dubious adventure."

"And if censure is your only reward?" asked Romo

Eros shrugged, indifferently. "Only those who warrant censure will receive it. I will place myself at the disposal of the emperor and senate should they require my assistance in identifying the miscreants."

"They are certain to prize your input," Romo dryly noted.

Eros frowned. "You seem little troubled about how the senate is likely to view your failure to safeguard the emperor's beasts, Romo."

"Neither the verdict of the senate, nor the emperor, concern me, Eros. Should they? By your own admission, you 'have done as much as anyone to ensure the success of this dubious adventure', such as it has been."

"That is, indeed, true, Romo. Having faithfully complied with all of your orders, however unwise, without hesitation, my constancy cannot be gainsaid...a fact I intend to acquaint the senate with."

Crixus began laughing. "Yes, of that I have no doubt. To further buttress your status with Titus and the senate, perhaps you should also volunteer to suck their cocks!"

Romo interrupted the taunting exchange between the two men. "While you ponder your report to the senate regarding my conduct, Eros, we must determine the number of beasts that remain alive. You and Crixus will canvas the Africans tomorrow about it."

"I will do as you wish," Eros shrugged, "provided any of the worthless cowards are still alive or have not already fled back to their villages, to their fat wives and squalling brats." He cast the bone he'd been gnawing into the fire.

"Such beasts as remain alive must still be conveyed across the great bog," Crixus reminded Romo, "though, as Eros said, the Africans will probably show no willingness after today."

Romo thoughtfully nodded. "If, as it appears, the gods decreed their destruction, we will proceed to Rome, with or without the beasts."

"And what, pray, is to prevent Crixus from also fleeing?" Eros asked.

"Nothing, save the certain destruction of his comrades at the *castrum.* If Crixus flees, it will be because the gods willed it," Romo responded. "No one may guess the gods' fancies."

"It is certain to require several days to locate the remaining beasts," Crixus matter-of-factly spoke. "Even then, there may be no Africans left to tend them."

Romo nodded in the dying light of their campfire. "If the Aethiops fled, find others to replace them and use them to locate the surviving beasts."

"And if there are no 'surviving beasts'?" Eros smirked.

"Then, it will not matter. We will remain here only until all the remaining beasts have been located and secured, whereupon we will resume our journey to Rome."

"How do you intend to explain the loss of the emperor's creatures?"

"As I said, Eros, if their destruction is ordained, we are powerless to avert it. That is a matter between the *Pontifex Maximus* and the gods."

“So, you intend to answer for your failure by blaming the gods, Romo? I sincerely congratulate you on your creativity, for the senate is certain to prove more deferential to the idiosyncrasies of the gods than to the ineptitude of cowardly, lazy Aethiops and the blunders of their commander.”

“’Their commander’”? Romo snorted. “Are you not sufficiently courageous to speak my name, Eros?”

“It not my responsibility to affix blame, Romo,” Eros shrugged. He wiped his greasy chin on the sleeve of his tunic. “That remains the province of the emperor and senate.”

“Just so. And, as you said, you remain prepared to place yourself at their disposal should your assistance be required,” Crixus sarcastically observed.

“Even, undoubtedly, if is not,” Romo added.

“What Roman would not do as much?” Eros yawned.

“To say nothing of a Gaul who pretends to be a Roman.”

ONLY ABOUT ONE-QUARTER of the animals remained alive, the rest having drowned, torn to pieces by crocodiles, or simply vanished. A depressing number of the survivors were not ambulatory due to broken or dislocated limbs, particularly the juvenile antelopes whose delicate legs were as thin as pipestems. Most of the surviving porters and servants had decamped during the night.

"Slaughter all the beasts that are unable to walk unaided," Romo directed. "We will smoke their flesh and survive on it for the remainder of our journey to Rome. Inform the remaining Aethiops that they are no longer needed and instruct them to return to their villages. Retain only as many porters as you think necessary."

"All will expect to be paid," Eros asserted.

"Their expectations must go unrequited, for I have nothing with which to pay them. Tell them to present their grievances to Corvo, for I will not suffer them."

"I have a better idea," Crixus quietly spoke. "Dismissing the Aethiops wholesale may prove unwise, for it is not impossible they will be needed to protect the column from bandits we may yet encounter during the remainder of our journey. The tombs near Meroe, an area through which we must pass, abound with such wretches. Slaughtering all the injured animals may also prove imprudent," Crixus continued. "It still remains to cross the Sudd with the beasts that remain, though we are no closer to surmounting that obstacle now than we were yesterday."

"So?" Eros impatiently interjected.

"I suggest we cast a number of them into the water some distance from where we intend to cross. Because they are lame, the animals will be unable to escape. Their clamorous exertions in trying to save themselves will excite the attention of the crocodiles and lure them away from us."

"You are a fool," Eros derisively scoffed.

Romo was less dismissive. "No, Crixus' words are prudent. The crocodiles must be dealt with, else we will be marooned here indefinitely."

"Had you not ordered them released in the first place, we would not be 'marooned here' at all," Eros reminded them.

"There were crocodiles here before we released ours," commented Crixus.

"That is unknowable, though this is not the time to debate it," Romo said. "Unlike you and the gods, Eros, I make no claim to prescience. I have no doubt, however, that you will acquaint the emperor and senate with my innumerable failings upon our arrival in Rome."

"As I stated before, I am at their disposal. I make no secret of it."

Romo ignored him. "Collect the remaining animals. Some we will butcher, others will be saved for the crocodiles, as Crixus suggests. Only those beasts able to walk unaided will be spared. Enlist the aid of those Aethiops who have not already fled. If they prove reluctant, remind them that their wives and children, whom they left behind, remain answerable to Rome; that will likely shake them from their sloth."

Crixus grunted, settled into his bedroll, and turned away from the campfire. Eros only scowled.

THROUGH THE HEAVY-HANDED application of bribery, threats, and cajolery, most of the remaining Africans were reluctantly persuaded to continue on the northward trek.

"I can take care of myself, but do not wish my family to be menaced by the Romans," was the universal lament.

"Because you have shown yourself to be a steadfast friend to the Roman people, you need have no concern for your family's welfare," they were assured. "Rome is generous toward its friends and amply rewards them with an open hand."

Crixus knew better. Rome's friends and enemies alike could, with equal probability, expect to be requited with the sting of the Roman lash, at best, or the clout its iron fist, at worst. Despite this, Crixus mouthed the platitudes as though his life, and the lives of his friends who remained behind at the *castrum*, depended on it. Because they did.

"How many beasts survive?" Romo asked late that afternoon.

"The Aethiops are still gathering them, but I daresay that most are dead," Eros informed him.

"That much I already knew. I require an exact count. What of the Aethiops?"

"What of them?"

"You convinced them to remain?"

Eros shrugged. “Some. The more cowardly ones disappeared into the bush before they could be caught and punished.”

Romo turned to Crixus. “What have you to say?”

“Most of the porters will accompany us to Rome. They otherwise fear for the safety of their families.”

“The Aethiops are more useless than even the stupid beasts!” Eros laughed. “Their anxieties are warranted, for they absolutely refuse to work unless made to understand that their families will suffer for their disobedience.”

Romo ignored the harangue. “Crixus, have you learned anything of the number of surviving animals?”

“As Eros said, the Africans continue their search for them, though I fear that a great number perished yesterday. On the other hand, we will now be able to travel more swiftly because there are far fewer animals to feed and attend to.”

“When will we be able to leave here?”

“Two more days, perhaps three,” Crixus speculated. “It will take the porters at least that long to locate and secure the remaining animals.”

Romo nodded in silence as he pondered the revelations.

“Inform the Aethiops that we depart for Rome in three days with whatever beasts they manage to corral,” he finally said. “In the interim, slaughter as many of the lame animals as you see fit and smoke their flesh over fires. Provide only enough forage to the remaining cripples to keep them alive until we feed them to the crocodiles. Attend to it."

LESS THAN 50 ANIMALS, representing a handful of species, remained ambulatory, most of them juvenile herbivores. In addition, the porters managed to recapture a few carnivores, as well: ratels, civets, some cheetah cubs, a serval. Herd animals like eland and impala instinctively congregated together, making them easier to round up. The fact they were young, weak, hungry, and terrified contributed to their docile recovery. As for mature, caged, carnivores, they had previously either succumbed to disease or starvation or the porters had simply abandoned them to the Sudd during their mad flight to escape.

"How many porters remain?" Romo asked Eros.

"Ask Crixus," shrugged the latter.

"Where is he?"

"It is not my turn to watch him. Last time I saw Crixus, he and some Aethiops were attempting to gather some antelope."

"You did not think to assist them?"

"Why should I? I am neither an Aethiop nor a captive," Eros replied before squeezing a mouthful of tepid wine from a bota.

"Do you know many beasts they have succeeded in capturing?" Romo scowled.

“Ask Crixus,” Eros repeated, taking another guzzle of wine. It drizzled from the corners of his mouth.

“Where is he?”

“Out there.” Eros extended his bota and vaguely gestured.

“Fetch Crixus and bring him here.”

Eros slowly lowered his arm and looked sourly at Romo. “He will return soon enough.”

“Your stubbornness does you no credit,” Romo snapped.

“Admittedly. But I would gladly forgo any amount of valueless credit in exchange for a fistful of Roman silver,” Eros rejoined with a smirk. “Though I will not begrudge it in the slightest should all credit for this catastrophe accrues entirely to you, Romo. Indeed, I would have it no other way.”

“Of that I have no doubt. While you ponder the fables you intend to spin before the emperor and senate regarding my stupidity, I will locate Crixus myself. Where did you see him last?”

“He and the Aethiops were grappling with a sable near the water’s edge over there,” Eros pointed, “though I daresay the sable appeared to be getting the better of them. The gods, alone, know how many of the buffoons have already been gored.”

“If it does not prove too much of an imposition, undertake the organization of our camp. I will inform Crixus that we leave for Rome on the morrow.”

Eros was unable to conceal his surprise. "It is not likely the Aethiops will succeed in rounding up all the stray beasts by then."

"I am beyond caring. It is profitless to remain at this place any longer. Most of the beasts have already perished or fled and surely will not return. It therefore does not matter whether we depart tomorrow or a month hence."

"As you wish," Eros shrugged as Romo turned away. "If you chance into any Aethiops while searching for Crixus, order them to return here. I will put them to work clearing the camp."

SEVEN

"PROFESSOR HUBERTUS AGREED to meet us on Thursday," Dunn exuberantly informed Laidlaw.

"I hope he's more helpful than the British Museum was."

Dunn chuckled over the phone. "Based on what you told me, that's apparently a pretty low bar. Did you end up buying a bunch of souvenirs in the museum's gift shop?"

"As a matter of fact, I bought you a talking Paddington Bear that says 'blimey!', 'pip-pip', 'bloke', 'mate', 'wanker', and 'bloody'."

"I'll treasure it. It will have pride of place on my bookshelf, right next to my miniature guillotine."

"Perfect!" Laidlaw laughed. "A tour of major European capitals in five seconds! Where are we meeting the professor? The university?"

"Yeah, at his office there."

"Am I picking you up, or are you picking me up?"

"I'll take an Uber to your hotel around 9'ish on Thursday. We'll head over to the university from there."

"Anything special I should say or do once we're there?"

"No, just don't forget the knife. I'll be there to translate."

"Hubertus really knows his stuff, huh? Think he'll be able to identify it?"

"Like I said at Harry's, Professor Hubertus is the preeminent French authority on ancient Roman arms and weaponry, maybe the world authority. If anybody can identify the knife, he can. I tried to describe it to him when we talked, but he said that he couldn't express an opinion regarding its age or provenance until he actually examined it."

Laidlaw unconsciously nodded. "Speaking of Harry's, you free for a beer?"

"I'm teaching a class until six, then I'm done for the week...except for our meeting with Professor Hubertus."

"How 'bout we meet at Harry's around seven? My treat."

"As my sainted grandmother wisely counseled, 'Never turn down free beer'. I'll see you at seven."

Laidlaw terminated the call, put his cell phone aside, and grabbed his laptop. He figured that, if Hubertus was, in fact, "the preeminent French authority on Roman weapons", there must be some info about the guy on the Internet.

Leo Hermann Hubertus, Professor Emeritus of Classical and Roman History at the *Sorbonne Universite'*, was born in Vienna in 1936. The author, contributor, or editor of numerous scholarly texts, author of dozens of academic papers, Hubertus also served as the primary consultant and collaborator on various documentaries about ancient Rome aired over the years on the BBC and other media outlets in both Europe and the United States.

Laidlaw closed his laptop and leaned against the headboard of the bed. Dunn hadn't exaggerated. Hubertus was evidently the real-deal. He glanced at his watch: four hours before he had to be at Harry's. Plenty of time for a little siesta.

LAIDLAW SPOTTED DUNN STANDING at the bar, chatting with Anatole, the moment he entered Harry's, his extraordinary height rendering him difficult to miss.

"Mr. Alex!" Anatole beamed as he approached them. "The professor and I were just chatting about you."

"It's 'Pierre', not 'professor', Dunn laughed.

“Of course,” Anatole smiled. “Harry’s is simply glad to see you both.”

Laidlaw shook hands with the both men. “I’ll have my usual, Anatole, plus Pierre needs a refill of whatever he’s drinking.”

“Certainly.”

Dunn grabbed his half-glass of Grimbergen and trailed Laidlaw as he headed for a table in the corner.

“So, where’s my Paddington Bear?” Dunn demanded once they were seated. “I cleared a spot for him on my shelf.”

“I decided to keep it for myself...a memento of my unproductive trip to London.”

Anatole arrived with Laidlaw’s Blood Mary and a fresh beer for Dunn. “Gentlemen,” he said as he slid the drinks onto their table before retiring.

“Cheers.” Laidlaw held his drink aloft.

“To London: bad food and worse weather,” Dunn reciprocated as they touched glasses.

Laidlaw sampled his Bloody Mary. “One of the sublime pleasures of life.”

“It’s too bad that your trip to the British Museum was a bust.”

“Not completely,” Laidlaw disagreed. “It’s been a long time since I’d been there and I enjoyed poking around. Can’t say that the hired help was particularly friendly, or helpful, though.”

Dunn nodded. “Yeah, the Brits tend to act like they’re doing you a favor just by talking to you.”

“Years ago, I had a hunting client from Manchester. He said the difference between a Brit and an American is that a Brit walks into a room like he owns it, while an American walks into a room like he doesn't give a damn who owns it!"

"I think that pretty much sums it up," Dunn concurred.

"So, how does a Frenchman walk into a room?" Laidlaw inquired.

"With a beautiful woman on each arm. How else?"

"Yeah, I should've guessed," Laidlaw chuckled. "I'm embarrassed that I even asked."

"I'm confident Professor Hubertus will prove much more helpful," Dunn asserted.

"I don't think he could be any *less* helpful."

Dunn drained his Grimbergen and wiped his mouth on a paper napkin. "Well, at least he won't ask you to buy a toy bear...a Sorbonne t-shirt, maybe."

"In that case, I'm already ahead."

THE TALL SHELVES OCCUPYING EACH wall sagged beneath the accumulated weight of books that were haphazardly crammed onto them. Laidlaw could only surmise that, if one dug deeply enough, a desk would probably emerge from beneath the welter of papers that occupied the center of the floor.

The three of them...Laidlaw, Dunn, and Hubertus...were crammed into the professor's surprisingly incommodious office at the Sorbonne.

Hubertus looked like someone a Central Casting Office would provide a motion picture director following the latter's request for, "somebody who looks like a college professor." Wizened, small in stature, bent, with a fringe of unruly white hair, Hubertus bore more than a passing resemblance to Albert Einstein. More-or-less what Laidlaw had expected.

"This is the gentleman I was telling you about," Dunn explained in French. "The American who found the knife."

"You are a hunter?" Hubertus inquired as Dunn interpreted.

"Yes," Laidlaw smiled. "In Africa."

Hubertus gazed out the window. "I hunted as a boy in my native Austria," he wistfully reminisced. "Not the huge creatures that you are accustomed to, of course," he smiled to himself. "Nothing more dangerous than rabbits, which my mother would cook for us."

Laidlaw smiled and nodded because he didn't know what else to do.

"May I see the piece?" Hubertus abruptly turned his attention to the matter at hand.

Dunn looked at Laidlaw, who wordlessly handed the academic the briefcase containing the dagger. Hubertus took it and carefully placed it on his lap. Snapping the latches, Hubertus lifted the case's lid and peered inside over the top of his bifocals.

Laidlaw had previously trimmed a block of Styrofoam to snugly fit the interior of the briefcase. Having done so, he sculpted a depression in the center of the foam to accommodate the dagger. Loosely swathed in the oily scrap of old bath towel, the relic rested in the resulting concavity.

Hubertus looked up from the briefcase. "May I?"

"Absolutely."

Hubertus used both hands to gingerly lift the shrouded relic from its receptacle. While the old man held it aloft, Dunn reached across and shut the briefcase. Hubertus lowered his hands until the dagger rested on its scuffed lid. Plucking a pair of lintless cotton gloves from the frayed pocket of his tweed jacket, he tugged them on as Laidlaw and Dunn watched in silence.

With meticulous exactitude, Hubertus began to unwrap Laidlaw's dagger. "There is a hand lens on the bookshelf," he murmured without looking up. "Please hand it to me."

Dunn glanced around the cluttered room until he spotted the magnifying glass. He rose to retrieve it and handed it wordlessly it to Hubertus.

"Thank you."

The dagger lay uncovered on Hubertus's lap atop Laidlaw's briefcase. A tiny smile, nearly imperceptible, flickered across the venerable academic's face.

"Lovely," he murmured, seemingly transfixed by the object.

"Do you recognize it, professor?" Dunn softly inquired.

Appearing not to hear, the old man simply stared at the dirk without touching it. Laidlaw glanced at Dunn, whose attention remained focused on the old man. Using the magnifying glass, Hubertus began to scrutinize the relic in greater detail.

“I have seen a similar specimen once before, in a collection in Budapest,” he finally responded as he continued his examination. “Although not identical, it exhibited a clear affinity with this example.”

“What can you tell us?”

Hubertus carefully turned the dagger over in order to examine the reverse side. “Its style is characteristic of the late Republic or early Roman Empire,” he continued, “though this particular knife is not of Italic origin. The Romans utilized only bronze or, rarely, meteoric iron, when fashioning weapons. For all their accomplishments, the Romans never figured out the intricacies of forging Damascus steel, which was utilized in this piece. Indeed, Damascus steel was something of a trade secret in the ancient world, confined to a comparatively few regions in the Near East and carefully safeguarded in order to maintain a monopoly on the process of fabricating it. This was undoubtedly a bespoke piece forged for a specific individual.”

“How can you be certain of that?” Laidlaw blurted as Dunn translated the professor’s remarks into English.

“As I said, its style is clearly Roman.” Hubertus paused and smiled, mischievously. “But the mystery conclusively reveals itself because of an inscription on the blade.”

“No kidding? I didn’t even know it had an inscription!”

"Oh, yes," Hubertus assured him. *'Hoc pertinet ad Crixo, civi Romano.'"*

"Meaning?"

"'This belongs to Crixus, a Roman citizen,'" Dunn interpreted, unbidden.

"The inscription is very faint," Hubertus continued. "The craftsman who engraved this weapon was extremely skilled, for he was able to cleverly integrate the owner's name into arabesques on the blade itself, features that are unique to Damascus steel."

"Wait," Laidlaw frowned. "If the knife is made of steel, which is obviously hard, how could he have inscribed anything onto it? What kind of tool did he use?"

"Damascus steel is, indeed, extremely robust. It was, and is, renowned for its ability to hold an edge and resist bending and shattering. My guess is that whoever engraved this dagger probably utilized some form of acid to etch the blade. In fact, the English word 'corrosive', as well as the French '*corrosif*', are derived from the Latin *corrodere*, which means 'to gnaw', in the sense of gnawing away at things. The use of sodium hydroxide, ordinary caustic soda, for that purpose was well established among the Romans, for example."

"Can you show me the inscription?" Laidlaw eagerly asked.

"Of course. I don't wonder that you were unable to see it unaided. It's integrated into the rippled texture of the blade and isn't especially pronounced. Time and erosion have further effaced it."

Laidlaw and Dunn simultaneously stood. The professor handed the magnifying glass to Laidlaw, who bent forward to scrutinize the relic. Hubertus angled the knife first one way, then another, in an effort to highlight the inscription in the imperfect light. Dunn watched over his shoulder.

"You were right about it being indistinct," Laidlaw muttered as he peered through the magnifying glass. "I don't see anything except swirls."

"Yes, the inscription is extremely faint," Hubertus acknowledged, "but rest assured it's there." He tilted the dagger slightly, hoping the shifting light would accentuate the contrast between the patterned blade and the lettering.

"Oh, I see it now," Laidlaw softly declared. He straightened and looked at Dunn, beaming, and passed him the magnifying glass. "Check it out. It's very small and hard to distinguish."

They switched places and Dunn leaned down to examine the knife. "Yes, I see it," he said after only a moment. "I'd never have guessed it was there." He straightened and returned the glass to Hubertus. "Have you ever seen anything like this before, professor?"

Hubertus shook his head. "Roman tourists and bored legionnaires routinely inscribed their names, as well as ribald graffiti, on every available surface, exactly like modern tourists. Many ancient Egyptian monuments, such as the Colossi of Memnon on the west bank of the Nile opposite Thebes, are replete with such impromptu carvings, which span several centuries. But I've personally never encountered a declaration of private ownership inscribed on the blade of a Roman weapon. In my experience, this is unique. But this particular knife was not the standard bronze *cultro* routinely issued to every Roman soldier. Given the costly material from which it was fashioned and its obvious quality, this piece was forged at the order of a specific individual, presumably Crixus, who evidently possessed sufficient financial resources to commission it."

"Do you think he was a soldier?"

"Impossible. An ordinary soldier could never have afforded such a weapon," Hubertus explained. "Ordinarily, I'd say that Crixus was a probably a diplomat stationed in Roman Judea. But, were that the case, he'd have had, at a minimum, both his praenomen and his cognomen inscribed on the blade. Because he used only his praenomen, I can only surmise that Crixus, whoever he was, was probably an ordinary Roman citizen, albeit a relatively wealthy one, perhaps a merchant of some sort. What he was doing in Judea is anyone's guess."

"Why would he have had this knife made?"

The old man smiled. "Because he could. However, it's equally likely that he acquired the knife from its original owner and simply had his name engraved on it." He paused. "Refresh my memory, please...where did you find it?"

"Central Tanzania, about 80 miles northeast of Mpanda."

"I'm not familiar with that area. I presume it is essentially wilderness?"

"Might as well be on another planet," Laidlaw confirmed. "Some migratory tribes...that's about it. I've never hunted in that area because no roads or rivers run through it."

Hubertus looked thoughtful. "That would certainly explain why this piece lay undiscovered until now."

"According to my tracker, the local tribes avoid the whole area because of some ruins, which they evidently consider bad medicine."

"Oh?" Hubertus raised an eyebrow, his interest piqued. "Characteristic of pre-industrial, animistic, societies are their embrace of particular taboos, which may include proscribed physical spaces, alimentary restrictions, prohibited articles of clothing, restrictions on bodily ornamentation, prescribed personal hygiene rituals, or forbidden verbal or written expressions, because of presumed supernatural or religious connotations. In many civilizations, including both the ancient Hebrews and Egyptians, for example, it was forbidden to utter the name of God. Herodotus also informs us that the ancient Egyptians refused to eat beans, as well as certain species of fish, because they considered them unclean. Even today, the consumption of certain foods remains forbidden in some cultures and religions. Until comparatively recently, only royalty was permitted to wear certain items or colors of clothing. Anthropologists and sociologists have largely succeeded in identifying the practical basis and rationale for most of these conventions, which are often puzzling when encountered in isolation, divorced from their historical context."

Laidlaw struggled to remain attentive to the professor's scholarly disquisition, though Dunn appeared to be genuinely interested.

"These ruins, they are Roman?" Hubertus asked.

"That remains unclear, Professor," Dunn interjected. "The ruins Mr. Laidlaw speaks of have apparently never been excavated, though they contain some Latin inscriptions."

Hubertus unconsciously nodded. "That would be consistent with the engraving on Mr. Laidlaw's knife, combined with its Romanic design. I daresay someone, perhaps 'Crixus' himself, transported the knife to Africa from the Near East where it was originally fashioned. Do you know whether the government of Tanzania has granted authority to excavate these ruins, Professor Dunn?"

"Mr. Laidlaw is not convinced that the Tanzanian authorities are even aware of their existence."

"Indeed? That is most curious. How extensive are the ruins?"

Dunn looked expectantly at Laidlaw, who responded. "It's hard to tell, as a lot of them have basically sunk into an old, dry river bed. If I had to guess, I'd say at least a hectare, maybe more."

Hubertus was puzzled. "It is a matter of historical record that, particularly under the Empire, Rome sent its legions very far afield, including into Mediterranean Africa at least as far south as the Second Cataract. I am unaware, however, of any systemic Roman penetration into sub-Saharan Africa. If you are correct that the ruins are Roman, a surmise bolstered by the Latin inscription on this marvelous piece, a significant Roman presence in that region seems apparent. How is it possible the Tanzanian government is unaware of this site?"

"That was precisely my question when Mr. Laidlaw informed me of its existence," Dunn noted. Both he and Hubertus looked to Laidlaw for an explanation.

Laidlaw smiled, thinly. "You're probably already aware that Ruth Schurr characterized French history as 'a series of dictatorship interrupted by riots', which also pretty much describes politics in third-world Africa, too. Governments have more important things to occupy their time than old ruins. Like politicians everywhere, their primary concern is to stay in power. If something doesn't accrue to their immediate personal benefit, it gets ignored. Being of no practical value, a scattering of ruins out in the middle of nowhere, Roman or otherwise, are nothing more than an irrelevant distraction. The first order of business for the majority of African politicians is to position themselves most favorably in anticipation of the next election, or the next revolution, whichever appears imminent."

"I share your disdain for the notorious venality of politicians. Still, it remains a strange business," Hubertus mulled. "Based on nothing more than this knife, one would expect that commercial treasure-hunters would already be on site, carting away artifacts to sell on the black market."

"I don't think treasure-hunters are even aware of the ruins' existence. The locals are tight-lipped about them. They're remote, isolated, and difficult to get to."

"Perhaps the Sorbonne could contact the appropriate authorities to secure the permits necessary to undertake excavation of the site?" Dunn hopefully prodded.

The old man wistfully smiled. "Unfortunately, my excavating days are behind me. I must devote what little time I have remaining to the completion of academic papers already promised to several professional journals. Furthermore, if Mr. Laidlaw's pragmatic assessment of the current political situation in Africa is accurate, which I have no reason to doubt, I suspect that attempting to secure authorization to dig will prove a convoluted and protracted exercise requiring very deep pockets...merely identifying the appropriate department, cabinet, or minister is, by itself, likely to prove a frustrating process. Should the chancellors of the university wish to pursue the matter, that is, of course, their affair. I wish I were thirty years younger," he sighed.

"What about UNESCO?" Dunn probed.

"What of it?" Hubertus scoffed. "The UNESCO trustees, like university dons, devote the preponderance of their resources to flitting about the globe, staying in first-class hotels, mingling with other like-minded bureaucrats, attending interminable symposia, and eating shrimp cocktails. UNESCO is only concerned with preserving sites that do not require preservation but look impressive on travel posters: the Taj Mahal, Copan, Machu Pichu, Victoria Falls, Mont-Saint-Michel, Pasargadae. A dreary pile of stones located in the middle of the African savanna will not excite UNESCO's interest...you will receive no assistance from that quarter, I assure you. I should know, as UNESCO is headquartered right here in Paris, at the *Place de Fontenoy.*"

"What, then, do you recommend?"

"I will approach the university's trustees about Mr. Laidlaw's ruins though, for the reasons we've been discussing, I would not expect my overtures to be greeted with an outpouring of enthusiasm." Hubertus paused. "Have you considered soliciting private or philanthropic donations? There are several international foundations that might be willing to provide financial or technical assistance."

Dunn glanced at Laidlaw. "I don't think Mr. Laidlaw has considered that option," he responded with some hesitation.

"I will have one of my staff prepare a list for you, in English. In the interim, what do you intend to do with this piece?" Hubertus nodded toward the dagger that still rested atop Laidlaw's briefcase. "Any number of museums around the world...Paris, of course, but also London, Berlin, Vienna, New York, Rome...would be pleased to add it to their collections."

"Yeah, I'll bet," Laidlaw dryly remarked following Dunn's English translation. "I think I'll hang on to it for a while."

Professor Hubertus handed the dagger back to him. "I would do exactly the same thing," he confided.

LAIDLAW SAT AT THE BAR IN Harry's, waiting for Dunn to arrive after wrapping up his afternoon class at the Sorbonne. The place was empty but for him and a twenty-something female sitting alone at a table, drinking a club soda. The bartender, whom he didn't recognize, ignored them from the opposite end of the bar. In the background, Bobby Hatfield warbled 'Unchained Melody' on the jukebox.

He'd not decided what to do about his dagger and wanted to kick it around with Dunn. Even if he managed to inveigle some private foundation into bankrolling exploration of the ruins, it was certain that he'd promptly be horned out of the picture and reduced to a footnote, at best. Some pin-headed academics would immediately seize control of the whole enchilada and, with it, the resulting fame, prestige, and dollars that would inevitably follow. Laidlaw didn't give a damn about fame or prestige, but he sure as hell wouldn't turn his back on a few shekels.

"Hello."

He turned to his right. The twenty-something stood next to him.

"I thought you might like some company," she explained in a British accent.

"I already have company." Laidlaw indicated his Bloody Mary. "But you can join me if you want."

She slid a stool out and plopped down, placing her purse atop the bar. "I'm Bonnie." Laidlaw didn't bother to introduce himself because he didn't want to appear conversational.

They were everywhere in Europe, wherever rich Americans, or at least Americans perceived to be rich, congregated. Those from Great Britain were invariably "Bonnie" or "Daisy." Their English-speaking French counterparts, "Dominique." In Germany, "Anna" or "Eva." Not exactly prostitutes, for they didn't necessarily sell sex, they glommed onto unaccompanied American males to offer their services as tour guides, translators, local experts privy to otherwise "unknown" hotspots, or simply "companions." They usually claimed to have a friend or relative who worked at this-or-that museum or attraction, willing to sell admission tickets to the naïve American at a huge discount, or place him at the head of a queue, absolutely gratis. Flattered and grateful, trusting American men were happy to reward their beautiful new best-friend with crisp greenbacks, dinners, or more. Alternatively, Bonnie/Daisy, Dominique, or Anna, would tearfully confide that their boyfriends had abandoned them and they needed "just a few Euros" to survive until their families wired enough money for them to return home.

It was 100 per-cent bullshit, of course. Nine times out of ten, the women were in cahoots with bartenders, hack drivers, and hotel concierges, who steered them to potential marks and split the ensuing take. Anatole wouldn't tolerate the presence of such grifters in Harry's, but this was evidently his day off; the unknown bartender was undoubtedly a party to the present scam.

"I love this song," Bonnie sighed as 'Unchained Melody' concluded with Hatfield's incomparable tenor crescendo. "It makes me want to dance." Failing to prod a response from the taciturn Laidlaw, she forged ahead, undeterred. "Do you like to dance? I know some lovely dance clubs nearby."

"Dancing's an idiotic waste of energy appropriate only for drunks and children's birthday parties."

Bonnie was taken aback by Laidlaw's unexpected rebuff. "It can be very sexy," she pouted.

"Yeah? Wanna know what's *really* sexy?"

"Tell me," she cooed as she leaned closer.

"Sex."

She feigned offense. "Are you trying to solicit me?"

"No, just stating a fact."

"You're from America?"

"*Mea culpa.*"

"Your accent and your mannerisms," she revealed. "Is this your first time in Paris?"

"Yeah," he lied.

"How are you enjoying 'The City of Lights'?"

"It's okay. But, aside from this place, nobody here has the courtesy to speak English."

She looked confused. "Are you in Paris for business or pleasure?"

"Yeah."

"I'm sorry, which?"

"Yes."

"What do you do?" she persevered.

"About what?"

Her face bore a pained expression as she struggled to stimulate a conversation. "No, no. What do you do for a living?"

"I'm a piano player in a whore house." Laidlaw drained his Bloody Mary.

Like most Europeans, she was finding the irreverent American difficult to plumb.

"What about you? Do you live here?" he agreeably inquired, thereby sparing her the necessity of trying to figure out whether he was serious about anything or merely spoke in jest.

Her face instantly assumed a sorrowful mien. "No, I'm from Liverpool. My wanker boyfriend and I were on holiday when he dumped me the day before yesterday...ran off with some French tart. I'm waiting for my mum to send me money so I can go home. It's been a struggle for her to come up with it, though, because of dad's illness."

"Sorry to hear that. But I suppose there are worse places to be marooned," he commiserated.

"Not when you don't have even a single sou for a hotel! My boyfriend took all our money when he left and, because I couldn't pay the bill, our hotel threw me out. I've been sleeping in a park until mum's money arrives, which is very dangerous, as I'm sure you can appreciate. I don't even have enough money to pay for one of those street corner WC's, so I can relieve myself in private. I have to do it behind bushes in the park."

"Bummer. Harry's has a toilet. I'm sure your buddy, the bartender, will let you use it if you ask real nice."

"My 'buddy'?" she huffed. "I don't know the gentleman!"

"Ok, my bad," Laidlaw shrugged. "Well, you're easy on the eyes. I'm sure there's no shortage of horny tourists you can put the bite on," he helpfully suggested. "Sorta payback for your boyfriend."

Frustrated, Bonnie tried another tack. "Would you like to buy me a drink?" The bartender would serve her another club soda and ding Laidlaw $25 for it.

"No thanks, I'll pass. But I appreciate your offer to allow me the privilege."

"Yes, of course," she responded because she didn't know what else to say. She stood, grabbed her handbag, and forced a smile. "Lovely chatting with you."

"Wish I could say the same. Hope you get the money from your mom sooner, rather than later. Sleeping in a park sounds uncomfortable, and damp, though you look no worse for it. Take good care of yourself," he amiably replied.

The puzzled bartender looked toward them as Bonnie walked back to her table. She returned his glance with a frown and he resumed polishing glassware with a dishtowel.

Laidlaw checked his wristwatch before tapping the rim of his empty Bloody Mary glass. "Next time, try being a little more discreet," he advised after the bartender clumped over to refresh his drink.

In Primis Anno Regnantibus Imperator Caesar Titus Vespasianus (79 CE)

"GET OFF YOUR WORTHLESS ASSES!" Berossus roared. "The Aethiops are en route with beasts they captured, for it is plain that Rome's finest are too lazy, or too stupid, to do it. It sickens me that legionnaires are content to be bested by savages. It is well that the emperor chooses to remain in Rome, rather than travel here, for he would weep torrents after witnessing the shameful state of *Legio Bestia XVI.* I swear by the gods, were it my decision, I would have every one of you fucking idlers fed to the beasts."

Neocles, Aulus, and the remaining legionnaires slowly bestirred themselves.

"You are a fool, Berossus," Neocles sluggishly commented. "Why should we risk life and limb to capture beasts when the Aethiops show themselves willing to do it? What sorts of creatures do they bring?"

"What does it matter? Even if the Aethiops deliver only a single, dead, beast, that will surpass anything you idlers have accomplished."

Neocles stretched extravagantly. “No, Berossus, you are wrong. We have managed to stay alive. That, alone, is commendable. But you did not answer my question. What sorts of beasts do the Aethiops bring?”

“Panther and cheetah cubs, antelope fawns, wild dog pups, a collection of venomous serpents, even some young elephants, according to the messenger sent to Corvo by their king.”

Neocles removed from the sheath that hung at his side the knife that Crixus had given him prior to his exile. He casually began to peel a plum-sized marula with it. “Have Romo or Eros also dispatched a messenger with news of their progress?”

“You surely speak in jest, Neocles, for how would it be possible for dead men to send a messenger anywhere? Not even the gods could accomplish such a marvelous feat,” Berossus derisively responded. “Either their Aethiops already slit their throats or Romo, Eros, and the rest have succumbed to banditry, starvation, or disease.”

Neocles resheathed his knife and took a bite of the piquant fruit. “You are probably right, though it seems to me that Titus is unlikely to be very much pleased by your indifference to the fate of an expert he specifically directed you to provide.”

“Your friend, Crixus?” Berossus scoffed. “That slacker was an ‘expert’ only on the subject of insolence. I’m certain that Titus has already forgotten and moved on from him. Indeed, for all anyone knows, Titus has already suffered the fate of Galba, Otho, and

Vitellius. It is anyone's guess who the current emperor is, though that is not your concern. Your concern is to ready the pens for the Aethiops' beasts once they arrive at the *castrum.* If any creatures currently confined in the pens are sick or dead, throw them into the river and make such repairs as are necessary."

The *Acta Diurna* was a daily, handwritten broadsheet emanating directly from Rome and conveyed to the far corners of the Empire via the official Roman courier service, the *Cursus Publicus Velox.* Like any newspaper, the *Diurna* reported happenings in the capital; gossip; details of quotidian urban fires; obituaries of leading citizens; accounts of military victories; the results of chariot races and other items deemed worthy of note. Galba, Otho, and Vitellius were opportunistic generals who, prior to Vespasian's ascendency and with the backing of the legions directly under their respective commands, successively ascended to power in the chaos following Nero's suicide. All of them met violent deaths, which would have been duly reported in the *Acta Diurna.* Because of its remoteness from the capital, however, arrival of the *Acta* at *Legio XVI Bestia* was invariably delayed for months, if it ever arrived at all.

"When will the Aethiops arrive?" Aulus asked.

"Tomorrow, the next day, the day after that," Berossus shrugged. "It is all one to you. Get to it." He turned on his heel and stalked off.

"THAT FUCKING ELEPHANT HAS no trunk."

Abbo followed Berossus' outstretched finger. He pointed to a baby elephant with long strings of bloody tissue dangling from its head. Not yet weaned, it vainly attempting to feed by kneeling and placing its mouth in a large pottery dish of sour goat's milk that one of the Africans had placed on the ground.

"Oh, that one," Abbo indifferently noted. "A crocodile bit it off when it attempted to drink. We had to spear its mother."

"How do you expect it to eat?"

Abbo watched with curiosity as the starving animal overturned the bowl, slopping milk onto the parched earth. It finally collapsed in frustrated exhaustion. "I expect nothing, Roman. Since you are the masters of the earth, figuring out how to feed an elephant should be a trifle to you."

"I have no interest in being a wetnurse," Berossus sneered.

"If you do not wish to be bothered with the creature, kill it," Abbo proposed. "One elephant will make no difference, as we have already supplied you with a multitude of other beasts which will more than compensate for its loss. On the other hand, if you can keep the creature alive, the people in your capital may reward you for its novelty."

"Elephants are noble beasts. Romans admire and feel a rightful kinship with them," Berossus responded with disgust. “They will have no interest in such a disgusting cripple.”

Abbo clasped his assegai and strode wordlessly to the prostrate young elephant. With two hands, he drove the spear’s fire-hardened point into the fallen animal’s earhole and leaned on it until it crunched against bone, killing the feebly squirming elephant.

“I spare you unease by resolving the dilemma for you, Roman,” he said as he placed his knees against the dead animal’s head and tugged his assegai free. “Your delicate Roman sensibilities are once again secure.”

“I trust the other beasts you supplied are in better condition.”

“We would not have to supply beasts if you Romans were not so lazy,” Abbo laughed. “But, if our offerings displease you, we will gladly stop providing them. My people can easily find less irksome activities with which to occupy themselves.”

Berossus looked scathingly at him. “I will let you know once Corvo reviews your latest offerings. The decision is his alone.”

“As you wish,” Abbo replied as he shouldered his assegai. “I will inform Jugurtha.”

“HOW MANY ROMANS ARE there?”

Abbo looked into the distance as he reflected. “Not very many...perhaps thirty men lounging about. I

do not know how many others were elsewhere in their compound or out hunting, but not many."

Jugurtha nodded to himself. "The men you saw...did they appear robust and in fighting mettle?"

"Just the opposite," Abbo scoffed. "Romans are already lazy and the heat renders them even more sluggish and idle."

"Were they armed?"

"None."

"Not even their headman?"

"Berossus, their centurion, told me that their headman's name is 'Corvo', though I have never seen him. As for Berossus, I am not sure that he even knows the proper end of a sword to grasp!"

"But you are convinced that the Romans possess a plenitude of arms?" Jugurtha probed.

"In abundance: swords, pikes, bows, slings, darts, javelins, leather and hammered armor. They secure everything in a special room, under guard."

"You have seen this room?"

Abbo shook his head. "No, though I know where it is located within their compound and what it contains. Other legionnaires previously described it to me. So confident are the Romans of themselves that a single legionnaire, armed with only a sword, guards their cache of weapons."

Jugurtha eyed him, dubiously. "Perhaps you are not as practiced in the Romans' tongue as you believe yourself to be. Or perhaps the legionnaires who described this room to you were lying in hopes of overawing you."

"That is possible," Abbo conceded. "But my knowledge of Latin notwithstanding, I possess eyes as well as ears. Even if the Romans lie, my eyes do not."

"Romans are resolute fighters with many victories."

Abbo laughed. "Of course! It is only necessary to ask them! But I do not think these Romans know how to fight. Besides, it will not be necessary to defeat them by force of arms when deception is all that will be required." He briefly paused to assess Jugurtha's reaction. When none was forthcoming, he continued. "I informed Berossus that we will return to the Romans' compound a few days hence with additional beasts for their arena. We will arrive at daybreak, when all but a handful of Romans will still be sleeping. All of us will be armed with knives beneath our cloaks. When the careless Romans admit us to their compound, we will spring on them and slit their throats. By the time the stunned Romans realize their blunder and attempt to resist, we will have already have seized their armory. With their weapons in our hands, the entire garrison will quickly surrender."

"The Romans prohibit the introduction of weapons into their *castrum*," Jugurtha reminded him.

Abbo laughed. "They do not bother to search us. The Romans do not care a straw for such restrictions."

"And if the Romans stand their ground after you have seized their store of arms?"

"Let them...it will do them no good. The Romans are lions possessing neither teeth nor claws. With what will they defend themselves? Their bare hands?

What good are bare hands against their own weapons? The entire garrison will fall in less time that it takes to tell. Aside from finally ridding ourselves of Roman scum, we will also possess all their weapons! So armed, neither the Romans, nor any of our other enemies, will be able to stand against us! And, if you wish to take some Romans hostage, rather than slaughter the lot of them, Rome will pay liberally to ransom them, especially their headman, Corvo."

"It is a sensible plan, Abbo," Jugurtha approved, "though the Romans will undoubtedly send new legions to avenge themselves on us."

"I hope that occurs, for I would welcome it. If Rome is so foolish as to send new legions, they will find us fully armed with their own weapons. When the Romans first arrived here, we knew nothing about them. Now we know much: their language, their tactics, their strengths, their weaknesses. Even if they flatter themselves able to punish us, which is far from certain, it will be many months or years before replacement legions are dispatched. By the time they arrive here, those legions will have been depleted through accident, disease, and desertion, making them even less formidable. The Romans will be far from home and surrounded by implacable enemies." Abbo paused. "The blood of one's enemies creates a most pleasing stain."

"Your words are alluring," Jugurtha conceded.

"The arrogant Romans fancy themselves heirs to the accomplishments of their illustrious forebears," Abbo resumed, "though they otherwise share no bond with them. They consider themselves invincible by arrogating to themselves the conquests of their ancestors."

"They harbor no suspicions of your ruse?"

"Aside from heaping us with insults, the Romans turn their backs and pay no attention to us once they admit us to their *castrum*. Their complacency will be their undoing."

"How many men will you need?"

Abbo reflected before responding. "Only those who wish to cover themselves in glory. Twenty, certainly. More, if possible. It is essential that we overwhelm the Romans quickly, before they realize what has befallen them and are able to mount an organized defense."

Jugurtha held up a cautionary hand. "Restraint, Abbo. You propose to best an entire *castrum* of legionnaires using a mere handful of men?"

The other man smiled, slyly. "A greater number will excite the Roman's suspicions. The Romans are woefully understrength. They are also unmotivated and not disposed to fight, especially if taken by surprise by those they consider their inferiors. They will quickly realize the folly of resistance and will yield in the expectation that their lives will be spared."

"You have spoken to the men of the kraal of this?"

"It was my wish to secure your approval before all else, Jugurtha. The approbation of others is a meaningless trifle if not accompanied by your blessing."

The tribal leader narrowed his eyes. "That is prudent, for no man in my kraal who values his life is reckless enough to undertake such a bold enterprise without my personal sanction."

"For no other reason do I humble myself before you, Wise One. The power of your words, without more, is enough to assure our success." Abbo took a step rearward and kneeled, placing the palms of his hands, as well as his forehead, on the earth. He remained immobile as Jugurtha, using his gemsbuck flywhisk, ritually leaned forward and flogged Abbo's naked back.

"The gods, alone, know the fate of all men, yet your desire to purge the loathsome Romans from our land is highly pleasing to them," Jugurtha spoke. "Bomu Rambi delights in their deaths. Let those who would seek the gods' favor, no less than their gratitude, contribute to that laudable enterprise, for the gods have decreed that our triumph over the pale heathens is ordained." He continued to lightly strike Abbo as he intoned the benediction.

"*Takatifu, takatifu, takatifu,*" Abbo softly chanted.

"You will adorn my kraal with Roman heads," Jugurtha continued. "Spare none of the invaders."

"*Takatifu, takatifu, takatifu...*"

"THE AETHIOPS HAVE PROMISSED to bring more beasts to the *castrum*."

"Of what type? Why?" Corvo sighed. He took another tug of wine and wiped his mouth. "We are scarcely able to feed the beasts already here."

"I did not think it prudent to discourage the Aethiops' display of initiative," Berossus opined. "And, if the beasts die, it is because the gods will it."

"Have we enough pens?"

"We will combine like beasts together in a few pens to create extra space for the new animals. If necessary, I will instruct the men to construct additional pens for them."

Corvo nodded in satisfaction before squeezing another drink of wine from the bota and passing it to Berossus. "Dispose of any creatures already dead and slaughter those that are diseased. Feed the men as much of the meat as they can hold and give the remainder to the Aethiops. Also, instruct the Aethiops not to bring additional beasts to the *castrum* until we direct them to do so. I have had my fill of tending beasts for the emperor's foolish games. Let them all die, for all I care."

"I will begin on the morrow," Berossus assured him. "Do you intend to unburden yourself by sending a second caravan of creatures to Rome?"

Corvo shrugged as he again reached for the bota. "Rome has not deigned to communicate its wishes, one way or the other, regarding beasts. Nor have I any inkling of the present circumstances of the caravan that is presently en route to the capital. I am reluctant to dispatch another until learning its fate, for *Bestia* is already undermanned and I have no desire to further deplete it. It is a most hazardous thing, Berossus, to engage in conjecture regarding an emperor's wishes...more than one senator and consul have been deprived of their heads for having guessed wrong. I have no desire to add to that list." He leaned back in his chair and silently nursed the wineskin.

Berossus' face assumed a pained expression. "What, then, do you desire, Pompeius? Is it your intention that *Bestia* passively languish in this Gehenna until all of us are dead from disease or the attacks of wild animals, condemned to oblivion and despised by both Rome and the gods? Would it not, on the contrary, be more fitting to conduct ourselves like Romans?"

"Continue," Corvo invited his garrulous companion, whose tongue was lubricated by wine.

"The Aethiops have long treated us with derision, considering themselves our equals. It is only with the greatest reluctance that they supply us with beasts and, even then, the animals are often sickly juveniles that are not worth the keeping. Worse, they openly mock our impotence by bearing arms inside the castrum."

Corvo blinked and sat up. "The Africans are armed while in the *castrum*? That is forbidden, Marcus."

"The Aethiops are aware, yet brazenly flaunt our decrees by possessing weapons."

"How do you know this?"

"I have an informant among them," Pompeius," Berossus explained. "He makes me aware of these things."

"Why have you not put an end to the practice?"

"To what end? I saw no point in confronting the Africans because as you, yourself, just said, *Bestia* is already undermanned. How would it profit us to antagonize them?"

"But you are suddenly of a new mind?" Corvo skeptically inquired.

"The men of the *castrum* are becoming restive. They no longer consider themselves Romans, but zookeepers. It is time they once again comported themselves as Romans."

"How do you propose to make zookeepers into Romans?"

"They are Romans already. It is only necessary to remind them who their enemies are and nourish their roots with their blood."

Corvo looked pensive. "Killing Aethiops is not without hazard, Marcus."

"What, then, would you have me do?"

Corvo reclined in his chair and took another quaff of wine. "When do you next expect the Aethiops?"

"Their courier assured me they would return with new animals within the next several days."

Berossus looked longingly at bota cradled in the other man's hands.

Corvo nodded and extended the wineskin to his subordinate, who eagerly leaned forward to retrieve it.

"Do what you think best to restore my Romans to me," instructed the former.

Berossus tipped his head back, placed his lips over the mouth of the bota, and avidly squeezed its remaining contents into his mouth. A thread of wine trickled from the corner of his mouth and dripped from his stubbled chin onto his tunic.

"You may rely on me," Berossus answered after wiping his chin on his sleeve.

IT WAS STILL DARK WHEN Abbo drew up to the castrum's gate. With him were a dozen discretely-armed warriors from Jugurtha's kraal, listlessly herding a mixed bag of enfeebled antelopes and goats.

"Hail!" he called to the sentry.

"Who approaches?"

"Abbo, with animals for your emperor."

"The Watch Commander did not notify me of your coming."

"That is of no moment, for I am obviously here. Moreover, we are acquaintances."

"I must summon the centurion," the sentry announced.

"The centurion? There is no need to disturb his slumber, nor that of anyone else," Abbo countered. "Admit us and we will quickly convey these beasts to the holding pens in your *castrum* and return to our kraal."

“I am under orders to admit no one,” the guard deferred.

“Of course,” Abbo smoothly responded. “It is wise to deny entry to those you do not know. But I am a friend to everyone in your *castrum*, including your centurion, Berossus.”

“I will summon him at once,” the sentry repeated. “He is nearby. Await my return.”

“What is the delay, Abbo?” one of his men grumbled in the gloom, though the sky was already beginning to lighten.

“It is nothing. The guard is just too stupid to open the gate. All will be well.”

“Do the Romans suspect treachery?”

“The Romans are as innocent as children,” Abbo scoffed. “They suspect nothing.” The heavy bolt being drawn from within the *castrum* terminated further conversation. “Be prepared to strike on my signal,” he hissed.

The portal groaned slowly open. Arrayed in the breach were Berossus and a squad of grim, armored legionnaires clasping pikes in a vertical position. Beyond them, on the *castrum's* parade ground, additional legionnaires were gathered, armed with pikes and short swords. In the damp early-dawn air, *Bestia's* standard, the image of a wild boar emblazoned against a red background, drooped from a pole in the center of the yard.

“Greetings, Berossus,” a startled Abbo managed to stammer. “I desired that the guard not disturb you, as we are merely conveying some additional beasts to you with Jugurtha's compliments."

"Welcome, Abbo. As you see, your arrival occasioned no disturbance, as my men and I were already about."

Abbo glanced uneasily at the handful of men crowded around him. Armed only with concealed daggers, they nervously shifted their weight from one foot to the other.

"How is it you are already up at this hour?" Abbo forced a conversational tone.

"I was previously notified of your coming." Berossus nodded his head slightly as he spoke. The squad strode forward in silence and, still holding their pikes vertically, stood loosely behind the knot of Africans gathered at the castrum's gate. Abbo pretended not to notice but could scarcely believe that his ruse had been exposed.

Noting with satisfaction the look of confusion that flickered across Abbo's face, Berossus feigned surprise. "Do you not know that *Bestia* has eyes and ears inside your kraal and that nothing occurs there without our knowledge? Jugurtha, your headman, has long shared with us matters of mutual concern."

Abbo narrowed his eyes. "You are a despicable liar, Roman." he sneered, dismissive of Berossus' outlandish claim. "What motivation would Jugurtha have for communicating with you?"

"Jugurtha fears your ambition, Abbo, and is mindful that you lack adequate wisdom to lead his kraal. Your presence here this morning, and that of the men who agreed to join you on this mad adventure, is abundant proof that Jugurtha's anxieties are warranted. It was he who requested that we temper your imprudent zeal."

His chief's betrayal stunned Abbo.

"Your words have no merit," he feebly asserted.

Berossus smiled without humor. "How, then, did we possess knowledge of your arrival here this morning? Haruspication?" As the two men tensely conversed, no one attempted to prevent the hodgepodge of goats and antelope from simply drifting away. "Your foolish plot to attack our *castrum* by stealth has come to nothing, Abbo." As he spoke, the remaining legionnaires moved forward as a unit and formed up on either side of the Africans.

Abbo feigned indifference. "No rational person would consider attacking the invincible Romans." He paused to mentally assess the most promising avenue of escape. "But I weary of your slanders. Allow us to return to our kraal." He turned as if to leave, though the soldiers surrounding them remained immobile.

"Gladly," Berossus responded with a tiny smile. "You and your men may demonstrate your amicable intentions toward us by opening your cloaks, after which you will be free to return home." In a single motion, the encircling legionnaires lowered their pikes until they were horizontal, their glittering bronze points directed toward the Africans.

Abbo faced his accuser. "Our cloaks?" he snarled. "This is how Romans treat their brothers?"

“One does not enter his brother’s house with the secret intent to slay him as he sleeps.”

“We did not enter your house, Berossus,” Abbo temporized. He gestured toward the threshold of the *castrum*, across which none of the Africans had been allowed to step. ”As you see, my men and I stand outside its gates, having wrongfully been denied entry. Nor have we ever desired to harm our Roman brothers. Allow us to depart in peace.”

“In peace?” Berossus scornfully responded. “Our *castrum* has been spared only because of the solicitude of the gods and our own vigilance. But we are not so foolish as to grant you fresh opportunities to practice further mischief.” Berossus impassively surveyed the poised legionnaires ringing Abbo and his men. “Kill them.”

Beginning with their left foot, the infantrymen took one step forward, which forced Abbo’s alarmed men to crowd closer together to avoid being injured by their pikes. Other legionnaires shifted right or left in order to plug gaps created by the movement of their fellow troops.

One of Abbo’s men whipped a dagger free and brandished it as he frantically back peddled. In response, the legionnaire nearest him plunged his lance into the soft flesh of the man’s side. Shrieking, the man dropped his knife and collapsed to his knees. The soldier yanked his pike from the man’s body, along with a string of his entrails. The watching Romans cheered.

Emboldened, the remaining legionnaires automatically tightened their ring around the entrapped Africans and began to indiscriminately stab them with their pikes. Surrounded and armed only with knives, Abbo and his men were unable to break free. Those that attempted to defend themselves by lunging at the Romans with their daggers were pierced by a hedgehog of bronze spear points.

The slaughter was over in less than two minutes, the Africans sprawled on the bloody earth at the legionnaires' feet. A few moaned in pain.

"Well done. Throw the corpses to the beasts," Berossus instructed. "Polish your weapons and eat breakfast afterward. I will report to Corvo what transpired here." He turned back toward the *castrum.*

"THOUGH WE HAD LITTLE CHOICE, I fear that we may have exchanged one viper for a more lethal one, Marcus," Corvo remarked.

"How so?"

"You have stirred the fire with a sword, for Jugurtha will welcome news of Abbo's death. He considered Abbo too headstrong and a threat to his throne. With Abbo's death, Jugurtha's power and influence now stand unchallenged. The sole remaining impediment to Jugurtha's hegemony is Roman. He will recruit other tribes in the vicinity to join him in attacking us."

"Perhaps," Berossus conceded, "though Jugurtha is an ally who apprised us of Abbo's perfidy."

"He is an ally only so long as it serves him. Jugurtha betrayed Abbo because he feared him and desired to be rid of him. He will declare to his brethren that his hands are unstained by Abbo's blood, which will enhance his prestige in their eyes."

"If the Aethiops are reckless enough to attack the *castrum*, we will defend it," Berossus shrugged, unconcerned. He reflected on the unexpected ease with which his men dispatched Abbo's small party that morning.

"How many men have we?"

Berossus performed a mental calculation. "In fighting condition, perhaps 50. In total, a tithe more."

"That is inadequate to thwart a wholesale assault, Marcus. Even if the Aethiops do not succeed in overrunning us, they will simply lay siege to the *castrum* until they starve us out."

The other man remained silent. "So, what is to be done?" he finally asked.

"*Bestia* must abandon the *castrum* and return to Rome," Corvo replied. "Otherwise, it is destined to be annihilated by the Africans. There exists no alternative."

"You must communicate this to the senate."

Corvo shook his head. "It is my decision, alone. If the senate chooses to sack me for acting unilaterally, I am powerless to prevent it. But I would rather die a disgraced pauper in Rome than at the hands of savages in Africa."

“I understand, Pompeius.”

“It will take time for Jugurtha’s runners to inform other tribes of Abbo’s death at our hands. But the storm is coming, Marcus, make no mistake. How quickly can the men be made ready to leave?”

EIGHT

DUNN'S ANOMALOUS HIGHT aside, Laidlaw spotted him the moment he stepped into Harry's because, other than the bartender and Bonnie, the place was empty.

"Greetings," Laidlaw smiled as Dunn approached the bar.

"What're we drinking?" the other man inquired.

"Just finished a Bloody Mary but could probably gag down another one. The bartender ain't too friendly, though." Laidlaw caught the latter's eye and held up two fingers. The bartender nodded.

"She's cute." Dunn nodded toward Bonnie, who pretended to ignore them.

"That's Bonnie. She needs money to return to her long-suffering, devout, mother and crippled father in England."

Dunn rolled his eyes. “She already tried to sting you, huh? I shoulda guessed.” He surveyed the lifeless room. Looks like slim pickin’s today for the prodigal daughter.”

“Don’t worry, some horny American frat boys will drift in before long. Anatole usually gives ‘em the heave-ho, but this must be his day off.” The substitute bartender approached with their drinks and placed them on the counter. Laidlaw lifted one and turned toward the vacant interior, sweeping his arm across it. “An embarrassment of riches. Shall we snag a table?”

Dunn grabbed the other Bloody Mary. “I’ll follow you...as far away from Bonnie as possible, if you please.”

The two men skirted Bonnie’s table and headed for a small booth near the window overlooking the sidewalk in front of Harry’s. She glanced at them without speaking when they passed, though Dunn smiled at her cordially.

“So, have you had a chance to look over the list of institutions that Professor Hubertus prepared?” Dunn asked after easing himself down.

“I gave it a once-over, but I’ve only heard of a couple of ‘em. Most are European. I’ll review it more carefully once I get back home.”

“Any of ‘em look promising?”

“Hard to say. At the threshold, I’ve gotta figure out what strings are attached. There’s no free lunch.”

“I’d be happy to write a letter of introduction for you,” Dunn volunteered. “Might help get your foot in the door.”

Laidlaw sipped his drink as he reflected. “That, actually, might be a good idea, Pierre. Give me some credibility. I’ve gotta head home at the end of this week, though. Got two safari clients arriving and the Minister of Wildlife emailed me about some kind of conference with all the licensed professional hunters operating in-country.”

“That sounds ominous.”

Laidlaw shook his head. “Naw, the government’s just trying to figure out a strategy to combat poaching. The minister wants to pick the brains of professional hunters ‘cause we’re out in the field every day and have a better feel for the poaching situation than out-of-touch bureaucrats or deranged anti-hunting fanatics.”

“Elephants?”

“Rhinos, mostly. Elephants are smart, which makes ‘em dangerous. Ivory is also difficult to transport because of its bulk. Rhinos are dumb and their horns are relatively light, easy to transport, and worth exponentially more than ivory of the same weight.”

“What do people want with rhino horn?”

“Asians think powdered rhino horn is an aphrodisiac and in some Arab countries, especially Yemen, rhino horns are used make ornamental dagger handles.”

“That’s it? They kill rhinos just for that?”

Laidlaw shrugged.

"Can they be hunted legally?"

"In a couple of countries but, because of their scarcity, only sultans, movie stars, and politicians can afford to legally shoot one. I say 'shoot' because rhinos don't require much actual hunting. Besides being dull-witted, they can't see worth a damn, although they hear and smell pretty well. All ya basically gotta do is sneak up on 'em and bang 'em. You wouldn't know it by watching nature shows on television, which wring their hands over the supposed plight of the poor elephant, but elephants are highly adaptable and relatively common throughout much of sub-Saharan Africa. The Romans eliminated elephants everywhere else in Africa, millennia ago. Rhinos are, and always have been, a different story. I can't speak to the prospects of the Indian rhino, but I suspect he's faring no better than his African cousins."

"Why are rhinos so scarce?"

"Rhinos have been lurching toward extinction, and their numbers have been declining, for centuries. Aside from having long lifespans and low reproduction rates, rhinos seem fundamentally incapable of wrapping their brains around the most rudimentary demands of their environment." Dunn looked puzzled, prompting Laidlaw to continue. "Here's an example. When a drought sweeps through their territory, elephants either dig for water with their tusks or, failing that, round up the whole gang and everybody hot-foots it to greener pastures. No big deal. Not rhinos, though. As Capstick characterized it, when drought hits a rhino's territory, he looks around, dumbfounded...'Who turned out the lights?'...until he eventually just keels over. An oversimplification, sure, but not by much. Rhinos just don't possess enough moxie to cope with the rigors of existence."

Dunn made a wry face. "Sounds like you don't think much of rhinos."

"Not at all. It's not a value judgment, just a statement of fact. I've no skin in the game, rhino-wise, one way or the other."

"Hunting them certainly can't help their numbers."

Laidlaw nodded in agreement. "You're right, but the volume of legal rhino hunting is so insignificant as to be inconsequential. As a species, rhinos have had one foot in the grave and another on a banana peel since day one, irrespective of hunting. Poaching hasn't exactly given 'em a boost, though. That's why the Minister of Wildlife wants to have a sit-down, to see if anything can be done to, essentially, save rhinos from themselves."

"Can it?"

"Honestly, I think in fifty years, there will be no rhinos left in the wild. The only ones that survive will be in zoos and preserves. Hell, we're almost there now! Beyond the elementary ability to put one foot in front of the other, rhinos just aren't equipped to deal successfully with the challenges of living. They look like something nature cobbled together as a prank during the Miocene Era, then moved on and forgot about. Rhinos have been fighting a losing battle against oblivion ever since. I'm surprised they've managed to hang on as long for as they have."

Dunn drained his Bloody Mary. "I think that's very sad."

"Me, too. I've always felt rhinos to be the unloved red-headed step-children of the animal world and would love to come up with some way to increase their numbers, but I'm not sure that's possible." A droll smile flickered across Laidlaw's face. "But I've been wrong once or twice in my life. Maybe this'll be my third time."

"When are you scheduled to meet with the minister?"

"Don't know yet. He's apparently in the process of sending feelers out and asked me to contact his office when I get home. Like I said, I also have two safaris remaining this season."

"Rhino hunts?" Dunn dryly inquired.

"You obviously weren't paying attention to the sermon I just delivered," Laidlaw laughed. "One guy's on a standard plains-game hunt...basically an assortment of garden-variety antelope...and the other one hopes to take a big kudu."

"What's that?"

"Kudu? Big, stately antelope with corkscrew horns."

"They're not endangered?"

Laidlaw shook his head. "Not quite dime-a-dozen, but fairly abundant. Record-book specimens are a different story, of course." He pointed to Dunn's empty glass. "You ready for a refill?"

"I'm good but could use something to eat. You hungry?"

"Yeah. Eat here or go somewhere that serves actual food?"

"There's a café near the university, *'Le Petit Rendezvous'*, that makes outstanding *soupe à l'oignon* if you don't mind a cab ride."

"I have no idea what that is, but I don't think the French are capable of making a bad meal." Laidlaw scanned the empty interior of Harry's. "I was gonna invite our friend, Bonnie, to join us but she seems to have taken a powder."

"Too bad...she could have taken you home to meet mama afterward," Dunn grinned.

"I said I'd treat her to lunch, not marry her," Laidlaw clarified, standing. He headed for the bar to pay their tab.

"I'll grab a taxi and meet you outside," Dunn said.

ONION SOUP.

"This is sure as hell better than the canned stuff I've had everywhere else," Laidlaw pronounced after finishing a second helping.

"It's amazing how speaking French instead of English improves the flavor of everything," Dunn laughed. "But that aside, the *soupe a l'oignon* here is outstanding in *any* language."

"Can't argue with that." Laidlaw leaned back in his chair and sipped a glass of Beaujolais. The café, having only four cheek-by-jowl tables, all of them occupied, was practically little more than a luncheonette.

"The chef that owns this place trained at *L'ateliers des Chefs*. He keeps prices low by limiting his menu, but everything is prepared in-house. *Le Petit* is popular with everybody at the *Sorbonne*, faculty and students alike."

"If the rest of his bill of fare is half as good as his soup, I can understand why. This place is confirmation of what I said earlier: I don't think the French are capable of making a bad meal. Seriously." Laidlaw tore a chunk off a baguette, smeared it with butter, and contentedly began munching.

"You have to return home at the end of this week?" Dunn asked, abruptly changing the subject.

"Yeah."

"Do you have Internet there?"

"In Dar but not out in the bush."

"I'd like to take some pictures of your knife, from different angles, before you leave. I'll continue to research it in your absence. I'll also draft the *lettre d'introduction* we talked about. Is there a way I can get hold of you when you're out hunting?"

"Satellite phone, but that can get pretty spendy."

Dunn laughed. “No problem. I’ll bill it to the university. Just text me the number before you leave Paris.”

“When do you want to photograph the knife?”

“Whenever it’s convenient for you. I only teach three classes this week, so my schedule is pretty much open.”

“How ‘bout tomorrow morning?” Laidlaw shrugged. “We can head over to Harry’s for a hotdog afterward. I want to say my goodbyes to Anatole before I leave, anyway. Hopefully, he’ll be working tomorrow.”

“Might I suggest that you leave the knife in Paris while you’re in Africa? Doesn’t make sense to risk carting it halfway ‘round the world…God only knows what could happen to it in transit.”

“Yeah, I already planned on doing that,” Laidlaw informed Dunn. “I was gonna ask if you could recommend a reputable, secure place that won’t gouge me an arm and a leg.”

“Absolutely!” Dunn enthusiastically responded. I’ll go with you to check some of them out if you like. You’ll probably want me to interpret, anyway.”

“Whoa! Ain’t nuthin’ gonna divert me from a Harry’s hotdog tomorrow!”

“Of course!” Dunn laughed. “I have no intention of putting myself in harm’s way by getting between you and Harry’s!”

“Now, if Harry’s would only add some of this soup to his menu…” Laidlaw wistfully commented.

“Are you mad? It would absolutely cease to be Harry’s! It would be the equivalent of *Le Petit Rendezvous* adding hotdogs and Bloody Marys to its menu.”

Laidlaw looked thoughtful for a moment. “You’re right. *Touche’*.”

The two men held their glasses of Beaujolais aloft in a mutual toast.

LAIDLAW RECLINED HIS BUSINESS class sleeper on the Air France flight from Paris to Dar es Salaam and closed his eyes. He favored Air France because its flight crews spoke English and French with equal facility and the food was pretty good. The previous morning, Dunn had conducted him to the city’s *La Defense* business district, where Laidlaw opened a private safe-deposit box in an imposing glass-and-steel skyscraper. Wrapped in a soft cotton cloth impregnated with oil, his dagger would rest securely until he decided what to do with it. Between safaris and the sit-down with the wildlife minister, whenever that finally occurred, he intended to return to the Mara ruins and poke around some more. Meantime, he’d vet Hubertus’ list of philanthropic institutions.

Both of Laidlaw’s two upcoming safari clients were Americans. One was a returning hunter while the other was a newbie. Laidlaw generally disliked first-timers because most of them had never hunted anything larger than deer, which they typically shot from an elevated stand while sitting on their butts. Like George Pyper, they quaked at the prospect of actually having to track a wild animal and pull the trigger on their brand-new, heavy-recoiling, safari rifles. As a consequence, the majority of tyros couldn't shoot accurately under actual field conditions. Having absorbed a pile of books and websites about safaris, however, they invariably considered themselves experts on African big-game hunting, despite never having been to, much less hunted in, Africa. Offsetting their fatuousness, neophyte hunters typically weren't too fussy, trophy-wise, and were usually content to shoot mediocre specimens...anything to hang in their man-caves. Their lack of discrimination made Laidlaw's job easier and, at the end of the day, their money was green.

Laidlaw's other client was a seasoned African hunter who sought only a record-book kudu. Laidlaw and his trackers would have to devote appreciably more time to him because of the specificity of his intended quarry. Cautious and secretive, kudu are notoriously challenging to hunt, their dusky pelage providing superb camouflage in the scrubby woodlands they inhabit. Hence, their nickname, the "Grey Ghost." Record-book Kudu don't get to be record-book by being brazen. Fortunately, Laidlaw's client could shoot accurately, didn't engage in vacuous chitchat, and wouldn't require any handholding. And, like his inexperienced counterparts, his money was also green.

"Would you like a drink, sir?"

Laidlaw cocked one eye open. A female flight attendant with a forced smile hovered over him. He punched a button on the armrest and his seat glided to an upright position.

"Sure. A gin and tonic, please."

"Of course," she chirped before scuttling off.

Laidlaw lowered his tray. Because business class only had five other passengers, he figured she was eager to get the obligatory booze ration distributed, pronto, so she could plop down in a jump-seat and bullshit with the other flight attendants until it was time to serve dinner.

"Here ya go." She returned and handed him a tiny napkin, a plastic glass with two ice cubes in it, a chilled aluminum can of tonic water, and a miniature bottle of Beefeater. He was obviously expected to mix his own drink. He'd always considered flight attendants to be little more than glorified waitresses but was beginning to think even that dubious assessment was probably overly generous. "Can I get you anything else?"

"How about a couple more napkins and something to stir it with?"

"With pleasure."

Laidlaw looked around the cabin while he waited. Three passengers wearing earbuds appeared to be engrossed by whatever was being shown on their individual television monitors, one guy was working on a laptop, and a woman wearing an eye mask was already sleeping. Laidlaw was apparently the only one imbibing. The flight attendant quickly returned with the additional items he'd requested.

"Anything else?" She interrupted his reverie.

"No, that should do it, thank you."

"My pleasure," she lied before hurrying back to her jump-seat near the galley.

After mixing his own drink, Laidlaw reclined his seat slightly in order to savor it. He'd spend that night in Dar, at a hotel near the airport, before taking a chartered bush flight to his safari camp the following morning. Although it was possible to drive directly to the camp, doing so would require an entire day because of its remoteness and the uncertain condition of the primitive dirt roads leading to it. Better to take the 45-minute flight in a light plane. One of the staff would hear the aircraft's approach and drive a bakkie out to retrieve him from the dirt airstrip.

Laidlaw finished his drink and placed the empty glass on his tray table. He glanced at his watch: just under seven ticks before they touched down in Africa. Plenty of time for a little siesta, at least until the flight attendant woke him for dinner. He closed his eyes and was sound asleep in exactly three minutes.

IT WAS DUSK WHEN THE AIRBUS finally lumbered up to the terminal at Julius Nyerere International Airport.

All of Laidlaw's effects were contained in a large duffle bag that he'd managed to cram into one of the oversized luggage cubicles available to business-class passengers. Once the Jet Bridge angled into place, he'd grab his bag and hustle to the cab-stand immediately outside the terminal. Although he didn't have a reservation, he was a regular guest at the Hotel Europa and could count on the staff setting him up with a room.

The cabin lights brightened, the "Fasten Seatbelt" sign flicked off with a soft chime, and the Airbus's engines began to power down.

"Will there be anything else?" the flight attendant inquired as she made her final walk-through of the cabin.

"No, thank you."

"Thank you for choosing Air France," she smiled. "*Merci.* We look forward to seeing you again soon."

"Yeah, you, too," Laidlaw mechanically responded. He stood, popped open the overhead luggage bin, and grabbed his duffle bag. He was eager to deplane before the jostling queue of coach passengers effectively blocked him in.

Laidlaw slipped the strap of his carry-on over his shoulder and strode to the front of the cabin, where the flight attendant posted at the exit stiffly wished him a good evening. He stepped across the threshold to exit the aircraft onto the Jet Bridge. Shifting his duffle bag to his opposite shoulder, he clumped along the narrow, sloped, tunnel toward the terminal. Once there, he threaded his way through swarms of milling travelers, past the baggage carousels, toward the building's exit.

The twilight air was warm and humid. A line of cabs snaked along the curb in front of the terminal and Laidlaw headed for the taxi at the head of the line. Opening the rear passenger door, he tossed his duffle bag onto the seat before slamming the door shut and clambering into the front passenger's seat.

"Hotel Europa."

"Yes, sir." The driver punched a button to reset the meter and pulled away from the curb. "Your first time in Tanzania, sir?"

"No, no," Laidlaw laughed. "I'm returning home from a short trip to Europe."

"I would like to go to Europe. I want to see the Eiffel Tower," the other man wistfully confided as he drove.

"It's pretty impressive. Actually bigger in real life than it appears in pictures."

"My brother lives in Paris. He has seen it, I think."

"What does your brother do?"

"He drives a taxi, like me, but I have not seen him for a while," the cabbie said. "I like driving a cab but the hours are very long and I miss my family. You have stayed at the Europa before?"

"Yes, many times. It's a nice place. What's your name?"

"My name is 'Benedict', sir."

"I'm 'Alex', Benedict. It's a pleasure to meet you." Laidlaw extended his hand, which the driver warmly grasped with his free hand. "Is this your cab?"

"Yes, sir," he responded with pride. "If you ever need a taxi, it will be my pleasure to serve you. Please take one of my cards from the console."

Laidlaw slipped a couple of Benedict's business cards into his shirt pocket. "I'll keep you in mind."

"Thank you, sir. We are here." Benedict swung his cab into the Europa's parking lot and pulled to the curb at the front entrance. He put the cab in 'park' and took his foot off the brake. "I hope your stay is a pleasant one. If you go into the bar, the bartender's name is 'Woodson'. Tell him that your first drink is compliments of Benedict."

"I'll do that." Laidlaw automatically handed the driver 100,000 Tanzanian shillings before opening the passenger door and sliding from the cab. Stepping to the rear door, Laidlaw opened it, dragged his duffle bag from the seat, and hoisted it onto his shoulder. He walked to the open driver's-side window. "Take good care of yourself, Benedict."

"God bless you, sir. Maybe we meet in Paris, at the Eiffel Tower, one day."

"You never know, Benedict, stranger things have happened," Laidlaw smiled. "Be well in the meantime."

"And you, Mr. Alex. Please do not fail to call me if you need a taxi in the future. I am at your service 24/7, day or night."

"Your wife must love that!" Laidlaw chuckled.

"My children cannot buy their own food, Mr. Alex, yet they still must eat. My wife understands this."

"Of course. I have your card, Benedict. Next time I need a ride, you'll be the one I call."

"Thank you, sir. I hope to see you again."

Laidlaw turned and headed for the Europa's modest lobby. The uniformed female behind the registration desk looked up and smiled as he stepped through the sliding glass doors of the entrance.

"Good evening. Welcome to the Hotel Europa. How may we serve you?"

"Good evening," Laidlaw reciprocated. He approached the desk and lowered his duffle bag to the floor. "I'd like a room for tonight only, please."

"I am so sorry, but we have no rooms available this evening."

Laidlaw frowned. "Hmmm...who is the night manager on duty tonight, please? I'd like to speak with him."

"Mr. Egebe is on duty this evening. It will be my pleasure to ring him for you. Who may I say is inquiring?"

"Egebe? That no-good, worthless bum! Tell him that Alex Laidlaw demands to see him immediately!"

The young woman was taken aback by Laidlaw's aggressive demeanor. "Of course, sir." She angled her body slightly away and, lowering her voice, quickly spoke into the tiny microphone pinned to her lapel. "Mr. Egebe will be right out."

It was clear the young clerk was nonplussed but Laidlaw's grim countenance did not waver as he awaited the arrival of the night manager. Presently, a large man with a pockmarked face, wearing an open-necked shirt and linen blazer, emerged from a door behind the registration desk.

"What is the problem here?" he boomed, a frown darkening his face.

"I demand a room for the night," Laidlaw barked, unintimidated.

Egebe strode around the registration desk to confront Laidlaw.

"Demand? As the young lady informed you, sir, we have no rooms available," he scowled.

"Hold on! You're telling me that, if the president showed up tonight and asked for a room, you'd turn him away? Really?"

Ebebe looked quizzical. "Of course, we would accommodate the president." He looked askance at the young assistant standing beside him.

"Well, I'll take his room since he's not coming."

Egebe glared at the Laidlaw in steely silence. Then he burst into a hearty laugh.

"Alex, it has been far too long since you darkened our doorway!" he grinned. "How are you, brother?" Egebe stepped from behind the counter and embraced Laidlaw in an impromptu bear hug.

"I'm fabulous," Laidlaw chuckled after they released one another. "I've missed you, Mosi."

"And I, you," the other man assured him. "*Of course*, we have a room for you." He turned to the receptionist, who'd watched the entire charade in astonishment. "Charlotte, this is my dear friend, and unrepentant rascal, Alex Laidlaw."

"Hi, Charlotte." Laidlaw extended his hand. "Sorry if I alarmed you."

"Well, I *was* becoming a bit uncomfortable," she confessed as she shook his hand.

"Alex spends most of his time in the bush," Mosi explained, "so it is a rare treat when he stays with us. What rooms have we available, Anna?"

She tapped a few keys on her computer and scanned its monitor. "Rooms 402 and 411, Mr. Egebe."

He turned to Laidlaw. "402 overlooks the parking lot and 411 the pool. They are otherwise identical, though 411 is probably a little quieter. Both have a single queen bed."

"I'll take 411."

"Done. Do you need help with your grips?"

Laidlaw shook his head and pointed at the duffle bag at his feet. "No, I think I can handle it."

"Anna, please check Mr. Laidlaw into room 411," Egebe instructed. He reached back over the counter, ran a plastic room key through the electronic key reader, and handed it to Laidlaw. "Hasten upstairs with your bag and meet me in the bar. We'll have a drink or two and exchange lies."

"A man who doesn't lie has nothing to say," Laidlaw chuckled.

"Yes, precisely! We clearly have many lies to share, my friend!" Egebe paused. "I heard the wildlife minister wishes to pick your brain, though I fear that may prove a fruitless undertaking."

"Where did you hear that?"

Mosi winked. "Tanzania is a rather parochial country and the Europa is popular with diplomats and other undesirables...one cannot but hear things."

"It's not just me. The minister wants a sit-down with all the registered hunting outfitters in the country. Gonna try to figure out a way to save the rhinos."

"While he's at it, please suggest to the minister that he formulate a strategy for saving all the unicorns, as well," Mosi amiably suggested. "But enough dreary talk of business. Join me downstairs as soon as you've settled in."

"Is Woodson bartending tonight?"

"Yes, why?"

"A mutual friend wanted me to say hello for him," Laidlaw smiled.

"Splendid!" Mosi beamed. "I'll see you in the bar."

In Primis Anno Regnantibus Imperator Caesar Titus Vespasianus (79 CE)

IN THE TWENTY-FIRST YEAR OF his reign, about 727 BCE, King Piankhi invaded Egypt from the south and established a new dynasty, the twenty-fifth in Egypt's immeasurable history. A succession of Nubian autocrats, emanating from what is now Sudan, thereafter governed the Two Lands. Nubian domination of Egypt was brief, however, ultimately collapsing during the reign of the last Nubian pharaoh, Taharqa, around 664 BCE, the consequence of unrelenting assaults by the Assyrian Empire. The Assyrians, themselves, were thereafter conquered by the Persian king, Cambyses II, in 525 BCE, the Persians benignly ruling Egypt for the next two-hundred years until the ascendancy of the Macedonian, Alexander the Great. Following Alexander's death, on June 11, 323 BCE at the age of 32 in Babylon, and the resulting disintegration of his empire, Egypt became a province of the Roman Empire.

Like many ancient and, indeed, modern cultures, the Nubians avidly embraced and mimicked the accomplishments of Egypt's great "Pyramid Age." However, Crixus considered the curious sandstone pyramids of Meroe, in Nubia, poor facsimiles of their massive counterparts to the north. Small and steep-sided, many of them flanked by carved sandstone pylons, hundreds of them dot a large area along the eastern bank of the Nile. Intended as tombs for Nubian royalty, the small pyramids had long ago been looted of whatever treasures they once held. The expansive burying ground was now a wasteland teeming with renegades, cutthroats and bandits, who appropriated the former crypts as convenient dwellings.

Crixus, Eros, and Romo crouched atop a low bluff abutting the Nile, *Nilus* to the Romans, and surveyed the quondam necropolis displayed below them. They could see abundant human activity and scatterings of goats and horses. The scent of cooking fires wafted through the scorching air.

"So, that is the fabled Meroe," Eros disdainfully commented. "A dunghill far from what I was led to believe we would encounter."

"Nubians, not Egyptians, erected these pyramids. I think it was their desire to duplicate the splendors of the Egypt, but they did not possess sufficient knowledge or resources," Crixus responded.

"That much is obvious."

"The Egyptian pyramids are much more impressive."

"I should hope so. I have seen termite mounds more imposing than those," Eros rejoined as he gestured toward the scattering of modest pyramids stretching into the distance.

They were about half-way through their journey. Though the deadly Sudd now lay behind them, few creatures, and fewer native laborers, survived the final crossing of the deadly swamp: two dozen small antelope, three starving cheetah cubs, one juvenile giraffe, a giant anteater, several mongooses, a yearling elephant, two haggard aardwolves, a flea-ridden hyena cub. Additional men and animals would undoubtedly perish before the attenuated caravan finally managed to limp into Rome.

"Our strength is much reduced," Romo stated. "We will be overmatched by the robbers who Crixus says occupy this area. We dare not risk an engagement with them."

"Why would robbers even bother to attack us?" Eros scoffed. "We possess nothing they would want."

"The robbers do not know that," Crixus said. "Furthermore, we are Romans and barbarians believe that all Romans are wealthy."

"Is it possible to skirt them entirely without alerting them of our presence?" Romo asked.

"I was told that a path meanders behind the cliffs adjacent to the river," Crixus replied, "though I have no personal knowledge of it. Assuming such a path exists, it will be necessary to cross the *Nilus* a considerable distance upriver to avoid the bandit patrols that range through the area."

"How far upriver?"

"I do not know…two miles? Three? Four?"

"That is a fool's errand," Eros snorted. "Because he possesses no *virtus,* Crixus shamefully urges us to slink away like base cowards, backtrack far out of our way, and risk yet another hazardous river crossing, simply because he fears a handful of miserable rabble. Romans have never shrunk from crossing swords with such vermin!"

"Crixus' words are not prompted by cowardice, but by prudence. We are few and they are many. Swords are not less keen when wielded by rabble. What would you have us do, Eros?" Romo questioned.

"The *banditti* must be taught that Romans are not to be trifled with," Eros confidently asserted.

"Indeed? And how effective will be such instruction prove if the mutilated corpses of their Roman tutors litter the ground, their blood staining the earth?" Crixus inquired.

"Extremely effective," Romo answered. "For we will have educated the barbarians that the myth of Roman invincibility is a laughable farce." He turned to Eros. "We will do as Crixus suggests. Instruct the men to begin transporting the remaining creatures southward. We will cross the river when a safe distance from Meroe."

"You are unworthy to be called 'Roman'," Eros mocked.

"I am unworthy of most of the boons of life," Romo sighed. "One additional blunder will not make a mite's worth of difference, one way or the other, though I am comforted by the certainty that you will not fail to make the senate aware of my infinite failings. Until then, see to it that my orders are promptly carried out."

Eros stalked off.

"He will ensure that you have much to answer for in Rome," Crixus softly commented.

Romo shrugged. "My duty is to conduct you and the beasts, or what remains of them, to Rome. I do not have the luxury of fretting over what Eros may do once we arrive there and, in any case, am hopeful the senate, despite the venality of its members, will prove able to fairly judge the merits of Eros' accusations against me, whatever they may be. Wisdom does not lie in seeing things, but in seeing through things."

"I have heard the emperor and senate accused of many things, though 'wisdom' was notable for its absence," Crixus laughed. "However, you may rely on me to disabuse the senate of any misapprehensions it may entertain regarding your conduct and diligence in the performance of your duties."

"I wonder how persuasive the senate is likely to find the testimony of my nominal prisoner," Romo mused.

NOTHING MORE THAN A NARROW goat path meandering through dense thickets of thorn bushes and brambles, the rocky trail leading northward was sandwiched between two ranges of cliffs that paralleled the *Nilus'* eastern bank, a quarter-mile to the west. Porters transported the smaller animals in wicker baskets strapped to their shoulders or balanced on their heads, while larger creatures were goaded with whips.

"If any of the beasts emits a sound, slit its throat," Romo directed in the suffocating heat. "I do not wish to announce our presence to the barbarians, else they will slaughter all of us in a heartbeat."

"Indeed, Romo, because we comport ourselves as contemptible women by skulking about, rather than as Romans, the barbarians will undoubtedly treat us accordingly," Eros mocked.

The stumbling train of humans and animals ranged along the uneven terrain for a distance exceeding four hundred yards. Blinding sunlight caromed off the steep bluffs that reared skyward on either side of the narrow path, intensifying the already stultifying heat. Thistles and dry brush snagged the clothing of the men and abraded their unprotected limbs. Romo and Crixus trudged at the van, while Eros trailed the column.

"Will this path take us as far as the Great Cataract?" Romo panted, referring to the span of whitewater rapids demarcating Nubia from Egypt. He used the back of his hand to wipe accumulated sweat from his forehead. Salt in his perspiration stung the cuts in his skin that were inflicted by the thorny scrub through which they pushed.

"I do not know," Crixus admitted. "I know only of its existence, not its measure. Once we reach the

Fifth Cataract, though, we should be clear of Meroe and its bandits. We can then angle back toward the river and simply follow it all the way to Egypt."

Their conversation was interrupted by a shower of pebbles cascading down a sandstone bluff that pinched the trail. Romo paused and looked upward to scan the adjacent cliff-side in an effort to identify the source of the disturbance.

Hunkered on a sloping ledge thirty feet above them was a man. Having been spotted, the interloper pressed himself against the face of the soaring rock, as if to render himself invisible. Realizing the futility of this stratagem, he promptly scampered along the ledge with the agility of a mountain goat until hurling himself into a vertical fissure in the cliff face.

"He will return with others to attack us!" Crixus barked.

"This path is not wide enough to accommodate a defensive *testudo*, nor have we time to properly synchronize one," Romo quickly determined. He grabbed the African attendant nearest him. "Race to Eros and inform him that an attack is imminent. If he thinks it feasible, instruct him to press forward here as rapidly as possible. Otherwise, he must organize a defense at his present position as best he can. Go!" Romo roughly shoved the man toward the rear of the column.

"The bandits will attempt to crush us by dislodging boulders and hurling stones from the heights," Crixus predicted. "A *testudo*, even if possible, would present an easy target. We must, instead, make haste along this path before they can get fully into position."

The men within earshot at the head of the column milled around in consternation, while those farther back continued to trudge forward, ignorant of developments at the front. It would not be long before the entire convoy learned of its peril.

"This path is tortuous and narrow. Your advice is ill-considered because the men and animals must pick their way slowly and with caution," Romo protested.

"That would be true under ideal conditions, Romo. Your options, therefore, are these: order the entire column to remain where it is, virtually immobile, to be shattered by falling rocks. Alternatively, allow at least some of the men to survive by flight. I submit those are your only choices unless the gods, themselves, deign to rescue us."

"You are truly a paradox, Crixus, for you do not even believe in the gods! Yet, you urge me to abandon my men so that a few may live?"

Crixus spoke quickly in response. "It is of no moment that I disavow the gods because *you* believe in them. Furthermore, I 'urge' nothing. I merely point out the most expedient resolution to your present, unhappy, dilemma, though even those few options diminish as we speak. I am your captive, Romo, and have no voice in the matter. I must do as you command. Irrespective of your decision, you must render it at once, before escape by *any* of the men becomes impossible."

Romo scanned the anxious faces surrounding him.

They were hemmed-in by steep cliffs that appeared unscalable, certainly not by men encumbered with animals. Crixus was undoubtedly correct when he opined that their assailants would simply pelt the slow-moving column with heavy stones from positions concealed on the soaring walls of rock. Mounting a viable defense against such an attack would prove impossible. Their attackers, high overhead, were virtually invisible to the men stranded on the ground. Moreover, the narrow, twisting path on which the convoy was marooned severely restricted its freedom of movement. The rough terrain, combined with the language barrier between the Romans and their African menials, rendered effective communication problematical.

Romo was reluctantly forced to conclude that Crixus was correct. Only through immediate flight could any of them hope to survive the coming onslaught.

"Gather the beasts and hasten down the trail as quickly as possible," he finally ordered the men gathered around him. "Your comrades will join you shortly." He turned to Crixus. "We will await Eros' arrival from the rear. Until then, assist the men to depart." Romo turned to assess the defensive potential of the surrounding area.

"By the gods, where is Eros?" he growled above the murmuring porters. "The bandits are preparing to spit us with arrows!"

"No, they will not squander arrows when mindless boulders will kill us with equal efficiency," Crixus noted, laconically. "Eros remains at the extremity of the caravan and is probably ignorant of our plight because your runner appears to have decamped rather than delivering your message."

Romo collared another underling, shouted orders at him, and propelled him in Eros' direction at the rear of the column. Aided by Crixus, other men from the line broke ranks and began streaming along the path, distancing themselves from the expected attack. Ahead, the beetling cliffs sloped away from the trail, minimizing the likelihood of an ambush from that quarter. Although the porters were charged with safeguarding the various creatures in the pack train, Crixus had little doubt they would jettison the animals at the first opportunity. Were he in their position, he would do the same thing.

A large boulder thumped onto the desiccated earth, causing the ground near them to shudder. The porters shrieked in alarm.

"It begins," Romo grimly remarked. "We must decrease the size of the target, Crixus. Ensure that the men do not bunch together. Disperse them along the path, some distance apart, and keep them moving. I will locate Eros and swiftly return." He raced away.

Amid the bellowing and screeching of frightened animals, Crixus redirected his attention to the confused throng of men milling in disorder around him. Indiscriminately grabbing one after another, he pointed down the trail and shoved them in that direction, urging haste.

With accelerating intensity, stones rained from above onto the trail. The shower of rocks plummeted haphazardly into the helpless men and animals, knocking them off their feet, breaking limbs and cracking skulls. Confined by the encroaching cliffs, the narrowness of the trail prevented the men from spreading out laterally, rendering them easy targets from above.

Feverishly pushing men along the path, Crixus scanned the heights in an effort to isolate the source of the barrage. If he could spot their assailants, the few bowmen still with the column might be able to wound, even kill, some of the marauders. He saw nothing, save a storm of rocks hurtling earthward.

"Abandon the beasts!" Crixus bellowed. "Look only to save yourselves!" There was no sign of Romo or Eros, prompting Crixus to fear that most of the column had already been annihilated.

He leaped aside to avoid a large stone that bounced off the jagged path and caromed toward him. A dozen steps away, a bearer attempting to release mewing cheetah cubs from their wicker container was not so lucky. As he bent forward to free them, a rock larger than a man's head hurtled into him. Crixus heard the audible crack of the man's splintered backbone as his contorted body was propelled into the ground.

Crixus strode to the crate containing the cheetahs and flicked its latch open, allowing the captive animals to scramble out. Though they would probably die, anyway, Crixus figured it was better to perish while attempting to reach safety than be crushed while imprisoned in a spindly box.

"Crixus!"

His head snapped upward. Romo and Eros were running up the trail, making directly for him while attempting to dodge the stone missiles that soared from the cliffs.

"I feared for your safety," Crixus confessed when the two men finally panted to a halt. All around them, babbling, terrified Africans jostled and shoved as they streamed down the path, distancing themselves from the chaos, uncaring for the Romans' exalted status as their purported masters.

"All is lost," Romo informed him, dispensing with salutatory formalities. "Many have fled, more than a score are dead."

"The time for talking and cowering like animals is past," Eros interrupted. "We must launch an immediate counterattack to prevent our utter ruin!"

Crixus looked at him incredulously. "A counterattack? We already know that you possess a glib tongue, Eros. Do you also possess wings?" A boulder crashed into a spindly dead tree near them, obliterating it.

"A sortie is impossible because our assailants are entrenched far above us and completely inaccessible." Romo curtly stated. "The best we can hope for is to save from destruction as many men as possible."

"Your shameful cowardice dishonors the gods, Romo," Eros sneered. "Romans have never surrendered the field of battle to its enemies. Though I expect nothing from the worthless Africans, who are less than women, it is your duty to stand and face your adversaries!"

"There exists no 'field of battle'," Crixus caustically interjected. "Only a cramped ravine where men are being slaughtered in droves even as we speak."

Romo looked about at the mayhem enveloping them. "Do not lecture me regarding 'duty', Eros. Crixus is right. There is no dishonor in declining to engage an enemy that one cannot even see. Assist Crixus to evacuate the remaining men."

Scarcely had he finished speaking when a massive chunk of falling rock bounced from the sunbaked earth and struck Romo's left leg. He crumpled to the ground.

Crixus rushed forward and kneeled beside him. From knee to ankle, Romo's leg was split open, the jagged bones of his tibia spiking through the flesh, evidencing a compound fracture. There was as yet little effusion of blood.

Romo propped himself up on his elbows to evaluate his injury. "I am dead," he stated without emotion.

"Your impiety has obviously angered the gods, Romo," Eros stoically observed. "Your life is now forfeit because of your imprudence."

Romo ignored him. Gripping Crixus' forearm, his eyes beginning glaze from pain, he began to speak. "Hear me," he began in a voice loud enough to be heard above the ambient clamor, "Crixus shall, from this moment forward, assume command. You, Eros, will obey Crixus with exactitude and fidelity, as if he were me. Swear now."

"You are delirious. Rome will hear of this outrage," Eros spat.

"Your oath!" Romo hissed between teeth clenched in pain. Blood had begun to flow from his wound, running down his splintered leg and dripping onto the ground. "Tell Rome whatever you wish, but at this moment, before the gods, swear it, Eros!"

"I will do as you ask, Romo," Eros stated, "and declare before the gods my vow to comply with Crixus' orders insofar as they are compatible with my duties and honor as a Roman."

"That will have to suffice," Romo sighed. He slowly lowered himself to the earth and looked directly at Crixus. "End my pain."

Crixus seated himself on the ground next to the injured man. Sliding his hand beneath Romo's sweaty head, he gently lifted it and cradled it in his lap.

"All will be well," he said, stroking Romo's damp hair. "The gods impatiently await the opportunity to embrace you as their brother. I will ensure that Rome is made aware that you discharged your duties with honor and diligence."

Almost imperceptibly, Romo nodded and closed his eyes. Crixus slid his hand beneath Romo's chin and eased his head backward. With his other hand, he removed the bronze cultro from his waistband and, displaying no hesitation, slit Romo's throat. He shifted his legs slightly to avoid staining his garment with the blood that bubbled from the wound. Crixus carefully lowered Romo's head to the ground before standing.

"Our desperate circumstances make it impossible to mourn Romo, nor do we have the luxury to properly attend to his corpse," he said. For once, Eros didn't argue. Together, they dragged Romo's body into the brush along the path, concealing it as best they could. Dwindling numbers of men continued to jostle past, scarcely noticing. It seemed to Crixus the volume of falling rocks had diminished, though he couldn't be sure.

"I will remain here to superintend the stragglers," he told Eros. "Hasten to the front to assess the situation, rally the survivors, and determine the number of surviving animals."

Eros cocked his eyebrow. "I will do as you request, but do not grow easy with giving orders," he cautioned. Crixus turned away.

Only a handful of men continued to struggle along the path. The remainder had already perished beneath the barrage of stones or managed to make their way to safety. Crixus was reasonably confident their assailants were not so imprudent as to risk a confrontation with, for all they knew, a full contingent of trained Roman legionnaires escorting a pack train. They would, instead, content themselves with stripping the corpses of those already slain.

Crixus toyed with simply deserting the caravan altogether and making his way to Roman Syria. However, his comrades, Neocles and Aulus, remained hostage in the *castrum*, their survival entirely contingent on his arrival in Rome. Of no less consequence, Romo had entrusted him with safeguarding the entire enterprise for the duration of the expedition. He reluctantly abandoned all thoughts of flight.

The remaining portion of the journey to Rome would prove long and arduous. Crixus glanced toward the dry undergrowth that half-concealed Romo's body.

"Damn you," he muttered.

In Primis Anno Regnantibus Imperator Caesar Titus Vespasianus (79 CE)

RELATIVELY FEW MEN REMAINED TO fill *Legio XVI Bestia's* ranks. Given its significantly reduced size, Corvo elected to ferry his surviving legionnaires to Italy via the Red Sea. Unsure of the reception *Bestia* would receive once its bedraggled troops finally limped into Rome, he none-the-less decided it could be no worse than simply whiling away time in the *castrum*, waiting to die from disease, or worse, far from home.

Since being posted in Africa, *Bestia's* ranks had been enormously depleted, primarily from disease. Desertions, animal attacks, native raids, and accidents also contributed to the death toll. Jugurtha's inevitable retaliatory raid on the *castrum* following Abbo's murder would result in the certain annihilation of the legionnaires who had, up until then, managed to stay alive. Berossus required only two days to ready the men for departure, so eager were they to decamp. Now, they found themselves sloughing eastward through East African scrubland, toward ports on the Red Sea and a voyage homeward.

Neocles bore a sour expression and had been noticeably uncommunicative since they vacated the castrum two days previously.

"Your long face distresses me, my friend. Pray, what troubles you? One would think you regret leaving this damnable place," Aulus remarked as they trudged.

"You will think me a fool," Neocles grunted.

"Undoubtedly, though your follies will take my mind off my painful feet and give me something to laugh about."

The two men paused to rest.

"You will recall that, before he was carried off to Rome, Crixus presented me with a knife."

"I remember."

"I cannot find it."

Aulus shrugged. "Knives are easily replaced." He tapped the sheath at his side, which held a standard bronze Roman *cultro.*

Neocles shook his head, sadly. "No, not this knife. It was forged from materials unlike anything ever seen, its edge as thin as a blade of grass and as keen. It bore a design that recalled a turbulent, foaming sea. Its loss grieves me, for I believe it irreplaceable."

Aulus patiently listened. "When did you last see the knife?"

"During our preparations to evacuate the *castrum*. I wrapped it in a cloth and placed it in my kit, or at least thought I did, but when I checked later it was no longer there."

“Could it have been stolen from your kit?”

Neocles shook his head. “My kit was always on my person, never out of my sight. Theft would have been impossible.”

“You merely thought you placed the knife in your kit, intending to do so, but forgot?”

“I confess my ignorance. I know only that it is gone, Neocles rued.

“Do not despair. It may yet surface,” Aulus commiserated. “It is not impossible that you merely overlooked it in your kit.”

Berossus materialized on the trail out of nowhere. “Move your asses! If the savages are trailing us, you two will be the first butchered. Every man will be required to defend the column, even worthless beggars like you! Move!”

Wordlessly, the two men returned to the path and resumed trekking eastward, toward the Red Sea and a waiting *navis oneraria*, fitted to ferry them to Rome.

“WHERE ARE THE ROMANS AT THIS moment?” Jugurtha demanded.

“They fled their compound like shivering whelps,” Yam replied, “and are now two-days hence.”

“Where do they go?”

"They slither eastward toward the Inner Sea, Lord. I believe it their intention to return to their hearths and their whores."

"How many men?"

"No more than two score."

Jugurtha smiled coldly as he reflected. "If the Romans succeed in reaching their homeland, they will eventually return in even greater numbers than before."

"*If*," Yam echoed.

"Can you interdict them?"

"With ease."

Jugurtha nodded. "Do so."

THE TRAIL DISEMBOGUED FROM mixed woodlands into a rolling plain of desiccated grass dotted with termite mounds and thorn trees. A herd of springbok grazed in the distance.

Corvo called the column to a halt. "We will bivouac here tonight," he instructed Berossus. "Make certain that watches are in place then gather the remaining men, as I wish to address them."

"Shall I first order them to dig a defensive moat and pile the soil into a berm?"

"No, I do not yet expect any attacks. I suspect the Africans but recently detected our absence and will require at least a day to track us, assuming that is their intention. Let the men rest tonight. They are fatigued from constant marching since departing the *castrum* and will require all their strength for the clash I fear is coming. But I will address the men before they sup."

"As you wish." Berossus strode toward the main body of men to convey Corvo's orders.

"WHY IN THE NAME OF JUPITER does Corvo waste time haranguing us?" Aulus groused as he smoothed a spot on the ground for his sleeping mat.

"It appears we will shortly find out," Neocles replied. "My only hope is that I manage to stay awake while he speechifies, else I may end up like Vespasian when he accidentally fell asleep during one of Nero's boorish musical recitals."

"What happened to him?"

"He suffered banishment. Vespasian was lucky that Nero didn't, instead, order him to open his wrists, as he did his tutor, Lucius Seneca. Vespasian was recalled from exile only because Nero was desperate for an experienced general to assume command of the legions stationed in the East before they were completely annihilated by the damned Jews."

"Ha!" Aulus scoffed. "In that case, it is a good thing, indeed, that Nero spared his life! The inscrutable machinations of the gods cannot be gainsaid, though Vespasian appears to have received the far better bargain. He died in bed, while Nero was struck down by his own hand!"

Neocles unrolled his sleeping mat a few paces from that of Aulus and plopped down. "Like Crixus said of the Jewish Wars, it is only the worms who should be celebrating since both men are equally dead."

Aulus nodded, thoughtfully. "You speak the truth. At what hour are we supposed to muster?"

Neocles clambered to his feet. "Now."

The two men sauntered toward the congregation milling about in front of Corvo's quarters, a rude tent fashioned of animal hides.

"What news?" he asked another legionnaire, named 'Senecio'.

Senecio shrugged. "Who, other than the gods, can say? All I know is that I am hungry, tired, and wish for nothing more than food and sleep. Instead, we are compelled to endure an oration."

Berossus parted the hides covering the doorway and, hunched, emerged from Corvo's cramped tent. "Form ranks!" he barked after straightening. "Your commander speaks to you!" He stood at rigid attention next to the tent's entrance.

Exchanging puzzled glances, the thirty-odd legionnaires shuffled more-or-less into a rough square. Presently, Corvo pushed aside the hides and emerged from his quarters. Berossus executed a smart Roman salute, his forearm horizontal against his chest, as Corvo stepped forward. In silence, he surveyed the restless company assembled before him.

"Bronze soldiers of Rome," he began in a robust voice, "even as I speak these words, we find ourselves marooned in a wilderness, in all probability pursued by murderous savages who wish for nothing more than to bathe their spears in Roman blood. But the entire earth, yea, even primitive barbarians inhabiting the fringes of the known world, tremble at the mere thought of Rome's invincible legions, mindful of Rome's universal renown for fielding the most formidable armies since the beginning of time. Yet, the savages who now long for our deaths dare not confront us as men, on the field of battle. No! The vile cowards proceed only by stealth for, possessing less intelligence than wild beasts, yet even they comprehend the suicidal folly of engaging legionnaires in open combat. But, as Romans, we rightfully laugh to scorn such impotent adversaries, knowing them to be scarcely worthy of that appellation. They are like little children merely play-acting at war. We welcome their assaults because such foolish burlesques provide us an opportunity to display our unrivaled martial prowess while, simultaneously, affording us matchless amusement. The gods have truly blessed us by supplying such buffoons for our swords to feast upon."

Corvo paused to assess the men's reaction to his declaration, though they remained stoical, if not more than a little bored.

"At first light, you will arm yourselves as legionnaires, girding yourselves for battle and assured of victory. *Bestia* will thereafter continue on its seaward trek, lusting to engage any adversary mad enough to challenge us."

"Who are we supposed to be fighting? Aethiops?" Aulus whispered to Neocles, who didn't respond.

Corvo momentarily scanned his impassive audience before abruptly turning to reenter his tent.

"Your commander has spoken!" Berossus announced. "Return to your duties!"

The legionnaires of *Bestia* began to drift away.

"I don't relish plodding through this damnable heat, bearing arms," Aulus complained as he and Neocles headed back to their sleeping area, "especially since we have no idea who we are supposed to be fighting."

"I daresay we will learn quickly enough the moment they attack us," Neocles reasoned.

In contrast to the ornate, sculpted ceremonial armor invariably worn by Roman soldiers in countless Hollywood 'sword-and-sandal' epics, the trappings of ordinary legionnaires, the basic design of which survived into the Middle Ages, typically consisted of either hammered scales of metal affixed to leather straps, or small interlocking iron rings fashioned into a tunic. Padded undershirts worn under either configuration minimized discomfort. Because of its low status, however, the accouterments of *Legio XVI Bestia* consisted only of a *lorica*, boiled and molded from thick bull hide, intended to protect the combatant's torso. Greaves made of the same material partially shielded the legs. A leather helmet and rectangular wooden shield emblazoned with the legion's device, a wild boar, completed their uniform. Each man was issued a *gladius*, a short sword that was both the primary weapon of the Empire and a brutal symbol of Rome's power, and a *cultro*. A few of the legionnaires also carried either a spear or a javelin. Disdained as a weapon for use only by cowards fearful of engaging in actual hand-to-hand combat, the bow was scorned, at least officially, though Roman commanders in the field did not hesitate to employ mercenaries accomplished in its use. The Persians, especially, were famed throughout the ancient world for their skill as archers.

Neocles and Aulus flopped onto their sleeping mats. "I am roundly sick of eating nothing but fucking dried goat meat and fish, the latter complained as he pawed through his tattered food sack. "Once we arrive in Rome, I swear by the gods the first thing I will do is get drunk. The second thing I intend is to fuck as many women as possible. Thirdly, I will kill anyone who dares offer me a damnable fish."

"What if it is one of the women you intend to fuck who offers it?" Neocles innocently inquired.

Aulus jammed a chunk of dried catfish into his mouth, reclined on his mat, and closed his eyes as he chewed. "That all depends on the size of her tits. If her tits are too small, I may kill her for that reason alone," he affirmed, causing Neocles to laugh. "Did you locate your knife?"

Neocles shook his head. "I fear that, in my haste to leave the *castrum*, I mislaid it. It is a grievous loss.

Hopefully, the Aethiop that finds my knife will properly care for it."

"Whether the savage does, or does not, is all one to you," Aulus replied. "It is foolish to mourn things over which one has no control. Crixus will be easy to locate in Rome because he will be attached to the emperor's court. Perhaps he can replace your knife with another like it."

"It is possible, though he is now greatly elevated above his previous station with *Bestia*."

"No doubt, though he is still our mate. Crixus will not turn his back on us."

Neocles stretched out on his mat. "I hope you are right. It would be gratifying to see him again and learn how he has fared since leaving us."

"'How he has fared'?" Aulus repeated in mock astonishment. "Do you not hear yourself, Neocles? Crixus exchanged Africa for Rome! That is comparable to exchanging Tartarus for Elysium!"

His friend chuckled. "You are right. It was for that reason that I questioned whether Crixus will remember his comrades."

"It is certain that our friendship with Crixus will open many doors for us when we get to the capital. You will then see that all your anxieties are for naught," Aulus assured him. He opened his eyes and swiveled his head to look at Neocles. "Want some fish?"

NEOCLES, AULUS, AND THE REMAINING MEN OF of *Legio XVI Bestia* grumbled when, at dawn, Berossus rousted them from sleep to resume their eastward trek.

"I hope the Aethiops attack us sooner, rather than later," Aulus grumbled as he buckled his *lorica.* "I am already sweating more than your sister when she confessed to your mother her ardent desire to become a whore."

"I have no sister," Neocles informed him.

"Well, it was *someone's* sister."

"Perhaps it was your sister," Neocles helpfully suggested.

Aulus shook his head. "No, my sister is not pleasing to the eye. She would be a failure as a whore."

"No matter. All women look alike upside down."

Aulus chuckled. "I daresay you are right!"

"You must inform your sister of this anatomical fact when next you see her," Neocles advised. "Perhaps it is not yet too late for her."

"I will do so, though I have not heard from anyone in my family for many years and am not certain any of them remain alive."

Crixus furrowed his brow, as if in thought. "Perhaps you can ask one of the whores you intend to fuck about your sister's whereabouts."

"You are positively brimming with excellent advice, my friend!" Aulus laughed as he adjusted the *gladius* hanging at his right hand.

After bolting down a breakfast of *piadina* dipped in olive oil, the legionnaires recommenced their trek, Corvo and Berossus at the van. Walking two abreast, the remainder of the column was trailed by lumbering supply wagons pulled by a teams of oxen. All the men were armed and, on orders from Berossus, passably vigilant.

The monotonous savanna through which they tramped was comprised of low, undulating hills with broad vales swathed in a golden sea of desiccated grass. A startled hornbill occasionally exploded from undergrowth, but there were otherwise no signs of animal life. The air was stagnant, and it was already becoming oppressively hot.

“If lions lurk nearby, their pelage will render them invisible until they pounce and devour us,” Aulus nervously commented, as he wiped perspiration from his face.

“It is not lions you need fear, but the vengeful Aethiops that Corvo fears are stalking us.”

“We have seen no Aethiops since leaving the *castrum*. For what reason would they seek to avenge themselves on us? We have done them no harm. Though Abbo's death occurred at our hands, it was occasioned by his own treachery. Corvo wrings his hands over foolish trifles like an old woman.”

“Perhaps, though savages do not reason like civilized men. They are mindless brutes.”

“Not even mindless brutes attack blindly, without provocation.”

“We shall see,” Neocles shrugged.

THE COLUMN HALTED TO REST after trekking four hours in sweltering heat, the weary legionnaires simply collapsing onto the baked earth.

"I feel as though I'm imprisoned in an oven," Alus complained. He loosened the straps of his *lorica* and tossed his helmet aside, his hair plastered to his head with sweat.

Neocles eased himself to the ground. Removing the bota slung over his shoulder, he grasped between his thumb and forefinger the cork that sealed its neck, wiggled it free, and took a long draught of wine liberally diluted with water. He handed the bota to Aulus, who flopped down beside him. The remaining legionnaires sprawled on the path in disordered nonchalance.

"How far do you think we are from the *mare*?" Aulus asked.

"I wish I knew. Too far," Neocles unhelpfully replied.

"I pray Corvo and Berossus come to their senses and allow us to travel unburdened by arms on the morrow. I am certain that I could not be any more miserable."

Neocles reclined and closed his eyes. "Miserable days and pleasant days are of equal duration. Both will become infinitely worse if one is impaled on an enemy's sword."

Aulus nodded, thoughtfully. "That is beyond dispute. Still, we have seen neither friend nor enemy since departing the *castrum*, nor do I think we are likely to."

Eliciting no response from Neocles, he glanced down at his companion. Neocles had fallen asleep and was gently snoring.

AT DUSK, THE LEGIONNAIRES FINALLY suspended their seaward march, having covered 25 miles that day. As they wearily unrolled their sleeping mats before consuming yet another cold meal, Berossus went from man-to-man, repeating Corvo's standing order to remain armed and vigilant when they resumed their trek at dawn.

"May the gods be damned if they expect me to sleep in this cursed thing," Aulus spat as he flung his *lorica* aside in disgust.

"I am so tired I could sleep without difficulty while standing upright," Neocles yawned.

Aulus settled onto his sleeping mat and stretched out. "If the barbarians are so treacherous, why did Corvo only now order us armed, days after we left the *castrum*? If they intended us harm, the savages would surely have attacked us immediately we departed, rather than wait until we were far afield! The idiocy of such a belated order should be obvious even to Corvo and Berossus."

"You make too much of it. Perhaps they are privy to information they have not communicated to us and issue the order out of an abundance of caution. Given a choice, I will gladly suffer inconvenience over death at the point of a barbarian spear."

"Death?" Aulus scoffed. "The only deaths we are likely to suffer are those occasioned by boredom or heat exhaustion!"

"If Corvo is truly convinced those represent the only perils for the remainder of our journey, I promise you he will rescind his order. But he will not do so tonight, so I suggest we get some sleep!"

"Not until I've dined on another exquisite supper of dried fish," Aulus deferred. Will you share my repast?"

"Gladly, if it will put an end to your grumbling."

"I make no promises," Aulus grinned as he handed a chunk to Neocles.

DAYBREAK FOUND *BESTIA*, ITS legionnaires fully caparisoned, following an old animal path toward a cluster of low hills blanketed with trees. In the distance, a mixed herd of zebras and wildebeests grazed unconcernedly in the fading shadows.

"The gods must have heard me, for it appears we may soon enjoy some respite from the heat," Aulus exulted as they marched.

“How could they not?” Neocles dryly rejoined. “You ceased complaining only when you finally drifted to sleep,”

Aulus ignored the barb. “It is yet cool enough and those hills are not far distant. At this pace we should reach them before the heat becomes intolerable.”

“Perhaps we will bivouac among trees tonight! It will be a welcome change from the heat and dust that has been our lot,” Neocles conceded.

Their steps unconsciously quickened as they strode toward the beckoning hills.

THE GENTLY SLOPING WOODLANDS were primarily comprised of fig, teak, and mopane trees, with a smattering of Aleppo pines. Subsidiary paths created by elephants shouldering their way through the forest branched from the main trail upon which the legionnaires marched. Colobus and vervet monkeys concealed in the trees eyed them in silence with a combination of curiosity and wariness.

“We will rest here until tomorrow,” Corvo informed Berossus. “Choose two or three men who are skilled hunters and instruct them to locate some game…forest hogs and apes surely inhabit these woods. And ensure that wine is delivered to my tent the moment it is erected.” He paused. “If the men wish to remove their armor, allow it.”

"As you order," his subordinate acknowledged.

"I THINK I MAY REMAIN IN THIS PLACE, rather than continue onward to Rome," Aulus sighed as he leaned against the trunk of a tree and stretched his legs out. His *lorica*, *gladius*, shield, and helmet lay in the grass beside him. Neocles relaxed nearby in the shade, still wearing his armor.

Neocles looked perplexed. "What about getting drunk, fucking women, and killing all those with small tits and anyone who dares offer you fish to eat?"

"I am rethinking those things. Luckily, I see no fish hereabouts."

"Nor any women, small-titted or otherwise."

"As I said, I am still at the reconsidering stage," Aulus reiterated. "It is not a decision to be rushed."

"I fear it unlikely that Berossus will agree to your proposed change of plans," Neocles laughed.

"What does Berossus care? If I happen to disappear one night, simply inform him that wild animals dragged me from my bed and ate me. In fact, why don't you join me? We will set up housekeeping together, find fat African wives, and produce many children!"

"If I join you, who will remain to explain that both of us were dragged from our beds and eaten?"

Their conversation was interrupted by a sharp yelp from a legionnaire a short distance away.

"Bowmen!" he cried. At that instant an arrow thudded into the tree against which Aulus reclined.

"By Jupiter!" he growled, leaping to his feet. "Will the gods never allow us ease?" He bent to retrieve his *gladius* and jammed his helmet on his head.

"Your *lorica*?" Neocles blurted as he, too, stood.

Aulus grinned and shook his head. "No time. We must hasten to kill some Aethiops before they slink back to the *cloaca* that produced them." He strode toward the rising clamor, Neocles at his heels.

The scene was one of pandemonium. Berossus was on site, barking orders, though there was no sign of Corvo. Two slain legionnaires already lay on the ground, spitted by arrows.

"I see no bowmen!" Neocles shouted above the tumult to no one in particular.

"They conceal themselves among the trees!" a legionnaire answered.

"Who are *they*?"

No one responded.

"*Testudo*!" Berossus bawled.

The legionnaires immediately formed themselves into a compact square, five men across and as many deep. Previously assigned stations near the center of the second rank, Neocles and Aulus scrambled into position. Berossus stood in the first row, directly in front of Aulus.

Each man at the front held his shield vertically before him, effectively covering his body from the bridge of his nose to his shins, which were protected by greaves. The resulting impromptu wall of overlapping shields created a barricade that was virtually impregnable. Those in the back ranks lifted their shields overhead, balancing them on the helmets of the men in front, thereby sheltering the formation from airborne missiles and arrows. Legionnaires along the sides of the *testudo*, and those occupying the last rank, faced sideways or rearward, respectively, their shields turned outward, to protect the perimeter. So robust was this defensive alignment that, when describing a campaign of Marc Antony in 36 BCE, the Roman historian, Dio Cassius, testified, "It is so marvelously strong that men can walk upon it and whenever they come to a narrow ravine, even horses and vehicles can be driven over it."

"Where is Corvo?" Aulus asked through clenched teeth as a deafening fusillade of arrows and stones rained down on the *testudo*, none of which managed to wound the men hunkered inside. The stones, propelled by slings, bounced harmlessly off their heavy wooden shields. Most of the arrows were equally ineffective, their sharpened points being merely fire-hardened and splintering on impact. A few costly bronze or iron arrowheads, acquired from Arabian traders, actually lodged in *Bestia's* shields, some even penetrating a half-inch or more.

"Drunk, in his tent, no doubt," Neocles muttered. Though he couldn't be sure, the volume of missles striking the *testudo* already seemed to be diminishing.

"They squander their darts foolishly," Berossus gloated. "Remain in formation and brace yourselves, for they are about to emerge from the woods in order to attack us. Do not yield! Grasp your swords firmly and keep your shields high. At my command, prepare to repulse them. Make ready, for our assailants die today."

Neocles, Aulus, and the other legionnaires of *Legio XVI Bestia* anxiously unsheathed their bronze swords and clutched them in hands slick with perspiration.

"I have not until now seen battle," Aulus nervously confided to Neocles.

Berossus overheard. "Nor will you today. You timid milksops are little better than effete slaves, fit for nothing more perilous than scything barley. Today you will, instead, find yourselves scything ignorant savages."

"Who attacks us?" Neocles asked.

"Africans. Whether sent by Jugurtha, or some other barbarian, I do not know, nor why. But I intend to find out."

"How many are they?"

"They are inferior to us in both number and daring. They hope to achieve by stealth what they cannot accomplish by valor."

The men waited anxiously as the drum of rocks and arrows against their shields further subsided. By listening intently to the sound of the projectiles striking the *testudo,* Berossus was able to discern the direction from which most of them were launched. He smiled, coldly.

"The savages are perplexed because we do nothing to repulse their attack," Berossus quietly informed the legionnaires on either side of him. "They are emboldened, flattering themselves that the suddenness of their raid has overawed us. Let us undeceive them."

"Where are they?" one of the men asked.

"Two *acti* distant. Having exhausted their missiles, the simpletons have left themselves no choice but to storm the *testudo*," Berossus confidently predicted. He increased the timbre of his voice, that his instructions could be heard by all the legionnaires. "Steel yourselves! Be resolute and do not waver! Strike between your shields and hack the bastards to pieces! Despise our enemies, not merely in spirit, but with the point of your swords. Do not falter, for our victory was preordained by the gods!"

At Berossus' command, the Romans' defensive formation would spontaneously dissolve as the men comprising it shifted their positions, thereby opening lanes the *gladius*-wielding legionnaires would utilize to repel their attackers. In effect, their assailants would plunge into a bristling hedgehog of bronze. The men of the *testudo* nervously fidgeted in place, readying themselves for impending hand-to-hand combat.

What arms do they bear?" Aulus nervously whispered to no one in particular.

“Spears and wooden cudgels,” Berossus shrugged. “Their weapons will disintegrate like melting wax beneath our swords.”

The soldiers of *Bestia* lapsed into anxious silence, breathlessly anticipating the imminent clash. Neocles was certain that those standing on either side of him could clearly hear the sound of his heart pounding through his *lorica*.

A collective, shrieking ululation interrupted his reverie as their assailants, heretofore concealed, surged forward in a single mass.

“Now!” Berossus bellowed. “Break ranks and slaughter them all! Whoever slays the first barbarian shall become my second!” He lowered his shield only slightly and stepped eagerly forward to meet the human onrush, *gladius* clutched in his right hand. An African brandishing a wooden knobkerrie, nude but for a kilt wrapped about his loins, sprang toward him. “Death opens its arms to welcome you!” Berossus gleefully cackled as he plunged his sword into the man’s unprotected abdomen.

In order to clear space in front of him as he simultaneously yanked his sword free of the African’s body, Berossus swung his shield in a wide arc. Next to him, a legionnaire hacked at the shoulder of another attacker before finally severing it from the man’s body. Behind them, other legionnaires pressed forward with varying degrees of enthusiasm to join the fray.

Neocles and Aulus found themselves among the crush of men near the heart of the disintegrating *testudo*, basically propelled forward involuntarily by their comrades behind them. Angling toward them from the side, Neocles spotted a young, slender African, little older than a boy, brandishing a long, pointed stave. *Gladius* at the ready, Neocles shouldered his way through the crowd to intercept him. Although he had not exerted himself significantly, adrenaline already surged through Neocles' veins and he struggled to catch his breath.

His adversary abruptly stopped and grinned at the legionnaire slogging through the confusion to reach him. He extended his free hand and flicked his fingers, inviting Neocles to engage in combat.

"Roman pig," the African sneered in garbled Latin.

Neocles hesitated. His adversary did not.

Agilely leaping toward him, the African sought to impale Neocles with his stave, though the latter easily turned it with his shield. Neocles retaliated by lunging forward with his *gladius*, but executed the maneuver with such clumsiness that his opponent nimbly sidestepped him.

"No!" mocked the African with a grin.

Though dimly aware of the cries and swirling maelstrom of clashing arms around him, Neocles' attention was riveted on his opponent. Both nervously gulped air as they stood, warily facing one another, undecided about how best to dispatch the other. Each stepped forward to make half-hearted feints with their respective weapons before scuttling back a safe distance.

Aulus appeared at Neocles' side out of nowhere. "It appears you have cornered one!" he panted. Neocles stole a quick glance at his friend, noting the blade of his *gladius* was smeared with blood.

"I am not certain which of us is cornered," Neocles tersely responded.

"I just killed one of the savages, by Jupiter," Aulus vaunted. "It was much easier than I expected, though mine was appreciably larger. Do you require assistance with yours?"

"I require nothing!" Neocles snapped, irritated by Aulus' braggadocio. Mindful of his friend's reproving presence, Neocles raised his shield and stepped boldly forward, firmly gripping his sword in his other hand. The young African answered by lifting his wooden spear and taking a half-step toward Neocles.

"His weapon cannot penetrate your *lorica*," Aulus coached from the sidelines, uninvited. "You need not fear him." Neocles ignored the unwelcome advice as he cautiously circled his opponent, who jabbed at him with his spear.

"The Aethiop is but a child! Move in and put an end to the game!" Aulus enthusiastically shouted.

Emboldened, Neocles abruptly changed direction and pounced. The African was caught off guard. He frantically backpedaled as he propelled his spear into Neocles' shield, though it bounced harmlessly off the stout wood.

"The fool has disarmed himself! Now you have him!" Aulus exulted.

Dropping his cumbersome shield and raising his *gladius* over his head, Neocles sprang toward the defenseless African, who flung his hands up in a vain effort to deflect the coming blow. His eyes were wide with fear, their luminous sclera vivid white.

"No, Roman!" he cried, this time without mockery.

Neocles wavered.

"Do not hesitate, Neocles!" Aulus exhorted from behind him. "The brutes have already slain too many of our brothers today. If you spare him, you merely place a sword in his hand with which to inflict further harms on us."

The African visibly trembled beneath Neocles' upraised sword.

"As you said, he is but a child, Aulus."

"A child who will happily slit our throats, given the chance."

Neocles slowly lowered his sword, though he did not take his eyes off his captive. "I cannot."

Aulus was clearly disappointed. "Your misplaced compassion smacks of cowardice and does you no credit, for one does not spare ravening beasts. The Aethiop will return to his village, where he is certain to boast how he bested the timorous Romans."

"So be it. Boastful words are without power to harm anyone and we will have returned to Rome by then, anyway." Neocles raised his chin to indicate the African was free to leave. He sheathed his sword and turned away.

"Then, by the gods, I will do it!" Aulus declared, stepping forward.

"No, let him live. The gods have heard my vow and it must be honored," Neocles sighed. He retrieved his shield and plodded toward Aulus, who observed his retreat with visible disgust.

The contest between Neocles and the young African appeared to be over.

Neocles trudged past Aulus without establishing eye contact, humiliated by his inability to execute the youth, who remained immobile and simply stared at the ground. Aulus continued to watch him with mistrust before turning away. He finally began to trail Neocles back to the main body of legionnaires.

Seeing his chance, the African swiftly bent to retrieve his weapon. He bounded toward the two unsuspecting Romans and, before either of them could turn to ascertain the source of the approaching footfalls, buried his spear into the right side of Aulus' back. With a groan, Aulus collapsed to the earth.

Hearing the sound, Neocles spun and witnessed the grinning African standing astride Aulus' prostrate body.

"Aulus!" he shrieked.

Neocles yanked his *gladius* from its sheath and sped back to his friend. Seeing this, his African counterpart jerked his spear from Aulus' body and retreated. Grasping its shaft in both hands he braced himself against Neocles' charge. Neocles paused only momentarily to assess the gravity of his friend's wound, then turned to retaliate against the treacherous youth whose life he had just spared.

Ignoring the African's lunges and uncaring of personal risk, Neocles attacked furiously with his *gladius*. Chopping in an irrational frenzy, Neocles managed to hack the fingers from one of his opponent's hands. His spear slipped from his grasp and Neocles kicked it aside. When the African sprang to escape, Neocles swung his sword in a wide arc and severed the tendons behind his knee. With a yelp of pain, he tumbled to the earth.

Raising himself on one elbow, the defeated African held his mangled hand aloft. Blood oozed from the amputated stumps of his fingers and streamed down his arm. Neocles loomed over him, blood seeping from a nick in his side inflicted by the African's spear.

"No, Roman," croaked the latter. "You swore."

Neocles stepped closer, shoved the man's head to the ground with his foot, and placed the point of his sword at this throat. The young African began to cry.

"The gods were witness to my promise of life," Neocles spat. "But even the gods acknowledge one's duty to avenge an unworthy death. I am hereby absolved of my oath."

With that, he placed both hands on the hilt of his *gladius* and shoved downward. A gurgling cough issued from the writhing African and an eruption of frothy blood burst from his nose and mouth. The sword's bronze point lanced through his trachea and esophagus before becoming wedged between his third and fourth vertebrae. Neocles firmly planted one foot on the dead man's face and, through vigorous twisting and pulling, managed to dislodge the blade. Removing his foot, he scuffed the leather sole of his *soleae* along the earth to remove blood and cleaned his *gladius* of gristle and tissue by wiping it on the young African's loincloth.

Neocles sheathed his sword surveyed the man's corpse with rueful melancholy before stepping away.

He walked to the body of his friend and knelt beside it. The African's spear had pierced one of Aulus' kidneys, killing him instantly. A thin trickle of watery blood oozed from the wound.

"You are avenged, my brother. Wherever you are, I hope there is no shortage of big-titted women." Neocles gently patted his friend's forearm before standing. The laceration in his side throbbed and was beginning to stiffen. He needed medical attention.

THE MEN OF *LEGIO XVI BESTIA* milled about and nervously sported about their prowess in surviving the attack they'd just repelled.

"Marcus nearly shat himself when threatened by two savages brandishing nothing more than sharpened sticks!"

"My aged grandmother would have fought more ably than these Aethiops!"

"Because there are undoubtedly many new widows in the savages' village, Quintus intends to take a wife from among them, mimicking the Sabine Women. His laziness will undoubtedly compel him to choose one already pregnant!"

"The lions and jackals will feast tonight, thanks to the valiance of Roman arms!"

Neocles hailed a legionnaire. "I have a wound. Where is the medic?" The other man pointed. "Corvo? Berossus?"

"I have seen neither of them since the fighting ended. Where is Aulus?"

"He sups with the gods tonight," Neocles stoically informed him. Around him, legionnaires dragged the bodies of slain Africans and heaved them into a pile. Neocles estimated they numbered more than twenty. After removing their armor, the Romans who died in the skirmish would be reverentially placed on a makeshift catafalque and a pyre made of their bodies.

He turned in the direction of the medic.

"YOU ARE FORTUNATE THAT nothing vital suffered harm," *Bestia's* medic remarked as he dressed with a plug of sphagnum the hole made by the African's spear. "I expect you will heal without difficulty, though you must change the poultice twice each day."

Neocles nodded. "How many Romans died?"

"I was informed of five, with as many wounded...none seriously, praise the gods."

"Six, with Aulus," Neocles corrected him. "And what of Corvo and Berossus?"

"Berossus survives. I know nothing of Corvo's fate."

"Where is Berossus?"

"Attending to the legion's welfare, I am sure."

"I would speak with him."

The medic rose from the stool on which he'd been sitting. "I am finished here. As I said, replace the poultice twice daily and all should be well."

Neocles departed the makeshift triage to search for Berossus. He did not have far to look, for the centurion stood chatting with two legionnaires only a few paces away.

"Hail," Neocles greeted as he approached them.

"Hail, Neocles," one of the soldiers responded. "It is good that I see you still among the living. Are you well? What of Aulus?"

Neocles joined the small circle of men. "A deceitful savage blindsided and slew him," he despondently revealed.

Berossus listened impassively. "I mourn that grievous news."

Neocles turned to look directly at Berossus. "What of Corvo?"

"The gods have welcomed Corvo into their company."

Neocles cocked a skeptical eyebrow. "Indeed? How did he die?"

“At the hands of a savage,” Berossus shrugged.

“A savage?” Neocles frowned. He found it more probable that the inconvenient Corvo met his fate at the point of Berossus’ sword during the turbulent swirl of battle.

“Who may gainsay the will of the gods?” Berossus gravely added.

“Where is his corpse?”

“His tent, where it is being prepared for immolation, along with our other fallen comrades.”

“Berossus now commands us,” one of the other men volunteered.

“‘Who may gainsay the will of the gods’?” Neocles dryly parroted. He turned again to Berossus. “What, now, are your plans for *Bestia*?”

“We shall resume our journey to Rome as soon as the necessary rites over our sanctified dead have been completed. Nothing has changed in that regard.”

Not yet, anyway, thought Neocles.

NINE

"SO, YOU FOUND THIS KNIFE in some ruins?" Mosi clarified.

"Yeah, about 80 miles from Mpanda."

The two men relaxed in a booth in the hotel's empty downstairs bar, having already consumed multiple beers.

Mosi leaned back with a thoughtful look on his face. "I think you already know that my family is from Stone Town…as far back as anyone can remember. I was born on the island. We came to Dar when I was a kid so my dad could work, though my roots still lie on Pemba. Because of that, I don't know a great deal about the interior of the country."

"I think the ruins are Roman," Laidlaw said.

"Roman! I didn't know the Romans penetrated this far into Africa!"

“Yeah, that seems to be the consensus of opinion,” Laidlaw wryly noted. “Everybody seems surprised when I tell ‘em.”

“I would love to see the knife.”

“I left it in a safe deposit box in Paris ‘cause I didn’t want to risk damaging, or losing, it. But I’ve got pictures of it.” Laidlaw fished his cell phone from his pocket and pulled up the photographs. He handed the phone to Mosi. “Swipe it to the left.”

The other man scrutinized the photos. “It looks almost modern, Alex. Not like the corroded artifacts one typically sees in museums. Perhaps it’s not as old as you surmise?”

“Maybe, but the design is classically Roman and it’s engraved in Latin with the owner’s name: ‘Crixus’. An expert who teaches at the Sorbonne thinks some rich Roman, maybe a diplomat, commissioned the knife. However you slice it, it's hard to explain how it ended up in the middle of Africa.”

Mosi drained his mug of Uhuru Lager and signaled the bartender. “Who else have you spoken to about it?”

Laidlaw shrugged. “Museum people, university professors, various brainiacs. The British Museum had a similar one on display.”

“What did they say about yours?”

“Nuthin'. A woman there suggested that I buy a toy replica in their gift shop,” Laidlaw chuckled.

Mosi looked again at the photos on Laidlaw’s phone. “The patterned blade is certainly striking. Do you know what it’s made of?”

The bow-tied bartender arrived with two frosty mugs of Uhuru and placed them on fresh napkins in front each man.

"Thank you, Woodson." The bartender smiled wordlessly before retreating with their two empty mugs.

Mosi grasped his fresh drink and held it aloft. "To mysteries, known and unknown, my friend." The men touched mugs.

Laidlaw took a long draught before responding. "The blade is Damascus steel, which is pretty rare. I'm sure that's why it didn't corrode much."

Mosi nodded, thoughtfully. "Who would own such a knife, especially one as old as yours? An ancient diplomat, as you say?"

"That's the rub. It's so unusual, possibly even one-of-a-kind, that I can't find much information about it."

"It must be very valuable, no?"

"I would think so, but really have no idea. The professor at the Sorbonne assured me that any number of museums would be happy to take it off my hands, though."

"Yes, I'm sure of that!" Mosi laughed. "So, what do you intend to do?"

"I have a safari client arriving in a couple of days for a 10-day hunt. I plan on headin' back out to the ruins after he leaves to poke around some more. Wanna come?"

"Absolutely!" Mosi enthusiastically responded.

ALTHOUGH A FIRST-TIMER TO Africa, Laidlaw's latest client, Al Garrett, was an experienced outdoorsman from Canada. Laidlaw met him and his 10-year-old son, Rocco, at their hotel and drove them three hours to the wilderness camp in his Jeep. Both father and son were euphoric about their first sojourn to the Dark Continent.

When booking his safari the previous year, Garrett made clear his primary goal was to bag an impala, the sleek, cinnamon-colored antelope ranging in herds across the broken woodlands and savannahs of south-eastern and south-central Africa. Two species exist, the more common southern impala and the larger, and rarer, black-faced variety. It has rightly been observed that, but for its prevalence, the graceful impala would be among the most prized of African trophies. Typically weighing between 120 and 150 pounds, only the males sport the sweeping, lyre-shaped horns that distinguish the species. The sheer abundance of the southern impala makes bagging a respectable trophy relatively straightforward. For that reason, Laidlaw suggested that Garrett add a few additional antelope to his license: wildebeest, bushbuck, blesbok, hartebeest, tsessebe.

A *sine qua non* before setting out on any hunt is the ritual of sighting-in one's rifle. Whether equipped with conventional "open sights" or a hunting scope, safari rifles tend to suffer a great deal of rough treatment while being transported halfway around the globe. Baggage handlers throw them about, multiple airline employees and agents drop them, functionaries at every level of various governments handle them, a multitude of inspectors scrutinize them. By the time the rifle actually arrives at its African destination, it has been repeatedly knocked about and battered, leaving its sights hopelessly deranged. Unless it is sighted-in afresh, it is likely that a hunter will completely miss his target animal or, much worse, inflict a painful, yet non-fatal, wound. Accordingly, it is absolutely essential that hunting rifles be checked to confirm their accuracy before heading into the field. This is typically done in the safari camp on the first day of the hunt.

Laidlaw was impressed when Garrett slid from its padded case a well-used bolt-action rifle in caliber seven-millimeter Mauser. Developed in 1892 for use by the German armed forces, the venerable "7x57" quickly became a popular hunting round worldwide. Renowned firearms authority, Frank Barnes, stated that despite its origins as a military cartridge, "the 7x57mm Mauser has proven to be one of the best all-round sporting rounds ever developed." In the wake of subsequent, trendier, and heavily-advertised hunting cartridges, the 7x57 fell largely into obscurity, though its effectiveness as a hunting round remained undiminished. Early in the 20th century, Walter Bell, a Scottish ivory hunter, bagged over 1,000 elephants using the seven-millimeter Mauser, most of them with a single shot. But elephant hunting was, and remains, exhausting work. Bell estimated that he walked an average of 73 miles per elephant and wore out twenty-four pairs of boots in a year.

Like George Pyper, too many first-time safari clients arrive in camp bearing flashy new rifles, many of them chambered in calibers Laidlaw had never even heard of but which are aggressively marketed by huge corporations in full-color ads in American hunting and gun magazines. Virtually all of them more-or-less duplicate the performance of cartridges that, like the seven-millimeter Mauser, have been in existence for well over a century. "All novelty is but oblivion," Francis Bacon observed some 400 years ago.

Garrett gently placed his rifle on a blanket spread across the hood of the bakkie. Rocco sat nearby in a collapsible camping chair and watched, entranced.

"Nice rifle," Laidlaw remarked with genuine admiration. "I've always liked the 7x57. You seldom see it used much anymore."

"It's my favorite. Okay to load it now?" It is standard protocol on safari to follow the instructions of one's professional hunter, thereby reducing the chance of accidents.

"Sure."

Garrett opened the action of his rifle and slipped a single brass cartridge into its chamber. Sliding the bolt closed, he clicked the safety on and hunkered over the rifle, preparing to shoot. A paper plate was tacked to a tree 100 yards away.

Using binoculars, Laidlaw focused on the target. “Any time you’re ready.”

In movies and television, actors blithely discharge firearms in closed rooms and automobiles. Aside from the death of the bad guy on the receiving end of the shot, this routine practice produces no apparent ill-effects. This scenario, like everything else that emanates from Hollywood, is fantasy. In reality, the explosion generated by a detonating cartridge is deafening, even painfully so, depending on the caliber. Countless people have been rendered permanently deaf from exposure to gunfire. As a consequence, Laidlaw, Garrett, and Rocco all wore hearing protection to shield them from the thunderous crack of the rifle.

Garrett clicked the safety off, took a deep breath, held it, and squeezed the trigger. His shot struck high, about three inches from the center of the paper plate. He slid the bolt rearward and ejected the smoking cartridge case.

“Not bad,” Laidlaw said with approval, lowering his binoculars. “Give it a couple of clicks down and try again.”

Garrett lowered the point-of-impact by slightly rotating a notched dial on body of the scope. He reloaded the rifle and reengaged its safety.

“Any time you’re ready,” Laidlaw repeated, again watching the paper plate.

Garrett flicked the safety off and aimed. His second shot landed less than one inch from the center of the plate.

"Perfect," Laidlaw smiled. "You're good to go. You'll be able to aim pretty much right-on at 200 yards." He lowered his binoculars, removed his ear plugs, and looked over at Rocco, who was grinning. He flashed a thumbs-up.

"Does Rocco want to shoot?" Laidlaw asked.

Garrett ejected the empty cartridge case and laid his rifle across the blanket. He left its bolt open so that it was obvious at a glance the rifle was unloaded.

"Naw, he's just here to enjoy watching his old man screw up!" he laughed as he, too, removed his hearing protection. Garrett looked over at his son. "C'mon on over here, boss! How'd I do?"

Rocco jumped up and ran to the two men. "Great, dad!" he laughed as he hugged his father.

"Why don't I have the kitchen whip up something before we head out to find your impala," Laidlaw affably suggested. "What are you hungry for, Rocco?"

"Elephant stew?" the boy mischievously suggested.

"Well, I don't think that's on the menu, but I'm sure we can find something you'll like. How does a buffalo burger sound?"

"Great!" Rocco beamed. "I don't suppose you have Cokes out here in the sticks?"

"Are you kidding? We have enough Cokes to fill a bathtub! Milk shakes, too! As soon as your dad packs up his rifle, we'll head back to camp and you can see for yourself."

THROUGH BINOCULARS, LAIDLAW and Garrett watched a large herd of grazing impala. To minimize the risk of spooking the animals, Laidlaw suggested that Rocco remain behind in the bakkie, parked 250 yards away. He provided the boy with binoculars so he could follow the stalk. Laidlaw knew that Moses and Smoke, though nowhere in sight, were also not far away.

"There's a couple of decent rams in there," Laidlaw whispered as he surveyed the herd. "Nothing record-book, but passable." He lowered his binoculars. "We can do better."

"They all look record-book to me," Garrett muttered as he watched the antelope through his binoculars.

"Yeah, I get that a lot," Laidlaw chuckled. "Let's see what your son thinks."

The two men crept through the brush back to the vehicle, where Rocco impatiently awaited their return.

"Dad!" he blurted as soon as they emerged from the bush. "There were some monsters in there!" he panted, wide-eyed.

"I thought so, too, but Mr. Laidlaw thinks we can do better. Could you see them okay?"

Rocco nodded enthusiastically. "Easy. These binoculars are the bomb! Impala look kinda like deer, but their horns are different."

"What else did you see?" Laidlaw inquired.

"Just some birds way over there." Rocco pointed. "I think they were buzzards."

"Ya know, I think you're right," Laidlaw concurred. "There are lots of buzzards in Africa. You thirsty? We've got water and soda in the cold box and the kitchen also packed some sandwiches and other goodies in there, too."

"Naw, I'm good for now," Rocco grinned. "I wanna see some more animals."

Laidlaw looked expectantly at Garrett, who unloaded his rifle and slipped it into a zippered case before depositing it in the vehicle. "I could use a bottle of water."

No sooner had Laidlaw flipped open the lid of the cold box than the two trackers materialized from the bush.

"Salam aleikum," Moses greeted them.

"Habari," Laidlaw responded. He handed bottles of cold water to Garrett, Moses, and Smoke. "What of the impala?"

"They were not special," Moses stated, nonchalantly. "There are many more impala."

"Yep, that was my thinking, too." Laidlaw turned to Garrett, who was chugging water. "I think we should look for a better ram. We might run into some of the other species on your license at the same time. We'll stay at it until dinner time, if you're agreeable."

"Sounds like a plan. What do you think, Rocco?"

"Let's hit it! Maybe we'll see a lion or some elephants!"

"Well, I guess the boss has spoken," Garrett laughed.

AVAILING THEMSELVES OF THE tracking skills of Moses and Smoke, they located two additional herds of impala, though neither of them contained rams satisfactory to Laidlaw's practiced eye. At dusk, he suggested that they return to camp, clean up, and relax over a dinner of gazpacho, broiled springbok filets, fresh vegetables, and crusty bread hot from a stone oven. The kitchen staff also baked chocolate éclairs for dessert. As they bounced back toward the boma in the fading light, Laidlaw overheard Rocco quietly ask his dad whether he thought it possible to get a dish of ice cream, too.

Laidlaw frowned. "Ice cream? In the middle of Africa?"

"Well, I was just wondering..." Rocco haltingly began.

"*Of course* we have ice cream!" Laidlaw heartily laughed. "In fact, we have the makings for hot-fudge sundaes and banana splits, too, if you want one of those!"

Rocco grinned from ear to ear and turned to Garrett. "Dad, let's go on safari again next year and bring mom."

IT WAS THE THIRD DAY of Garrett's safari and, before leaving camp after breakfast, Laidlaw informed Garret that Smoke had chanced upon the tracks of a bushbuck ram that morning. Judging from their size, the animal might be of record-book size. Laidlaw proposed they try to locate the animal, a suggestion to which Garrett excitedly agreed.

While neither as large nor as striking as the dazzling kudu, sable, or gemsbuck, the humble bushbuck is remarkable for its extraordinary fearlessness. Inherently shy and solitary, bushbuck rams have been known to attack, even kill, leopards, dogs, and human beings. Though ubiquitous throughout much of sub-Saharan Africa, bushbucks ordinarily remain unseen because of their wooded habitat and secretive nature. All of their senses are well developed which, combined with the bushbuck's natural courageousness, makes hunting them a daunting challenge.

With Smoke's help, they tracked the bushbuck ram for nearly three hours before finally spotting him.

"He's browsing right at the tree line," Laidlaw whispered as looked through his binoculars. They were hunkered behind a termite mound 400 yards away. "See him?"

As he did the previous day, Rocco waited in the bakkie, parked a half-mile away. He happily used his binoculars to scrutinize the area around the vehicle for wildlife. Laidlaw instructed Moses to remain in the vicinity of the vehicle, out of sight, to ensure Rocco's safety.

"No. All I see are trees and shadows. Where is he?"

To the left of that big tree. He's old 'cause bushbucks get darker as they age and he's almost completely black. Got a nice set of horns on him, too…eighteen, maybe nineteen, inches."

"I still don't see him," Garrett groused.

Laidlaw lowered his binoculars and reached across to Garrett. He clasped his client's head in his hands and gently rotated it slightly to the right. "See him? He's right beneath that big tree."

"Hang on." Garrett slowly rotated the focusing ring on his binoculars to sharpen the view. "I think so. Hang on," he repeated in a tense whisper. "Yeah, I see him now."

"He's looking right at us. Stay still."

The two men remained motionless. Sweat poured into Garrett's eyes, burning them, and dripped onto his shirt. Nervous excitement and the tension of holding his binoculars to his face, immobile, caused his hands to tremble.

"You okay?" Laidlaw murmured without looking at him.

"Yeah."

"He's still staring in our direction. If the wind shifts and he catches our scent, he'll bolt for the trees and disappear. Do you feel confident enough to take your shot from here?"

"I'm not sure. Can we get closer?"

Laidlaw silently assessed the intervening landscape. "There's nothing to hide behind if you leave the termite mound, but you can try to creep closer. Can you shoot prone?"

"Yeah."

"Okay. Get ready and I'll tell you when to start. Stay flat on the ground and don't hurry. If he looks in your direction, freeze. Animals notice movement but don't pay much attention to stationary objects. Take your shot whenever you feel comfortable doing so."

"Okay."

Garrett handed his rifle and binoculars to Laidlaw and slowly lowered himself to the ground. Laidlaw reached down and handed him his items then turned his attention to the bushbuck. He refocused his binoculars on the ram.

"He's resumed eating. Go!" he hissed.

Clutching his rifle in his right hand, Garrett wriggled awkwardly forward on this stomach. He'd slung his binoculars backward over his neck and they rested in the center of his back as he crawled.

Jagged stones abraded Garrett's unprotected arms as he inched forward, his heart pounded, and he was sweating profusely. After less than a minute of struggling he paused to rest and cautiously raised his head to peer over the expanse of parched grass that interrupted his view.

The bushbuck remained so distant that Garrett couldn't see it with his naked eye. He wished he'd kept his binoculars in his other hand, but it would have been too awkward to crawl holding both rifle and binoculars. Nor could he easily retrieve them without spooking the ram. He craned his heard rearward and was dismayed to see the termite mound scarcely twenty feet behind him.

Garrett was faced with dilemma. At his current pace, it would take him forever to reach the bushbuck, which might simply wander off in the interim. If he moved too quickly, however, the animal would probably spot him and flee, anyway. He slowly dragged his rifle toward his body, intending to use its telescopic sight to locate the animal.

Slowly raising himself onto his forearms, Garrett rested his cheek on the stock of his rifle and squinted through its scope toward the large tree beneath which, hopefully, the bushbuck continued to browse. The scope's lenses were covered with dust from scraping it along the ground. Not that he could see much though the scope but the blurry stalks of dry grass directly in front of him.

Garrett adjusted his position slightly and pursed his lips to gently blow the accumulated grime from his scope as best he could. He peered through it again.

The bushbuck had wandered several feet from the tree and stood frozen in position, staring squarely at him.

"Shit," Garrett muttered through gritted teeth. He instinctively held his breath as he continued to watch the transfixed bushbuck through his scope. A meat hornet, attracted by the salt of his perspiration, landed on his glistening face. Garrett didn't flinch.

Behind the termite mound twenty feet away, Laidlaw switched his gaze between Garrett and the wary antelope. He could easily hit the bushbuck with his .375 from his position but, except in the case of a wounded animal high-tailing it into next week, as in the case of George Pyper, or to prevent a client from being gored by a charging animal, shooting a client's trophy *for* him is absolutely unacceptable. "One does not hunt in order to kill; on the contrary, one kills in order to have hunted," said Jose' Ortega y Gasset.

Given the distance, the wariness of the bushbuck, and his torturous progress, Garrett feared it would prove impossible to get within shooting range before the animal raced away in alarm. His shoulders and wrists were starting to cramp because of the strain required to maintain his current rigid posture on the ground. He had to do something.

The meat hornet sauntered down Garrett's face and began to burrow between the collar of his shirt and his sweaty neck. A second became entangled in his hair. Garrett squirmed slightly in the baking sun. He again squinted at the antelope through his scope, its lenses still clouded by a translucent film of dust.

Motionless, the bushbuck continued to stare in his direction though it had resumed chewing the twigs in its mouth. It was quickly becoming apparent to Garrett that further attempts to worm his way closer to the antelope would only frighten it away. His choices under the circumstances were either to terminate the stalk altogether or try to shoot from his present location. Because he might not get another opportunity at a trophy bushbuck, Garrett chose the latter course, though he had never previously attempted such a long shot in the field.

With his right hand, Garrett retracted the bolt of his rifle. With painstaking slowness, he then slid the bolt forward, where it locked into place, thereby allowing a live round of ammunition to slide into the rifle's chamber. Resting the forepart of his rifle in his left palm, he pressed his cheek against its stock and clicked its safety off with his right hand. He could feel the meat hornet roaming along his spine beneath his shirt. As soon as the insect figured out that it was essentially trapped, it would wallop Garrett with its powerful sting. Adjusting his head behind the scope, Garrett settled into a shooting position.

The antelope had wandered even farther from the tree and now stood half-shielded behind a thick thorn bush. Garrett was shooting bullets of relatively light weight, 139 grains, which could easily be deflected by the thin, stiff branches of the thorn bush should it strike one before hitting its intended target. Were that to occur, Garrett's shot might easily go awry. Still, he had little choice.

Laidlaw continued to monitor developments from his vantage behind the termite mound. Realizing that Garrett was about to shoot, he trained his binoculars on the grazing bushbuck.

Garrett clasped his rifle tightly and reconfirmed his target through the scope. He took a deep breath, held it, and squeezed the trigger.

The rifle lunged rearward at the instant of detonation. Although the 7mm Mauser is not a particularly heavy-recoiling caliber, a stationary shooter lying prone, like Garrett, must absorb the totality of its jolting kick directly on his shoulder. The column of scorching gas that erupted from the muzzle of the discharging firearm created a billowing cloud of dust and twigs that momentarily engulfed Garrett.

Garret scrabbled for his rifle, clicked its safety on, and sat up. He'd momentarily lost sight of the bushbuck and anxiously squinted through his scope, trying to locate the animal. Laidlaw appeared at his side.

"Clean miss," he informed Garrett, who'd climbed to his feet. Garrett could feel the meat hornet making a transit of his waist beneath his shirt. He handed his rifle to Laidlaw, rapidly unbuckled his belt, dropped his pants, and lifted his shirt to allow the insect to escape before it stung him. The meat hornet previously exploring his scalp had apparently already decamped.

"You sure?" Garret pulled his trousers up, tucked his shirt in, and buckled his belt.

Laidlaw handed Garrett his rifle and binoculars. "Yeah. Your shot went low." Seeing Garrett's dismay, Laidlaw placed his hand on his client's shoulder. "Don't beat yourself up. It happens to everyone. It was a difficult shot."

Using binoculars, Garrett scanned the area where he'd last seen the animal. In vain…the unharmed bushbuck had clearly taken flight. "Shit!" he groused.

"You'll have other opportunities," Laidlaw consoled him. "Don't engage in post-mortems…they'll just make you feel worse. Let's go check on Rocco and grab something from the cold box. We've still got a lot of daylight left to hunt."

On cue, Smoke emerged from the bush and strode toward them.

"It was a hard shot, mabwana," he commiserated. "Do not feel bad."

"Where is Rocco?" Garrett blurted.

"He is with Moses," the tracker smiled. "They are watching giraffes. Do not fear. Come."

The three men headed back to the vehicle, Smoke leading.

"We may run into another herd of impala, so stay alert," Laidlaw instructed Garrett as they walked.

"DAD!" ROCCO SQUEALED WHEN he saw them emerge from the scrub. He was standing in the bed of the bakkie, his binoculars dangling from his neck. The boy jumped to the ground and raced over to greet Garrett and Laidlaw, Smoke having melted back into the bush a few moments earlier. "Didja get anything?"

Rocco panted with excitement. “I heard a shot a little while ago.”

“We saw a nice bushbuck, but I missed him.” Garrett hugged his son. “I heard you and Moses saw some giraffes.”

Rocco glanced around. “Yeah, he was just here...where’d he go?”

“Those lads have a tendency to just disappear,” Laidlaw laughed. “They’re here one minute then, next time you turn around, they’re gone! But they’re never far away.”

“Tell me about the giraffes,” Garrett urged.

“They were huge!” Rocco grinned. He pointed. “They were right over there. They just wandered out from the trees and stood there, starin’ at me like it was nuthin’!”

“How many were there?”

“Two. I was kinda nervous at first, but Moses was here, so it was okay.”

“Moses was here with you the whole time?”

“Not at first...it was just me. But then I saw the giraffes and he sorta appeared out of nowhere! It was funny!”

“The boys were keeping an eye on Rocco even though he didn’t know it,” Laidlaw informed Garrett. “You needn’t worry.”

“Were you scared?”

“Are you kidding, dad? They were the coolest! A million times better than a zoo ‘cause the giraffes were right there, lookin’ at me like it was nuthin’! Moses told me they were both boys but I didn’t even see ‘em, even with binoculars, until they walked out of the trees. They were *huge*!" he laughed.

"Mr. Laidlaw thought it best that you wait here for us while we went hunting. I hope that was okay, Rocco."

"'*Okay*'? I would have missed the giraffes if I hadn't been here while you guys were gone!"

"You hungry?" Garrett asked.

"I'm still full from breakfast, but a soda sounds good," Rocco said. Breakfast that morning consisted of fresh fruit, juices, milk, pancakes, bacon and eggs, hash browned potatoes, and hot bread with fresh butter and blackberry preserves. "I wish we could eat like this at home!" Rocco had exclaimed.

Laidlaw flipped open the lid of the cold box and scanned its interior. "Let's see, we've got sodas, milk, juice, water, and some Red Bulls. What sounds good, Rocco?"

"Okay if I have a soda, dad?"

"You bet!"

"Help yourself," Laidlaw invited. "An embarrassment of riches."

Rocco frowned. "What's that mean?"

"It means that there's lots to choose from," his father laughed. "Pick one you like, son."

Rocco leaned over the cold box and eyed its contents. "I think I'll try this one." He lifted a bottled soft drink from the chilled receptacle.

Laidlaw fished two beers from the cold box and handed one to Garrett. "Cheers."

Garrett seemingly just noticed the absence of the trackers. “Where are Smoke and Moses?” He popped the tab of his beer and took a sip.

“Tracking. They’ll report back by the time we finish here.”

“What are they tracking?”

“Impala, hartebeest, another bushbuck…everything that's on your license.”

Garrett nodded appreciatively. “Those guys are amazing.”

“'Amazing' is the word,” Laidlaw smiled.

In Primis Anno Regnantibus Imperator Caesar Titus Vespasianus (80 CE)

PARALLELING THE GREAT RIVER inland, Crixus and his surviving band limped northward. Their Meroe attackers didn't bother to pursue them, evidently content to merely strip the bodies of those slain in the ambush. The brooding Eros scarcely communicated following Romo's death, merely emitting little more than sullen grunts in response to Crixus' directives.

"How far before we reach the Fifth Cataract?" Eros finally growled.

"I am not sure, though I do not remember the distance separating the cataracts being excessively great," Crixus replied. "Once we reach the Fifth Cataract, there will be boats to carry us down the *Nilus* to Pelusium, where we will find *navis oneraria* waiting to convey us to Rome.

"With what do you expect to pay them?" Eros scoffed. "We have no coin."

"We have the remaining beasts to barter. We will also make it known that our business is that of the emperor. Crews will gladly transport us because of their eagerness to ingratiate themselves to Titus.

They will also be assured of liberal compensation by the senate once they reach Rome."

"When we arrive in Rome without the beasts, what then?"

Crixus looked askance at Eros. "Having fulfilled your duty to conduct me thither, you will have discharged your obligation. I will place myself at the emperor's disposal, as I was directed to do. What do *you* intend?"

"I intend to present myself to the *cohors praetoria*," Eros haughtily replied, referring to the elite clique that ostensibly served as the emperor's personal bodyguards, though more often utilized as a goon-squad to intimidate, or kill, the emperor's personal and political enemies. "By Jupiter, I will not return to *Bestia*!"

"I daresay the emperor's bullyboys will happily welcome you into their fraternity," Crixus dryly responded.

"You will be undone by your impudence, Crixus, nor shall I mourn your destruction" Eros spat. "Why should they not embrace me as a brother? The *cohors praetoria* is especially favored by the emperor and will gladly welcome someone of my stature into its ranks."

"I am sure you are correct. Since Sejanus' time, the *cohors praetoria* has been populated with thugs and cutthroats who devote themselves entirely to bouts of drinking and whoring. They no longer have the slightest interest in safeguarding the person of the emperor but, instead, conspire to ensure the installation of emperors who promise them generous rewards, and the elimination of those who do not. You will most assuredly be embraced by the *cohors praetoria* as a brother. I fear, however, that you will find yourself their reluctant tutor, for am quite certain that, the assassin's knife being their primary weapon, they are unschooled in the use of the *gladius.*"

"They will not find me loath to demonstrate its proper use. Indeed, I eagerly look forward to your presence on that occasion." Eros smiled, coldly, at Crixus. "Unless, of course, the emperor finds it impossible to conduct pressing matters of state without you."

"It was not my doing to undertake a journey to Rome in order to join Titus' court. Romo ordered me there at Berossus' urging."

"You have enjoyed perfect freedom since departing the *castrum.* But for your cowardice, you could have escaped at any time."

"It is not cowardice that restrains me, but anxiety over the welfare of my comrades who remain behind."

Eros clucked his tongue. "You are both a coward *and* a simpleton, Crixus. Berossus will not spare your comrades. Though Corvo is nominal commander of *Bestia*, he is a drunken fool who allows Berossus to do as he pleases."

Crixus nodded, thoughtfully. "Perhaps, but that is now beyond my control. The more interesting question, which has clearly eluded you, is why you, Romo, and the others were chosen to escort me on this doomed mission in the first place. I was banished from the *castrum* purely because of Berossus' animosity. It would appear that you, Romo, and the rest are objects of his disdain no less than myself."

Eros narrowed his eyes. "What are you talking about?"

"Are you so ignorant that you are unable to comprehend that Corvo and Berossus entertained no expectation that any of us would actually survive this wretched misadventure? I, at least, am sufficiently intelligent to recognize this obvious fact."

"You are a perfect fool, Crixus. Though you are expendable rubbish, I am invaluable to *Bestia*."

"Indeed? Why, then, are you here rather than at your ease in the *castrum*?"

"For what reason would either Corvo or Berossus wish me dead?" Eros challenged, undeterred.

"I do not pretend to know," Crixus responded. "It is a simple matter to explain my expulsion from *Bestia*. In your case, perhaps you did something to displease Berossus. Or perhaps he feared your ambition. Either way, Corvo and Berossus sleep in comfortable beds, enjoying copious amounts of wine, while you are stranded in a treacherous wasteland, herding beasts in the manner of a slave and struggling merely to survive from one day to the next. I confess that is not an easy thing to credit your assurances of Corvo's and Berossus' esteem for you," he concluded.

Eros was momentarily silent. "The gravity of the mission required someone of my stature to lead it," he finally responded, somewhat lamely.

"It is an admirable thing to retain one's sense of humor in the face of adversity."

"I do not speak in jest," Eros scowled.

"Oh? Forgive me, but I am quite certain that it was Romo, not you, who was burdened with the duty of leading this sorry expedition. From its inception, its insignificant and haphazard character deprived it of any pretensions of importance."

"The emperor and senate give the lie to what you say, Crixus. *Bestia's* fame reaches every corner of the Empire. That is why the emperor personally sought *Bestia's* aid for his upcoming games."

"Before joining his father in the East to fight the Jews, Titus found himself unable to keep his cock out of other men's wives, including those of senators. He populated Rome with an abundance of both bastards and enemies. Those who felt themselves aggrieved nurture durable memories and, now that Titus is emperor, pour honeyed words into his ear."

"So?"

"Titus is a soldier who knows less than nothing about staging *venationes*. He must rely on the advice of others, a great number of whom have long hated and envied him. His own brother, Domitian, may be counted among them. The emperor's enemies know less about the games than even *he* does and possess no incentive, and less desire, to be of service to him. Titus was led to *Bestia* on the advice of those who hate him."

Eros narrowed his eyes. "How do you pretend to know these things?"

“I fought beside the emperor and his father, Vespasian, in the East, where Titus’ youthful extravagances were the subject of much ridicule. His brother’s hatred, though, springs from their father’s insistence that Titus would succeed him as emperor, or no one at all.”

“Why should I believe anything you say, Crixus?”

“You have been too long in Africa, Eros. For what reason would I care to deceive you? It is all one to me whether you believe me, or otherwise. All that is certain is that Titus’ countless enemies in Rome remain sanguine that we will fail to arrive there, which will prove a great embarrassment to the emperor. Nor do Corvo or Berossus have the slightest interest in our fate, only availing themselves of a timely opportunity to rid *Bestia* of troublesome beasts and disposable men.”

Eros forced a laugh. “You are the disposable one, Crixus, not I.”

“I suspect Romo believed the same thing. I would fain ask him, were he still alive.”

“No matter,” Eros sniffed. “Though Romo’s judgment was clouded by pain when he appeared to place you in command, he was clearly manifesting his desire to shield me from censure for the disastrous fate of this expedition. It is plain that you hope by your words that the emperor and senate will be moved to grant you absolution for your countless blunders. By defaming *Bestia* and, by extension, me, you will succeed only in exposing yourself as a base liar. Nor should you flatter yourself clever enough to spin your fanciful tales before the *cohors praetoria* in a vain attempt to discredit me, for you will find them far less clement than am I."

Crixus began laughing. "Romo placed me in command only because he witnessed your daily ineptitude, though you obviously feel yourself abused by my unexpected promotion. I did not solicit it and hereby surrender to you all authority delegated to me by Romo. Upon our arrival in Rome you, alone, shall be the beneficiary of the emperor's boundless thanks"

The other man looked at him, skeptically. No, Crixus. I decline your invitation to share in your obloquy. Nor do I welcome your attempt to foist infamy onto my shoulders, for none but you and Romo shall bear responsibility for this laughable farce."

"I daresay Romo was not disposed to laugh while he lay dying,"

"The gods were kind to Romo because, by his timely death, he was spared the condemnation of the entire senate for his clumsy mishandling of his duties. While Romo has escaped reproach, you will not be so fortunate. All of Rome will know of your failures, to say nothing of your treachery."

"Yes, I am quite certain of your eagerness to inform all who will listen," Crixus sighed.

THE SURVIVING REMNANTS OF the caravan continued to limp northward through a broad, sandy *wadi.* To their left, dizzying sandstone cliffs reared skyward; to their right, a series of low, scorched hills marked the distant horizon and shimmered in the incandescent sunlight. Beyond them lay the Red Sea.

"It is time that we turn in the direction of the Great River!" Eros demanded. "I weary of this endless plodding in the relentless heat."

"I think you are right," Crixus concurred. "We will do so when we next encounter a corridor through the bluffs, unless you fancy scaling them."

Eros eyed him with suspicion. "It is not like you to be so agreeable. Have your brains been addled by the heat?"

"Hardly. We have now traveled far enough from Meroe that we are unlikely to suffer another attack from that quarter. As for my being agreeable, even an old, blind hog blunders onto an occasional acorn, Eros."

Eros ignored the barb. "How distant is the Fifth Cataract?"

"The Great River flows just beyond the bluffs," Crixus gestured west, "and we are approaching the vicinity of the Fifth Cataract. The next passageway through the mountains will lead us there."

"And you are certain we will find enough boats there to transport us to the *Mare Nostrum*?" Eros anxiously pressed.

"For good or ill, there remain comparatively few beasts and men that require transportation. There will be ample boats with which to do so."

"How long will the journey downriver take?"

"A month, perhaps more."

"What of pirates?"

"They base themselves on Elephantine Island and generally confine their raids to the waters in the immediate vicinity. Because we have no coin and pirates have no interest in playing wet nurse to a collection of half-starved animals, I am hopeful they will not molest us. We may also be able to add some mercenaries to our retinue once we reach the Great River. How many men-at-arms have we still?"

"Three legionnaires and a handful of askaris. The remainder are porters or camp staff and a few hunters. The rest of the worthless Aethiops either died or fled."

"Aside from the legionnaires and askaris, how many men, total?"

"Twenty, more or less."

Crixus reflected a moment. "See to it that all of them are armed for the remainder of the journey."

"For the remainder?" Eros scoffed. "Why have you waited until now?"

"Many of those previously slain by the boulders that rained down on them from the heights bore arms. Pray, how did their weapons profit them?"

"They were blameless for their impotence," snapped Eros. "The terrain rendered it impossible for our comrades to see and engage their adversaries."

"Just so. Henceforth, our enemies will be unable to effect ambushes from hidden positions. They will have no choice but to show themselves and confront us on the field of battle, as men." Crixus cocked his eyebrow. "Now, if you have finished second-guessing me, collect the remaining men into a compact body, count them, and issue arms to them. Having done so, ascertain the number and condition of the beasts."

Eros began to speak again.

"Now!" Crixus barked.

THE VESTIGES OF *LEGIO XVI BESTIA*, Berossus commanding, resumed its northward march.

"How far do you think we remain from the *Pontus Herculis*?" Senecio asked Neocles, referring to the Red Sea, as they plodded.

"I wish I knew," Neocles conceded. "I do not fancy another engagement with savages."

"I fear *Bestia* will prove unable to repel another attack because our numbers are much reduced. But neither do I relish climbing aboard a leaky *navis* for the return voyage to Rome. The gods seemed determined to ill-treat us, though I do not know why."

Neocles did not respond.

"THE ROMANS HAVE BEEN ANNIHLATED, Great One," Yam announced.

Though slumped on his throne, Jugurtha listened attentively. "How many?"

"At least two hundred. Perhaps more."

'"Where?"

"The burnt hills. The Romans panicked when our warriors burst upon them. We scattered them like a whirlwind and speared them like rabbits as they fled."

"How many survive?"

Yam smiled, coldly. "No Romans remain to seek vengeance on us. Hyenas and jackals feast upon their corpses as we speak. Nor will their countrymen learn of their inglorious deaths for a long time. You shall not hereafter be troubled by the Roman pigs, Great One."

A cold smile creased Jugurtha's leathery face. "You did well, Yam. *Ubarikiwe, kutakaswa.*"

A NARROW CORRIDOR, ERODED by wind and water through the porous sandstone cliffs over millennia, led to the riverbank three *stadia* north of the Fifth Cataract. A series of ramshackle structures, constructed of driftwood, palm fronds, mud, and stones, occupied a narrow stretch of the shoreline. Lashed to makeshift piers, a hodgepodge of watercraft of various sizes and configurations bobbed in the Nile's gentle current. Other boats were simply dragged onto the shore. Fishing nets fashioned of stringy palm fibers, and that day's catch of perch, bream, and catfish, were draped over boulders to dry in the baking sun. Nude children gamboled and splashed in the river near the shore while adults suspended their activities to observe in silence the arrival of the Romans. The entire tableaux reeked of fish and wood smoke.

Eros paused and surveyed the placid scene with disdain. “By the immortal gods, does this pigsty have a name?”

“If it does, I do not know it,” Crixus replied.

“Who among you speaks Latin?” Eros abruptly bellowed. Eliciting no response, he attempted another tack. “Who here speaks Greek?”

“I speak passable Latin, Roman.”

Startled, Eros and Crixus turned toward the speaker, an ancient, bent Nubian clad in a torn and dirty djellaba. A fringe of white hair ringed his bald head like a circlet and he leaned heavily on a wooden staff. Not a square inch of his scarred and wrinkled skin remained undamaged by decades of exposure to the ferocious sun.

“Who are you, old man?” Eros demanded.

“I am Ra,” he revealed, “headman of this village. What is your business here?”

Crixus intervened and took over the conversation. “I am Crixus and these are my men. We seek transportation downriver.”

Ra frowned. “What distance? The Mother of Rivers flows into tomorrow and many days after that.”

“To Alexandria or Pelusium. Do you have boats enough to transport all of us?”

Ra looked over Crixus' shoulder, to the knot of armed men and exotic animals gathered on the shoreline. “You are many. What have you to barter?”

“Barter!” Eros barked. “Perhaps we will simply take your boats and women, leaving you to barter for your lives.”

The old man nodded, thoughtfully. “Aye, that lies within your power. Yet, you do not strike me as much of a sailor, Roman. Do you know how to safely guide a craft to the destinations you seek without foundering? Do you even know how far distant those ports are, where they are located, or how to navigate around the raging waters of the many cataracts that yet remain before you? And what of the brackish waters of Lake Mareotis? Do you know how to avoid becoming lost among the canals that lead from it, or how to find your way through the innumerable channels that wend their way through the featureless Delta? ”

Noting Eros' lack of response, Ra turned again to Crixus. “Again, I ask: what have you to barter?”

“You will be paid upon our arrival at our destination.”

Ra shook his head. “No, Roman. I place trust in only the gods.”

Crixus thought quickly. “Fresh meat. As you see, we have many live beasts.”

Ra surveyed the collection of animals scattered among the interlopers, many confined to rude cages, others docilely led on halters.

“Your beasts in exchange for conveying you and your men to your desired destination,” the old man proposed. "As I said, you are many and will require several boats, as well as food and provisions for the journey.”

“*All* the beasts?” Eros exploded. “That is madness! It is clear that you do not know with whom you are trifling, old man. The Divine Titus, personally, commissioned us to transport these beasts to Rome!”

“Then let the Divine Titus retrieve you,” Ra shrugged. “But without boats, neither you nor the beasts will see Rome. Those are my terms, Roman.” A collection of Nubians had gathered near them, appearing more curious than menacing.

“I must discuss your proposal with my men,” Crixus said.

“Of course,” Ra concurred. “While you do so, the universal laws of hospitality compel me to bid you welcome and invite you to be at your ease. My people will provide refreshment for you and your men.” He turned toward the growing crowd of onlookers and spoke a few words. The audience quietly began to disburse.

“The old bastard thinks he has us over a barrel,” Eros muttered.

“That is because he does,” Crixus stoically replied.

"We should just put them all to the sword and take their boats."

"I would expect no better advice from you, Eros. What then? As the old man said, we are not sailors."

"The beasts are not ours to dispose of. They belong to the senate and people of Rome," Eros protested.

"It is all one whether the beasts escape, die of starvation, drown, or are eaten by savages. Irrespective, they will be no less dead. None of them is likely to survive what remains of the journey to Rome. If the senate and people wish to safeguard their property, I encourage them to take personal responsibility for doing so."

Eros scowled. "You seem to have forgotten, Crixus, that it is at the emperor's direct order that we convey the beasts to Rome."

"No, Eros. We travel to the capital because *Bestia* was ordered to provide someone to advise Titus on his upcoming games. I was picked only because Berossus disliked me. It is obvious that you and Romo were chosen to conduct me thither because Berossus holds you in equal contempt. The inclusion of beasts were merely an afterthought. The senate and people of Rome know little, and care even less, of our existence."

"So, you simply intend to yield to the old man?"

"I intend to consult the men. They will decide how best to proceed, for it is their lives which are at stake."

"You are determined to secure your own destruction," Eros groused as he stalked off.

"THE BEASTS ARE A BURDEN that mean nothing to me," a legionnaire named Quintus affirmed. "I would cook and eat them myself. If those are the barbarians' terms, give the creatures to them."

"Quintus' thoughts are a reflection of my own," added an animal handler. Several others nodded in agreement.

"I can scarcely credit what my ears are telling me. None of you is worthy to be called 'Roman'," Eros snapped. "Crixus urges you to meekly barter your honor for a crust of bread and you show yourselves willing to comply without protest! Better that we slice the noses and ears from the womenfolk of these worthless savages who make bold to dictate terms to the masters of the world. Every one of you curs has taken leave of both his senses and his courage!"

"Do you know how to pilot a boat, Eros?" the animal handler pointedly asked, "for I do not."

"I am a soldier, not a hireling," Eros scowled. "After witnessing the mutilation of their wives, daughters, and mothers, however, you will find the remaining savages eager to convey us wherever we dictate."

"Like as not, they will promptly abandon us on a sandbar at their earliest opportunity, leaving us stranded and helpless. Or, more likely still, they will barter us to pirates," Crixus remarked. "What then?"

"We then slit the throats of as many of the bastards as necessary to convince them of their folly."

"And, when we finally run out of throats to slit, will we remain less stranded?" one of the men asked.

"Pirates will undoubtedly slit *our* throats first," another added.

"Men," Crixus counseled, "it was merely a caprice of fate that Romo chose me to lead you in his absence. But he appointed me your guide, not your lord. I know better than to request, nor do I expect, that you sacrifice your honor for an illusory gain. It is for that reason that I earnestly solicit your guidance on the matter presently before us. If it is your recommendation that we follow Eros' advice, notwithstanding how imprudent I may personally find it, and secure the barbarians' cooperation by force, you will find me ready to comply. You need only advise me. Otherwise, inform me how you think it best to proceed."

Quintus was the first to respond. "Eros' suggestion, though appealing to my martial instincts, is certain to harden the Aethiops against us. Moreover, most of the animals have already perished, so the loss of the rest will be a small thing. As I stated before, those still alive are a hardship that serve only to impede us. I see no disadvantage to giving the surviving beasts to the savages if doing so will expedite the completion of our journey."

"We have no assurance that the barbarians will honor their word," Eros countered.

"That cannot be gainsaid. But, in that event, they still have throats to slit."

Another spoke up. "Quintus speaks prudently. If we spurn the barbarians and proceed blindly northward, the remaining animals will die, anyway, and we will have received nothing in the bargain. We have not fared well on this mission and may suffer the same fate as the beasts without the assistance of the Aethiops."

"We, ourselves, can eat our remaining animals if we resume the journey to Rome on our own," a third opined. "We do not need their help."

"We are still very far from Rome," Crixus responded. "All the animals will be consumed long before we arrive there. What, then, shall we eat? In addition to transport, our hosts promise to feed and provision us for the entire journey upriver to the *Mare Nostrum*. Furthermore, they undoubtedly know the location of channels that can be used to skirt the pirates on Elephantine island."

"You are all fools. Especially you, Crixus, because you pretend to lead these men."

All eyes turned toward Eros.

"Do you not hear yourselves? Why do you even consider striking a bargain with these savages? The best way to secure the cooperation of Rome's enemies is at the point of a sword, not through idle words and discourse."

"I have seen nothing to convince me these people are either the enemies, or the friends, of Rome. Enmity is one thing, indifference, another."

"Indeed? Why, then, do they not offer to assist us unconditionally?"

"Because, unlike you, Eros, they are shrewd. It is plain their headman cares more about the welfare of his people than about Rome's prestige, an *ultra mare* of which he knows only by reputation through the tales of travelers."

"Yet, you would treat with such ignorant brutes?" Eros laughed with scorn.

"I would treat with anyone who expresses a willingness to keep us alive and aid in the completion of our mission."

"The old man simply tells you what you wish to hear," Eros rejoined.

Crixus shrugged. "As I said, he is shrewd. If you possessed a tithe of that old man's cleverness you, also, would tell me what I wish to hear."

"I am certain that you have no desire to hear my words, Crixus, though they hardly remain a mystery to you."

"What of the beasts?" another legionnaire interrupted the barbed exchange.

Crixus turned to him. "We will do what is best for all of us."

"It is best for all of us that we proceed to Rome straightaway," the other man declared.

"I AM CERTAIN I CAN SMELL the sea," Senecio excitedly remarked.

"I think we are still far distant," Neocles tiredly responded as they plodded northward.

"Perhaps, but the air seems different: denser, heavier. You cannot sense it?"

"I sense only my blistered feet."

Four days had passed since Yam's assault on the column. Although the men of *Bestia* now marched in formation and fully armed, and Berossus established a perimeter with pickets each night, no further attacks had occurred, nor had the men encountered any additional native peoples.

"I overheard Berossus say that it is probable the Aethiops will attempt another ambush before we reach the coast. I hope he is wrong."

"I do not understand 'probable'," Neocles replied. "The probability of anything occurring remains an immutable constant because it is always 50-50. Either something will occur, or it will not. The barbarians will attack us, or they will not...it is impossible to act by halves. It is foolhardy to brood over something that is as likely never to happen as to happen."

Senecio frowned. "I confess I never thought of it in that manner. Do you think Berossus a fool because he remains vigilant against another attack?"

"No. It is equally probable that the barbarians will attack us as that they will not. Berossus is certainly no fool because he is mindful of that possibility. That is the least of it. He is a fool because he betrayed his only stalwart friend."

"What are you talking about? Who did Berossus betray?"

"Corvo."

"Corvo?" Senecio exclaimed. "He was killed in the barbarians' raid!"

"Just so, though I believe it unlikely that Corvo died at their hands."

With that pronouncement, Neocles lapsed into silence.

TEN

"YOU WERE NOT KIDDING WHEN you said your ruins were a million miles from anywhere!" Mosi shouted over the engine noise of the lurching bakkie.

"Yeah, they're pretty hard to get to," Laidlaw responded through gritted teeth as the vehicle bottomed-out in a hole. "I wouldn't even have known about them if Moses hadn't told me."

Mosi glanced rearward where Moses and Smoke sat, gripping the roll bar of the bucking vehicle. Smoke grinned at him. Laidlaw downshifted as he guided the vehicle down a steep bank into a dry riverbed.

"Still, it seems odd that no one has been to them before," Mosi continued.

"Moses' people have been to them, of course. Undoubtedly other tribes, too. I just don't know how many Anglos have visited the ruins over the years 'cause the locals are tight-lipped about them and they're hard to get to." Laidlaw looked at Mosi and smiled. "As you see!"

"Why are the locals so protective of them?"

Laidlaw guided the vehicle around a boulder in the dry stream bed. "Not sure 'protective' is the right word. More like 'afraid' of them. Moses told me that his people consider the ruins taboo, bad medicine. I think because they're so old, but who knows?"

"So, why did Moses tell you about them?"

"He said there was lots of game in the vicinity of the ruins because nobody hunts there. Guess he figured I could finally be trusted with the secret."

"Have you taken any clients out to them yet?"

"Just one. A client from Russia who I've known forever and trust absolutely."

"Well," Mosi smiled. "It appears that I am in exclusive company, indeed! I'm flattered, Alex. Really."

"Well, irrespective of whoever originally built them, the ruins are your patrimony, Mosi. Who could possibly have a better claim to them?"

Mosi swiveled his head around to scan the surrounding terrain. "Are we getting close?"

"Kinda." Laidlaw slowed in order to guide the vehicle over a berm and out of the riverbed.

Mosi laughed. "'Kinda'? How far is that, exactly?"

"Well, we'll get there before nightfall, anyway," Laidlaw assured him.

THE SUN DIPPED BELOW THE horizon twenty minutes before they finally bumped to a dusty halt. Moses and Smoke immediately sprang to the ground from their cramped perch in the rear of the bakkie. Both glanced warily at the ruins, fifty yards away. Laidlaw and Mosi climbed from the vehicle more slowly.

With his hands on his hips, Mosi surveyed the site in the fading light. "So, these are your ruins. I'm not sure what I expected, but I'm surprised to see intact walls, or at least portions of them."

Laidlaw walked to his side. "As far as I can tell, the surviving walls are mud brick coated with gesso, which more-or-less protected them from the elements. That's my guess, anyway."

"And you're convinced they're Roman and not, say, Arab?"

"Well, my buddy, Greg, and I found a bunch of Latin inscriptions. And, like I said, the knife I found is inscribed in Latin with the name of the guy who owned it."

"That is amazing, Alex. It must be thrilling to actually hold something that was owned by an ancient Roman!" Mosi paused and grinned. "Or an ancient someone, anyway! What do you suppose the Romans were doing so deep into Africa?"

"That's the $64,000 question. All I can figure is that they were collecting animals for the *venationes*."

"The animal fights?"

"Yeah. Don't know why else they'd be here. Why don't you poke around a bit while I set up camp and there's still a little light?" Laidlaw suggested. "We can start exploring in earnest tomorrow morning."

"Splendid! I would like to find a knife like yours."

"Well, I make no promises, but ya never know."

Mosi paused. "Alex, are we doing anything illegal just by being here?"

"Honestly, Mosi, I have no idea. But it seems to me these ruins belong to your country, and by extension, you. Provided we don't do anything to damage them which, of course, we won't, I don't see a problem."

The other man nodded, thoughtfully. "Do you intend to tell anyone else about them?"

"At some point I'll probably have to. But the moment that happens, they'll be cordoned off while the powers-that-be...governments, universities, museums, galleries, bureaucrats, collectors, grifters and hustlers of every stripe...start jockeying for control of the ruins so they can snag their share of the antiquities racket, carve out a piece of the action, and cash-in on the resulting profits. This may be one of the last times anyone actually gets to visit these ruins before they're officially declared off-limits. The Egyptian government long ago sealed off all but a handful of pyramids and temples in that country. If you want access to any of the remaining sites, and there are hundreds of them, you have to apply for special permits, pony-up hefty fees, hire and pay for official government escorts, and jump through a bunch of bureaucratic hoops, hat-in-hand. Everybody and his brother is dining at that trough and there are still no guarantees that your application will be approved. Everything depends on greasing the right palms."

"I fear you may be right about the fate of your ruins," Mosi sighed. He began picking his way toward them. "Keep an ear out in case I bump into the ghost of an ancient Roman! Perhaps even the fellow who owned the knife you found!"

"Will do," Laidlaw laughed as he began dragging camping supplies from the rear of the vehicle.

DINNER CONSISTED OF IMPALA steaks broiled over the campfire, baked potatoes, and hot bread, all washed down with plenty of cold beer. Mosi leaned his head back in his camp chair and stared at the glittering firmament. An ember popped from the fire and landed on the toe of his boot. It glowed momentarily before fading to nothingness. Somewhere in the darkness a solitary lion moaned, followed by a chorus of howls from jackals.

"I tell you, my friend, this is the life," Mosi murmured. He lifted his head after a moment and took another sip of beer. “Where are Moses and Smoke?”

“They always camp off by themselves. They don't like being too close to the ruins and Moses complains that I snore louder than a chainsaw,” Laidlaw chuckled. “We'll see 'em in the morning.”

“Speaking of sleeping, do we have to worry about being eaten by anything during the night?”

“I'll keep a small fire going all night. Aside from disliking the smell of humans, animals, including carnivores, are afraid of fire. They'll leave us alone.”

“Excellent. I do not relish having my face eaten off by a hyena while I sleep,” Mosi declared.

“You've been watching too many Jungle Jim movies,” Laidlaw smiled. He squatted next to the fire and poked at it with a stick, causing a swirl of sparks to float upward like stars. He tossed another chunk of mopane wood onto the embers before resuming his seat. “You gettin' sleepy?”

“Not a bit. Just relishing the evening and your company.” Mosi paused to drain his beer. “But who is 'Jungle Jim'?”

“Originally, a comic strip, then a bunch of old movies about the adventures of an African 'white hunter'. The movies regurgitated just about every cliché about Africa you can think of: cannibals, head-hunting savages boiling people in big pots, shrunken heads, poisoned darts, rampaging elephants, ferocious gorillas, gigantic boa constrictors, you name it.”

“You will forgive me, Alex, but these ruins almost sound like a cliché: an ancient, forgotten city discovered in the heart of contemporary Africa. How many Hollywood films do you suppose have been produced with that as a plot element?"

"Well, I can think of one right off the top of my head," Laidlaw mused. "*Legend of the Lost*, with John Wayne and Sophia Loren. I probably saw that movie a dozen times as a kid just to ogle Sophia Loren's cleavage!"

Mosi laughed. "I daresay there exists no better reason for a young man to attend the cinema."

"Or, for that matter, an *old* man," Laidlaw added.

Mosi reached into the cooler next to his chair, fished out another can of beer, and held it aloft. "To old men," he toasted.

"To old men and old friends," Laidlaw reciprocated.

MOSES AND SMOKE MATERIALIZED in camp just before dawn the following morning. From the battered and blackened steel pot resting on the coals of the campfire, Laidlaw automatically poured two mugs of hot coffee and handed one to each of them. He then settled into his camp chair and sipped from his own mug. The two trackers walked to the bakkie and sat on its bench seat, where they conversed in low tones while drinking their coffee.

Mosi wandered over, plopped into a canvas chair, and yawned.

"How'd you sleep?" Laidlaw inquired.

"Like a dead man. I am very happy to report that a hyena did not eat my face off as I slept."

"I got up during the night to attend to the fire and startled a serval that was checking out the camp." Laidlaw took another sip of coffee. "But no hyenas."

"What was he doing?"

"Just nosing around, bein' a cat. He split the instant he saw me."

"They're not dangerous?"

Laidlaw shook his head. "Naw. A lot of people keep 'em as pets."

Mosi poured himself a cup of coffee and sampled it. "You make excellent coffee, Alex."

"I can't take any credit for it. Everything tastes better outdoors."

The men sat in contemplative silence, staring into the small campfire, the murmured conversation of the two trackers in the background the only sound. Moses must have said something funny because Smoke softly laughed.

"What shall we do today?" Mosi roused himself from his pleasant reverie.

"Well, I'll start breakfast in a coupla minutes, then we'll check out the ruins. You hungry?"

"I could eat a hyena!" Mosi declared.

"Unfortunately, hyena isn't on the menu. How 'bout scrambled eggs, fried potatoes, and hot bread? I know it isn't hyena, but think you could gag some of it down?"

"I suppose I have no choice but to make do because I'm at your mercy," Mosi sighed with mock solemnity. "If I make too much of a fuss, you may simply abandon me out here." He leaned forward in his chair, retrieved the coffee pot from the coals, and topped-off his mug. "I'll just have to console myself with your splendid coffee."

"We have plenty of coffee" Laidlaw laughed, "in the event you require extra consoling."

"I WONDER WHEN THIS PLACE was built," Mosi pondered.

"It looks smaller than when Greg and I first saw it. Maybe it's the time of day or we were just overwhelmed by it."

"It *is* overwhelming, Alex. Think about it. Just like we were talking last night...an actual lost city! It's like something from a novel or a movie."

The two men stood atop a slight rise more-or-less in the center of the ruins. They'd spent the morning exploring the site, though had failed to find anything as spectacular as Laidlaw's knife. There was, however, no shortage of broken stone blocks, all of them eroded and most of them half-buried in the soft earth.

"Look." Mosi pointed northward. "That line of trees follows an old river bed. At some point, the river probably flowed right past this place, which would make sense. The ground is swampy because the water table is still quite shallow, even though the river no longer flows above ground."

"What do you suppose this place was, Mosi?"

"I'm no scholar, Alex, but I agree that it looks Roman. Everything we've seen is in Latin, including what you said about the writing on the knife you found. I think what you said is probably right. It was an entrepot for the collection of animals. What else could it have been? The Romans wouldn't have built a town so far from anyplace else...what would be the point? Besides, from what I can see, it really doesn't look big enough to have been a city...perhaps it was a fortress of some kind."

"That's what I think," Laidlaw concurred. "Nothing else makes sense. How big do you think it was?"

Mosi surveyed the ruins in silence before responding. "Not very. A hectare? It's hard to say."

"I wonder what ultimately happened to it."

"Well, it was undoubtedly abandoned at some point, but experts will have to determine when and why."

Laidlaw smiled, dourly. "Yep. Of course, once the 'experts' take over, it'll all be over but the crying because they'll immediately put out the 'No Trespassing!' 'Violators Will Be Prosecuted!' signs. Nobody but the highest bidders will be able to get near this place."

"I never took you for such a cynic, Alex!" Mosi laughed.

"Cynic or realist. I get those two things mixed up," Laidlaw shrugged.

"If this place was a fort, who do you suppose 'Crixus' was? Its commander?"

"Maybe. But I can't believe he left his knife behind on purpose. Something must've happened."

"Would that your knife could talk." Mosi spoke for both of them.

"Let's keep looking around. Who knows what's still here that we may yet stumble onto. If it was a fort, they may have left behind other knives or weapons."

"I would not mind finding something remarkable like that," Mosi confessed.

"There's a shovel in the bakkie if you need it."

THEY PROBED THE RUINS UNTIL midday, when they took a lunch break. Laidlaw stood at a folding table to prepare cold sandwiches using the leftover meat from the previous night's antelope. Mosi relaxed in a camp chair with a can of cold beer.

"I tell you, Alex, I could probably be persuaded to lug off one of those carved lintels for my garden. The problem is getting the damned thing to my house." He looked around. "Where are my brothers, Moses and Smoke? I've not seen any sign of them since breakfast."

"Out scouting," Laidlaw responded without looking up. "Like I said, they don't like hanging around the ruins. They'll be back for supper." He carried a plate containing a sandwich over to Mosi, who placed his beer on the ground beside his chair. Holding his own plate, Laidlaw plopped into the chair next to Mosi.

"Although I really didn't expect to find another knife, I'm still slightly disappointed," Mosi confessed before taking a bite of sandwich.

Laidlaw took a drink of bottled water. "Well, we'll get back at it after we eat. The last thing I want is to listen to you complain about it all the way back to town!" he laughed.

Mosi chewed contemplatively. "So, my friend, what do you intend to do after today? About these ruins, I mean. They've evidently managed to stay under wraps since forever...do you hope to maintain the *status quo*?"

"I've been going back-and-forth in my head about that. Before I do anything, I'll have a sit-down with Moses and Smoke. They're the ones who originally told me about this place and I need to know what they think about it. Even though the local tribes have probably known about these ruins since the day they were built, they've managed to keep 'em a secret. If they want to keep it that way, that's fine by me."

"And if they don't?"

Laidlaw unconsciously frowned. “I haven't gotten that far, Mosi. If Moses, Smoke, or any of the tribes don't give damn, one way or the other, I suppose my civic duty as a good citizen is to inform the world about the ruins. But I'm torn because I'm afraid that, once the bureaucrats and academics get wind of this place, the graft-machine will kick into overdrive. The ruins have been here, minding their own business, for as long as anyone knows. I'm inclined to keep it that way.

“I understand your ambivalence, Alex. I don't know what I would do in your place, but I share your distrust in government and academic hotshots.”

“Well, I'm just gonna back-burner the whole thing for the time being 'cause I have bigger fish to fry,” Laidlaw commented.

Mosi's curiosity was piqued. “Oh? What's going on?”

“That conference the Minister of Wildlife is putting together...the one we talked about.”

“Saving the rhinos and unicorns?”

“That's the one. All licensed professional hunters in the country, plus the usual assortment of citizens-for-good, are supposed to be there: academics, various self-appointed experts on who-knows-what, activists, hangers-on, political wannabes, bureaucrats, businessmen. I expect it'll turn out to be your typical symposium where there's plenty of speechifying, nothing gets accomplished, and everyone agrees to meet again in the near future so they can get more face-time on the local media and load up at the buffet."

"Yes, I know exactly what you are talking about!" Mosi laughed. "My tax dollars at work. Please enjoy a cucumber sandwich for me, Alex, so I can at least get some vicarious pleasure from the affair."

"Of course. I'll think of you as I help myself to seconds on the brie."

Mosi finished his sandwich and drained his beer. "When is the Minister's bash supposed to happen? I've heard none of the details."

Laidlaw shrugged. "It's still in the talking stage...they're probably in the process of finding the right caterer. But I want to get the conference behind me before I do anything about these ruins, if I do anything at all."

"I agree. 'God is with those that are patient', the Holy Quran reminds us," Mosi smiled. "The ruins will still be here."

THEY COMBED THE RUINS UNTIL TWILIGHT, finding nothing new. The two men trudged back to camp, where a smiling Moses and Smoke lounged in the bakkie.

"Salam aleikum," Smoke greeted them.

"Salam aleikum," Mosi responded.

"What did you find, mabwana?" Moses inquired from his perch.

"Just some carvings and whatnot. No piles of gold or bags of jewels, I'm sorry to say."

"There is nothing at this place but dead men and ghosts, mabwana."

"Moses, do you know how old these ruins are?" Mosi interjected.

"Jinns built them at the beginning of time," Moses solemnly replied.

"All the carvings we found are in Latin. Do you know if Romans ever lived here?"

Moses shook his head. "No Romans. Only jinns."

"Well, if jinns built this place, they packed their bags and blew town a long time ago," Laidlaw laconically observed.

"Have your people ever found things here?" Mosi continued to probe.

"My people do not come here. No one comes here."

"Moses, if only jinns lived here, why do you say they're inhabited by ghosts and dead men?" Laidlaw interjected. "What men?"

"My grandfather told me stories about this place that his grandfather told him. He said that his fathers before him saw men here but did not know who they were." Moses paused. "They were not men, mabwana. They were jinns."

"Could've been just about anybody at any time during the last coupla centuries, or even prior to that," Laidlaw reasoned aloud to Mosi. "Other tribes passing through the area, hunters, explorers...who the hell knows? On the other hand, it's just as likely that Moses' grandpa was creeped out by the place and was just whistlin' past the graveyard. He saw what he expected to see."

Perhaps," Mosi said, "though it seems unlikely that absolutely no one ever blundered into these ruins after they were abandoned by the Romans." He paused. "Or by whoever abandoned them."

"Yeah, that's where those 'experts' we talked about come in."

"You are referring to the army of rogues and scoundrels that will descend on this place once people learn of its existence?" Mosi grinned.

"Yeah, *those* experts. There are as many opinions as there are experts, 100 per-cent of whom agree with whoever happens to be funding them. To use one of Henry Kissinger's expressions, an expert is 'someone who articulates the needs of those in power'. That, of course, includes the need to enlarge their bank accounts."

Mosi mocked surprise. "You can't possibly be suggesting that experts are no more than hired guns!"

"You're absolutely right, I would never suggest such a thing...far from it. I'm explicitly stating it," Laidlaw corrected him.

"I fear that I may be unable to resign myself to such disappointing news."

"Shocking, I know, old friend. It's almost too much to bear. I suggest we commiserate over a cold beer," Laidlaw proposed.

“Alex, you read my mind!” Mosi clapped him on the shoulder and headed for the beer cooler.

In Primis Anno Regnantibus Imperator Caesar Titus Vespasianus (80 CE)

"YOU HAVE MADE A FAIR BARGAIN, Roman," Ra cackled.

"Do not fool yourself," Crixus responded. "Had my men decided instead to cut your throat and take your boats, I would have done so with alacrity. You were fortunate they urged a more clement resolution."

Ra smiled, cunningly. "Your shabby host seems scarcely able to fend for itself, far less to coordinate such an attack. But, no matter. We have struck a bargain."

"How soon will we depart?"

The old man rubbed his grizzled chin as he thought. "Two days hence. You may set up your camp near the river until then. My people will provide food for you. Do not allow your men to approach the village."

"Agreed."

With that, Crixus turned to report to his companions.

"TWO DAYS?" EROS SPAT. "The old man is playing us for fools, Crixus. Worse, you indulge it. The barbarians will seize our beasts and give us nothing in return.

"Do you seriously believe they intend to kill all of us in exchange for a few starving beasts?" Junius asked. "For what possible reason would they risk such a foolish stunt? The barbarians are not so stupid that they would even attempt it."

"Because slaughtering us will render it unnecessary for the barbarians to transport us to the *Mare Nostrum*, you fool!" Eros snarled.

"Yes," Junius acknowledged. "But they would also risk the annihilation of their entire village should they fail."

"The savages betray their contempt for Roman arms, " Eros asserted. "They need to be disabused of their impudence."

"Have you so quickly forgotten, Eros, that I made an agreement with the old man?" Crixus asked. "You would have me violate my oath with blood?"

"An 'agreement' with Aethiops is not worthy of the name. One might just as well compact with a pig or a toad. Such bargains may be safely ignored because they are *void ab initio.*"

"Explain to me how slaying the barbarians will profit us, Eros," a legionnaire invited. "By doing so, would we not deprive ourselves of the services of those who have placed themselves at our disposal to safely pilot us downriver?"

"That is my thinking, also," Crixus concurred, "though Eros would have us believe it the very pinnacle of wisdom to piss in our own well."

"I expect they will either poison us or attempt to slaughter us while we sleep," Eros grumbled.

"We will post sentries to ensure we are not molested during the night. As for poisoning us, you need not eat any of the food they prepare for us, Eros. In any case, I would not have entered into any agreement with them without the consent of all present. The matter is therefore settled. Move the men a *stadion* upriver and erect camp," he directed.

Eros started to reply, thought the better of it, and stalked off.

A HANDFUL OF SCRUFFY EMISSARIES from Ra's village appeared at dawn the following morning to collect the surviving animals.

"What do you intend to do with them, you stupid ape? Eat them?" a legionnaire amiably inquired of a bearded man clad in a tattered djellaba. The man, unable to understand Latin, stared at him without comprehension. The Roman gestured toward a flimsy cage containing mewing serval cubs, two of which were already dead, and tried again. "Will you eat them?" Still no response. He turned away in disgust.

"Eros is right. These fucking Aethiops are the stupidest, sorriest lot I have ever seen," he muttered.

Ra's envoys half-herded, half-dragged the ambulatory animals back to their village. The sole remaining elephant calf, sickly and reduced to a mockery of jutting bones and flaccid skin, trundled after them. Other men carried in their arms, or in woven baskets or cages, creatures too weak to stand unassisted, most already near death because of starvation and dehydration.

"Good riddance to the beasts *and* the barbarians," the legionnaire glowered to a companion who joined him to watch the transfer.

"What do you suppose they want with the beasts?" mused latter.

"I asked one of the ignoramuses but he only gaped at me as though stupefied. I thought the fool had taken leave of his senses."

"The gods have not seen fit to favor savages with the power of reason," the other legionnaire stated with authority.

"Damn them. I hope they choke on the beasts."

"No, not before they conduct us away from this place, unless you fancy spending your remaining days marooned in this *Avernus*."

THE FLEET THAT RA ASSEMBLED to transport the Romans downriver consisted of a decaying *melange* of watercraft: decrepit boats, open to the elements, lacking both decks and cabins; lumbering rafts fashioned of woven reeds and sticks, possessing neither sails nor rudders. Some of the boats possessed rudimentary keels and proto-lateen sails, others were simple coracles.

"The barbarians expect us to travel in these?" Junius sputtered, incredulously.

"None will survive the voyage," Eros laconically observed. "It is unfortunate that you fools did not heed my warnings. You will have ample time to rue your stupidity, at least until you drown."

"So, Eros, you decline to accompany us to the *Mare Nostrum*?" Junius asked in surprise.

"Don't be an even greater fool! I can remain behind in this wilderness and be shamefully murdered and eaten by heathens, or I can die among my comrades as a Roman. Which alternative do you suppose I will choose?"

Both men lapsed into silence as Crixus approached. Eros pointed to the collection of watercraft dragged halfway up the bank of the *Nilus*.

"The fruits of your shrewd bargain with the savages," he mockingly laughed.

Crixus surveyed the eclectic flotilla. "I suppose we are fortunate they were able to scrape together this many."

"Just so, provided you consider a death-sentence 'fortunate'." Eros said.

Crixus turned to him and cocked his eyebrow. "You cannot swim?"

"Had I wished to swim, I would have chosen to be a *nautae*, not a legionnaire."

Their discourse was interrupted when Ra shambled up. “Greetings, Romans.”

Eros immediately confronted him. “You expect to convey us to the *Mare Nostrum* in these?”

“I expect nothing, Roman,” Ra shrugged. “You may swim downriver if you find that more to your liking. It is less than nothing to me.”

“How will you guide rudderless rafts once they are laden with men and supplies?” Crixus asked, dubiously.

“My men will pole the rafts in the shallows. They will be towed behind other boats, or controlled directly from the shore by means of ropes, in deeper, swifter water,” Ra replied.

“What of the cataracts?”

“What of them? The most fearsome cataract is easily circumvented. The others are of no consequence and there are channels in the river to bypass even those,” Ra assured him. “Do not concern yourselves.”

“You will accompany us?”

Ra shook his head. “Though I have made the journey northward countess times during my long life, I am now an old man and of meager use. One of my sons will serve as your guide, along with other men from my village.”

“How do we know they can be trusted and will not simply abandon us in transit?” Eros snapped.

Ra grinned a toothless grin. “Travelers with empty pockets can whistle in a robber's face. Putting aside our bargain with your headman, you are impoverished dross possessing nothing that we desire. Our only wish is to be rid of you. Furthermore, what possible fear could valiant Romans have for a smattering of unarmed Africans? Do you feel yourselves unequal to the challenge of protecting yourselves against any threat they might pose? I fear more for my kinsmen that you do for your companions."

"Do not taunt me, old man," Eros retorted. "It is not fear that prompts my words, but prudence. In contrast to Romans, the treachery of savages is well known."

"Having never been to Rome, I know little of treachery or savages," Ra replied. "But why would we risk betraying you, Roman? Conducting you to your destination is a trifle compared to provoking the fury of the gods arising out of the betrayal of our word."

"The old man speaks true," Junius declared. "Though I do not know what gods these barbarians recognize, *no* god will tolerate such a breach of trust." Curious members of their caravan who drifted over nodded in silent agreement. They looked expectantly at Eros.

"For all any of us knows, these barbarians worship their own anuses," the latter scowled. "I have already voiced my opposition to this whole mad enterprise, but honor compels me to accompany all of you to your deaths at the hands of these wretches."

"'Honor', or the prospect of being murdered and eaten by heathens should you remain behind?" Junius pointedly inquired. Eros cast him a withering look.

“At what hour do you suggest we depart?” Crixus asked Ra.

“It does not matter, for the Iteru flows ceaselessly. However, it will prove easier to navigate the waters during the daylight hours.”

Crixus turned to Eros. “Assemble the men. We cast off as quickly as they collect their things. Ra's people will provision the boats in the meantime.”

“Did you not just hear the old man say that it is best to delay our departure?” Eros rejoined.

“No, that is not what I heard. Of course, you are welcome to linger as long as you desire.” Crixus turned back to Ra. “Gather your pilots and lay adequate food aboard the boats. We leave forthwith.”

The old man nodded and shuffled away.

Crixus frowned at Eros. “Why do you remain here, standing about? I have issued orders. Obey them.”

“Your play-acting as commandant is becoming wearisome, Crixus,” Eros snapped.

“I previously invited you to assume command, though you lacked the will to accept. Do you still?”

“I do not intend to pollute my record by sharing your blunders, Crixus. The senate will hold you, alone, responsible for those.”

“Of that I am mindful and do not require your gloating reminders. While you hungrily await the senate's imprecation, however, see to it that my orders are promptly obeyed.”

With that, Crixus turned and strode away. He ardently hoped Neocles and Aulus remained safe at the *castrum*.

RA'S SON, HARKUF, A MAN OF about 40, distributed Crixus' men across the various watercraft. Most of the supplies for the voyage downriver...burlap sacks of barley and dried goat meat, piles of firewood...were lashed to the rafts. The men, themselves, were seated in the boats' cramped interiors. Ra stood close by, superintending the preparations as the *Nilus* gently lapped against the hulls of the watercraft.

"By Jupiter, this is the most disagreeable conveyance I have ever been forced to suffer!" one of the men loudly complained. "I feel as though I am wedged into a coffin and can neither stand upright nor change my position to ease my suffering. I see, too late, that Crixus was played the fool by these barbarians, exactly as Eros warned!"

"No one is compelling you to proceed by boat, Roman. I invite you to proceed to your destination afoot, if you believe that to be preferable," Ra suggested.

The other man glared at him. "Does your son at least speak our tongue?"

"He speaks it well enough, though he is not as adept as me," Ra informed him. "All of the men from my village who go with you speak at least a little of your language."

"Will we actually be able to communicate with any of them?"

"I am confident you will manage," Ra shrugged. "Is there no obstacle the invincible Romans have proven unable to surmount?"

Hearing the squabble, Crixus approached. "What is the reason for this clamor? How quickly do we depart?"

"No clamor, Roman. One of your men was merely speaking to me." Ra glanced at the surrounding bustle. "You will be ready to embark shortly."

"How long will the voyage take?" the first man interjected. "I will not be able to maintain this painful body position for very long."

"Harkhuf will regularly beach the boats to enable you to relieve yourselves and move about. And you will also camp each night on dry land," Ra informed him. "Notwithstanding your carping, you will not be as uncomfortable as you suppose. Did I not know better, I would think I was transporting a bevy of quarrelsome women rather than a company of Roman legionnaiers."

Crixus laughed aloud at Ra's riposte. "How long will the journey take?"

"Two months, perhaps more, perhaps less."

"You have provided adequate food for that period?"

“There is food enough,” Ra said. “Nor does the Iteru want for fish. Your men will not starve.”

“Your men have made this trip before?”

Ra smiled, wistfully. “Countless time, Roman. I, myself, first made the journey upriver while I was still sucking at my mother's tit.”

“For what purpose do your people travel the river?”

“Trading, ferrying travelers from the interior to the cities that line its banks.”

“Are there many such travelers?”

Ra eyed Crixus with suspicion. “What is that to you, Roman?”

“Nothing,” Crixus indifferently responded. “I ask only because we encountered many perils and suffered greatly over the course of our trek. But I expect that is the lot of all who undertake hazardous journeys.”

“I know not and care even less,” Ra distractedly informed him. “If wayfarers arrive here and desire transport downriver, we will accommodate them...provided they possess either coin or goods to barter. Whatever travails the gods have decreed for them before they reach my village are not my concern, for we are mere playthings to them.” He turned to face Crixus. “Gather your remaining men. You are ready to leave us.”

Crixus glanced about for Eros, who was not within sight. “Yes.” He hastened off.

“I AM SURE OF IT NOW,” Senecio confidently asserted.

“Of what are you sure?”

“The sea. You cannot help but sense it.”

Neocles stopped mid-stride and cocked his head slightly. “If you say so.” He resumed walking.

“We have traveled at least 150 miles since we were attacked, I am sure of it! Unless we have been traveling in circles, we must be nearing the sea.”

“As I said, if you say so. I know only that I am tired of marching,” Crixus muttered.

“I wonder if Berossus has ships already awaiting our arrival?” Senecio pondered.

“How could he?” Neocles scoffed, “unless he rode Pegasus to the sea and returned while we slept. I do not expect to find any ships present if and when we finally arrive at the *Pontus Herculis*, nor do I know how many of us will even survive to seek passage on such ships as may exist.”

Though it had engaged in only the single skirmish since vacating the *castrum*, the ranks of *Legio XVI Bestia* continued to wither. Six additional men had succumbed to disease, infections, or accidents since Yam's ambush.

“That does not matter, Neocles, for the gods continue to favor you and me. It is plain they intend to preserve us for some purpose known only to them.”

“If the gods wish to do us in, they first make us stupid,” the other man dryly remarked.

"Undoubtedly," Senecio acknowledged, "though I would much rather be a live fool than a dead philosopher."

Neocles nodded. "It is a fact that security comes too late to the dead."

"My only desire is to secure a berth on a *navis oneraria* and hie myself back to Rome," Senecio countered.

"Will you ask to be reassigned to another legion?"

"Of course. I have but six years of service remaining. After that, I will be awarded my *praemia*. I will then take a fat wife who will produce many children to take care of me in my old age."

"I overheard Berossus say there is a surfeit of land in Africa," Neocles jested.

Senecio scowled. "I have had my fill of Africa...*more* than my fill."

"A man with wife and children does them no service," Neocles affirmed, "for they are mere playthings to the gods."

"It is not *their* weal that concerns me, but my own," Senecio snorted. "How long do you think the voyage to Rome will take?"

"All depends of whether there will be ships to carry us, or how long we will have to wait until there are. After that, the gods, alone, know."

"What will you do in Rome, Neocles? We should seek reassignment together."

Neocles reflected before responding. "I intend to reunite with Crixus, if he is still alive."

"Why would he not be? But, how do you propose to locate him in Rome?"

If he still lives, Crixus will be attached to the emperor's court. He and Titus fought cheek-by-jowl against the Jews. Whatever his other failings, Titus does not forget his mates."

"'If he still lives'...you fear Crixus dead?" Senecio asked in surprise as they walked.

"Though unencumbered by beasts, we have not had an easy time since quitting the *castrum*. Crixus is certain to have suffered immeasurably more. Berossus never intended him to survive the journey to Rome because he held Crixus and Corvo in equal contempt. Sending Crixus to Rome solved one-half of his problem. Romo's convenient death solved the other half."

"No, you are wrong, Neocles. Berossus held no animosity toward your friend."

"Berossus has animosity toward anyone he considers a threat to his ambitions."

"What 'ambitions'?" Senecio frowned, puzzled.

"It is no secret that Berossus longs to command a legion."

Senecio shrugged. "So? With Corvo dead, perhaps Berossus hopes the senate will appoint him commander of *Bestia*."

"Is it not remarkable how the gods' wishes align themselves so closely with our own?" Neocles wryly noted. "But, Berossus has no interest in *Bestia*. He has his eyes set on a legion quartered in a wealthy province like Egypt or Syria, not in an impoverished backwater like Africa."

Senecio shook his head. "Perhaps, but several others were ordered to Rome in addition to Crixus. Berossus would surely not sacrifice his own comrades in a fit of pique."

"'Pique' has nothing to do with it," Neocles explained. "Berossus desires his own command and will do whatever is necessary to secure it."

"I daresay we will learn soon enough, once we finally reach Rome and you are reunited with your friend."

Berossus stalked down the column, cursing the marching legionnaires.

"Close your fucking mouths!" he roared. "I will personally cut the tongue from the next man who speaks."

Neocles and Senecio cast their eyes downward and marched in silence.

CRIXUS' MEN PUSHED OFF THE eastern bank of *Nilus*, into the river's sluggish current. The muddy water swirled and eddied around the hulls of their watercraft.

"I feel like one of those ancient pharaohs on his fancy barge," Junius beamed to the other men who shared his boat. He swiveled around in an effort to see where the remainder of his companions were arrayed along the surface of the river.

Another legionnaire looked up at the barefoot Nubian who stood at the stern, guiding their craft with a long pole. “What distance will we travel today?” The man ignored the inquiry.

“I do not think he speaks our language,” Junius helpfully suggested.

“All the better. A barbarian has nothing intelligent to say, anyway,” the other man reasoned.

“I think I could quickly get used to this mode of travel,” Junius continued. “This is but the second time I have been on a boat, though it seems to me much preferable to ceaseless overland marches”

“When was the first time?”

“When I crossed the *Mare Nostrum* on a *navis oneraria*. I puked my guts out,” Junius matter-of-factly confided. His companions in the boat nodded but did not otherwise respond.

The men were scattered among watercraft of various sizes and configurations. Crixus occupied one of the larger boats with Junius and two other men. Eros and two of his friends claimed another, smaller craft, for which Crixus was grateful. He was tired of Ero's constant carping.

When Drusus, one of Eros' companions, stepped aboard he looked contemptuously at their boatman. “Can you even read, barbarian?” he sneered.

“No.”

“Then, half your life is wasted,” Drusus scornfully laughed.

The boatman did not deign to respond.

In Crixus' boat, one of his men turned to Harkhuf, “What is the distance to the next cataract?”

“Four or five days,” he sullenly replied.

“Is it perilous?”

“Not for me.”

“You have navigated the cataracts before?”

“Many times. As you see, I am still here, Roman.”

“Are the other boatman as skilled as you?”

“If they survive the cataracts, they are as skilled,” Harkhuf sensibly responded. He turned his attention to guiding their craft.

THE SMALL FLOTILLA DRIFTED DOWN the wide, torpid river, the silence broken only occasionally by the sound of a fish splashing on the surface or the men's muted voices hanging in the humid air. Thick masses of papyrus reeds and water lilies choked the shallows on both sides, while groves of date palms crowded the riverbanks. Resembling massive tree trunks, innumerable crocodiles basked on the shore, the mouths of many of them frozen in a wide yawn, allowing small birds to confidently enter the primordial reptiles' mouths to clean their teeth of accumulated matter. The placid water swirled and eddied around the long poles used by the boatmen to ensure the vessels remained centered in the *Nilus*' deeper, main channel. High above the red sandstone cliffs that paralleled the river, the silhouettes of hawks and vultures could be seen wheeling in the cloudless sky.

"Why are there no hippopotamus?" one of Crixus' colleagues asked Harkhuf.

"Many crocodiles. Crocodiles do not trouble adults but eat their babies. Hippos farther upriver."

"I am told the Egyptians worship crocodiles."

Harkhuf made a wry face. "What do the Egyptians *not* worship? Insects, kine, birds, jackals, stones...I do not understand Egyptians."

"How will we protect ourselves from crocodiles when we camp each night?"

Harkhuf looked at the Roman, incredulously. "We camp where there are no crocodiles. We make fire. All animals fear fire." He paused. "Romans worry too much. Like women."

Though his companion scowled at the rebuff, Crixus laughed out loud.

"These ignorant Nubians forget who they are addressing," the former grumbled.

"No, they know perfectly well," Crixus corrected him. "They are addressing a group of foreign vagabonds who appeared at their village to ask for help and who are at their mercy."

"We are Romans, not 'vagabonds'," the other man snapped.

"Do you suppose it matters one whit to them? For all they care, we could be insects, kine, birds, jackals, or stones."

“Exactly!” The other man triumphantly cried. “You have just confirmed their stupidity, Crixus.”

Crixus laughed again. “For myself, I look forward to being worshiped by the Egyptians.”

IT WAS EVENTIDE WHEN THE remnants of *Legio XVI Bestia* finally surmounted a low, sandy hill and, in the failing light, encountered the wine-dark sea spreading to the horizon before them. In the distance, scattered pin-pricks of campfires glittered on its indistinct shore. Since repelling Yam's attack over two weeks previously, *Bestia's* procession to the east coast of Africa had been uneventful. Still, Berossus remained vigilant. He directed the men to dig a shallow dry moat around the perimeter of their camp each night and posted sentries.

“We will rest here for tonight and march to the sea at first light,” Berossus ordered. “It is certain we will find ships willing to convey us to Arsinoe.”

“So much for having vessels awaiting our arrival,” Neocles muttered to Senecio.

“I am roundly sick of standing guard when I should be sleeping,” Senecio retorted.

“Provided there are actually seaworthy ships down there, this may be the final night we will be forced to do so.”

The two men removed wooden digging tools from their packs and wearily trudged over to join their comrades as they began to excavate the defensive moat that would encompass their camp that night.

Hopefully, for the last time.

ELEVEN

THE CONFERENCE WAS HELD OVER two days in a ballroom at the Airport Hilton, which offered “exceptional room rates,” as well as discounts “to our esteemed guests on our full suite of hotel amenities and services, excepting only the Cleopatra Day Spa and Prester John's Tavern.” The sponsors of the symposium, in conjunction with the Hilton, grandly assured attendees of their unshakable commitment to global sustainability. Consistent with their vow to 'Save the Planet', no printed materials or documents, though highly pertinent to the various presentations at the symposium, would be provided. Attendees were invited to download and print the voluminous materials at their own expense, though there would be no corresponding reduction in the cost of attending the symposium. It was a complete sham, of course, a cost-shifting stratagem intended to fob the burden of printing from the sponsors onto the attendees. No trees were saved, no streams unpolluted, no carbon emissions reduced. Quite the contrary. But a reassuring, if vacuous, pledge of concern for a greener world was apparently all that mattered.

Laidlaw's bland room was located on the sixth floor, two doors down from a clanking ice machine. Although the Minister of Wildlife invited him to attend the symposium more-or-less as a complimentary observer, Laidlaw knew that his professional hunting license, issued by the ministry, would be at risk should he decline to pay his way. Accordingly, he dutifully shelled-out the exorbitant registration fee, which was divided between the ministry, the Hilton, and various other sponsors, to reserve a seat. Laidlaw debated whether to pay extra to copy the reams of symposium materials, but ultimately decided against it. He was dubious of the actual usefulness of scores of white papers, abstracts, studies, diagrams, graphs, pie charts, and Venn diagrams ostensibly analyzing the current status of African wildlife. He figured he could ascertain its status just by looking out the flap of his tent, which is more than most eggheads did.

The Hilton's ballroom had been converted into a lecture hall, with a rostrum at one end and folding banquet tables, one optimistically holding multiple large stainless steel coffee urns and boxes of donuts, occupying much of the room. Additionally, a dozen smaller tables, round and covered with white tablecloths, were aesthetically scattered about. Whoever was in charge of seating arrangements placed Laidlaw at one of the round tables with three strangers. Two of them were black Africans wearing business suits, while the third, Anglo and appreciably younger, was dressed like George Pyper: three-day-old beard, bush jacket with multiple empty cartridge loops and matching khaki shorts, hat with a faux leopard-fur hat band and its brim turned up and snapped to one side, gaiters and hiking boots. He looked like a caricature of what a New York advertising agency trying to sell men's cologne thought an African hunter ought to look like.

"Gentlemen," Laidlaw nodded as he slid his chair out and plopped down.

Thin cardboard rectangles, folded like miniature tents, identified his table companions. The names of the two black guys were both preceded with "Honorable," so they were evidently bigwigs of some kind, though Laidlaw had no idea who they were or what country they hailed from. Both completely ignored him.

The George Pyper lookalike thrust his hand across the table like a spear. "Jocko Vanderbeeke," he announced in a distinct South African accent.

"Alex Laidlaw," he responded as he warily shook Jocko's hand. "Pleasure."

"The pleasure is entirely mine," Jocko assured him, enthusiastically pumping his hand. "I've been looking forward to meeting you, mate...okay if I call you 'Alex'?"

"Might as well...everybody else does," Laidlaw shrugged. He wrestled his hand away. "Why did you want to meet me? Do I owe you money?"

Jocko guffawed. "No, not at all, mate! I'm simply honored to be seated at the same table as someone of your professional reputation."

Laidlaw found his admirer's enthusiasm puzzling. "Well, thank you," he managed to respond. "You're a PH?" Laidlaw made a show of looking about the room, as if searching for someone. He was eager for the symposium to begin, so it could end and he could return to his room at the Europa.

"Not yet. Still jumping through all the hoops."

All African nations which allow sport hunting have established policies and protocols for licensing professional hunters, which vary by country. At the threshold, all require months of rigorous classroom instruction on applicable game laws; import/export regulations; animal identification, morphology, biology, taxonomy, and behavior; firearms and ballistics; emergency medicine and first aid; field preparation and transportation of trophies; and taxidermy. Following successful completion of the academic component of the process, candidates must then serve an apprenticeship under the tutelage of an established professional hunter lasting a few months or, depending on the particular country, several years. Only after successful completion of both the classroom and field portions of the course are they eligible to apply for their PH license. None of this comes cheap. Given that Vanderbeeke was a newbie apparently still in the classroom portion of the curriculum, it was no surprise that Laidlaw had no idea who he was. It also explained why Jocko was dressed like the Crocodile Hunter.

"Well, good luck," Laidlaw lamely responded. He was already bored with his chatty tablemate and hoped the introductory speaker would soon kick things off.

"I expect to finish my classroom studies in a few months and am looking for an established PH to host me," Jocko hinted.

"Uhhhh, yeah. Well, I've been thinking about retiring and am not sure how much longer I'll be in the business. Why don't you look me up when the time comes?" Laidlaw deferred. He had no interest in nursemaiding Jocko, or anybody else.

If Jocko was dismayed by the rebuff, he didn't show it. "Great! Okay if we stay in touch in the meantime?"

"Sure. Everybody knows how to find me." Hopefully, Jocko would find some other chump to put the bite on in the interim.

The low hum of chatter in the room tapered off as the Minister of Wildlife, who was evidently MC'ing the event, entered the room through a side door. Wearing a dove-gray bespoke Hugo Boss suit and a silk shirt with a contrasting Stefano Ricci tie, he clumped up the steps and strode to the lectern. Predictably, the minister tapped the microphone to confirm that it was functioning properly, grasped both sides of the podium, and leaned forward. He gravely surveyed the assemblage seated before him.

"*Salamu* and warmest greetings, dearest friends and colleagues," the minister beamed. "It is with greatest pleasure that I welcome you to the First Annual African Wildlife Conference and Symposium." He paused to assess the audience's reaction before launching into his substantive remarks. "Foremost among the innumerable blessings endowed by our Creator on the African continent are its extraordinary people. It is our intention to make this conference and symposium an annual celebration devoted to the continued existence and prosperity, for our grandchildren and their grandchildren, of Africa's second exceptional resource: its abundant and incomparable wildlife."

He was interrupted by the smattering of polite, obligatory, applause that rippled through the crowd. The money machine will henceforth be a permanent annual fixture, Laidlaw concluded.

The minister continued to address his audience in the same platitude-heavy vein for the next forty minutes before introducing the symposium's first academic expert, "the distinguished Doctor Nicholas Goldman." Accompanied by tepid applause, a slender, middle-aged man with a goatee and obligatory ponytail, carrying a file folder, stepped to the rostrum. Taking advantage of the momentary break in the action, Laidlaw scanned the ballroom.

The coffee and donut station at the rear of the room was already doing a brisk business, where several attendees were absorbed in looking at their cell phones while holding a donut in their other hand. A few members of the audience folded their arms on their tabletops and rested their heads on them, though Laidlaw was unable to determine whether they were actually sleeping. Three guys were reading newspapers at their tables, while another removed a stack of papers from his briefcase and was furiously using a pocket calculator, pausing only to periodically flip through his papers. Like Laidlaw, several people in the audience simply gawked about, probably wondering when and where the line for the lunch buffet was supposed to form. Four or five people in the audience actually seemed interested in Dr. Goldman's presentation, who was using a laser pointer to explain a confusion of graphs on a large projection screen. Either because he wasn't wearing a lapel microphone or, if he was, it wasn't working and his back was toward the audience, his accompanying exposition was inaudible.

It seemed impossible to Laidlaw that the soporific conference would lure many attendees back for a second day. He mildly regretted his decision to forego printing the formal symposium materials, though not enough to purchase the bound copy displayed on a table at the entrance to the ballroom.

A sprinkling of applause caused Laidlaw to direct his attention back to the speakers' platform, where Dr. Goldman had just concluded his presentation. He and the wildlife minister were switching places at the lectern.

"Before our next speaker, let's take a little break," the minister announced to the grateful audience. "Please be back in twenty minutes."

Laidlaw pushed his chair away from the table and stood. He figured he'd head to the men's room before Jocko buttonholed him.

"Where ya headed, mate?" Too late.

"Uh, I gotta go see a guy about a dog."

"A dog?" Jocko exclaimed. "One of my mate's bitches just whelped...Aussie Shepard mix. I'll set you up if you'd like to check out the litter."

This guy is as dense as a pallet of bricks, Laidlaw thought. "Naw, I've got it taken care of. Thank you. Excuse me." He pulled himself away from the garrulous Vanderbeeke.

"Alex!"

Laidlaw heard his name called above the milling crowd and looked in the direction of the hail. The wildlife minister was picking his way through the crowd, directly toward him. It was obvious Laidlaw wasn't going to have time to use the head.

"Hello, Robert," Laidlaw greeted the minister as he extended his hand. "It's been too long."

The minister huffed to a stop and clasped Laidlaw's hand. "Indeed, it has, Alex. I wasn't sure I would see you here at the symposium, as I heard you were out of the country."

"Just a short trip to Paris for a little R&R. Nothing too exciting."

“It is essential to get away now and again,” the minister stated. “All work and no play makes Jack a dull boy and there is much to like about Paris.” He finally noticed Jocko standing, dumbly, near Laidlaw. “Robert Mwanajuma,” the minister introduced himself. He reflexively shook the South African's hand before effectively dismissing him by turning back to Laidlaw.

“Pretty good turnout,” Laidlaw blandly observed, looking around the room.

“Yes, I'm very pleased.” Mwanajuma placed an avuncular hand on Laidlaw's shoulder, leaned closer, and lowered his voice. “There is a particular matter I would discuss with you, Alex. How long before you head back into the bush?”

“I'll be in the capital at least a few more days. I'm at the Europa.”

“Splendid! Please call my office on Monday with your schedule. I'll have my driver pick you up at the Europa at your convenience.”

Laidlaw was puzzled. “Is this something that can be handled over the phone, Robert?”

The other man shook his head. “It is better if we discuss it face-to-face. I can think of no one in whom I repose more confidence than you.” Mwanajuma removed his hand from Laidlaw's shoulder to consult his Cellini Moonphase, his 18 karat cufflinks glinting. “I must introduce the next speaker, Alex. Please call me on Monday, yes?”

“Ok,” Laidlaw sighed.

“Excellent! I hope you enjoy the rest of the symposium.” The minister patted Laidlaw's shoulder before heading back to the speaker's platform. Laidlaw wearily resumed his seat.

"Who's he?" Jocko asked.

"Minister of wildlife. Didn't you recognize him from your classes?"

"We don't really get into politics," Jocko responded with indifference. "You guys mates?" Laidlaw looked at him, dubiously.

"I wouldn't exactly say we're 'mates'. But if you expect to get a PH license anywhere in Africa, you sure as hell better get to know the people who issue them. Guess they don't teach that in PH school, huh?"

"Well, not exactly," Jocko chafed. "Hey, where'd you go to school to get your PH license?"

"Didn't need any formal classroom instruction when I got my license...just had to apprentice for a year under another PH."

"No kidding? Who'd you apprentice under?"

"Old-timer named 'Nicobar Jones'. Jones hunted all over Africa for sixty years. There was nothing about animals that old man didn't know," Laidlaw fondly recalled. "I was blessed to have known him."

"What happened to him?"

"He died a long time ago."

"Well, that's exactly what I wanna do, mate!" Jocko enthusiastically affirmed.

"Die?"

"No, learn the ropes under somebody like that."

Laidlaw didn't take the bait. Wordlessly, he directed his attention to the next speaker mounting the steps to the lectern.

LAIDLAW ESTIMATED THAT symposium attendance plummeted more than fifty per-cent by its second, and final, day. Like rats deserting a sinking ship, attendees began slipping out after lunch the previous afternoon. The exodus greatly accelerated as the session wore on. By the time everyone drifted back from the buffet, it was obvious that many had taken the opportunity to bail. When the symposium convened on the morning of its second day, the MIA's included the annoying Jocko, though Laidlaw's remaining two, stony-faced, table mates inexplicably returned for the remainder of the proceedings. Laidlaw made a bet with himself that, by the afternoon session, only about four or five tables would still remain occupied. The symposium was clearly a bomb and he actually felt sorry for Minister Mwanajuma, who clearly entertained high hopes for its success.

There was always next year.

The final speaker was a Professor Ledwaba, a faculty member at South Africa's University of Mpumalanga. Professor Ledwaba's area of expertise was Africa's mega-fauna, specifically, its two species of rhino.

Though designated "white" and "black", both species of rhinoceros are actually battleship-gray in color. The white is the larger of the two, its name derived from the English mistranslation of the Dutch "wijd", meaning "wide", and refers to the animal's broad mouth. This characteristic also led to its nickname, the "square-lipped rhinoceros." White rhinos are exclusively grazers, bulk-feeders cropping the grasses of Africa's vast savannas. Because of their relative abundance and docility or, less charitably, stupidity, white rhinos are invariably the species on display at zoos and animal parks around the world.

The white rhino's cousin, the black or "hook-lipped" rhinoceros, acquired its moniker by further compounding the confusion arising from the former's "white" appellation. It was reasoned that, if a "white" rhino existed, nature's inherent symmetry must necessarily have likewise created a "black" counterpart. *Viola!* The black rhinoceros was born. No one appeared to notice, nor seemed particularly troubled, by the fact that the white rhino isn't white, nor the black rhino, black. Aside from their diametrical names, however, the black rhinoceros is, fundamentally, an entirely different creature altogether from its benign cousin.

Unlike the white rhino, the black rhino is not a grazer, but a browser, subsisting on thorns, bushes, twigs, shrubs, trees, and the like. And, though smaller than its white cousin, the black rhino is irascible, short-tempered, and unpredictable. Verified accounts of enraged black rhinos spontaneously attacking people, trees, automobiles, even locomotives, are legion. Neither species can see worth a damn and each reacts to perceived threats differently. Discretion being the better part of valor, the ponderous white rhino generally prefers to high-tail it to safety when imperiled. Not the black. The black rhino's policy is to charge first and ask questions later. Hence, its well-attested propensity for aggression, notwithstanding that it usually comes off the worse for it.

Poaching represents the primary threat to the survival of both species. Throughout the 20th century, the black rhino was the most numerous of the two; as late as 1970, there were an estimated 65,000 black rhinos in the wild. By 1992, that number had plummeted to around 2,400. It is estimated that only about 5,500 black rhinos currently exist in the world. Meanwhile, the historically rarer white rhino experienced a renaissance, with nearly 20,000 animals now ensconced in various conservatories and refuges, the vast majority of them located in South Africa.

Poachers have little interest in rhinos per se, but kill them primarily for their horns. Like the horns of other mammals, rhino horns are composed of keratin, though they lack a bony core and are not attached directly to the animal's skull. Instead, they rest on nasal and frontal-bone pedicels. Rhino horn is, literally, worth its weight in gold throughout Arabia, the Middle and Far East, and India. It is especially prized in Yemen, where it is carved into ornate hilts for ceremonial daggers. In China, powdered rhino horn is sold as a cure for arthritis, cancer, diabetes, impotence, depression, and a host of other ailments. East Indians grind rhino horn into a powder, boil it in wine, and sell the concoction as an aphrodisiac.

In an effort to discourage poaching, the handful African countries where rhinos can still be found have undertaken to remove the horns of adult rhinos by sawing them off. The process doesn't harm the animals and may well save their lives.

In addition to their horns, rhinos were historically killed for their thick hides, which were fashioned into native shields, breastplates, sandal soles, retaining straps, and pails...anything that could withstand hard usage. And, in the 19th and early 20th centuries, rhino hams were widely esteemed the finest in the world.

But few people are aware that the most highly valued part of the rhino is its penis.

The most vicious whip on earth, the *sjambok*, also called a *kiboko*, was a favorite of 19th century Prussian and Belgian army officers, who used them with brutal efficiency on native Africans. One lash from a *sjambok* lays the flesh of a man open to the bone. While some *sjamboks* are fashioned from the hides of hippos, giraffes, or rhinos, the most desirable are those made from stretched and sun-dried rhino penis.

To make a *sjambok*, a two-or three-pound weight is tied to the small end of the penis, which is then suspended from its opposite end in the sunlight. It stretches from day-to-day, growing increasingly slender in the process. South American *vaqueros* make a lighter, but no less lethal, *sjambok* from the penis of an ordinary bull. When thoroughly dried, trimmed, oiled, and polished, a *sjambok* is sleek and beautiful. And deadly.

Professor Ledwaba's address was a straightforward presentation of the current status of both species of African rhinoceros. The good news is that white rhinos continue to rebound and black rhino populations in Zululand are actually increasing in the same reserves they share with white rhinos. Because one is a grazer and the other a browser, the two species do not compete for food. The bad news is that, notwithstanding the good news, black rhino numbers continue to dwindle overall. In a word, the black rhino is rapidly approaching extinction. No one possessing an ounce of humanity or compassion can feel anything but profound sorrow over the passing of these magnificent relics from a bygone age.

Provided one is willing to pay the cosmic fee charged by the South African government, it still remains possible to hunt a white rhino. According to what Laidlaw was told by a couple of guys who actually did so, however, bagging the dull-witted beast is akin to shooting a cow in a pasture. In an innovative program intended to allow the South African government to have its cake and eat it, too, “green” white rhino hunts have also been introduced. After paying the requisite, exorbitant fee, clients are provided an air-powered rifle with a tranquilizing dart, an escort/"guide", and a tracker. Once the quarry is located, which usually doesn't take long because rhinos are creatures of habit, the client creeps up and pops the rhino with the tranquilizer dart. The rhino snorts, peers around, sniffs the air, then makes a mad dash of about fifty yards before keeling over. Everyone then races up to snap photos of the client posing beside the incapacitated, semi-conscious animal. Once that ritual is concluded, a revivifying drug is administered via syringe and everyone beats a hasty retreat. Concealed in the nearby brush, they keep an eye on the rhino until, after several minutes, it more-or-less regains its senses. The dazed animal then heaves itself to its feet and unsteadily lurches off. Wildlife biologists are divided on the issue of the long-term effects of repeatedly tranquilizing rhinos but, because "green" hunting has proven to be extraordinarily profitable, the practice is unlikely to be reduced or terminated, irrespective of its potential deleterious effect on the animals.

Given their tenuous hold on life, Laidlaw had never hunted either species of rhino, nor entertained any desire to do so. The only time he'd even *seen* a rhino, of either variety, was during visits to game reserves. And, although hunting the white rhino's more dangerous cousin would prove, at least in theory, more challenging, the black rhino's scarcity and protected status renders any legal hunt, even a "green" hunt, an absolute impossibility at any price.

“SO, DID YOU AT LEAST ENJOY the buffet?” Mosi chuckled. They were sitting at a table in the Europa's empty bar.

“It was adequate, though it could have used more cheese dip,” Laidlaw replied.

Mosi nodded, gravely. “Where lunch is provided gratis, corners will be cut,” he philosophically intoned. “But, seriously, how was the conference? Was Mwanajuma there?”

“Yeah, along with a bunch of other politicos.” Laidlaw took a sip of beer. “He managed to round up a pretty fair number of speakers, a couple of whom actually seemed to know what they were talking about.”

“Like all politicians, Mwanajuma is a bandit, though one cannot help but like him. He occasionally stayed at the Europa while campaigning, but his tastes currently run more to the Hilton and Four Seasons. A real man of the people!”

“You're too hard on Robert,” Laidlaw responded. “I think he's doing the best he can with the limited resources he has. At least he appears to be trying.”

Mosi chuckled. “And, in politics, appearances count for far more than actual results. It is enough that one is well-intentioned."

“Speaking of Mwanajuma, he buttonholed me at the symposium,” Laidlaw revealed.

“You exchanged pleasantries?”

“That, but Robert also asked me to make an appointment to see him at his office.”

"The meeting about which rumors have been swirling?"

"I guess. I'll know for sure when I talk to him.

Mosi signaled the bartender and held up two fingers. "When are you supposed to call on him?"

"I told him I'd telephone his office tomorrow."

"Do you need a lift there? I'll drive you."

"No, Robert said he'd send a car."

Their conversation was interrupted when the bartender arrived at their table with a tray bearing two fresh glasses of cold beer. He slid them in front of the men, retrieved their empty glasses, and departed.

"A car? I had no idea you were such a VIP," Mosi grinned.

"Yeah, that makes two of us, although some kid at the symposium just about peed his pants for the privilege of sitting next to me," Laidlaw laughed.

"Who was he?"

"Damned if I know, though he knew who *I* was. Said he was studying for his PH license. Surprised he didn't ask me for my autograph!"

"You see, my friend?" Mosi exclaimed. "You are far too modest! Your fame clearly preceded you."

"My 'fame' and 5,000 shillings will get you a cup of coffee," Laidlaw dryly responded.

"Nonsense. At the Europa Hotel, we charge celebrities only 3,500 shillings!" Mosi grinned.

"So, I've just achieved celebrity status? But I'm only talking about the price of a cup of coffee, not the whole damned hotel!" Laidlaw furrowed his brow. "I may ask Mwanajuma if he'll let me bunk with him over at the Four Seasons in the future."

"Unfortunately, I don't think the Four Seasons offers roll-away beds. You may be stuck here at the Europa for the duration!" Mosi gravely counseled.

Laidlaw pretended to scowl. "I don't mind the overpriced coffee, the intolerably thin mattresses, the incessant noise, the limitless bugs, or the indigestible food served in your restaurant. It's the watered-down beer that really hurts."

Mosi laughed uproariously. "The Europa prides itself on consistency. However, as a demonstration of our unwavering commitment to the absolute satisfaction of our guests, I have instructed Woodson to dilute your beer by only one-half, rather than our customary two-thirds. As an additional courtesy, there will be no corresponding increase in price."

"Business school clearly wasn't wasted on you," Laidlaw remarked.

"Oscar Wilde said that 'nothing worth knowing can be taught'. I immodestly take credit for all the cost-saving measures implemented by the hotel."

"And, all this time, I thought you were manager because of your sparkling personality!" Laidlaw laughed.

"My 'sparkling personality' and 5,000 shillings will get you a cup of coffee," Mosi said with a wink.

"I'll drink to that."

The two friends lifted their glasses of beer in a toast.

"MR. MWANAJUMA WILL BE pleased to see you at your convenience," the secretary informed Laidlaw over the telephone.

"I'm pretty much available whenever he is."

A paused ensued while she checked the minister's calendar. "Does tomorrow morning at 8:00 work for you?"

"Perfect."

"Very good. If you'll give me your address I'll send a car for you." Laidlaw complied. "Thank you. The minister is looking forward to seeing you."

"I'll be there."

"See you tomorrow, Mr. Laidlaw."

IN THE MOVIES, MAFIOSI and government officials, often times indistinguishable, are invariably shown chauffeured about in new, gleaming black SUVs with darkened windows. A four year-old Nissan sedan arrived at the Europa to conduct Laidlaw, who stood outside the hotel's front entrance, to the offices of the Ministry of Wildlife.

"Mr. Laidlaw?" inquired its young driver as he emerged from the vehicle.

"That would be me." Laidlaw stepped to the curb and waited while the man opened the front passenger door and held it open for him. He slid into the vehicle, the interior of which reeked of men's cologne.

“Do you like the Europa, sir?” the driver conversationally asked after resuming his seat and pulling away from the curb. He rested the crook of his left arm on the ledge of his open window.

“Very much. It's my go-to hotel whenever I'm in town.”

The Nissan merged into heavy traffic and headed downtown. “I am told you are a hunter, sir.”

“Yeah.”

“I would like to do that one day, I think,” the young man mused. “But I would not like to be eaten by a lion!”

“Well, I've managed to avoid that so far but the day ain't over yet," Laidlaw laconically responded. “What's your name?”

The driver laughed. “My name is 'Leo'. The minister speaks very highly of you.”

Laidlaw nodded, absently. “Yeah, we go back a long way. You work for him long?”

“No, not long. I attend university and intern at the ministry. I hope to work in government when I graduate.”

“How much longer do you have?”

“At university? A year and a half.” A battered Ford, smoke boiling from its engine, darted in front of them, forcing Leo to instinctively wrench the Nissan's steering wheel hard to the left with both hands. The Nissan bounced into a deep pothole and shuddered as it sprang back onto the roadway without slowing down.

"Many bad drivers here," Leo muttered by way of apology. Laidlaw merely nodded.

THEY ARRIVED AT THE DETERIORATING bunker-like edifice that housed the offices of the Ministry of Wildlife forty minutes after leaving the Europa. Mwanajuma's office was located on the second floor.

Leo pulled into a 'No Parking' zone directly in front of the building. He left the Nissan's engine running as he exited the car. Stepping to the passenger's side, he opened the door and Laidlaw swung his legs from the idling vehicle.

It was a great pleasure to meet you, sir," Leo grinned as Laidlaw straightened. "If you have not been to the minister's office before, it is at the top of stairs you will see as soon as you enter. It is impossible to miss." Throughout the Third World elevators are not the norm, regardless of a building's height.

"Thanks, Leo. You won't be taking me back to the Europa?"

"I regret not, sir. I must get back to university. Someone else will drive you to your hotel following your meeting with the minister."

"I understand. No problem." Laidlaw extended his hand. "Good luck with your studies."

"Of course, sir. Thank you."

The men shook hands and Laidlaw turned to enter the building, curious to learn what the Minister of Wildlife was so eager to discuss with him.

"ALEX! MWANAJUMA EFFUSIVELY greeted him as he stepped from behind his desk.

"Robert. Good to see you again." Laidlaw shook the other man's hand.

"Sit, sit," Mwanajuma invited, gesturing toward two overstuffed chairs. He grasped Laidlaw's elbow and propelled him across the room. "Thank you for coming."

"No problem." Laidlaw eased himself down.

"Can I get you anything? Water? Coffee?"

"No, I'm good, thank you. Already had too many cups before I left the hotel."

"I understand," the minister smiled. "Where are you staying?"

"The Europa."

His host smiled, broadly. "Yes, of course. I remember your informing me at the symposium...the venerable Europa. Truly, one of the city's gems."

Laidlaw recalled Mosi's droll remark about Mwanajuma's preference for the Four Seasons. "That it is," he amiably concurred.

Mwanajuma angled his chair to directly face Laidlaw's, sat, and using an ornate desk lighter, stoked a fat *La Aroma de Cuba Reserva Pomposo.*

"Before we begin, how did you find the symposium? I was gratified by the turnout." He admired the *Pomposo* at arm's length as he spoke.

"It was good," Laidlaw lied. "Some speakers were better than others, of course, but that's to be expected."

"Of course." The minister tapped the ashes from his cigar into an ashtray. "But you are no doubt wondering why I wished to speak with you today."

"It crossed my mind."

"It was not by accident that Professor Ledwaba spoke at the symposium," Mwanajuma confided as he contentedly puffed his cigar.

"Oh?"

"Under Ledwaba's oversight, the ministry is developing a pilot program to establish breeding herds of black rhinos."

Laidlaw nodded. "Great! Where?"

"The Selous and Bukoba, initially. Perhaps other preserves later on, depending on how matters progress."

The Selous Game Reserve, named for famed British explorer, hunter, and conservationist, Frederick C. Selous, is the largest game reserve on the African continent. Permanent human habitation within the Selous is prohibited, which contributes to robust populations of lion, elephant, leopard, buffalo, giraffe, zebra, and other indigenous species.

"I'm happy to hear that, Robert," Laidlaw said. "Whatever you can do to give 'em a boost. You're getting initial breeding stock from South Africa?"

The minister nodded as he gently ground his cigar out. “It will be a cooperative effort.”

“Okay, so what's this got to do with me?”

Mwanajuma leaned back in his chair as Laidlaw listened in silence. “We needn't discuss in detail the growing problem of rhino horn trafficking. We fear that, even in the isolated Selous, the herd will not be safe from poachers.”

“Put armed game rangers on 'em, like they do in South Africa. I guarantee about a dozen field executions will put a serious dent in the poaching. If nothing else, there will be a few less poachers.”

The other man looked grim. “That is exactly the rub, Alex. The ministry does not repose absolute confidence in its game rangers.”

Laidlaw cocked his eyebrow. “But you apparently do in me.”

“Exactly!” Mwanajuma beamed. “I cannot entirely blame the rangers, though. They have families to support and the work is dangerous and pays little.”

“Robert, I have no interest in babysitting a herd of rhinos, or a gaggle of venal rangers.”

“Nor do I have the slightest intention of asking you to do so. I ask only that you make some unannounced visits for the purpose of assessing the welfare of the rhinos, nothing more. If the rangers know they are under the watchful eye of Alex Laidlaw, they will be less likely to succumb to the blandishments of poachers.”

“I don't know about that. What about just cutting the animals' horns off?”

"Shall we cut their penises off, as well? Even hornless rhinos will be killed to make *sjamboks*. So much for our breeding program!"

Laidlaw sighed. "Robert, if it were even remotely possible, I'd be happy to help. But I just have too many irons in the fire right now. I'm sorry. I'm sure there's another PH who would be willing to help you out."

Mwanajuma shook his head. "We have learned that cartels are actively recruiting PH's. There are already comparatively few licensed PH's in the entire country and their fidelity cannot be assured."

"But mine can?" Laidlaw scoffed.

"I don't know...can it? Are you in communication with poachers or smugglers?"

Laidlaw looked at the other man with irritation. "You know better than that."

"Precisely," Mwanajuma smiled, expansively. "While we're on the subject, I checked the ministry's records and noticed that your PH license will soon be due for renewal. Under ordinary circumstances that would simply be a routine housekeeping matter."

"Seriously?" Laidlaw retorted. "You're stooping to extortion now, Robert?"

Mwanajuma feigned offense. "You cut me to the quick, Alex," he protested. "I remind you that one hand washes the other. It is just a fact of life."

Laidlaw slowly shook his head. "It would seem that you have me, and my PH license, over a barrel."

"The Ministry neither solicits, nor expects, charity. You will be compensated for your assistance.

Of far greater importance, you will be making an inestimable contribution to the propagation of an iconic African species, for your children and their children."

"I don't have any children. At least none that I'm aware of," Laidlaw scowled.

Mwanajuma chuckled. "For *my* children, then!"

In Primis Anno Regnantibus Imperator Caesar Titus Vespasianus (80 CE)

A PATCHWORK OF IMPROVISED dwellings ranged along the desolate fringe of the Red Sea. They included simple dugouts scraped from the earth and lined with sea grass, rough piles of stones, tangles of driftwood covered with palm fronds, or the upturned hulls of small boats. Offshore, a collectiom of dilapidated vessels bobbed in the crystalline waters, none nearly large enough to accommodate the soldiers of *Legio XVI Bestia.* The legionnaires were mobbed by a score of naked children as they plodded down the beach toward the settlement.

"By Herakles, I would fuck that one," one of them said, indicating a girl perhaps ten years old, her skin bronzed by the sun.

"I think your horse-cock would likely kill her, Antonius," one of his comrades guffawed. "Besides, she has no tits. Now, her *mother...*"

"Shut your yapping maws!" Berossus bellowed.

"So, those are supposed to carry all of us to Rome?" Senecio whispered to Neocles. With his chin, he pointed to the eclectic offshore flotilla.

Berosses halted. "Who here can speak?" he shouted toward the gathering crowd. The assemblage stared in silence at the strange apparitions which had materialized in their midst. No one volunteered.

"Which of you stupid bastards can speak?" he again demanded. Still, no one stepped forward. A baby began wailing somewhere. Even though it was only mid-morning, the heat was already intense. The restive legionnaires began shifting their weight from one foot to the other as the cluster of people continued to dumbly gawk at them.

A bearded figure appearing to be in his mid-30's emerged from the crowd.

"What do you want?" he asked in flawless Latin. It was obvious he was a deserter from an unknown Roman legion, though Berossus didn't recognize him. Prudently, he chose to ignore the man's problematic origins.

"We require transport to Arsinoe."

"Arsinoe is very far from here and we have no boats. Leave us."

Berossus looked at him skeptically. "You may have no boats, but traders from Arabia that call on you have boats."

The man swept his arm across the open sea. "Do you see any traders, for I do not."

"When were traders last here?"

The man turned back to Berossus. "Many months.

"How often do they call?"

"Sometimes not at all. The gods, alone, control such things."

"How distant is the next settlement?" Berossus probed.

"A day." The man gestured vaguely southward.

"How many people are there?"

"I do not know."

"Is there nothing to the north?"

"You asked about the next settlement, which lies in that direction," the man reminded Berossus.

The latter eyed him, skeptically. "What is your name?"

"I am called 'Carpio.'"

"What lies northward, Carpio?"

"Other people."

"How far?"

Carpio furrowed his brow. "Two or three days. More, perhaps."

"Do traders call there, as well?"

"I cannot speak to who calls there. You must inquire for yourself."

Berossus glanced rearward, toward the restless, edgy legionnaires gathered behind him. The surrounding throng of villagers listened to the tense exchange between Carpio and Berossus without comprehending their words.

"We have been marching for weeks and have suffered much," Berossus said. "We are fatigued and require food and rest."

"Food we gladly provide. You must look to the gods for all else, who grant repose to those who warrant it."

"It was the gods who directed us hither," affirmed Berossus.

"Whether your gods are mild or ill-disposed, we freely offer food to all, for the gods possesses long memories."

"We would take our ease and refresh ourselves before resuming our journey," Berossus informed Carpio.

The latter man nodded. "There is room aplenty. To ensure harmony, conduct your men along the beach a quarter-league northward, where you will encounter an estuary. You will be able to refill your water containers from the stream flowing into the sea at that place. We will bring food while you rest."

"Food and women," Berossus clarified.

Carpio narrowed his eyes. "Our women are chaste and have no desire to entertain your men."

"Indeed?" Berossus mocked surprise. "I see many young girls hereabouts. If your wives decline, you will bring them in their stead. It is one thing to profess a desire for harmony, but quite another to furnish tangible proofs of it."

"We trust in our gods to shield us from the afflictions of those who would harm us," Carpio avowed.

"Your gods? Pray, how many pikes do your gods wield?" With that, Berossus turned on his heel and strode away to assemble his men.

SWARMED BY GNATS AND MOSQUITOES, the watercraft floated downriver for three monotonous days. The previous afternoon, they drifted past the remnants of a former settlement: a few collapsed hovels made of sticks and the deteriorated husk of what had once been a boat. It was impossible to ascertain whether its quondam inhabitants had intentionally abandoned their homestead, or simply succumbed to disease or animal predation.

The region abounded in wildlife: innumerable crocodiles, pods of truculent hippos, herds of elephants, numberless birds, uncounted antelope and baboons. On one occasion a pride of lions comprised of an old, scarred, black-maned male, three maneless juveniles, and numerous lionesses and cubs, lined the shore to lap water from the river. They watched in idle curiosity as the Roman flotilla drifted past. While thus distracted, a fourteen-foot crocodile slowly propelled itself toward the incautious lions, only its eyes and nostrils protruding above the surface of the river. Approaching the shallows, the reptile paused in order to isolate a target animal among the drinking lions. With a sweep of its powerful tail, the crocodile surged forward, nearly exiting the water in the process and, with an audible thump, engulfed the entire head of the nearest lioness in its jaws. The remaining lions instantly scattered while, with a startled roar, the lioness sought to free her herself from the crocodile's grasp by frantically backpedaling in the sand.

For naught. Outweighing its hapless prey by a half-ton, the crocodile easily dragged the doomed lioness beneath the swirling surface of the Iteru.

Because the structure of their jaws renders it impossible for them to chew, crocodiles must either consume their prey whole or in large chunks, which they simply gulp down. Crocodiles easily ingest dog-sized animals and swallow waterfowl whole, feathers and all. Nor are they deterred by horns, bones, or hooves. But, the lioness being too big to swallow in a single gulp, the crocodile would first try to tear chunks from her. Failing that, he'd carry her to the bottom of the river, shove her in the mud, and wait for her body to decompose. Once the lioness' rotted remains floated to the surface, the croc would consume them with ease.

Even today, the number of people killed and eaten by crocodiles every year in Africa is unknowable...scores, certainly; hundreds, probably. Children are attacked while playing in rivers and streams; women killed while washing clothes near riverbanks; men seized and dragged overboard while paddling boats; the unwary caught by their hands or heads while scooping water from a river to drink, savaged while fording streams, or dragged to their deaths while walking carelessly along marshy or overgrown riverbanks.

Death in Africa is always lurking just out of sight.

ON THE FOURTH DAY, A MUTED roar rumbled through the heavy air.

Quintus was dozing but bolted upright. "Listen!" He looked anxiously toward Harkhuf, who appeared oblivious. Quintus turned to Crixus. "It is an earthquake!"

"It is not an earthquake, fool," Harkhuf contemptuously spat. "It is the cataract."

"It is near?"

"Yes, near."

"How dangerous is it?" Quintus anxiously inquired.

Harkhuf appeared confused. "There is no danger."

Having experienced first-hand the Iteru's six major cataracts during his previous voyage upriver, Crixus was aware that their fearsome reputation was invariably exaggerated by those who had never actually navigated them. The only genuinely hazardous cataract was the First, in Upper Egypt near its border with Nubia. A constriction in the Iteru compelled watercraft transiting the First Cataract to proceed with caution because of a series of enormous submerged boulders. While this did not present an insuperable peril to experienced sailors, river pirates based on nearby Elephantine Island took advantage of the slow-moving boats' vulnerability to attack them. Thus, it was not the cataract, itself, that was intrinsically dangerous, but its collateral infestation by freebooters.

"I agree the cataract we are approaching is a trifle. But, make no mistake," Crixus sharply informed Harkhuf. "I have also traversed the Great Cataract, which swarms with cutthroats. How do you intend to deal with them?"

Harkhuf poled their drifting craft away from the riverbank before responding. "You speak true, Roman," he said, impressed with Crixus' evident knowledge of the river. "But I know a way around the pirates."

Crixus looked at him dubiously. "How?"

"There is a path along the western edge of the Iteru. We will land upriver from them and carry our boats overland, past the Great Cataract, until we are beyond the pirates. Though their boats do not draw much water, the pirates cannot sail on dry land. We will be safe."

Crixus' skepticism was not assuaged. "You, personally, have done this?"

Harkhuf nodded. "Many times."

"Do you suppose the barbarian is telling the truth," Quintus asked.

"How would it profit him to lie? Pirates' swords make no distinction between barbarian flesh and Roman flesh."

"Does it not occur to you that the barbarian conducts us *to* the cutthroats, rather than away from them?"

Crixus nodded. “Yes, that is a possibility. Pray, what would you have me do, Quintus? Shall I order the barbarian to beach us at this spot, here and now? What then? If it was your desire to complete less than half our voyage before abandoning it, why did you urge that we undertake it in the first place?”

“I freely admit that I am of two minds,” a chagrined Quintus confessed.

“Have you forgotten Pompey's astonishing success against the Cilician pirates, whom he completely swept from the *Mare Nostrum*? Do we, Pompey's heirs, possess less *virtus* than did he? Pompey did not quail at the prospect of crossing swords with a shabby collection of beleaguered pirates, especially on dry land! No, he eagerly welcomed it. So shall we.”

Quintus looked doubtful. “As you say, Crixus, Gnaeus Pompeius vanquished the Cilician pirates. However, the senate placed at Pompey's disposal hundreds of ships and thousands of men-at-arms with which to accomplish that task. We are few in number and our vessels, if they may truly be called that, are laughable. Furthermore, the unlimited resources that Pompey commanded enabled him to remain on the offense against the pirates while, contrariwise, we will be the quarry.”

“So much the better,” Crixus assured him, “for a surfeit of vessels will prove an encumbrance to us. We are legionnaires, not sailors! If the pirates are foolish enough to mount an attack on land, thereby abandoning the safety of their ships, we will have succeeded in luring them to fight at a place of *our* choosing, on *our* terms. Like the Spartan, Leonidas, we shall defeat the bastards while standing securely on dry land in the shade!"

CONSONANT WITH CARPIO'S directions, Berossus ordered the legionnaires to march north along the beach until they reached the estuary. It was approaching noon and the heat was already stifling.

"I hope there are trees where we are going," Senecio muttered as they marched.

"If there are, they are likely to be mangroves," Neocles reasoned.

"I do not care what kind of trees they are as long as they provide shade."

"Shade, yes, but I long to bathe in the sea. I have not seen a bath in nearly two months."

"Bathing is imprudent. You should be more mindful of your health," Senecio pontificated. Neocles ignored his counsel.

As Carpio assured them, a march of three-quarters of an hour brought the legionnaires to a sandy plane crisscrossed with numerous small rivulets that flowed into the sea. Because it was low tide, the frothy surf line was visible only in the distance. Tangled masses of mangrove trees sprouted here and there across the broad estuary and scores of gulls patrolled its damp sands, searching for crustaceans, buried mollusks, and stranded fish.

"Go to higher ground!" Berossus barked. "The tide will otherwise swamp us when it returns."

"You will have to slog at least a league just to reach the sea from here, Neocles! So much for your ablutions," Senecio laughed.

His companion shrugged. "I have waited two months and can wait still longer. The tide will turn in a few hours."

Bestia pivoted inland before finally halting on a barren, gritty incline sprinkled with patches of dry grass above the high-tide mark. A brisk wind swept landward from the sea.

As one, the exhausted legionnaires sank to the earth. Berossus strode among them, hurling invectives. Although the shallow, frangible soil rendered it impossible to dig a protective moat or erect a rampart, Berossus ordered that a defensive perimeter be established. He directed some legionnaires to locate the source of the rivulets that carried fresh water seaward, while others set to work erecting shelters against the blistering sun. The remaining men set out to scrounge for wood or, indeed, anything that would burn, for cooking fires.

"When is that barbarian supposed to bring food?" Senecio asked no one in particular as he began to tug desiccated grass from the sand to use a fuel.

"Food?" another guffawed. "You can have my portion! I am more interested in the women!"

"I cannot eat a woman," Senecio grumbled.

"If that you believe that, I invite you to watch me tonight. You are certain to learn much." the other retorted.

"I would be surprised if we are provided either food *or* women. The barbarians would promise the moon and stars if they thought doing so would induce us to depart."

"We will know soon enough," Neocles commented. "*Mulier profecto natast ex ipsa Mora.*"

The third legionnaire placed his hands on his hips. "And you, Neocles, are you also a *eunuchus* who favors food over women?" he inquired with mockery.

"All depends on the circumstances," Neocles indifferently replied. "For the nonce, I favor appeasing Berossus by setting camp and collecting firewood. Everything else will come in time, if the gods will it."

His interrogator merely grunted in response.

"OUR WIVES, SISTERS AND DAUGHTERS are pure and, by the gods, shall remain that way," one of the men grimly avowed. "None shall be defiled at the hands of a Roman." The assembly murmured its collective approbation.

"I agree with all my heart," Carpio assured them. "My words were intended only to lure the vile Romans away from us."

"Perhaps, though, your artifice accomplished nothing. The murderous swine are now camped nearby, fully expecting to be provided both victuals and women! If we fail to comply, we will be worse off than before because they will return, seize our women, and slaughter the rest of us!" The other men nodded in silent unison.

Carpio extended his arms, palms toward his audience. "Hear me! Having for the nonce relieved ourselves of the Romans' presence, we are at leisure to discuss a resolution to our predicament. While the Romans idle away their time, we remain free plot their destruction."

"And how do you hope to accomplish that?" the other man challenged.

"I hope for nothing. It is a far better thing to plan ill for our enemies, rather than simply hope for it."

"I hear brave words, yet we and our women remain no less menaced."

"As you said, we have already promised to feed the Romans. We will do so, though I daresay the food we provide will not be entirely to their liking."

"How so?"

"The Romans are hungry and stupid, in equal measure. We will serve them the flesh of the globefish, which they will consume with relish. The fools will happily poison themselves with their own hands!"

The globefish, or puffer, is a common species throughout tropical seas worldwide, including the South Pacific and Indian Oceans, the Red Sea, and the Sea of Cortez. Although its flesh is considered a delicacy throughout Asia, particularly in Japan, it contains tetrodotoxin, a neurological agent also known as TTX. Studies have revealed that TTX , for which no antidote exists, is more lethal than cyanide because it prevents the flow of sodium to the skeletal muscles and heart. As a consequence, eating globefish prepared by someone without specialized training on how to eliminate the toxin can be fatal. Symptoms of globefish poisoning, which typically begin to manifest themselves within a half-hour of consumption, include tingling of the lips and face, ultimately spreading to the limbs; dizziness; abdominal pain with diarrhea and vomiting; respiratory failure; slurred speech; even paralysis. Severe cases inevitably lead to seizures, coma, and death.

Carpio was gratified to discern the murmurs of approval that rippled through the gathering.

"What makes you confident the Romans will eat?"

"Why would they not? As I said, they are as hungry as they are stupid. Hunger never saw bad bread."

"And if the Romans suspect something is amiss?"

"They will not. The fish will be seasoned so as to cloak all traces of poison. We will also give the Romans honeyed wine, which they believe increases their sexual vigor. Together, the food and drink we provide the Romans will combine to ensure their rapid deaths."

"Carpio speaks wisely," a listener volunteered. "His is the only proposal that will safeguard us."

“Perhaps, but the Romans expect both food and women. They will be enraged if we arrive at their camp bearing only the former,” said another.

“We will remind them of the poet's words: 'Without food and drink, love will grow cold',” Carpio explained. “We will further assure the Romans that, while we assemble the most desirable women for their pleasure, they are at liberty to rest, eat, and refresh themselves. For the nonce, we must set about preparing a feast of globefish for them. Hie to your nets and ensnare as many of them as possible without delay, before the Romans' impatience is transformed into violence.”

With that, the gathering quickly disbursed, determined to permanently rid themselves of the unwanted interlopers from the interior of Africa.

CARPIO AND THREE OTHER MEN arrived at the Romans' camp three hours later. Between them, they lugged copper cauldrons brimming with fish stew, which they carefully lowered to the ground before Berossus. He surveyed the offerings with skepticism.

“I see no women,” he said.

“Our women have agreed to entertain your men. They ask only that you allow them time to prepare for, as you know, women are vain creatures. We will conduct them to your camp once your men have eaten and refreshed themselves,” Carpio responded.

Enticed by the arrival of food, a crowd of legionnaires gathered. They listened intently to the terse exchange between the two men.

"Where did these ignorant brutes acquire cooking pots?" Unius whispered to Neocles.

"Traders, no doubt...they certainly did not fashion them themselves."

"My men are adequately rested," Berossus informed Carpio. "Conduct your women here without further trickery!"

"There is no trickery," the other man protested. We will deliver them to your camp this eventide. In the meantime, please avail yourselves of our hospitality." Carpio executed a slight bow.

Berossus glanced at the cauldrons of soup. "I would have you sup with us."

"These victuals were prepared especially for our venerated guests. We not wish to dishonor you by presuming to reclaim them," Carpio deferred. "I invite you and your men to enjoy this humble token of our esteem."

"As you wish," Berossus shrugged. "Ensure that your women are conveyed hither without further delay."

"Of course." Carpio motioned to his companions and they turned to leave. Berossus watched in silence as they departed.

"I do not trust them," he commented to a legionnaire standing near him.

"They do not appear threatening," the man replied with indifference.

“It is obvious the one who speaks for them is a deserter. Such faithless traitors are never to be trusted.”

The legionnaire gestured to the basins of soup. “It is a strange foe who willingly provides food to his enemies.”

Berossus turned toward him. “You are right, Silvanus. Either they are not our foes or their gift is a deceit. Which do you think most probable?” Silvanus did not respond.

“Pour the barbarians' swill onto the earth. Do not allow any man to eat it,” Berossus swiftly ordered. “Instruct them to consume only such food as they personally carry with them. Having done so, make ready to march on the barbarians' camp. We will repay their treachery, like for like.”

TWELVE

THE MINISTRY OF WILDLIFE established two rhino sanctuaries, one in the Selous and the other in the extreme north of the country, near Bukoba. Either way, they were a pain in the butt to get to.

While the fringes of the Selous Game Reserve, where virtually all Western tourists flock for upscale camping "adventures" and photo safaris, are accessible by road, its interior largely remains a trackless wilderness devoid of human settlements. In order to monitor its nascent rhino herd, Laidlaw would be forced to charter a light aircraft to transport him from his camp on the Rufiji River deep into the reserve, where he would be deposited on an isolated air strip. He would then use a walkie-talkie to inform the assigned game rangers of his arrival and, at some point, they would eventually arrive in a bakkie to retrieve him.

Aside from females with calves, rhinos are solitary by nature. Notwithstanding that each wore a radio collar, it would require a greater or lesser amount of time to locate the scattered animals across thousands of hectares of extremely rough country. While onsite, Laidlaw would bunk with the rangers in their clapboard shack with electricity provided by a gasoline-powered generator. Once he was satisfied that the herd was intact and healthy, Laidlaw would radio for the plane to return. That might take a day or a week.

While Bukoba was not quite as remote and readily accessible by an ordinary vehicle, it was much farther away. Thus, as between the two sanctuaries, Laidlaw basically considered it a case of damned if you do, damned if you don't.

Although his role in the rhino project was, according to Mwanajuma, confidential and his spontaneous visits to the rhino sanctuaries unannounced to anyone in the field, the two uniformed rangers stationed at the Selous were already waiting at the airstrip when his plane touched down. Obviously, someone had tipped them off that he was coming. Once he returned to the capital, Laidlaw had the unhappy duty to inform Mwanajuma that moles had apparently infiltrated his ministry, as well as other entities including the air taxi service.

"Welcome, Mr. Alex, sir," one of the rangers greeted him as Laidlaw hopped from the Cessna. In the background, his associate slouched against a roofless bakkie. “My name is Israel. My companion is Jahi.”

Laidlaw turned and dragged his duffle bag from the plane before shaking the man's outstretched hand. “How did you learn of my arrival, Israel?” The ranger grabbed Laidlaw's bag with his free hand and slid its strap over his shoulder.

“We received a wireless message.”

“Oh? When?”

“Yesterday afternoon.” The same day, coincidentally, that Laidlaw radioed the air taxi service to arrange for transportation from his camp to the Selous. The cartels moved fast.

“Who sent the message?”

“I don't know, sir. Jahi took the message and told me of your coming.”

Laidlaw glanced at the other ranger who still lounged near the bakkie, smoking a cigarette.

“Well, show me around, Israel. I'll check out your digs afterward. How are the rhinos faring?”

“They are fat and healthy,” Israel assured him as they walked toward the bakkie. The Cessna pilot waited for them to clear the plane before restarting its engine and trundling down the airstrip, preparatory to taking off.

Jahi finished his cigarette and flicked the butt away as Israel and Laidlaw approached.

“This is Mr. Alex,” the former revealed. Jahi half-heartedly shook Laidlaw's hand as the other man placed the latter's duffle in the rear of the vehicle.

“Israel tells me that you were informed I would be arriving today,” Laidlaw casually remarked.

“We were instructed to greet you here.”

“By who?”

Jahi narrowed his eyes. “We received a wireless transmission yesterday.”

“From who?”

“The ministry, I think. I do not know where it came from.”

“No one but the minister knew I was coming.”

“Then, you have answered your own question,” Jahi shrugged. “But, you are here now.” He turned away, slid into the bakkie's driver's seat, and cast an expectant look at him.

Laidlaw walked to the opposite side of the vehicle and climbed into the passenger's seat. Israel clambered into the bakkie's rear jump seat.

“Let's go,” Laidlaw directed.

“Mr. Alex wishes to see the rhinos,” Israel elaborated. Jahi wordlessly depressed the clutch and started and vehicle. They swung in a wide arc and headed south.

TWO BLACK RINO COWS, one with a calf, all wearing large plastic ear tags and electronic collars, nipped at a stunted brachystegia tree fifty yards away, grasping its brittle stems with their prehensile upper lips.

"How many total cows in the reserve?" Laidlaw asked Israel in a low tone while, from the bakkie, they watched the rhinos feed.

"Now?"

"Yeah, now. When did you think I was talking about?" Laidlaw peevishly responded.

"Three black cows and eight white ones. There were originally had five black and ten white rhino cows, but poachers killed them."

"And bulls?"

"One black and three white."

"Calves?"

"That one and two white."

Laidlaw nodded. "How often do you do a head count?"

"Twice daily, once in the morning and again in the evening. All of them wear collars, which makes them very easy to track on GPS."

"I'm guessing the calf's mother ran the old man off?"

Israel grinned. "You know something of rhinos, Mr. Alex."

In his iconic *Behavior Guide to African Mammals*, biologist Richard Despard Estes notes that, "Of all the carnivores, cats are the most committed meat-eaters." Despite this predilection, every owner of a domestic house cat knows their beloved Whiskers or Cosmo will avidly eat vegetation, as well: catnip, obviously, but also raw spinach, parsley, clover, fresh grass, melons, herbs, and various flowering plants. This can sometimes be their undoing, however, because many such plants, such as poinsettias, are toxic. Nor are house cats the only carnivores to readily consume greenery. Aside from the family dog, lions, wolves, coyotes, foxes, weasels, jackals, badgers, ferrets...virtually all carnivores supplement their diet with plants, either occasionally or regularly. The surprising, to most people, converse is that many herbivores supplement their diets with meat to a greater or lesser extent,. Rodents such as ground squirrels, hares, and rabbits, and even bigger species like deer, do so regularly, typically by consuming road-kill. In Africa, classic herbivores like hippos and rhinos are opportunistic meat-eaters. Hence, female rhinos with young will not tolerate the presence of males because the bulls sometimes kill, and eat, the calves.

"A little," Laidlaw admitted. "Have you seen any hunters or campers?"

Israel shook his head. "No one."

The taciturn Jahi lit another cigarette and reclined his seat slightly. He lowered the bill of his cap over his eyes and appeared to doze.

"Any vehicle tracks? Old campfires? Gunshots?"

"Nothing. It is very boring here."

Laidlaw looked over at Jahi. "What about you?"

"I have not seen anyone, either. There is no one out here but us," he mumbled without lifting his cap from his eyes. The smoldering cigarette bounced between his lips as he spoke.

Laidlaw turned his attention back to the rhinos.

Both cows had wandered farther from the vehicle, followed by the calf. Aside from physical, temperamental, and behavioral differences, a distinguishing characteristic between the two species of African rhinoceros is that black rhino calves trail their mothers when walking, while white rhino calves invariably lead. The trio was now busy sampling a whistling thorn bush. Heedless of three-inch-long spines capable of penetrating the sidewall of an automobile tire, the rhinos swung their massive heads from side-to-side as they tore the prickly branches free.

"How far away are the whites?" Laidlaw inquired.

"The herd was about two miles west of here this morning," Israel replied. "I reckon they are probably still in that area."

"Let's go find out. I also want to check in on the black rhino bull."

"Of course," Israel enthusiastically responded.

Jahi raised his cap, returned his seat to an upright position, and cranked the bakkie's engine to life.

"LOOK." LAIDLAW POINTED OVER the windshield toward the horizon, where a column of vultures soared atop the thermal updrafts.

Israel followed his gaze from his perch in the back of the vehicle. "Something dead."

“Not just 'dead' but big, too, judging from the number of vultures.”

“Could be anything. A lion probably killed a buffalo,” Jahi commented. He sharply yanked the steering wheel to avoid clipping a termite mound.

“Yeah, maybe,” Laidlaw frowned. “Head over in that direction,” he directed. He leaned back in his seat, a growing sense of unease gnawing at him.

THE RHINOCEROS COW SAT on her rump, front legs extended in front of her. Blood seeped from the multiple bullet holes that riddled her body, creating dark rivulets that streaked her mud-caked hide. The poachers hadn't waited to remove her valuable horn; they simply used a hatchet to chop it free and lift it from her skull as she sat, her life dwindling. They'd also used bolt cutters to disable, then remove, her electronic collar. Blood flowed from the wound where her horn had previously rested; it dripped onto the ground, where it mixed with frothy blood that bubbled from her nose. Squabbling vultures hopped clumsily about, stirring up dust and twigs with their wings, and three jackals lingered nearby. All impatiently waited for the rhino to die.

She lifted her sagging head and groaned softly when she saw the three men approach.

“One of the white cows.” Israel stated the obvious.

Like most of their ilk, the poachers used Chinese-made AK-47 automatic rifles to indiscriminately shoot the rhino until she collapsed. Because of the intervening distance and the bakkie's engine noise, neither Laidlaw, nor the two game rangers, heard the multitude of shots that were undoubtedly expended. Ordinarily, the poachers would have dispatched the wounded cow by shooting her in the head while she was slumped, incapacitated. Once she was dead, they would certainly have removed not only her horn, but also some internal organs, such as her spleen and gall bladder, which were believed to possess medicinal properties. However, one of the poachers' lookouts must have spotted the bakkie's approach, forcing them to abandon their task half-done.

"Bring me the rifle from the bakkie," Laidlaw ordered.

Israel scuttled back to the vehicle and lifted a battered Mauser bolt-action rifle, in the venerable 9.3 x 62 caliber, from a welded metal rack. He hastened to the side of stricken rhino with it.

Laidlaw stood next to the doomed cow, gently talking to her and scratching behind her ears. Jahi hadn't moved from his previous spot.

"I'm sorry, old girl. You didn't deserve this," Laidlaw murmured. She slowly blinked her glassy eyes and her head sank lower. Blood continued to ooze from her nostrils; she snorted, spraying foamy blood onto the earth. Israel wordlessly handed the rifle to Laidlaw and retreated to stand near Jahi.

Laidlaw retracted the Mauser's bolt, chambering a cartridge, and slid the bolt home. He took a step rearward, placed the muzzle of the rifle in the rhino's right ear, and touched off the shot. She collapsed in a heap.

The jackals fled at the report of the rifle. The vultures remained, but flapped their enormous wings and glared at Laidlaw.

“What do we do now?” Israel asked, after a moment,

Laidlaw ejected the spent cartridge case from the Mauser and clicked its safety on. He bent to retrieve the brass casing from the ground and slid it into his shirt pocket. “Take a blood sample and report what happened to the ministry. But start by checking the area for tyre tracks. Other than that, there's not much else we can do. Are there any villages in the vicinity? If there are, we'll let 'em know about the poached rhino, so they can haul ass out here and butcher her before the scavengers eat everything. And we've gotta locate the other rhinos, pronto.”

“There is a village about 20 kilometers from here, just outside the preserve's boundary,” Israel informed him.

“Okay. We'll head there on our way to check on the rest of the animals.”

Laidlaw carried the rifle to the bakkie and returned with a blood kit. He cut the rhino's ear tag off and, while he extracted a blood sample from her body, the other two men scoured the area for tyre impressions. They hoped to identify where the poachers came from and the direction they headed after poaching the cow. Although they found generic tracks, the imprints revealed nothing.

"Let's head to that village," Laidlaw finally said. "That meat's gonna start to go bad in this heat." They trudged back to the vehicle.

THE MASAI VILLAGE WAS A hodgepodge of cinder-block structures with tin roofs, interspersed with small garden plots containing corn, cabbages, bananas, and various root vegetables. Goats, a couple raw-boned cattle, and chickens roamed the dirt streets. Rap music and a televised soccer game blared from the paneless windows of several buildings.

"I know the headman of this village," Israel said. "I will speak to him of the rhino."

Jahi navigated the bakkie through the narrow, muddy lanes before drawing to a halt before a combination mini-mart, barber shop, and tavern. He killed the engine.

"Their headman owns this place. Even if he is not here, they will know where to find him." Laidlaw nodded, while Jahi appeared indifferent.

Israel jumped to the ground and disappeared into the noisy, smoky interior of the tumbledown structure. Several young males loitered outside the protean building and eyed the waiting Laidlaw and

Jahi with suspicion. The latter lit another cigarette and reclined his seat.

Israel returned five minutes later.

"The headman is inside and is very grateful for the rhino. I gave him the GPS coordinates and he is gathering men at this moment. I told him that he must hurry, before the heat and scavengers degrade the meat. I also asked whether he had seen any strangers pass through the village recently, but he said he had not."

"Either that, or he's in bed with 'em," Laidlaw responded. "Either way, we're done here. We need to check on the other rhinos asap."

Jahi sat up and started the engine as Israel climbed into the rear of the bakkie.

IT WAS DARK BEFORE THEY FINALLY bumped back to the rangers' camp, a ramshackle collection of small block buildings, resembling bunkers, arranged in a tight semi-circle. The remaining rhinos had proved to be unharmed, though it had taken several hours to locate the scattered animals. Jahi pulled in front of one of the structures and left the bakkie idling, its headlights illuminating a tiny building directly in front of them.

"Bunkhouse," he grunted.

"You will be comfortable here," Israel assured Laidlaw, more amiably. He climbed from the rear of the vehicle and reached back to grab the latter's duffle bag. “There is no electricity, but there is a gas lantern inside. I will show you.” Carrying Laidlaw's bag, he headed for the building's steel door.

Laidlaw stepped from the vehicle. Jahi released the bakkie's clutch and pulled away from the bunkhouse.

The one-room structure was scarcely large enough to accommodate the narrow mattress resting on a thick sheet of plywood eighteen inches above the concrete floor atop stacks of bricks. A rickety dresser occupied the wall opposite, with a narrow passage between them. The propane lantern, and a pasteboard box of wooden kitchen matches, sat on the dresser. A small window, only partially covered with a diaphanous curtain, completed the picture. Israel dropped Laidlaw's duffle bag onto the bed.

“The privy is next door,” he said. “Tomorrow morning, I will start the petrol generator and you can use the wireless to inform the ministry of the rhino's death. I will light your lantern and bid you goodnight, Mr. Alex.”

The lantern was fed from a small cylinder of propane attached to a coupler. Israel removed a match from the box, dragged it across the splintered dresser, and held its wavering flame beneath the lantern's mantle while slowly opening a valve on its base. The lantern emitted a quiet hiss before flaring into a soft glow with a soft 'pop'.

He turned to Laidlaw. “Will there be anything else, Mr. Alex?”

“No, I'm good for now. Thank you, Israel.”

“Of course.” The other man turned to leave, then paused. “Though I am saddened by the cow's death today, I am glad the poachers did not kill any of the other rhinos.”

“Well, not yet, anyway,” Laidlaw said, “though it wasn't through want of trying.”

“How do you mean?”

“I mean the poachers will be back.”

Israel nodded, thoughtfully. “Goodnight, Mr. Alex.”

“Goodnight, Israel. Thank you, again.” In the morning, Laidlaw would use his sat phone to place a direct call to Mwanajuma, informing him of the loss of the rhino cow.

THE THREE MEN BREAKFASTED IN a tin-roofed structure with no walls. Israel had not yet powered up the gasoline-powered generator, as they were able to heat water for washing, and cook their morning meal, using the camp's bulk propane tank.

"How long will you be here?” Jahi casually inquired while he sipped an enamelled mug of coffee.

“Not sure yet.”

“You live in Dar?”

“No, I've got a permanent camp here in the Selous.”

“The Selous? I thought no one was allowed to live here.”

“I have a permit from the ministry.”

"So, you and the minister are friends?"

Laidlaw smiled, ruefully. “I thought we were.”

“But you are no longer?” Jahi probed.

“No, we still are.”

“What will you tell the minister about the rhino cow?”

“I already called him this morning and told him she was killed by poachers. There was nothing more to tell.”

“What did he say?”

“What *could* he say? He was dismayed, of course.” Laidlaw laid his fork aside and looked directly at Jahi. “There were originally several more rhinos in the preserve. Were you here when they were poached?”

Jahi eyed him, mistrustfully. “No. I was assigned to this post only recently.”

Laidlaw turned to Israel, who'd been quietly listening.

"What about you?”

“Not for very long.”

Laidlaw tilted his head. “What does that mean? Were you here when the other rhinos were shot?”

“Yes.”

“You two know each other before either of you were assigned here?” Both men shook their heads in the negative. “What about the rangers you replaced. Did either of you know them?”

“I knew one,” Israel replied. “We were stationed together for a short while at Mkomazi.”

"Do you know where he is now?"

"No."

The coffee in Laidlaw's mug had grown tepid. He flicked his wrist and splashed the residue onto the ground. "Well, you might as well fire up the gen."

"Of course." Israel stood to comply. Because of the reverberating din produced while in operation, the generator was housed in a shack at the periphery of the compound. As Israel plodded to the generator, Laidlaw carried his mug to a dishpan of water. He rinsed the cup before placing it on the draining board. Still seated at the breakfast table, Jahi watched him, wordlessly.

"If you already talked to the minister why do you need the generator?" Jahi finally inquired.

"Charge my sat phone."

Jahi nodded and Laidlaw resumed his seat at the breakfast table. "Do you have a family?"

"A wife and four children," he acknowledged.

"Must be tough...kids are expensive and this job doesn't pay much."

"It is enough."

"What about Israel?"

"What about him?"

"Does he also have a family?"

"A wife and a baby, I think. We talk little of such things. He is from a different tribe."

"What do you guys do all day out here?"

"We find the rhinos on the GPS, then drive out in the bakkie to wherever they are so we can check on them. As Israel told you yesterday, twice each day we do this and make a notation in a logbook."

"And you've never encountered any other people? Hunters? People from that village?"

"No one."

"How often do you talk to people from the village?"

A puzzled expression crossed Jahi's face. "I never go to the village. Only Israel sometimes."

Laidlaw unconsciously frowned and gazed across the packed earth of the compound's yard. Israel had not yet returned from his mission to start the generator.

He looked back at Jahi. "Any idea who killed the rhino cow?"

The other man was silent for a moment. "Bad men," he finally said.

"Do you know any bad men?"

"Everyone knows bad men. The world is full of them." Jahi didn't elaborate further.

In Primis Anno Regnantibus Imperator Caesar Titus Vespasianus (80 CE)

HARKHUF SHEPHERDED CRIXUS' ragtag armada through the five cataracts immediately south of the first, or “Great Cataract" suffering the loss of only a single boat, and one legionnaire, in the process. The doomed craft began taking in water shortly after its Nubian pilot successfully guided it through the murky, frothing water of one of the lesser cataracts.

"Romans, can you swim?" the pilot snapped at his passengers.

"I cannot!" Ero's friend, Drusus, cried in alarm.

The pilot laughed, disdainfully. "In that case, I submit that *all* your life is wasted."

Saying nothing further, he dove into the river and began to swim for shore, closely followed by Drusus' fellow legionnaires. Terrified, the latter clung desperately to the gunwale as the listing boat whirled in the current. Moments later it, and Drusus, disappeared into the choppy water.

Each evening, after endless days of floating downriver, the men beached their watercraft before fishing for Nile perch, and netting birds, for their evening meal. Crixus recalled Aulus' vow never to eat another fish and smiled, forlornly.

"How long before the Great Cataract?" he asked their guide one evening.

"Two days, perhaps three," Harkhuf replied.

From the dawn of pharaonic civilization, the foaming waters of the Great Cataract represented the physical barrier separating Egypt from Nubia and the interior of Africa, the demarcation between the known and the unknown, the border separating order from chaos, safety from danger. The ancient Egyptians believed the jumbled heaps of massive granite sarsens that formed the Great Cataract, their lacquered surfaces gleaming as though polished by the hand of God himself, gave birth to the Nile. The Cataract's churning waters and surging currents were thought to boil to the surface from deep within the earth, one half flowing northward until ultimately losing itself in the numberless channels and inlets that crisscrossed the pathless Delta, the other half struggling south, to the Sudd and the uncharted vastness of the African interior.

Located mid-river at the northern terminus of the First Cataract, Elephantine Island derived its name from the cluster of boulders, resembling a herd of elephants, massed along its periphery. Opposite the island, on the eastern bank of the Nile, lay the ancient city of Sunu, biblical 'Syene', now the sprawling metropolis of modern Aswan. Though only 3,900 feet long and 1,300 feet wide, Elephantine Island is one of the oldest continuously inhabited sites in Egypt, a palimpsest reflecting a succession of civilizations spanning millennia: predynastic and dynastic

Egyptian, Nubian, Jewish, Levantine, Assyrian, Persian, Greek, Roman, Christian, Arab. It was the pharaohs, however, who were the first to recognize the island's strategic importance. Predictably, they erected a fortress on its southern end in order to monitor, and tax, the riverine traffic.

Both Elephantine Island and Sunu were important trade entrepots in antiquity. However, the practical Romans quickly concluded that Sunu, not a geographically insignificant mid-river speck girded by submerged boulders, represented the far more promising locus. At the expense of Elephantine Island, the Romans devoted all of their resources and energies toward developing the riverside town. Ships bearing goods from sub-Saharan Africa...exotic animals; ostrich feathers; gold; malachite, turquoise, and lapis lazuli; leopard, lion, zebra, and giraffe hides; spices; slaves...regularly called at Sunu to barter. Because of its strategic and economic importance, the earlier Ptolemies erected a wall five miles long, thirty feet high, and fifteen feet thick at its base, to shield from bandits the portage road that ran from Sunu northward, paralleling the river. In addition to repelling occasional border raids, the later garrison of Roman troops ensured that taxes and import duties were duly paid on all shipping that managed to successfully navigate the Great Cataract.

Minuscule Elephantine Island, marooned in the center of the Nile's main channel and left to its own devices, became little more than a footnote of the Empire. A backwater, both literally and figuratively, the islet attracted a kaleidoscope of dispossessed and rootless migrants of varying proclivities. Provided the settlers acknowledged Rome's nominal suzerainty and posed no overt threat to the *Pax Romana*, they were largely ignored by the Imperial government, irrespective of whatever nefarious activities they otherwise engaged in. As a consequence, Elephantine Island inevitably became a haven for waterborne piracy.

"How far below the Great Cataract is the path you spoke of earlier?"

"Not far. It lays at the foot of sandstone bluffs that range along the Iteru's western shore, beginning less than a quarter league from the near end of the cataract. The path is invisible from the river," Harkhuf informed him.

"By using this path to travel overland past Elephantine Island, the pirates may be entirely skirted?"

"Just so."

Crixus looked at the other man with suspicion. "The pirates must be aware of the path and surely post spies to intercept those who would use it."

"There is no want of trade vessels for them to seize on the Iteru. They have no need to seek plunder inland."

"Who knows of this path?"

"Those who value their lives but place no trust in the capricious gods. Not even the Egyptians will venture onto the west bank of the Iteru, for they believe it to be the abode of the dead."

“You know others who have availed themselves of the security afforded by this path?”

“Many,” Harkhuf affirmed, “though the path is of no use to merchants who travel with an abundance of wares. Those have no choice but to sail the Iteru and trust their fate to the gods. But, you are not them.”

Crixus sighed. They had traveled this far downriver without incident and Harkhuf had provided the Romans no reason to distrust him. Still, Crixus was conflicted and feared betrayal. He was apprehensive about the possibility of the Nubian leading the men directly into an ambush.

Harkhuf sensed his unease. “Do as you wish, Roman.” He turned to walk away.

“Wait! How long will it take the men to traverse your path?”

Harkuf paused. “If they porter their own boats and move rapidly, no more than two days. If it proves necessary to hire porters, at least two days more, for I must find men willing to help us. That will prove difficult, though, for you possess nothing with which to pay them.”

“We will haul our own boats over your path.”

“Two days, then.”

“I will inform the men this evening.”

Harkhuf shrugged. “Do as you wish, Roman.”

"SO, ARE WE NOW TO BE REDUCED TO the status of slaves?" Eros grumbled when informed of the details of Crixus' conversation with Harkhuf. "Why do we even have boats if we are expected to lug them overland? Perhaps I shall suggest to Crixus that we simply hump our boats all the way to Rome on our backs!"

"Indeed, Eros. Crixus does not appear to understand that boats are intended to carry, not *be* carried! Perhaps no one ever informed him," one of his companions laughed.

Eros frowned in anger. "Is it not finally clear to all but his craven toadies that Crixus' masquerade as a leader of Romans is a laughable farce? Romo was either out of his wits, or bewitched by Crixus, to have appointed him commander in his last extremity."

"What do you intend?"

"I intend to complete my sojourn to Rome via the *Nilus*, rather than entrust my life to a treacherous barbarian and traipsing cross-country, hauling a boat in the bargain! All who possess a mite of common sense will accompany me." Eros looked, expectantly, at the faces clustered around him.

"I will join you," a legionnaire named 'Fabatus' immediately asserted, "as will any Roman who despises taking orders from an effeminate Greek or a Nubian."

"I, too," another boldly announced.

"Aye, and me."

"Me, as well."

In all, the entire assemblage pledged its fidelity to Eros, representing a third of the surviving men under Crixus' command.

Eros smiled with satisfaction. "I will inform Crixus of your decision. We depart on the morrow. Use the rest of today to assemble and provision your boats."

"And if Crixus forbids splintering the group?"

"'*Forbids*'?" Eros scoffed. You speak in jest, Fabatus! Do you suppose I care a whit about what Crixus 'forbids'? Pray, how do you suppose he will prevent us from leaving? By ordering our comrades to physically bind us? Crixus and those who foolishly heed him are certain to suffer death long before they reach Rome. My only regret is that we will be deprived of the pleasure of seeing Crixus dragged away in chains after I denounce the poseur to the senate."

"How will we deal with the pirates that menace the river hereabouts?"

"Preying upon unarmed merchants is one thing, daring to trifle with Roman legionnaires quite another. Even ignorant freebooters are mindful of the dreadful consequences of such folly," Eros confidently declared. "Those vagabonds are hardly worthy of Roman bronze."

"And the Great Cataract?"

"It boasts terrors no greater than the relatively benign cataracts we have already encountered."

Fabatus nodded, thoughtfully. "Your words ring true, Eros. It is well that someone possessing true

Roman *fortis* has now vouchsafed to take charge before a new host of evils conspires to utterly ruin us."

"Aye. Though our venerated fathers counseled, 'through obedience learn to command', my patience with Crixus' treacherous ineptitude is finally at an end."

"YOU ARE AT LIBERTY TO DO AS you see fit, though I wonder at those who agreed to accompany you."

"I am far from surprised that you marvel at Roman *virtus*, Crixus," Eros sarcastically responded. "I would expect no less."

"You, and they, are prepared to battle the Great Cataract, to say nothing of the freebooters who swarm the area?"

"We are prepared to do battle with Jupiter, himself, if the gods will it."

Crixus nodded, thoughtfully. "Your valor, if not your prudence, does you justice, Eros. When do you leave?"

"The morrow."

"Whatever weapons and provisions you consider needful are at your disposal."

"I do not require your leave in such matters," Eros crisply responded.

Crixus arched his eyebrows at the sharp rejoinder. "How many boats will you take?" he smoothly transitioned.

“Four.”

“I hope we may greet one another as friends in Rome.”

Eros coldly smiled. “You were previously my prisoner, Crixus. Had Romo's wits not abandoned him, you would be, still. Though we may meet again in the future, it will assuredly not be as friends.”

“In that case, I wish you ill though I bear no enmity toward those you duped into joining you.”

“Roman courage requires no cajolery, nor cowardice, which you possess in abundance, any prompting,” Eros smirked.

“I do not mourn your leaving,” Crixus said, standing.

Eros laughed, derisively. “The gods truly have a sense of humor, for this is the first time we have been of one mind.”

A BOY CRABBING IN THE SHALLOWS was the first to spot the armed legionnaires advancing on the village. Flinging his basket aside, he sprinted homeward to raise the alarm.

“Romans! Romans!” he shrieked as he flew along the beach, his legs churning.

Hearing the tumult, Carpio rushed from his rondavel to determine its source. Spotting the frantic boy, he raced to intercept, and roughly collar, him.

“What is the cause of this disturbance?” Carpio demanded, cuffing the boy across his head.

“The Romans are coming back!” the boy panted, pointing northward.

Carpio released the boy and squinted in that direction.

“How far?”

“Near.”

“Many or few?”

“Many.”

In fact, Berossus had previously divided his command and only a portion of the Romans descended on the unarmed colony. A handful of men, including Neocles, were chosen to remain behind to guard the *castra aestiva.* The main contingent marched inland, southward. They would be further divided when they drew near the village, some positioning themselves below it in order to intercept any villagers who might attempt to flee southward. The main body, about 20 men led personally by Berossus, headed directly for the settlement.

Carpio thought quickly. Even if the villagers had time to gather their belongings, he knew the legionnaires would attempt to envelope them, thereby rendering flight an impossibility. Nor had they time to erect defensive works. As for mounting a meaningful defense, their knives and fishing spears would prove useless against the vengeful Roman's swords and bronze-tipped pikes. There remained but one alternative.

"Hasten to the village and gather all the woman and girls at once! There is not a moment to lose!" Carpio shoved the boy forward and he sped off.

Carpio rapidly scanned the quarter from which he anticipated the soldiers would appear. The enervated legionnaires were evidently proceeding at a leisurely pace, as there was yet no sign of them. The only advantage the villagers held over the Romans was their knowledge that an attack was imminent, thus depriving their enemies of the element of surprise. They could plan accordingly.

Carpio turned and strode back toward his village.

"THE FAITHLESS ROMANS BETRAYED betrayed our trust. They will slaughter us, violate our women, and sell our children into slavery. They march even now."

"How do you know these things?"

Carpio pointed to the boy. "Speak!"

"It is true. I saw them while crabbing. Armed soldiers come this way," he stammered.

The group of men exchanged worried looks.

"We will do battle with them," proposed one.

"And give the Romans the pleasure of butchering us at their leisure?"

"We have no choice but to flee," insisted another.

Carpio shook his head. "There is no time. The Romans will be upon us before our women are even able to organize themselves."

"The feckless gods have abandoned us to the savagery of the Romans," bewailed one of the men.

"No, the gods have not forsaken us," Carpio sternly retorted. "On the contrary, they vouchsafe the only honorable solution to our plight." The other men looked upon him dubiously.

"Speak plainly, Carpio."

"Gladly. The Romans disparage our men, covet our women, and will enslave our children."

"These things we know already."

"For all their boasting, Romans are frauds as soldiers and as men. The most stinging insult to them is to reveal their natural womanishness."

"While we may exceed the Romans in valiance, it cannot be gainsaid that we are inferior to them in weapons and numbers!" a man rued.

Carpio looked solemn. "*We* may be unequal to the Romans, but the gods are not.

"What is your meaning, Carpio?"

"The opportune appearance of the Romans was no accident, but irrefutable proof that the gods favor us. They have blessed us with an opportunity to expose the Romans as braggarts and blowhards by denying them the glory they covet. Is it not apparent that the gods desire that we do so? What could be more clear? We spurn the gods' generous gift at our peril!"

“Perhaps, but the gods are inconstant and changeable. If we fail, the Romans will avenge themselves on our wives and children.”

Carpio smiled, coldy, and shook his head. “We will deny them that pleasure by delivering our loved ones into the benevolent company of the gods.”

Uneasy murmurings rippled through his audience.

“What you are suggesting is no easy thing, Carpio,” one of them said.

Carpio shook his head. “You are wrong. When Caecina Paetus was ordered by the emperor Claudius to end his own life, he quailed at doing so. Paetus' wife took the dagger from his hand, drove into her own breast, and removed it. She then offered the dagger to her husband with the words, 'It does not hurt.' So, too, the noble wife whose husband's private parts festered with ulcers. Convinced that his condition was hopeless, she urged his honorable death. Nay, she became his boon companion and helpmate for, after binding herself to her husband, she flung herself from a height, drowning both of them in Lake Comum. It is no different here, for the gods will give us courage.”

“How is the deed to be done? We have but little time.”

“Go quickly to your homes and order your wives, sons, and daughters to this spot. After they depart your dwellings, gather your infants and smallest children and slit their throats. They will not resist, for they trust you. But take care not to spatter their blood on your clothing, that the others will not be alarmed.

Once you are done, return here and we will explain matters to the women. Know that no man is expected to destroy his own wife. But you must hurry!”

After a brief, tense discussion the men scattered. Carpio turned back to the boy.

“Go to the place where you last saw the Romans then return here to inform me of their progress.” The boy raced off.

ONLY THE MUTED KEENING OF A FEW children rent the lifeless air. Gathered on the beach a distance away, apprehensive women looked toward their village with dread.

“What is happening?” one, called 'Amina', wailed as they milled about.

“Where are our husbands and children?” another, Lelise, anguished.

“Why were we ordered to remain here?” demanded a third, her question directed at no one in particular. “Whatever is afoot, those Romans are to blame!” she snarled.

Collectively, the women again peered anxiously toward the village, where several observed their husbands emerging from their homes. The men huddled together and spoke in low tones, though the women were too far away to discern the subject of their conversation. Several of the men looked up during the course of their grim colloquy to glance in the direction of the women.

"Where are our children?" Lelise whispered under her breath.

Led by Carpio, the men broke their conclave and began striding toward the women clustered on the beach.

"Why are you behaving like fools? And where are our children?" one of the women angrily demanded of the approaching men.

Carpio drew to a stop before her. He surveyed the women's anxious faces before responding. "Your children are with the gods. Far better there than buggered by Roman scum or sold into slavery."

Only for an instant, silence prevailed. Then one woman began to scream hysterically.

"You are a liar!" the woman howled. Though her husband rushed to subdue her, she shoved him away. "A liar, Carpio, and a murderer!" she shrieked. "All of you!"

"We are neither," Carpio calmly responded. "By surrendering to the fulsome embrace of the gods, your children have been spared defilement at the hands of the Romans."

"But what are we to do without our children?" the woman wailed.

"You need not want for their loving kisses, for the gods invite you to join them, as well. But you must act quickly, for the Romans approach even now."

As they conversed, the men slipped closer to the group of women and children, knives concealed beneath their garments. Each man having reluctantly acceded to sacrifice specific individuals, they stood in trembling silence near their assigned victims.

"You are a blasphemous murderer!" a woman screamed at Carpio. "We are not Carthaginians! The gods do not demand that they be requited with innocent blood!"

"The gods seek to ensure that your children's blood remains untainted, though you will find the Romans less discriminating. They will not confine themselves to your children, but will violate you, your daughters, and your sons before slaughtering all of you. The gods have deigned to preserve your honor by preventing such outrages."

So saying, Carpio gave the prearranged signal, a slight nod of his head. Initially displaying some hesitancy, the anxious men stepped into the cluster of women and children. Abandoning their previous agreement, they began to madly, indiscriminately, slash at them.

With anguished cries of shock and horror, mothers futilely attempted to shield their children from the flashing blades wielded by fathers, husbands, brothers, and uncles.

The executioners' knives quickly became slick with spurting blood. Undeterred, the frenzied men continued to stab and hack the terrified women who, in their panic, unconsciously drew into an even tighter defensive knot. In his delirium, one man's hand slipped from the hilt of his knife onto its blade, amputating two of his fingers. He automatically changed hands and resumed his sanguinary task without pausing.

Screaming, weeping, mothers clutched their children as the latter stumbled onto the bloody sand. Still, the men continued to slash their defenseless victims without relent.

Finally, but for the ragged gurgling of a handful women sprawled on the earth, the massacre was over, seemingly as quickly as it had begun.

"Spare them needless suffering," Carpio directed.

Trembling as much from an adrenaline surge as from exhaustion, a few men began stepping gingerly among the prostrate bodies. When they found any still clinging to life, they cut their throats.

"What now, Carpio?" one of the men wept. He squatted next to the blood-soaked body of his wife, holding her dead hand.

"Now, we will ambush the Romans."

"How?"

Carpio's young scout lingered, diffidently, farther down the beach. "Come, boy," he called to him. The youngster momentarily vacillated before complying.

"Where are the Romans?"

The boy pretended to not to see the scattered bodies when he drew closer to the scene of the massacre.

"Very near."

Carpio turned to the men milling about the blood-soaked shoreline. "The Romans are, collectively, too strong for us to challenge. But, as a precaution against raids, their commanders leave a small detachment of men to guard their camp while the main body is afield. These we will best."

A man gestured to the corpses. "And our women?"

"We must leave them. The incoming tide will carry their bodies away and deny the Romans opportunity to defile them. Make haste and return to your homes to collect whatever weapons you have. We must make our way to the Romans' camp, and destroy them, before they return thither. Knives will not do for the Romans. We must use bows and darts to ambush them from a safe distance. Go now!"

Sorrowfully, the men abandoned the gore-spattered corpses of their loved ones and began to make their way back to their dwellings. Carpio looked down at the boy.

"Unless you wish to die today, you must flee this place. Do not return." He placed a rough hand on the youth's shoulder and shoved him. The boy looked confused. "You will die if you stay here. Go!" Carpio directed a kick at the boy, who began to whimper. He nudged a corpse with the toe of his sandal. "It is your desire to end up a piece of meat like this one?" The sobbing boy stumbled backward, never taking his eyes off Carpio. "Yes, go now, before the others return!"

With a wail, the boy abruptly turned and bolted. Carpio watched his exodus with melancholy. He turned away only when he heard the other men returning.

“We found arrows, slings, and darts,” one of them called, holding aloft a carved wooden bow.

“Excellent. Though the Romans do not anticipate an assault, they will assume it would come from the seaward side. We will therefore attack from the landward side. Let us go; the Romans are only moments away.”

The men headed inland.

“THE TIDE IS TURNING,” NEOCLES remarked, squinting eastward.

Senecio looked up from the fallen tree upon which he sat. “Perhaps you will only have to journey half a league for your bath,” he joked. “Either way, it is too far. I think I shall just sit here and await Berossus' return with women from that village. If you are not back by the time he does so, I will take *your* woman, leaving you to enjoy sloppy seconds!”

Neocles scowled at him. “I will return before Berossus does, as I have no desire to suffer abuse for leaving the *castrum* unguarded.”

“Unguarded? You do us a grave disservice! Your unbathed comrades and myself will ensure the security of the *castrum*.” Senecio spread his arms and beamed. “Who exists to attack us?”

Neocles did not directly respond. “I will return soon.” He turned and began walking toward the sea.

"There is no need to hasten! Your absence leaves a greater number of women for the rest of us to choose from!"

IT TOOK ONLY TWENTY MINUTES for the villagers to reach the *castrum* overland.

"I see five Romans," one of them whispered to Carpio as they hunkered in the surrounding brush, fifty yards away.

Carpio surveyed the camp. "I, also, count five, though others may yet be lurking nearby."

"What shall we do?"

"We will wait to attack until we are satisfied there are no additional Romans nearby."

"Their companions have certainly reached our village by now. They will be outraged when they see the bodies of our women and will seek to avenge themselves on us. We must attack now, before the others return in a rage!" the other man hissed.

The few inattentive legionnaires lounged about the *castrum*. Three of them played at knucklebones, while Senecio and another stretched out in the shade to nap.

Carpio continued to watch the unwary Romans in silence.

"I do not think there are others about," he finally whispered. He gestured to the villagers crowded around him. “Make ready. We must catch them unawares.”

The two archers nocked their arrows. Others slipped stones into slings or clutched hand-thrown missiles fashioned from dense wood. All carried knives or billhooks, as well.

“Bowmen, do not be profligate with your arrows, for you possess but few. Aim for the three Romans who remain awake,” Carpio whispered. “Darts and stones will suffice to kill the other two. We will hurl them the moment you release your arrows.”

“We will spit the Romans as we would a fish. Mark us,” one of the archers assured him, though his bravado was strained. All realized they were no match for trained legionnaires in close combat. As a consequence, the Romans had to be quickly immobilized, if not killed outright.

Because it was impossible to release their arrows from their current squatting position, both archers slowly straightened. With trembling arms they drew their bowstrings.

Fabius, one of the knucklebone players, looked up at that moment.

“Assassins!” he screeched, leaping to his feet and pointing wildly. He dove for his sword.

Instantly, the remaining four legionnaires sprang upward.

The archers released their arrows in a panic. Both shots went wide and the men fell back into the bushes.

"Now!" Carpio shouted as he sprang free of the vegetation and, wielding a billhook, began running toward the bivouac. He hoped the other men followed his lead.

The legionnaires, having meanwhile armed themselves, braced for the attack by grouping themselves into a compact defensive square.

"Which direction?" Senecio barked as a smattering of men from the village emerged from the brush and bounded toward them.

"West!"

"How many?"

"Few. Barbarians from that place, I think!"

A smattering of stones and darts thudded into the ground around the Romans, less than a dozen harmlessly striking their shields.

Quickly sensing the failure of their impetuous ambush, several of the villagers abruptly suspended their advance and began to fall back in confusion. Others, cautiously watching from the safety of the bushes, opted to exercise the better part of valor and took to their heels. Unaware of the assault's spontaneous disintegration, the small number of villagers in the vanguard aggressively pressed forward.

"The cowards are already retreating!" a legionnaire gleefully cried.

"Do not allow yourselves to be lured into a trap!" Senecio cautioned through gritted teeth.

The Romans broke formation and strode forward. Undeterred, Carpio angled toward the advancing Fabius and raised his billhook.

Utilizing his shield as an offensive weapon, Fabius reciprocated by thrusting it into Carpio's chest and shoving him backward. Frantically backpedaling, Carpio slashed downward with his billhook, though it merely glanced off the top of the legionnaire's shield. Fabius withdrew his shield with his left arm and robotically buried the point of his *gladius* into Carpio's unprotected side with his right. Carpio's legs buckled and he collapsed without a sound.

On his knees, Carpio's head slumped forward. Blood flowed from the fatal wound in his side.

"Your liver," Fabius informed him with the indifference of a clinician. He took a half-step forward, placed the point of his bronze sword near the base of Carpio's sagging skull, between the second and third vertebrae, and shoved downward, severing Carpio's spinal cord. His nearly decapitated corpse sprawled to the earth.

Because the majority of the frightened villagers had already fled, few remained for the Romans to dispatch in hand-to-hand fighting. The thick bullhide *lorica* of one legionnaire blunted the sharpened point of a stave wielded by a villager; the Roman casually lopped both of the villager's arms off at his elbows. The man writhed on the ground, groaning, blood oozing from the stumps. The remaining victims of the abortive raid, their limbs akimbo, lay scattered. The five legionnaires, though out of breath and shaking from exertion, were unharmed.

"Bastards!" on of them spat as he viewed the carnage with satisfaction. "It is not enough that the swine try to poison us. They also steal up on us like serpents!"

"Well, these will do so no longer," another said, sweeping his arm around the area. He looked at Senecio. "Should we pursue those that fled?"

Senecio shook his head. "Though they are terrified like rabbits, it is not impossible they might return. I do not wish to leave the camp unguarded, should they do so. They dare not go back to their village, though, because they will encounter Berossus, who will annihilate them. The barbarians have nowhere to run!"

Fabius laughed, nervously. "In his haste to preen, Neocles deprived himself of the pleasure of killing them."

"Truly," Senecio responded. "But let us make a pact, brothers. Do not inform Berossus of Neocles' absence during this skirmish, for he will be certain to mete out unjust punishment. Any of us could easily be the next to suffer Berossus' mercurial wrath. Swear to it."

The other men glanced, wordlessly, at one another before responding.

"Aye," they affirmed in unison.

A STUNNED NEOCLES RETURNED to discover the legionnaires had slain eleven villagers, two of them boys about ten years of age. They'd dragged the bodies several yards from the castrum and arranged them in a row.

"In your haste to undertake ablutions, you deprived yourself of some unexpected sport," Fabius chastened him.

Neocles viewed the line of corpses with skepticism. "Slaughtering rabble and children armed with sticks would seem to provide rather thin sport."

"Hardly, Neocles," Fabius stiffly retorted. "The barbarian scum attacked us and fought with vigor!"

"Indeed? All eleven of them?"

"I daresay you are hardly in a position to censure us, given that you were absent the entire time we were besieged. There were far more than just these few. The remainder of the horde abandoned the field when the tide of battle began to turn against them.

Senecio smoothly intervened. "You heard nothing of the recent tumult, Neocles?"

The latter shook his head. "I was too distant. I heard nothing but the hissing surf and the lap of the incoming tide. Have you news of Berossus?"

"None, though not even barbarians are foolish enough to match themselves against an entire Roman legion."

"Or, at least with what passes for a Roman legion," Neocles dryly commented.

"No matter," Fabius interjected. "Even if the barbarians slip Berossus' net, he will be gratified by our handiwork today."

"For once, I tend to agree with you," Neocles sighed.

THIRTEEN

"YOU UP FOR A ZEBRA?" ASKED Nicobar Jones.

"A zebra?" Laidlaw responded, as though unsure of what a 'zebra' was.

"They look like black-and-white striped horses. Figured you might have seen a picture of one in a book somewhere."

Laidlaw rolled his eyes. "I know what a zebra is."

"Oh. Wasn't sure from your reaction," Jones grinned. "Thought I might have to refresh your memory."

Laidlaw had been under Jones' tutelage for nearly four months and had already crammed five, going on six, notebooks with field notes: European colonial and African history; hunting and game laws and regulations; animal identification, behavior, taxonomy, anatomy, physiology, and reproduction; firearms types, calibers, and ballistics; bullet construction; geography, map-reading, and navigation; ecology; botany; meteorology; astronomy; marksmanship; first-aid; tracking and spooring; skinning, butchering, and preservation of hunting trophies; hunting scopes and binoculars; wilderness survival; languages; oenology; maintenance and repair of internal combustion engines; countless other subjects, great and small. He was astonished on a daily basis by Jones' seemingly limitless fund of knowledge on every conceivable subject.

"Your clients come from all over the world, so ya gotta know how to talk to pretty much anybody about pretty much anything," Jones explained. "Some guy from Spain ain't gonna give two shits about how the Yankees are doing or who some big-boobed Hollywood nobody has been sleeping with."

Laidlaw applied himself diligently to the task, trying to absorb everything he'd seen and heard, but the sheer volume of information was overwhelming. He'd be lucky to retain a quarter of it, even with his notebooks.

"Don't fret, son," Jones counseled, "you'll eventually get it. Nobody can teach experience. Wish I had a nickle for every screw-up I've had."

"Yeah, but..."

"'Yeah, but' nuthin'. You'll figure it out. It just happens. Kinda like ridin' a bike."

Although he and Jones had, of necessity, already engaged in a great deal of hunting together, they'd not yet gone after a zebra. Until today.

THEY PARKED THE BAKKIE IN THE shade of a marula tree. Jones and Laidlaw stood in the rear of the vehicle, monitoring through binoculars a distant herd of Burchells' zebra.

"Zebras are good eatin'," Jones murmured as he watched them. "Lions like 'em, too, especially the little ones."

"How can you tell the stallions from the mares?"

"Pretty much can't. Almost no dimorphism between the sexes. Stallions have thicker necks and broader muzzles. Quickest way is to look for udders on the mares, but even that ain't easy. Best way is to watch 'em when they're runnin'. The dominant stallion will almost always be at the rear of the herd. But ya gotta be careful 'cause he may lead the herd during its initial flight from danger."

"Christ! So, like I said, how are you supposed to tell 'em apart?" Laidlaw bemoaned.

Jones lowered his binoculars to look at his protege. "Like I said, I can't teach experience." He raised his binoculars again and resumed scanning the herd. "Zebras are pissy, aggressive animals," he said.

“They're always kickin' and bitin' each other, especially during matin' season. Clients usually want juveniles 'cause their hides are in better shape than those of older animals, especially stallions. Their hides can be pretty rough...old wounds, scars, and the like. Lot of 'em have even had an ear bit off by another stallion. Personally, I like the old boys. Their beat-up hides give 'em character.”

“See one you like?”

“It ain't me I'm lookin' for,” Jones replied without removing his binoculars from his eyes. “There's a nice looking one toward the back. Can't tell if it's a stallion or mare, but it don't really matter. You see the one I'm talkin' about?”

Laidlaw raised his binoculars and scanned the grazing herd. “Yeah, I think so. Toward the left in the rear?”

“Yep, that's him. Herd's about 600 yards away. You comfortable taking a shot from here or ya wanna move a wee bit closer?”

Laidlaw gulped. “I'm not real confident from this range, Nic.”

“Fair enough. If you start your stalk from here, it'll take a while and the herd might move off in the meantime. Let's try creepin' up a little closer in the bakkie and you can sneak up on 'em from there.” Laidlaw nodded. He was using his Remington .375 H&H, which had plenty of punch for a zebra stallion.

The men clambered into their seats and Jones cranked the vehicle's engine to life. Driving with agonizing slowness and taking advantage of natural declivities, trees, and termite mounds, they crept toward the unmindful zebras. Jones finally braked about 300 yards upwind from the herd and switched the engine off.

"If we get any closer we're liable to spook 'em," he whispered. "You ready?"

"Yeah."

Jones pointed to a truncated termite mound. "Steady your rifle on top of that and take your time. Wait 'till your zebra gets clear of the others...don't want a shoot-through," he recited for the thousandth time.

Laidlaw nodded and eased out of the vehicle. He hunkered down and began to edge his way forward. At the termite mound, he slowly retracted the bolt of his rifle and eased a cartridge into the chamber. Placing the Remington on 'safe', Laidaw peeped around the edge of his improvised rifle rest. Looking over the top of the mound would silhouette his head against the sky and alarm the herd into instantaneous flight.

In movies and on television, "snipers" are stereotypically shown using ominous-looking black rifles that they rapidly assemble while perched on a building rooftop in full view of God and everybody. The sniper then peers through a high-tech scope, with an abundance of hash-marks, at a politician or bad guy located at least twenty stories below and four blocks down the street. Movie snipers are so accomplished and confident that they have no need to conceal themselves, nor do they bother to use any sort of rest in order to brace their rifles for shots routinely exceeding 500 yards. They simply fire their rifles offhand and hit their targets with consistent ho-hum accuracy. Having done so, they disassemble their rifle before sauntering away from the scene by mingling with the panicked crowd. Such scenarios are, of course, ridiculous fantasies bordering on farce.

In order to ensure an instantaneous humane kill, experienced hunters steady their rifles against some sort of rest before attempting any shot at an animal, irrespective of the distance. They might utilize commercial bipods or shooting sticks, the branch or trunk of a tree, a fence post, a heap of soil or pile of rocks, a termite mound, even the shoulder of their guide or hunting companion. While field conditions sometimes render such precautions impossible, as when forced to take a snap-shot at wounded or fleeing game, hunters make every possible effort to eliminate errant shots. Compassion aside, hunters are required to pay for every animal they shoot, whether killed outright or merely wounded and lost.

The zebras continued to feed without apparent concern. The animal Laidlaw wanted had moved away from the rest of the herd and was grazing by itself around 350 yards away, plus or minus. A formidable distance by any standard.

Laidlaw glanced back toward the bakkie, where Jones watched through binoculars. The latter grinned at him.

Still on his knees, Laidlaw straightened, slightly, and gingerly began to lift his heavy rifle. He was careful not to bump or scrape it against the side of the termite mound; with their acute senses, the zebras would hear the anomalous sound and spontaneously bolt. He was already dripping sweat and his back, arms, and legs were beginning to cramp from strain.

Laidlaw inched the Remington upward and gently laid it across the top of the termite mound, muzzle toward the herd. He shifted his position and slowly stuck his head around the side of the mound again.

The preferred aiming point on any large animal is the broadside heart-lung region which, depending on the species, varies in size from a tennis ball to a dinner plate. A venerable, if counter-intuitive, axiom among experienced hunters is, "The bigger the animal, the smaller the target." Shots to the heart-lung area, even if not immediately fatal, will generally "anchor" the animal, prevent it from fleeing, and allow the hunter to place a rapid second shot to a vital area. However, the ideal heart-lung shot on a stationary animal is often not possible or practical under actual hunting conditions.

If an animal is not broadside to the hunter, shots to its brain, spinal chord, or kidneys offer an alternative which ordinarily produce instantaneous death. Despite this salutary affect, these aiming points are generally disfavored because they represent relatively small, difficult targets. If missed by even a fraction of an inch, the animal will, as likely as not, take flight in a rush of adrenaline and may never be found. Indeed, the creature may suffer no long-term debilitating effects after a botched shot to these areas.

Head shots on elephants are especially dicey because, in relation to their mass, their brains are relatively small. Moreover, an elephant's skull is a honeycomb of bone and empty air. A misjudged shot may miss its brain entirely but enrage the elephant, with lethal consequences to the hunter.

As it continued to crop the dry grass, the zebra wandered even farther away from the termite mound. It now stood at a shallow oblique, quartering away from Laidlaw, rendering a broadside shot impossible. Although the animal might change its orientation at some point, there was no way to predict this. Moreover, the entire herd could just as easily make a sudden mad dash for the hills if something happened to spook it, a happenstance more likely than not.

Shit.

Under the circumstances, Laidlaw decided to attempt an "off-shoulder" shot. That is, he would visualize and aim for the zebra's opposite front shoulder, notwithstanding that it was blocked by the animal's body and invisible to him. By placing his shot about a foot behind the animal's near-shoulder, the expanding bullet would angle diagonally though its chest cavity, resulting in massive hemorrhaging of heart and lungs, and exit the zebra through its opposite, "blind", shoulder. Not an ideal shot, but the only one to immediately present itself. Thus, Laidlaw had little choice.

Hugging the termite mound, Laidlaw inched his way upward. Reaching its crest, he grasped his rifle and lifted it toward him. Grazing, their heads lowered, the herd appeared not to notice. Placing the Remington's wooden forearm in his left palm, Laidlaw positioned his eye behind the scope and adjusted it to maximum magnification. He gently curled his right index finger around the trigger. Centering the scope's crosshairs a foot behind, and two inches above the zebra's near-shoulder in order to compensate for bullet drop caused by gravity, he flicked the safety off, took a deep breath, and held it.

Laidlaw touched-off the shot.

The herd exploded in a tempest of alarmed barking peculiar to zebras, flying hooves, and dust. In seconds, the animals, including Laidlaw's, had vanished.

Laidlaw didn't hear the distinct thump of his bullet striking home but, given the distance, didn't expect to. He straightened and looked toward the bakkie. Jones lowered his binoculars and shook his head.

A clean miss.

Chagrined and embarrassed, Laidlaw ejected the spent cartridge from his rifle and clicked its safety on. He bent to retrieve the brass casing from the ground before trudging back to the vehicle. Jones started the bakkie's engine as he approached.

“Let's check for blood-spoor to see whether you winged him,” he said after Laidlaw climbed in.

They bumped across the veldt and drew to a stop at the last location of the zebra herd. The men exited the vehicle and began to examine the grass stubble for blood.

"Ho!" Jones immediately exclaimed. He pointed to a mass of frothy blood on the ground. "I'll be a son of a bitch. You banged him, Alex," he grinned.

Laidlaw felt like laughing. "I'll be a son of a bitch," he echoed.

"He's hit hard," Jones said. "He ain't gonna get very far."

They followed the copious blood trail about 50 yards before coming upon the zebra. He lay on his left side in the brush beneath a mimosa tree. Jones knelt beside the body to examine the exit wound.

He looked up at Laidlaw. "Perfect shot, son. He was dead before he hit the ground... just didn't know it."

Though elated, Laidlaw tried to appear modest. "Well, I'd rather be lucky than good."

"Bullshit. Luck's got nuthin' to do with it. Your shot was right on the money."

"SO, YOU THINK ISRAEL OKUBUNA may be poaching my rhinos?"

"That's not what I said. I said he knows more than he's letting on."

Laidlaw reclined on a settee in Mwanajuma's second-floor office, cupping a zarf of thick, bitter Ethiopian coffee.

"I pulled his ministry file," Mwanajuma revealed. "He has an exemplary record."

Laidlaw shrugged. “That just means one of two things. Either he's the real-deal or he just hasn't been caught yet. Could go either way.”

“I swear, Alex, you are the most cynical fellow I've ever met,” Mwanajuma declared.

“Cynical or realistic, take your pick. How long's Okubuna been with the ministry?”

“Five years.”

“What did he do before that?”

“I have no way of knowing.”

“What about the other ranger, Okubuna's partner?” Laidlaw asked. He dipped his head and attempted to sip his scalding coffee. “He's tough to read.”

“Well, I pulled his file, too: Jahi Owusu.”

“What's his story?”

“He joined the ministry about a year before Okubuna. Otherwise, nothing.”

“Neither of 'em said they'd been at their present post very long, but certainly long enough to cozy up to the poachers that hang out in that village.”

“The ministry makes it a point to rotate its game rangers to different postings to prevent that from happening.”

Laidlaw raised an eyebrow. “Kinda like sending prisoners to different prisons to keep 'em from conspiring together or joining gangs.”

“That may be the practice in the States, but here we have neither enough prisoners, nor enough prisons, to play musical chairs,” Mwanajuma scoffed.

Laidlaw sat up and placed his feet on the floor. “How're the Bukoba rhinos faring?”

“Very well, indeed,” Mwanajuma beamed.

“Bingo,” said Laidlaw.

Mwanajuma reflected a moment. “Given your suspicions, I will immediately reassign or terminate Okubuna and Owusu,” he proposed.

“If you do that, we'll have overplayed our hand. They'll put two and two together and figure out that my visit was behind it. Once they realize that we're on to them, they'll warn their poacher-buddies to lay low. If the poachers go to ground, you may not be able to smoke 'em out again.”

The minister thoughtfully listened. “So, what do you suggest, Alex?”

“Do nothing. Maintain the *status quo* for the time being. I have a client coming in the first of the week for a ten-day safari. After he leaves, I'll pay another visit to Israel and Jahi. I would say a surprise visit but your mole, whoever and wherever he is, has probably made that impossible.”

Mwanajuma smiled, wistfully. “At the end of the day, we may have no rhinos left to protect.”

“I don't know what to tell you, Robert. You can do whatever you want but this may be your only bite at the apple. If the poachers get tipped-off and head down a rabbit hole, you'll be left holding the bag. And that's exactly what'll happen if you arbitrarily pull the plug on Okubuna and Owusu and send 'em packing. Hell, it won't even be necessary for them to give the poachers a heads up because, once they get wind that their ranger pals got the heave-ho, the poachers will know something's afoot. And, when that happens, adios poachers."

"Both men may be innocent of any wrongdoing," Mwanajuma said.

"All the more reason not to pitch them overboard by reassigning them for no reason, completely out of the blue. Let things play themselves out for now."

"I will do as you suggest, Alex. But inform no one of this conversation or about your future plans to visit the rhino preserves. We will let things ride for the time being."

MOST AFRICAN HUNTING IS CONDUCTED via the "spot-and-stalk" method. The quarry is identified, either from the safari vehicle or simply by hiking around, before being pursued on foot. Depending on the species being hunted, however, it is sometimes necessary to depart from this technique. Leopards and crocodiles, for example, represent notable exceptions. Although both species possess exceptionally keen senses, particularly sight and hearing, they otherwise appear at first blush to be polar opposites by every other conceivable metric. Despite this, leopards and crocs are often hunted in similar fashion.

Cryptic in both appearance and behavior, the solitary leopard is most active at night and seldom encountered during the daylight hours. This, combined with its inherently secretive nature, renders leopard hunting by the conventional spot-and-stalk method highly unproductive. Diurnal crocodiles, by contrast, flourish in open view throughout many of Africa's lakes and rivers. Notwithstanding their abundance, crocodiles are difficult to hunt in their natural, aquatic environment. If shot in the water, where they are most often found, crocodiles either dive to the bottom of rivers teeming with their voracious brethren or, if killed instantly, sink like a stone. Either way, the trophy is lost.

Surprisingly nimble swimmers, crocodiles are awkward and clumsy on dry land. Despite this, the cold-blooded saurians regularly drag themselves from the water in order to sun themselves on river banks or the shores of lakes, which are often lined with dozens, even scores, of the languid reptiles. In addition to their extraordinary eyesight and hearing, crocodiles possess the ability to discern vibrations in the earth and are thus able to detect the approaching footfalls of hunters or other threats. When this occurs, they scramble back to the safety of the river where, pell-mell, they hurl themselves into the water. Further compounding matters, only a shot to its golf ball-sized brain or spine will immediately incapacitate or kill a crocodile. Absolutely precise marksmanship is therefore imperative.

The leopard's furtiveness and the crocodile's watery habitat and preternatural ability to detect vibration compel the use of “blinds” or “hides” to successfully hunt either species. Using native vegetation, brush, and tree limbs, hunters erect crude shelters on the banks of crocodile-infested rivers or near particular trees known to be frequented by leopards. Hunters then conceal themselves in these makeshift hideaways and wait in perfect stillness, often for hours at a time.

Laidlaw's client was one such hunter.

Arthur “Patty” Perryman hailed from Liverpool and had come to Africa for the avowed purpose of bagging a Nile crocodile. His ruddy face nearly as red as his hair, Perryman informed Laidlaw that, “I've wanted a croc ever since I was a lad.”

Laidlaw considered “Patty” to be an especially juvenile sobriquet for an adult male standing six feet, two inches tall. He always thought “Patty” was a girl's name, anyway.

“The Rufiji's full of crocs. Shouldn't be much of a problem,” he responded. “How big you looking for?”

“The biggest ya got!”

“Big, old crocs don't get that way by being dumb or careless. The real monsters are older than your grandfather and crafty as hell. It'll take time, and some luck, to bag one of those brutes.”

“How big?”

“Well, a fourteen-footer is a big crock,” Laidlaw said. “Anything beyond that is pretty much off the charts. The official record is just over seventeen feet. Even bigger crocs have been reported but not confirmed.”

“That's what I'm looking for,” declared Patty.

“We'll see what we can do, Mr. Perryman. Any objections to shooting from a blind?”

“'Patty', mate. And, no.”

Perryman's excitable demeanor led Laidlaw to question his ability to remain silent and still in a hunting blind. George Pyper, Version 2.0.

“Okay, we'll start scouting tomorrow. If you don't see anything you like in the Rufiji, we'll move on to some other rivers. Crocs are territorial so, once you spot one you want, we'll construct a blind. There's no telling how long we'll hafta wait 'till you get a clean shot, though. Sometimes those old boys don't emerge from the river for days 'cause they're arthritic and weigh nearly a ton. It just requires too much effort to haul themselves around on dry land.”

“How 'bout I just pop 'im while he's in the river? No fuss, no muss.”

Laidlaw shook his head. “No way. Crocs are hard enough to kill when they're on dry land. You increase that difficulty tenfold when they're in the water. The probability is that your shot won't kill him and he'll dive for the bottom. Not only will you have wounded the animal unnecessarily, you'll forfeit your license fee on a trophy you have no chance of recovering.”

Patty took umbrage at Laidlaw's denigration of his marksmanship. “What are you talking about, mate? I'm a crackerjack shot!”

“Doesn't matter. It's one thing to punch holes in paper targets at a comfortable air-conditioned shooting range. It's something else altogether to hit a target the size of a golf ball 200 yards away, over water, from a cramped blind with flies and mosquitoes devouring you while the temperature's 45 degrees, Celsius. And, if the croc is partially submerged, your target will only be half the size of golf ball because much of his brain will be under water."

"That's duck soup for me, mate," Patty boasted.

"It might be 'duck soup', but you're not after ducks," Laidlaw laconically observed. "Even if you're lucky enough to actually pull off a killing shot, the croc will sink like a rock before you can scramble from the blind, with his croc buddies yanking chucks of meat out of him on the way down. Now what do you do? Ya still gotta pay for him."

Laidlaw's nonchalant deportment displeased Patty. "Mate, I think we need to get a few things straight, right from the off. I hired you; you work for me. Your job is to put me on an animal so I can shoot it. Don't forget that it's my money we're talking about here. It's actually pretty simple, mate."

Laidlaw sighed. "Since we're on the subject of not forgetting, my primary responsibility is to keep you alive: not gored by a buffalo, bit by a puff adder, run over by the bakkie, drowned, or accidentally shoot yourself or someone else. While I'm doing that, I'll guide you to the best of my ability to the trophy animals you specify. All the while, I must also ensure that you remain in full compliance with all game laws and regulations. Once we locate your trophy, I, alone, will determine when and where to pull the trigger. My decision will be based on a desire for a clean kill so as to prevent pain to the animal while maximizing your chances of collecting the trophy you want. It's actually pretty simple. Anything else, boss?" Laidlaw concluded with exaggerated solicitude.

Patty looked at him, sourly, but didn't respond.

"I'll see you at dinner," Laidlaw amiably continued. "The cook always makes something special for the first night of safari."

"THERE'S A COUPLE OF RESPECTABLE BULLS, but most of 'em are still juveniles," Laidlaw whispered as, through binoculars, he surveyed the shoreline, 100 yards distant. "I think we should check another spot."

"Whereabouts?"

Laidlaw lowered his binoculars and faced Perryman. "There's a big pool a couple of miles upriver with a lot of hippos and crocs. Normally, hippos will bully crocs and try to take over the entire pool. Crocs are intimidated by hippos and try to stay out of their way, but the pool's big enough to keep 'em separated."

"Why ain't there any hippos here?" Patty asked, pointing.

"River's too narrow and shallow. Won't accommodate their bulk."

"Why didn't we check out that pool to begin with?"

"'Because we're hunting crocs, not hippos," Laidlaw replied. He began to crawl rearward before standing while Perryman lingered and continued to scan the river. Laidlaw waited for him in the shade. Patty finally lowered his binoculars and retreated from the riverbank, huffing and puffing. The men walked to the bakkie without talking.

Perryman finally broke the silence as they bumped northward. “What do you think our chances are of finding a good croc at the pool?”

“Hard to say. Hippos don't hesitate to harass the hell outta crocs and are the only animals that crocs actually fear. Adult hippos outweigh crocs by a factor of at least three, so crocs give 'em a wide berth. In an row between a croc and a hippo, the croc always comes out second-best: either dead or badly injured. About the only time that won't happen is when you've got a big croc and a juvenile hippo...that usually ends in a standoff. Otherwise, crocs and hippos generally mind their own business, though they keep a wary eye on each other. But, to answer your question directly, it depends on the abundance of fish in the pool, which is the crocs' main food source, and the inherent aggressiveness of their hippo roomies.”

Patty nodded but didn't respond. He unconsciously patted the rifle resting between his knees, its chamber empty.

“THERE’S A BRUISER DOWN THERE...better than twelve feet and very broad across his back.”

"How can you tell?"

"The distance between a croc's eye and his nostril, in inches, is equivalent to his overall length in feet."

"Bollocks! No shit?"

"No shit."

"I thought you said a fourteen-footer is the minimum I should look for."

"I said that a fourteen-footer was a big croc, not the end-all and be-all. You'll know the one you want when you see him, whether he's fourteen feet or not. You see the one I'm talkin' about?"

A pod of honking, quarreling hippos occupied the pool below them. Perryman wiped sweat from his face and squinted through his binoculars, lenses fogged from humidity and perspiration. "I think so." He counted under his breath. "Fifth one from the edge of the water, toward the left?"

"That's him. Let's just keep watchin' him for a little while. We're in no hurry and I wanna get a better look at him.

"I'm good with that," Patty whispered. He was nervous and his heart was already beginning to race.

The two men continued to watch the basking crocodiles in silence. The reptiles held their jaws wide open, allowing Egyptian plovers to enter their cavernous mouths, where they picked food debris, leeches, and other parasites from between the crocodiles' teeth.

"Should I take him?" Patty hissed after a few minutes. His binoculars kept fogging up, he was hot, sweating profusely, and gnats from the river were swarming around his face and crawling into his nostrils and ears.

Laidlaw didn't lower his binoculars. “No,” he whispered. “I think we should keep looking. There's no hurry and you may see one you like better. If you don't, he'll still be here.”

“How do you know?”

“Like I said earlier, crocs are territorial. On top of that, he's the king and he knows it. He's smart enough not to trifle with the hippos, so they leave him alone. And, based on his size, there's plenty to eat here, to say nothing of lots of available ladies. He has zero incentive to pull up stakes and go somewhere else.”

“Makes sense,” Patty conceded. “I just don't want to return home without my croc.”

“Don't worry, there's no shortage of crocodiles. The trick is to find one you like and getting into shooting position to take him. We'll keep looking until you're satisfied. Let's go check out another honey hole I know.” Crouching, Laidlaw eased away from the river, Perryman trailing.

AFTER SIX DAYS OF HOT, GRUELING scouting, Patty finally found the croc he wanted.

Laidlaw led him through a wasteland of boulders and dense thorn bushes to what turned out to be no more than a shallow mud wallow fed by a sluggish rivulet. Although they'd seen more than a half-dozen large crocs in the intervening days, and Perryman had expressed satisfaction with two of them, Laidlaw always dissuaded him.

"I think you should hold off. We still have time to do more scouting," he reasoned. "These will still be here if we can't find a better specimen."

Perryman was so tired by that point that he was basically willing to shoot the next crocodile he saw, irrespective of size. His rifle was beginning to feel like it weighed a ton and all he wanted was to get out of the scorching sun, drink multiple cold beers, soak his feet, and treat his innumerable scratches and abrasions.

"Let's check one more place," Laidlaw urged. "It's a waterhole that's been on its last legs for months, though some pretty big crocs used to hang out there. I actually forgot about it until just now."

"I'd be happy just to go back to one of the places we already checked out," Patty deferred. "We saw some okay crocs and I'll just bag one of those."

Laidlaw resisted. "Look, this new place is pretty close. There's no downside to giving it the once-over. If it's dried-up or nothing's there, fine...we'll head back to one of the places we previously scouted and you can take your croc today or tomorrow. What do you say?"

"Okay, I guess," Patty yielded with a distinct lack of enthusiasm. He was tempted to simply wait in the bakkie while Laidlaw hoofed it in to check out the latest spot, but didn't want Laidlaw to think him a slacker.

They fought their way through the encompassing thicket and spilled into a small clearing. A seam, or “pan,” in the middle of the glade was occupied by a single, enormous crocodile, resembling a felled tree. He observed their arrival with a flinty eye, though the mud in the shallow depression was scarcely adequate to cover the massive reptile's feet. Laidlaw extended his arm to arrest Perryman's advance.

The latter drew a sharp breath. “Bloody hell!”

The two men stood, motionless, staring at the croc.

“That dude is ancient, older that you and me put together,” Laidlaw remarked. “This pan has been shrinking for months and all his pards split to find new digs a long time ago. He stayed behind to defend his territory. Trouble is, there's nothing left to defend, but that's irrelevant. He's been the king for so long, thirty or forty years, that this waterhole is all he knows. He won't budge from this spot until he dies, which won't be long 'cause there's absolutely no food here.”

“How big do you think he is?” Perryman whispered.

Laidlaw tipped his head slightly to assess the animal's length. "Thirteen, fourteen feet and north of a ton. The biggest croc we've seen, easy.”

“I want him.”

"You'll actually be doing the old guy a favor. If you don't shoot him, sooner or later the hyenas will start showing up and he's probably already too weak to fight 'em off. They'll start tearing him to pieces while he's still alive."

"Have you seen him before?"

"I don't remember him but, like I said, I haven't visited this waterhole in a while." Laidlaw shrugged. "Who the hell knows?"

"Well, I'm taking him. He's a behemoth, mate!" Patty declared.

"Yep, his hide will make a helluva trophy." Laidlaw quickly scanned the immediate area. "We won't need to construct a blind. Just move over there," he pointed, "and set up your shooting sticks. Crank your scope down to its lowest power and place the crosshairs on the point of the croc's 'smile'...you'll break his spine and he'll be dead before he draws another breath. I'll back your shot from here. The croc's way too big for us to handle by ourselves so, after you take your shot and we get some photos, I'll hike to the bakkie and high-tail it back to camp for a truck with a winch and some boards. I'll also corral Moses and Smoke and bring 'em back with me. Between the four of us and the winch, we'll get him loaded up. You okay with staying out here by yourself for a couple of hours while I go back for the truck?"

"You bet," Patty assured him. He was trembling with anticipation.

"Like you said, 'duck soup'," Laidlaw winked.

In Primis Anno Regnantibus Imperator Caesar Titus Vespasianus (81 CE)

AT DAWN, EROS GUIDED HIS WATERCRAFT from the shallows and floated on the gentle current toward the center of the Nile. He and those accompanying him occupied three small boats; a fourth, lashed to Ero's boat, was filled with foodstuffs and weapons. A handful of well-wishers gathered on the shore to watch, though Neocles was not among them.

"Farewell," one of them called to the departing men. "We will greet your arrival in Rome."

"Perhaps, though I do not expect you will make it that far," a response floated over the water. "Take comfort knowing that I will recall all of you with great fondness as I fuck every whore in the capital!"

"If we reach Rome before you, there will be no whores left to fuck!"

"No matter, for even whores have daughters!" The laughter of the departing legionnaire faded as Eros' boat yielded to the river's inexorable pull and began to increase momentum.

"I do not think they will arrive in Rome," one of the bystanders softly remarked as he watched the small craft bob in the current.

“Only the gods are privy to such things,” another commented. He turned to the legionnaire who had just spoken. “As they are to our fate.”

Harkuf approached and apathetically surveyed the legionnaires' departure.

“You will not see them again,” he stated.

“So, you now presume to speak for the gods?”

“The gods speak for themselves. They require no champion.”

“Indeed? Do they speak at this moment? If so, I am unable to hear them,” the Roman smirked.

“The gods speak to those who would listen, sometimes through men, other times through signs. They have decreed that your friends will die.”

Listening to the exchange, a nearby legionnaire interjected. “I do not know which gods this barbarian worships, neither does it matter. Though there exist many paths, there is but one destination and his words ring true. The omniscient gods reveal themselves at their pleasure. It is not for the hubris of men to dictate when, or in what manner, they do so. To presume otherwise is to risk invoking the gods' anger.”

“Admittedly, Lucanus, though the gods would not esteem as their messenger an ignorant savage in preference to a Roman.”

Harkuf laughed, harshly. “Roman fools! Is it not obvious that you enjoy the gods' favor? The gods have ordained that the anguished cries of your comrades will soon enough acquaint you with their unhappy fate. It is Romans, not me, through whom the gods speak, as you shall soon learn."

"The barbarian is our enemy and says only what he hopes will occur, not what the gods have decreed," a legionnaire growled.

Harkuf arched his eyebrows. "I am your guide, not your enemy, Roman. You are not worthy of being my enemy. *Your* enemy's name is 'Paneb'."

"Who, by Hercules, is *he*?"

"Paneb is the chief freebooter on Elephantine Island. Should your friends successfully navigate the waters of the Great Cataract, which is not likely, they are certain to make his acquaintance. The Romans will have eluded one trap only to jump into the jaws of another, one whose hospitality they will not find to their liking. But, as you say, only the gods are privy to such things," Harkuf concluded with a half-shrug.

The rudimentary armada having floated around a bend in the *Nilus*, the knot of legionnaires on the riverbank drifted away, disquieted.

"IF THIS IS THE GREAT CATARACT, I look forward to a tranquil sojourn in Tartarus!" Marius shouted to Eros over the bruit of the seething river. He gripped the vessel's gunwale with both hands to prevent being pitched overboard as the little boat bucked and spun in the increasingly turbulent current.

"I hope this is the worst of it," Eros responded through gritted teeth. He swiveled his head downriver, hoping to spot a quiescent expanse of water in the heart of the maelstrom. Massive black boulders, battered by foaming, swirling water, jutted from the Nile like dragon's teeth.

The roaring current heaved the legionnaires' watercraft about like the twigs, some becoming momentarily airborne. In vain the terrified helmsmen grappled with their oscillating rudders in a futile effort to avoid being dashed against another spinning boat or the glistening rocks. Water poured over the boats' gunwales, sloshing in their hulls and threatening to swamp them.

"Heave to shore!" Quintus implored above the din, as if that were even possible. His eyes were wide with fear. "Otherwise, we are all dead men!"

No one bothered to respond, his companions caring for naught but their own survival. Some, convinced that the surging water offered more safety than their fragile boats, rashly leapt into the river. They immediately disappeared from view and did not reemerge from the boiling undercurrent. Others, through fear of death, prayed to die.

Tossed helplessly about like the rest, Eros clung desperately to the gunwale of his boat. He and Marius were its only occupants, two others having already been washed overboard. The one-time cluster of watercraft was now disbursed haphazardly along the river; only one other boat remained visible to Eros, the disposition of the others uncertain.

"We angered the gods by abandoning Crixus and our mates!" his companion bawled as their boat whirled and spun in the current. "They punish us for our folly!"

"Do not blame the gods for separating the wheat from the chaff," Eros snapped. "In their infinite wisdom, the gods decided the only ones who will perish today are craven wastrels who will not be missed."

The other man lapsed into resentful silence.

AS QUICKLY AS THE TEMPEST BEGAN, it ended.

Two rudderless boats drifted along a broad sandbar just beyond the northern periphery of the Great Cataract. Eros and Marius occupied one of the vessels; the other held Quintus and another legionnaire. The remaining watercraft, and the rest of the men, were lost. Ahead of them stretched the tranquil *Nilus*, placid and unobstructed for nearly 1,000 miles until reaching the fertile Delta and ultimately debouching into the *Mare Nostrum*.

Eros hailed the other boat across the water.

"Let us beach here. We must recover from our ordeal and plan what next must be done."

"'What next?'" Marius scoffed. "Is it not obvious that we have no alternative but to wait here for our compatriots, who are likely to reenter this section of the river after skirting the Great Cataract overland?

We cannot resume our journey downriver because our damaged vessels can no longer be steered, Eros. Were that not bad enough, our arms and food lie at the bottom of the *Nilus*!"

Eros jumped into the muddy, waist-deep water and began to shove his boat toward the sandbar. Seeing him, Marius and the two remaining men in the other surviving boat, followed. After dragging both watercraft onto the wet sand, the four men collapsed in trembling exhaustion.

"What now, Eros?" Quintus asked, without opening his eyes, after a few minutes.

"Nothing has changed, save the gods have blessed us by eliminating those unfit to accompany us on the remainder of our journey. Our burden has thus been eased and our lot improved," the former reasoned. "We will resume as soon as we are rested."

"You must be mad, Eros. Is it not clear that we misjudged the ferocity of the Great Cataract, which severely damaged our boats, to say nothing of destroying two others? We are in no condition to risk the unknown hazards that yet remain before us. And, what do you propose we eat? Air?"

"We have scarcely begun, yet you whimper and carp like little children!" Eros snapped. "Perhaps the gods were too generous in sparing you, Quintus!"

Marius spoke, "No, even the gods know that Quintus speaks prudently. Mere bluster will not fill our stomachs, nor provide us weapons. We must wait here for the others, confess our imprudence, beg their pardon, and rejoin them. We are otherwise certain to perish, and that sooner rather than later."

Eros sat up and disdainfully surveyed the three exhausted men crumpled around him. "I believed myself in the company of Romans," he mocked, "but am very much mistaken. Romans possess *virtus* in abundance, while your cowardice sickens me. For myself, I decline to bend my knee and beg absolution from a Nubian savage and his Greek toady."

"We are all Romans, Eros," a legionnaire interjected. "As you suggest, let us rest and gather our wits. The infallible gods will direct us."

"How distant are Elephantine Island or Sunu?" Quintus asked. "Sunu has a garrison of troops. Would it not be safer to seek haven there?"

"Assuming our boats will make it that far without sinking, we will have to pass Elephantine Island, which swarms with pirates, before we reach Sunu," Marius responded. "We are few, slow, and weaponless. They are many, swift, and armed. We must avoid going anywhere near Elephantine Island. Better that we remain here."

"You may do as you wish, but I will not slink into Sunu to beg for sanctuary," Eros grunted. He reclined on the wet sand and closed his eyes.

PANEB AND HIS MEN REGULARLY PATROLLED the section of river between the northern terminus of the Great

Cataract and Elephantine Island, where they attacked vessels and expropriated cargoes. Alternatively, they extorted substantial tribute before allowing boats to pass through the waters surrounding the island. In addition, the pirates routinely seized entire crews and bartered them in the slave markets of Damascus and Emesa. The smashed remains of watercraft that failed to successfully navigate the treacherous shoals and boulders of the Great Cataract were scavenged for booty and survivors, the latter sold as slaves to nomadic caravans passing through the area.

And Paneb was on the prowl at that moment.

Eros and the remaining legionnaires finally roused themselves from their torpor and stood, still somewhat shaken from their recent ordeal.

"What shall we do?" Quintus addressed no one in particular.

"By Hercules, I already told you what I intend to do," Eros spat. "You *feminae* may either accompany me or remain here. It matters naught."

One of the men looked beyond Eros and pointed. "Look."

The others turned. A small ship with a fluttering lateen sail advanced upriver, against the current. Several dark-bearded men peered over the ship's gunwales toward the ragged men clustered on the sandbar.

"The gods see us and take pity! We are saved!" a legionnaire happily exclaimed.

Marius shielded his eyes from the sun and squinted toward the approaching vessel. "No, I do not think the gods pity us. Those are not our salvation, but our doom. They are pirates."

The interlopers' ship wallowed inexorably through the turbid water, directly toward the stranded Romans.

"We possess nothing the pirates desire," Eros asserted with confidence. "They are merely curious and will not trouble us once they see our dolorous condition. I will prevail upon them for some food before they depart."

"No, we possess the *most* valuable object," Marius commented under his breath. "Our lives."

As the Romans watched in apprehensive silence, the interlopers' disintegrating vessel plied the Nile's deepest channel. It lumbered beyond the sandbar before casting anchor and furling its sails, whereupon an equally dilapidated dinghy was lowered over one side. A number of men clambered in and pushed off. The dinghy drifted with the current toward the marooned legionnaires.

"What shall we do?" one of them whispered. No one responded.

"Greetings!" an occupant of the small craft hailed in a language none of them understood as he drifted toward them.

"Greetings! We are Romans!" Eros confidently responded in Latin.

The men in the boat quickly conferred.

"I speak your language, Roman!" another finally called out. "You are armed?"

"Fully!"

The pirate began laughing. “I think not, Roman! You seem to me stranded in the middle of the Great River with neither boats nor arms! But, no matter, for we have weapons!” he cackled as he held aloft a *lingula,* a short sword.

“They intend to kill us!” one of the legionnaires hissed.

Marius looked down and shook his head, sadly. “No, we are of no value dead. Our fate will be more wretched than that.”

The bobbing watercraft was now only fifty yards from the sandbar. The Romans could clearly see that it held a half-dozen pirates, all of them clutching curved swords.

"Let us rush them when their boat touches shore!"

"How do you propose we overpower them? With our empty hands? They are armed and their numbers are superior to ours. And, even if we succeed, there are more of them on their ship!"

“What, then?”

“I will speak to their headman,” Eros said with less bluster than before.

The dinghy slid onto the sandbar and its occupants leapt out. The Romans instinctively retreated into a smaller cluster.

“Put yourselves at your ease, Romans,” the pirate grinned. He had no front teeth and gripped his *lingula* in his left hand. His shipmates, brandishing cutlasses, were arrayed close by.

“I would speak with your chief,” Eros imperiously informed him.

“Of course! It would not do to ignore the demands of such redoubtable visitors,” the pirate leered. He turned his head, slightly, and uttered a few words to his companions. One of them sheathed his weapon and strode to the dinghy. He shoved it into the river, climbed in, and began rowing back to the immobile pirate vessel.

“You are surely hungry and thirsty,” their host said. Without taking his eyes off Eros, he raised his right hand and flicked his fingers. Two of the other pirates tossed a skin of water and some unidentifiable chucks of meat onto the sand at the legionnaires' feet. “Refresh yourselves. Penab will greet you shortly.”

None of the Romans moved.

“'Penab' is your chief?” Eros probed.

“He leads by common consent, aye.”

“What is your name?”

The pirate grinned. “I have no name.” He viewed the untouched food and drink laying at the legionnaires' feet and frowned. “Though I have never been to Rome, in my country it is considered a gross insult to refuse the hospitality of another.”

Eros glanced at the stoical men crowded behind him then turned back to their *de facto* captors. “We will eat.”

The nameless freebooter smiled, coldly. “I have been told that Romans are prudent.”

The prisoners sank warily onto the damp sand. Eros dragged the water skin toward him, took a cautious drink, then passed it to the next man. In the center of the river, the dinghy had nearly reached the pirates' ship. Aboard the latter vessel, his uncouth shipmates eagerly awaited his return with news of the legionnaires.

"We allow ourselves to be ordered about by barbarian savages?" one of the Romans hissed. "I have already endured too much of this charade." Ignoring a companion's restraining hand, he stood; Eros made no effort to intervene. "You!" He pointed to the toothless pirate who had previously spoken. "You are obviously unschooled regarding your betters. We are citizens of Rome, not the common river trash you are accustomed to dealing with. Our divine emperor, Titus, will swiftly punish any insult to our honor that we may suffer at your hands."

The pirate rapidly translated the legionnaire's scolding for the benefit of his associates, who burst into spontaneous laughter.

"I do not see your 'divine emperor' anywhere hereabouts," the pirate rejoined. "In any case, I am powerless to address your concerns and must await Penab's arrival. I am quite certain that he will requite them in a manner befitting your exalted rank. I invite you to take your ease until then."

Grumbling, the legionnaire resumed his seat in the sand. He continued to glare at the guards.

One of the other freebooters spoke, causing the lead pirate to turn seaward. The dinghy was returning with two occupants, one of whom was presumably their headman, Penab. The Romans didn't know whether to be encouraged or alarmed.

"Penab comes," the pirate confirmed.

Less than five minutes later the small craft made landfall. The pirate chieftain and his oarsman stepped onto the sandbar and sauntered to the assembled men, where he engaged in earnest conversation with his subordinate after barely glancing at the captive legionnaires.

Short and stocky, Penab was obviously a Nubian. Colored ribbons were woven through his gray hair and beard, both arranged into long plaits. Fingers on each hand were twisted and knotted from rheumatoid arthritis and two fingers on his left hand were mere stumps. Penab appeared to be in his mid-60's, perhaps as old as 70.

After conversing for perhaps two minutes, Penab stepped away from the other pirate and approached the seated Romans.

"Who leads you?" he unexpectedly asked in Latin. Eros concealed his surprise and stood. "You are Romans?" Eros nodded. Penab looked at the other pirates and said something in their native language. He turned back to Eros. "What legion?"

"Legio XVI Bestia."

Penab narrowed his eyes. "*Bestia*? A Roman legion comprised of only four men? And were are your beasts?"

Eros was unprepared for the canny pirate's question. "Our beasts perished," he stammered. "The Sudd."

"And the remainder of your legion? It, also, perished?"

"Yes. We are on our way to Rome and require food and weapons," Eros stated.

"And boats, as well, if I am not very much mistaken," Paneb playfully noted.

Eros nodded. "The senate and people of Rome are grateful for your assistance. Nor does Rome forget her friends," he added.

"Indeed? All sensible people vie for Rome's gratitude, which is of inestimable value. But the Damascus slave markets express their gratitude with coin, especially for Roman legionnaires." Paneb paused. "My men and I prefer coin."

Eros was taken aback. "What?"

Paneb abruptly turned away and motioned to his men. They strode forward and swiftly began to bind the legionnaires, who looked at Eros in helpless terror.

"Do not be a fool, Paneb!" Eros shouted as rough hands were laid upon him. "Rome remembers her enemies equally with her friends!"

"I have so far managed to prosper without Rome's friendship," Paneb shrugged. "It is more difficult to prosper without coin."

The legionnaires were dragged across the sandbar and unceremoniously shoved into the dinghy. They would eventually be transported via caravan to Damascus, where they would be placed on offer in one of the city's vast slave markets.

In a final irony, those legionnaires who didn't end up toiling, and dying, in Spanish or Thracian silver mines might ultimately find themselves serving in some Eastern warlord's mercenary army, locked in combat against their former Roman comrades.

BEROSSUS WAS SURPRISED TO FIND the seaside village completely deserted. He ordered his men to conduct a search of all its structures.

"Bring to me anyone you find," he ordered. The legionnaires fanned out and went from hovel to hovel to search for inhabitants. Berossus, himself, walked to the shoreline and looked seaward, hoping to spot fleeing boats.

Nothing.

A legionnaire hastened across the sand toward him. "Commander, you must see this," he announced when he drew abreast.

Berossus asked no questions, but followed the soldier to a dwelling comprised of the arched rib bones of a whale covered with palm fronds. His subordinate held aside its door of woven sea grass and Berossus bent to peer into its squalid interior.

Sprawled on the structure's dirt floor were the bodies of three small children, one an infant. From what Berossus could ascertain, the throats of the two older children were crudely slashed, while the infant's skull had been crushed. In the stifling air, clouds of black flies already swarmed around the corpses.

"Nearly every hut contains the same," the legionnaire informed him.

Berossus withdrew his head and stepped away from the dwelling. "Their parents?"

"They appear to have abandoned the village after slaying their children."

"Commander!" Berossus turned as another legionnaire hastened toward him. "We found more." He drew abreast of the other two men and pointed toward the beach. "Many adolescents and female adults."

Increasingly perplexed, Berossus followed him to the site of the *auto-de-fe'*.

"What is the meaning of this villainy?" he blurted upon seeing the mass of corpses. "Methinks these brutes are not human but raging beasts or demons let loose!"

"But where are the men among these bodies?" the puzzled legionnaire reflected, mostly to himself.

"They are at our camp!" Berossus spontaneously blurted. "They sacrificed their wives and children simply to spite us! Gather the men...we must hasten back to the *castra aestiva*!"

The legionnaires sprinted back to the village to locate the legion's trumpeter. Those still engaged in searching, and looting, the abandoned dwellings would automatically rally to the sound of his clarion. Berossus anxiously trailed them, alarmed that the unsuspecting handful of men left behind would be overwhelmed and slaughtered by the duplicitous villagers. To his immense relief, the harsh notes of the trumpeter immediately reached his ears.

The majority of the legionnaires had already assembled in the center of the deserted settlement. They were disgusted by the villagers' lack of worthwhile material possessions.

Berossus strode into the midst of the soldiers. “Having slain their loved ones, the remaining savages attacked the *castrum* in our absence. We must return thither at once!”

The legionnaires looked at one another in consternation, fell into ranks, and began an urgent march back to their largely undefended base.

THE ROMANS ARRIVED AT the *castrum* in double-quick time to find everything unexpectedly sedate.

“Greetings,” Fabius welcomed their return with a broad grin.

Berossus eyed him skeptically. “We feared you were besieged. It appears we were mistaken.”

“Your anxieties were warranted, for we were, indeed, attacked by the villagers.” Fabius pointed with pride to the place where the eleven bodies were arrayed. “They fell upon us like a tempest. There you will find the fruits of their audacity.”

Berossus and the other legionnaires crowded around the display of corpses.

"Eleven?" Berossus dubiously noted.

"Their numbers were incalculable," Fabius assured him, "the remainder fled like hares when greeted by Roman arms."

"What casualties did we suffer?"

Fabius shook his head. "None."

Berossus turned to Neocles. "What say you?"

"I was absent during the assault and cannot speak to either the villagers' numbers or their daring."

Berossus frowned. "Not present?"

Fabius quickly interjected. "The engagement, if it could truly be called that, was brief because of the skill with which we wielded our swords and the cowardice of the savages. Neocles had previously gone down to the sea and had not yet returned when the enemy descended upon us."

Berossus raised a skeptical eyebrow. "It is a most curious thing that a clash of arms against a hoard beyond counting ended so quickly and with such few casualties. How is such a thing possible?"

None of the sheepish legionnaires volunteered an explanation.

"Methinks this sham engagement was very far from what you profess, Fabius," Berossus continued. "I am less displeased by Neocles' fortuitous absence than by your fanciful account of what transpired during my absence."

Fabius gestured defiantly toward the bodies of the slain villagers. "Sham? Though mute, they bear abundant witness to the battle."

"You consider it valorous to have bested eleven lowly fisherman, three of them mere boys?" Berossus dryly remarked. "I do not wonder that Neocles absented himself from this farce, which does honor to none of you."

"What of their village?" Senecio deftly changed the subject.

"Like madmen, the men slew their wives and children before abandoning their homes. We feared they intended to annihilate the *castrum*," a legionnaire informed him.

"It was not through lack of trying that they failed to do so," Fabius stubbornly insisted.

"Dispose of the bodies in the sea," Berossus curtly ordered. "We leave on the morrow."

HARKUF IN THE VAN, CRIXUS AND THE remaining legionnaires hauled their watercraft along the trail at the foot of red sandstone bluffs that paralleled the Iteru's western shore. They repeatedly stumbled and twisted their ankles on the path's stony, uneven surface.

"By the gods, I think I would rather have taken my chances on the river," one of the men groused. Sweat streamed down his face, burning his eyes. He tripped over a rock.

"You would be dead by now, Roman," Harkuf laughed, "yet it is not too late!"

"How much farther?" Crixus asked.

Harkuf paused to scrutinize the cliffside. "Sunset, at this pace. We will camp away from the Iteru tonight and reenter it at dawn. The current will carry us beyond the pirates before they stir."

"Do you suppose Eros and the others managed to successfully navigate the Great Cataract?"

Harkuf surveyed Crixus in silence before responding. "The Great Cataract and Penab are one. Regardless of which is chosen, your friend's doom was ordained even before his departure yesterday."

"On what do you base your unhappy words? If they defeat the Great Cataract but are captured by Penab, he will simply kill them all?"

Harkuf laughed. "Penab is not a fool. He is shrewd. While killing Romans would undoubtedly give him great pleasure, doing so will bring him no profit. Penab will barter your friends to slave traders, for Roman legionnaires will prove a great novelty in the Syrian slave markets. Better for your friends to be dashed to pieces on the rocks of the Great Cataract."

"Is it not possible that Eros may yet prevail over both hazards?"

"Anything is possible, Roman, though it is better to trust in courage than luck. Your friend, the other Roman, did not appear to possess either in abundance."

Though he was glad to be rid of him, Crixus did not envy Eros' fate, nor that of the men whom he lured into participating in his ill-conceived decampment. He recalled the words of the Roman satirist, Decimus Iunius Juvenalis: we seek what will be our ruin.

FOURTEEN

ACCORDING TO OKUBUNA AND Owusu, somebody from the Wildlife Ministry radioed to inform them of his first impromptu inspection tour. Hoping to ferret out the mole, Laidlaw figured he'd start at the top and work his way down. During a pretextual call to Mwanajuma, Laidlaw offhandedly mentioned his intent to return to the Selous rhino preserve the first week of the following month. Having done so, he immediately contacted an entirely new air taxi service to book the short flight on a day the week prior. Although a clumsy attempt at subterfuge, spycraft was not Laidlaw's *metier* and it was the only stratagem he could immediately think of to identify the source of the leak. Notwithstanding his belief that it was extremely unlikely Mwanajuma was complicit in the tip-off, he couldn't play favorites and had to start somewhere.

“Can you radio them to tell them I'm coming?” Laidlaw shouted to the pilot over the roar of the plane's engine.

The pilot, a middle-aged white guy, nodded and began fiddling with the cockpit radio. Although the ambient noise rendered it impossible for Laidlaw to discern what he was saying, the pilot began speaking into his headset.

The pilot nodded several times as he listened, then turned to Laidlaw. “He said they didn't expect you 'till next week, but he'll pick you up at the airfield!” he yelled.

That was easy: Mwanajuma. Shit. Laidlaw absently nodded as he gazed out the plane's plexiglass window. The surface of the earth floating beneath them was brown and dry, interspersed here and there with isolated, scrawny trees. He saw no animals.

“WELCOME BACK, MR. ALEX,” Israel greeted him. Laidlaw had just climbed from the aircraft, which now trundled across the corrugated soil, kicking up puffs of dust, until it faced the slight breeze. The pilot powered-up for takeoff before releasing its brakes and bouncing along the rough ground.

“Yeah, thanks,” he responded, without enthusiasm. The plane lifted skyward, immediately above their heads. A vague feeling of disquiet gnawed at Laidlaw.

"We were not expecting you until next week but you are always welcome."

Laidlaw slipped his duffle bag from his shoulder into the rear of the bakkie. "Where's your partner?"

"Jahi is in the field, checking on some wildebeests."

Laidlaw slid into the vehicle's passenger seat. "How'd you know to expect me next week?"

"The ministry." Israel started the bakkie's engine and rotated its steering wheel in the direction of the base-camp.

"Somebody from the ministry contacted you on the radio?" Israel nodded but didn't take his eyes from the jolting dirt track they were traversing. "Who?"

"I do not know who it was. Maybe Jahi will recall."

"Who received the message?"

"I did, but the person at the other end did not identify himself."

"It that's the case, how would Jahi have any idea who it was?"

Israel didn't respond.

JAHI WAS ALREADY THERE WHEN they finally pulled into the rangers' tumble-down compound. He looked on with indifference as Laidlaw pulled his bag from the bakkie and placed it on the ground.

"Back already?" he inquired. Israel stepped around the front of the bakkie and stood near him.

"I heard you were expecting me."

"Not until next week."

"I'm surprised, since no one knew of my intended visit," Laidlaw said.

Jahi arched his eyebrows. "Well, *somebody* knew."

"And who was that?"

"The ministry informed Israel over the wireless a few days ago. They said you intended to arrive here next week."

"How do you know whoever you talked to was from the ministry?" Laidlaw continued to probe.

"They said so. Otherwise, we would have no way of knowing."

"Did the person identify himself?"

Jahi glanced at Israel, who shook his head.

"Did you recognize their voice?" Laidlaw asked the latter.

"Reception is very poor out here and messages are garbled. I gave no thought to it."

If, as it appeared, Mwanajuma was the source of the leak, Laidlaw knew the minister would take pains to ensure that his fingerprints were nowhere in the vicinity. He undoubtedly ordered some unassuming flunky in the ministry to radio the erroneous information about Laidlaw's upcoming visit. It would have been a miracle if Israel had recognized the speaker's voice, irrespective of the garbled reception.

Because he was getting nowhere, Laidlaw changed the subject. “How are the rhinos?”

“Prospering. None have been killed since you were last here. The calves are growing rapidly.”

“And the remaining species?”

“A sable bull. For its horns.”

“Any idea who killed it?”

The game rangers shook their heads in unison.

“Where's the body?”

“We gave it to the villagers for food.”

There was nothing sinister in that. It was standard protocol for the meat of poached animals to be given away, as was done previously with the poached white-rhino cow. But Laidlaw needed time to think.

“I'm tired and want to rest,” he said. “I'll take a look at everything tomorrow.”

“Of course,” Israel readily agreed. “Unfortunately, because we were not expecting you until next week, we have not prepared your sleeping quarters.”

Laidlaw shrugged. “Doesn't matter. I'll attend to it.” He hoisted his duffle bag and slung it over his shoulder. The rangers watched in silence as he walked across the hard-packed earth toward the spartan bunkhouse.

Opening its dented and rusted steel door, Laidlaw entered the bunkhouse and stepped into the tiny room. Tipping his shoulder, he let his duffle bag slip onto the stained, bare mattress. He sat down and slumped against the cinder block wall.

Based on his observations during his first visit, combined with what the rangers just told him, the Selous rhino preserve was being poached on a more-or-less regular basis. And, although Laidlaw hadn't yet visited it, if the Selous was the target of systematic poaching, it was certain that its counterpart at Bukoba was, also.

Less clear was the extent to which Mwanajuma, Okubuna, or Owusu knew of, or were complicit in, the trafficking of wild animal parts: horns, internal organs, pelts, skulls and other bones, teeth, penises, tusks, claws. Other than to caution the game rangers to lay low while he was on site, however, Laidlaw could think of no plausible reason for the exalted Minister of Wildlife to directly communicate with two low-level flunkies like Okubuna and Owusu.

Maybe Laidlaw was simply missing something. He sighed and sat up. Tomorrow, he'd scope-out the rhinos; meantime, he'd continue to ponder the situation.

JAHI WAS RIGHT. THE RHINO CALVES seemed to have doubled in size.

"They look fine," Laidlaw remarked as he watched two of the calves through binoculars. "How are the moms?"

"Very well," Israel assured him.

Laidlaw lowered his binoculars. "Any sign of intruders in the preserve?" He looked at both rangers as he spoke, both of whom remained stoical as they shook their heads in the negative. "Well, have you actually *looked* for any?"

"We would have seen evidence of intruders if there were any," Israel asserted. "We patrol the entire preserve throughout the day and periodically during the night. We have seen no sign of trespassers."

"Yet, a sable bull was poached right under your noses. How is it that you failed to detect the poachers?"

"They go to great lengths to conceal themselves. The preserve is very large and we are but two," Israel protested.

"What about the people in that village...the ones you gave the meat to. Did you talk to them?"

"Of course. They know nothing."

"Well, I guess the invisible poachers must have levitated in and levitated out," Laidlaw said in disgust. "Let's go check on the remaining rhinos. I also want to see where the sable was killed."

"Of course," Israel said again.

"SO, YOU BELIEVE MWANAJUMA IS trafficking animal parts?" Mosi and Laidlaw were drinking beer in the Europa's bar.

"It's kinda lookin' that way."

"What do you intend to do?"

Laidlaw sighed and sipped his beer. "Damned if I know."

"Go to the media?"

Laidlaw chuckled without humor. "What for? To blow the whistle on political corruption? What else is new? That's pretty much like bitching that the sun rises in the east and sets in the west. When did *that* bombshell become newsworthy? Even if I had absolute, irrefutable proof of malfeasance by government fat-cats, which I don't, and used a dead fish to slap people across their faces with the evidence, the response would be a collective yawn. Joe Six-Pack doesn't give two hoots about 'trafficking animal parts'. He's got rent to pay and a family to feed."

"Mwanajuma is a formidable man with many friends and connections," Mosi cautioned.

"Powerful people have far more enemies than friends. Robert didn't get where he is without climbing over a lot of other people."

"That is true," Mosi concurred, "though one must know how to distinguish one's friends from one's enemies. All cats are gray in the dark."

Laidlaw drained his beer. "Yep, that's the rub."

MWANAJUMA SNIPPED A *Ramon Allones Superiores LCDH* and held the blunt end beneath the quivering flame of a wooden match. "My desk lighter needs fuel," he explained, unbidden. He leaned back in his squeaky office chair, placed his feet on his desk, closed his eyes, and smiled contentedly as he sucked a mouthful of smoke. "Cuban. They only make 50,000 of these a year."

"Sounds expensive," Laidlaw remarked from across the desk.

"60,000 Tanzanian shillings. Each. But worth it."

"Too rich for my blood."

The minister opened one eye to look at Laidlaw. "Life is short, my friend. It is important to reward yourself now and again. Never forget that we die forever."

"Yeah, well...," Laidlaw let his voice trail off.

"I trust your visit to the Selous was productive? How are my rhinos?" Mwanajuma nonchalantly inquired as he puffed on the *Ramon Allones.*

"Who told you about my supposedly clandestine trip?"

"One of the rangers radioed the ministry to say you'd been there."

"You, personally, talked to him? The ranger?"

"Me? Why would I talk to him? I received the message through channels."

Laidlaw nodded. "More interesting is the fact that somebody tipped the rangers off about my trip in advance. The only thing they got wrong was the date, which I deliberately intended."

"I don't understand. What are you saying?"

"Look, Robert, it's pretty clear there's a mole somewhere in the ministry who's in cahoots with the poachers. Whoever it is tips 'em off about me, tells 'em when the coast is clear, and whatnot."

"Yes?" Mwanajuma leaned forward in his chair, planted his feet on the floor, and carefully extinguished his cigar in the ceramic ashtray on his desk before lovingly sliding it back into its aluminun tube.

"I figured I might be able to smoke the mole out by planting false info about the trip I just made to the Selous preserve." The minister didn't respond, so Laidlaw continued. "You're the only person I told about it before I left."

"I trust there is a point to what you are telling me, Alex?"

"I intentionally told you the wrong date, which was the date you provided Owusu and Okubuna when you radioed them to tell them I was coming."

"And why would I have bothered to do that?" Mwanajuma airily inquired.

"Because you're the mole, Robert."

The minister narrowed his eyes but, otherwise, remained impassive.

"So, you are accusing me of being in league with criminals, Alex?" he asked, coolly.

"Do you deny it? I'm just stating things as I see 'em, Robert."

"Would my denial make any difference? It appears you have already made up your mind."

Laidlaw reflected. "Pretty much."

"In that case, I await your evidence."

"Explain to me why you gave Owusu and Okubuna the heads up about my visit to the Selous preserve. We previously agreed that no one would be notified in advance."

"You are assuming that I spoke to the rangers about that matter," Mwanajuma replied. "That is your first mistake."

"You didn't talk to either of them?"

"I did not."

"They said somebody from the ministry radioed them with the date."

"'Somebody from the ministry', even if true, could have been anyone. And has it not occurred to you that it could just as easily have been someone masquerading as a ministry employee?"

"No, it couldn't. You were the only one I told about my phony plan to visit the Selous. Whoever radioed the rangers had to have obtained that info directly from you because you were the only one who knew it."

Mwanajuma was silent a moment. "Your allegations," he began, "for they are nothing more than that, mean nothing, Alex. As everyone knows, it is part of my job to regularly communicate with game rangers in the field. There is nothing inappropriate about my doing so."

“There is if your purpose was to give the heads up to poachers.”

The minister raised his eyebrows and smiled, provocatively. “You have proof of this, of course.” He awaited Laidlaw's response, which was not immediately forthcoming. “I thought not.”

“It doesn't take a whole lot of smarts to connect the dots, Robert.”

“I am fortunate that 'smarts' do not constitute proof. But, I am not sure you are thinking clearly, Alex. Should you consider going public with your fanciful allegations, who do you think will be believed? A disgraced professional hunter who slaughters animals for money, and whose government-issued permit has been suspended for malfeasance, or a selfless public servant who has devoted his entire life to safeguarding our precious wildlife?”

“What are you talking about? What 'malfeasance'? My hunting permit was never suspended!”

Mwanajuma smiled. “Nor, if you are sensible, will it be.”

Laidlaw began to feel sick. “By 'sensible', you mean I should just look the other way? That's how you intend to play this? We've known each other a long time, Robert...I can't believe you'd stoop to extortion!”

“Please, Alex, don't be naive. Besides, such sanctimoniousness ill-suits you,” Mwanajuma tut-tutted with equanimity. “We are both realists. Poaching of exotic African fauna is a fact of life that we must live with because we will never be able to totally eliminate it. The best we can hope for is to control or, if we're lucky, minimize it. And the best way of doing that is to take advantage of those who have something to gain.

“Make your point,” Laidlaw said.

“You'll remember that in World War II, your government, fearing Axis sabotage, held its nose and enlisted the Mafia to protect the dockyards of New York, New Orleans, and elsewhere. The thinking was that, because the Mafia already controlled them, it had a vested interest in safeguarding the dockyards. For the same reason, the United States government used the Sicilian Mafia to gather local intelligence prior to invading Italy.”

“I'm still waiting for you you to make your point.”

“The point is, like it or not, circumstances often create strange bedfellows. It is sometimes necessary to do repugnant things for the greater good.”

“What's that got to do with rhinos?”

“Though providing employment, being a game ranger pays little and all of them have families to feed. It is an open secret that some, maybe most, of our rangers are occasional poachers. Who could blame them for selling an occasional rhino horn, here or there? Such subsistence poaching does not threaten entire species. Wholesale butchery by organized gangs *does.*”

“You're telling me the game rangers are the ministry's 'Mafia'.

“Just so. The ministry is willing to allow the rangers to cull a limited number of animals. In exchange for this concession, the rangers keep the preserves free of roving armies of international poachers who indiscriminately slaughter everything with four legs. In a word, the rangers have a vested interest in keeping 'their' preserves free of competing poachers.”

“What does that have to do with me? It sounds like you've got everything figured out."

“When I initially approached you about assisting with the rhino project, I did so in good faith because your reputation for wildlife conservation and incorruptibility is well known. Your participation provides additional lustre and credibility to our preservation efforts, which will increase global donations. Furthermore, as I told you previously, if the rangers are convinced that the great Alex Laidlaw is looking over their shoulders, they will be less tempted to get greedy or succumb to the lure of commercial poaching. Rest assured that you are by no means mere window dressing, Alex. On the contrary, your cooperation is indispensable to the success of our entire breeding program.”

“Bullshit. What 'cooperation'? You hold me in such high regard that you threaten to ruin me professionally by suspending my license if I don't participate in your little charade? Is that how it works, Robert?”

"I do what is necessary," Mwanajuma shrugged. "I knew that, otherwise, you would be impossible to persuade."

"You're right about that much. I have no interest in being a party to your scheme, though I fully understand that it's essential for donations to the poor, beleaguered rhinos continue to flow into government coffers. Like you said, Cuban cigars aren't cheap."

"Your cynicism does you no credit, Alex. Donations to the rhino project are regularly audited. I purchase my cigars from my own pocket."

"You honestly believe that your professed altruism justifies manipulation and deceit? The ends justify the means?"

"As I said, I do what is necessary and do not seek your imprimatur for having done it."

"Jesus Christ, Robert! Do you even hear yourself? You sound like Joseph Goebbels or Mao!"

Mwanajuma ignored him. "So, we may continue to rely on you, Alex?" he asked with equanimity.

"What the hell choice do I have?"

"One always has choices. We must simply be prepared to live with the consequences."

"SO, YOUR INTUITION PROVED CORRECT' Mosi remarked. The two men were eating dinner in the Europa's bar: pork chops, mashed potatoes, and fried plantains.

Mosi was drinking a gin and tonic, Laidlaw a Manhattan.

"Sorry to say."

"His conservation model, such as it is, is a bit unorthodox, yes?"

Laidlaw rested his fork on the edge of his plate and stared into the distance as he thought.

"'Unorthodox'? It's way beyond 'unorthodox'. It's bizarre: implicitly encouraging game rangers to kill the animals they're responsible for protecting! And that's assuming Robert is actually telling the truth. If he is, his harebrained anti-poaching 'strategy', if it can be called that, sounds like something a committee of nitwits would dream up...and that's being generous."

"Nitwits or government bureaucrats," Mosi suggested. He sipped his cocktail.

"Six of one, half-dozen of the other. God only knows what kind of kick-backs Mwanajuma's getting from his little scheme."

"It seems that Robert may be crazy like a fox."

Laidlaw drained his Manhattan and signaled the bartender for another. "You must be clairvoyant. I was thinking the same thing."

"All of that is irrelevant," Mosi declared. "It does not matter how well intentioned Mwanajuma may be. He is blackmailing you. Such shabby treatment is unacceptable."

"I agree, but what am I supposed to do? I've known Robert forever and can't believe he'd treat me this way. But, if something happens it must be possible. Even if he's bluffing about suspending my hunting license, can I afford to take that chance? If I publicly call him out, he'll just portray me as a disgruntled anti-government nut job with an axe to grind."

Their bartender arrived with Laidlaw's fresh drink, placed it on the table, scooped up his empty glass, and disappeared.

"So, you intend to simply go along with Robert's institutionalized poaching, at least for now?

Laidlaw looked Mosi squarely in the face. "To get along, you gotta go along. If you've got a better idea about what I should do, I'm all ears. Otherwise, I'll keep monitoring the rhinos...if not me, who? I'm not the one holding hands with poachers. I haven't been up to the Bukoba preserve yet. Maybe things are different up there."

"My friend, when a dog breaks wind, the stench does confine itself to a small area, but fills the entire room."

Laidlaw began laughing. "Mosi, if nothing else, your aphorisms are certainly colorful!"

JOCKO VANDERBEEKE TAPPED THE driver's shoulder; the latter braked the roofless bakkie to a stop in a swirling cloud of dust and switched the engine off. Jocko stood and lifted to his face the binoculars hanging by a padded strap from his neck. Peering over the vehicle's bug-spattered windshield, he scanned a herd of impala 250 yards away.

"There's a couple of decent rams in there," he informed the driver, who didn't really give a damn. Jocko flopped into the seat and continued to survey the antelope through the windshield.

"What do you want to do, mabwana?" his driver finally asked.

Jocko lowered his binoculars. "Get closer but don't spook 'em," he ordered. The driver started the engine, released the clutch, and began to ease the vehicle forward.

Bolted to the bakkie's metal dashboard was a makeshift rifle rack. Jocko lifted a beat-up AK-47 from the rack, retracted its bolt, chambered a steel-cased 7.62 x 39 millimeter cartridge, and held the loaded rifle vertically in front of him with its butt resting on the vamp of his boot. The bakkie slowly bumped and swayed toward the impala.

Airport gift shops across sub-Saharan Africa sell a myriad of native African handicrafts to vacationing tourists: wooden carvings, furniture, clothing, rugs, paintings, textiles, but especially animal products, including hides, horns, and scrimshawed ostrich eggs. Zebra hides and rugs are, not surprisingly, hugely popular because of their striking beauty. Because the pelages of wild zebras are invariably blemished and scarred, thereby diminishing their commercial value, all zebra products sold in gift shops, or over the Internet, derive from semi-domesticated stock bred on sprawling South African commercial ranches. Only in such an assembly-line setting can the pristine condition of their hides be ensured.

Zebras and the large felines are relatively easy to raise and breed in captivity. Other African species prove less compliant, however. With the exception of the massive eland, they include virtually all varieties of African antelope, the beautiful impala among them. Irrespective, impalas remain highly desirable trophies because of the male's symmetrical lyrate horns and warm chestnut pelage. Notwithstanding their desire to impress others with tangible evidence of their manly ruggedness, many Zoomers balk at the prospect of having to actually shoot a rifle, or spend exhausting days in the field tracking an animal. Perfectly willing to pay the asking price, it is equally efficacious and far less hassle to simply purchase a set of poached impala horns and claim them as one's own.

Jocko Vanderbeeke and his ilk were a godsend to such armchair sportsmen.

Dispensing with such boorish formalities as hunting licenses, Vanderbeeke and his associates indiscriminately shot rhinos, elephants, lions, leopards, bonteboks, impalas, sables, kudus, warthogs, bongos, and pretty much anything else the horns, hides, teeth, or tusks of which promised to generate a profit. Fully-automatic AK's were indispensable tools for the job, their large capacity magazines and cyclical rate of fire obviating the need for precise aiming.

“Stop!” Jocko hissed. His driver braked and killed the bakkie's engine. They were less than 100 yards from the impala herd, which was interspersed throughout the brush.

Grasping the windshield frame, Jocko pulled himself upright from his seat and extended his arm. The driver wordlessly handed him the AK.

"I'll get $4,000 for those bloody rams and they ain't even record-book," he grinned. "The hides on the others will fetch another eight."

Legitimate sportsmen choose their firearms with great care and use only ammunition specifically designed for hunting. Jocko, however, was unencumbered by such considerations. His AK was loaded with cheap military surplus ammunition from Eastern Europe designed not to kill, but to wound. No matter. Assuming he was able to hit an animal a sufficient number of times, it would eventually die. If, instead, it managed to limp away and succumb to its wounds in some hidden location, Jocko would just chalk it up to bad luck.. He sure as hell wasn't gonna lose sleep over it. There were plenty of other targets of opportunity to cover the loss.

Jocko raised the rifle to his shoulder, pointed it in the general direction of the nearest impala ram, and squeezed the trigger. A stream of steel-jacketed bullets ripped through the intervening brush, stripping the foliage from the bushes before plowing into the antelope herd. The projectiles shattered delicate limbs; struck animals in their flanks, breaking their hips; and punctured internal organs without instantly killing.

"Taught those bloody cunts a lesson!" Jocko gleefully cried.

In Primis Anno Regnantibus Imperator Caesar Titus Vespasianus (81 CE)

MARCHING ROUGHLY PARALLEL TO THE Red Sea, Berossus and his legionnaires resumed their northward trek, still hopeful of securing maritime transportation to Rome. Since their departure from the *castrum* weeks, months, or years ago, the legion's number had been more than halved: disease, injuries, accidents, wounds, desertions. They had encountered no other individuals or settlements in the aftermath of their brief skirmish with Carpio.

"At this rate, none of us will remain alive to see Rome," Senecio grumbled. "We would have been better off remaining at the *castrum*."

"Too late hindsight gives us new eyes," Neocles said in response.

"What do you suppose will happen in Rome, assuming any of us actually arrives there?"

Neocles sighed. "Perhaps *Bestia* will be reconstituted. Perhaps it will be ordered back to Africa. Whatever the gods will."

"You are foolish, Neocles. Why would Corvo flee the *castrum*, and undertake a hazardous journey to

Rome, if he knew he would just be ordered back to Africa? The gods are not that inconstant."

"Corvo is dead. Besides, neither he nor the gods bear responsibility for the decision to abandon the *castrum*."

Senecio stopped mid-stride and frowned. "Who, if not Corvo or the gods?"

"Berossus, alone, will benefit following our arrival in Rome. *Bestia* surely will not."

"Berossus!" Senecio snorted. "How does *he* stand to profit?"

Neocles shrugged. "He is our commander. The senate will reward and promote him for preserving one of its legions from annihilation by African savages."

"Corvo, not Berossus, is our legitimate commander! He, not Berossus, warrants the senate's gratitude," Senecio affirmed.

"Corvo *was* our commander. Unfortunately for him, he is dead, leaving Berossus the beneficiary of the senate's praise by default."

"Berossus had no way of predicting the will of the gods," Senecio stated. "They do not confide such things to mortals."

"It takes but little effort to ascertain the will of the gods while holding a dagger to the throat of one's enemy."

Senecio looked incredulous. "You accuse Berossus of murdering Corvo?"

"Only if the gods willed it," Neocles responded with a tiny smile."

FIVE DAYS NORTH OF CARPIO'S VILLAGE, the weary residue of *Legio XVI Bestia* rested at the base of a low hill overlooking the *Pontus Herculis*, its face pocked with large black boulders. Berossus ordered a legionnaire named 'Frontius' to scale the promontory.

"Reconnoiter the area," Berossus instructed him. "It is only reasonable that there is a port hereabouts."

Frontius laid aside his pike and began to scramble up the hill while his colleagues watched in silence. One by one, the legionnaires collapsed to the earth, glad that it was Frontius who was chosen for the task instead of them. All were hot, tired, and weary of endless marching.

"The rocks on that hill resemble the heads of Nubians," Senecio idly observed as he watched Frontius ascend. "Though I think Berossus right."

"How so?"

"About a port being nearby. That barbarian told us there existed settlements to the north of his village."

"He said that in the hope of getting rid of us," Neocles sighed. "Besides, a 'settlement' could mean a family of naked savages living on the bare earth, subsisting on insects."

"I have yet to encounter a sea where ports are completely lacking, or people who live on insects...not even barbarians!" Senecio scoffed.

"I had never before seen a giraffe until being shunted off to Africa."

Senecio began to laugh. "By the gods, Neocles, I had not considered that! I suppose we shall see which one of us is correct when Frontius returns from his scout."

"I would happily confess my error if the penalty for being wrong is a berth on a *navis* for the remainder of our journey."

"That would be a fine penalty, indeed!" Senecio snorted. "Only the gods are sufficiently perverse to transform a penalty into a reward."

"We shall know soon enough," Neocles remarked. He gestured beyond Senecio, where Frontius was sliding and tripping down the hill's steep, rugged facade. Once on the ground, he hastened to Berossus.

"Commander." Berossus turned and coolly surveyed the panting legionnaire. "I saw an entrepot from the hilltop," Frontius reported.

"Which direction?"

Frontius pointed. "Northeast. Not far...perhaps two miles."

"Defended?"

"I saw no one armed, though the distance was great."

Berossus cocked an eyebrow. "How large?"

"Large. There are many *navii* in its harbor."

"Vessels adequate to carry us to Rome?"

"That and more," Frontius affirmed.

In point of fact, the substantial town Frontius spotted from the crown of the hill was Adulis, a significant trading hub now subsumed by the modern

Eritrean city of Zula. Adulis' coastal location, natural harbor, and relative proximity to Egypt, Greece, and the Arabian peninsula rendered it a major commercial center for merchants plying the waters of the *Pontus Herculis*. Records dating from as early as the 15th century BCE establish that the ancient Egyptians sent regular trading expeditions to Adulis, called by the pharaohs "The Land of Punt," where they obtained slaves, exotic woods, ivory, gold, turquoise, ostrich feathers, animal skins, and live animals.

"We will rest here until the morrow, whereupon we shall march thither," Berossus stated.

AFTER A DAWN BREAKFAST OF barley cakes and water, the legionnaires backtracked three-quarters of a mile in order to circumvent the range of hills that lay between themselves and the sea. Having done so, they resumed marching northward, along the rocky beach, toward Adulis. Their step was lighter in the expectation that the remainder of their journey to Rome was likely to be conducted by watercraft.

"How far do you suppose we have marched in total?" Senecio mulled.

"Since leaving the *castrum*, it feels as though we have marched to the end of the known world. Twice."

"We have suffered much. I hope the gods have finally wearied of toying with us."

Neocles did not immediately respond. He felt a profound emptiness when he reflected on the fate of Crixus and the deaths of Aulus and other *Bestia* comrades, events that seem to have occurred an eternity ago.

"For what reason do the gods strew our path with thorns? Have they nothing better to occupy themselves?" Neocles mourned.

"Men are without power to comprehend the gods. Their actions are beyond human understanding," Senecio lectured in response.

Neocles smiled, bitterly. "The gods are in an enviable position. When I enjoy good fortune it is because the gods are well-disposed toward me, for which I am expected to render copious thanks. Contrariwise, when I am beset with evils those, also, are the work of the gods, though I am too dull-witted to discern a rationale for the gods' displeasure with me. Notwithstanding the suffering I endure at their hands, however, I remain under an obligation to venerate the gods. That is akin to thanking a bandit for robbing me, which makes no sense."

"Your impiety is certain to offend the gods," Senecio cautioned. He edged slightly away from his friend, as though half-fearing an imminent, annihilating thunderbolt.

"If that is so, I will have at least provided them some justification for despising me. The gods should be grateful for my help."

Senecio thought it prudent to change the subject.

“What shall you do in Rome once we arrive there?” he asked.

“I am not sure, for I do not know how to lie,” Neocles shrugged.

Senecio began laughing. “By Jupiter, if I did not know better, I would swear that I was talking to our friend, Crixus, rather than to you!”

Hearing Senecio's words, Neocles felt a sharp pang of sadness.

“I would like very much to be reunited with Crixus in Rome,” he said, “though I now believe that we shall not see one another again.”

“You mock the gods, yet everything lies within their power.”

“For good or ill...” Neocles' voice trailed off.

WHILE AT NO TIME PROJECTING THE CONVENTIONAL IMAGE of polished Roman military splendor, *Legio XVI Bestia* had at least looked reasonably professional when it originally departed the *castrum.* The bedraggled collection of men that finally limped from the wilderness was a far cry from those heady days. Stretching before them along the arid coastline for a half-mile, and an equal distance inland, Adulis was, by a wide margin, the largest settlement the legionnaires had encountered in years. For a few, the largest they had ever seen.

Other than a scattering of date palms, the spongy wood of which is worthless as lumber, there were no trees in the vicinity. As a consequence, all of Adulis' dwellings were constructed of whatever materials were immediately at hand or could be scrounged or bargained: boulders; marine debris; the sawn and stacked trunks of palm trees; whale ribs and skulls; the upturned hulls of old boats; canopies woven of flax, camel or goat hair, or rags; planks of timber salvaged from wrecked ships; palapas of various sizes; and warrens of burrows and tunnels scraped from the bare earth and shielded from the blistering sun with layers of palm fronds. Dozens of vessels of varying configurations lay at anchor in Andulis' broad harbor and a multitude of emaciated dogs panted in what little shade was available. A few chickens and guineafowl pecked listlessly at the dirt. Given Andulis' seaside locus and status as a trading center, its eclectic population of traveling merchants and more-or-less permanent residents paid little attention to the legionnaires' arrival.

Senecio grinned as he gestured toward the harbor with a sweep of his arm. “There are *navii* aplenty here. Our days of endless marching are at an end!”

“There may be vessels enough, though an inadequate number of *nautae* to crew them,” Neocles responded as he scanned the desolate settlement.

“The *navii* did not sail here on their own,” Senecio chuckled.

Berossus bulled his way into the midst of the collected Romans, interrupting their conversation. “Slaughter the dogs and fowl and prepare them for our meal,” he barked at four of them. “For the rest, separate into squads and go to each dwelling. Collect all the adult men and, from them, assemble crews adequate to man the two largest vessels in the harbor. From each household, seize all foodstuffs, as well. We will require provisions for the voyage to Rome. If any of the people balk, inform them that you act under my direct authority and that of the senate and people of Rome.”

“And if they do not speak our language or are unwilling to comply?” asked a legionnaire.

Berossus looked at him, sourly. “Execute the first few that resist and display their corpses publicly. Their neighbors will soon enough learn the cost of defiance. I will meanwhile examine ships in the harbor to determine which are suitable to convey us to Rome.”

Neocles and Senecio formed a four-man squad with two of their friends. Berossus having disappeared, they stood around, uneasily, reluctant to implement his directive.

“Do no harm to any of the males,” a legionnaire proposed, essentially countermanding the order that Berossus gave only a few minutes earlier. “They may be necessary to crew the *navii.*”

“What of Berossus' instructions to execute *all* who resist?”

The other legionnaire reflected a moment. "If it proves necessary to compel the barbarians' obedience, secure it by means of their wives and children. Compassion is a pernicious luxury that will ensure our ruin."

The squads split up and began to distribute themselves throughout the inoffensive community. Although unspoken, most of the legionnaires hoped no bloodshed would result.

Not surprisingly, Adulis was home to multiple polyglots. They were promptly conscripted for use as translators as the Romans went door-to-door to levy crews for the voyage to Rome. The legionnaires' overtures were initially greeted with incredulity, followed by anger, then categorical rejection by the Andulites.

"Even though they are barbarians, I have no desire to kill them. They have done us no harm," Senecio confided to Neocles as they sauntered down a dirt lane between shanties.

"I will walk the remaining distance to Rome, or take my leave entirely of *Bestia*, before staining my hands with innocent blood, even that of barbarians," Neocles agreed.

Senecio dipped his head toward the other two men in their squad, who plodded a few yards ahead. "And them?"

"Unless I am wrong, they appear in no great hurry to begin cutting the throats of women and children."

"Even so, Berossus will rightly expect that his orders are strictly obeyed."

"Do not concern yourself. *Bestia* has no shortage of lickspittles who will happily comply with his orders, so eager are they to ingratiate themselves with Berossus. Having unintentionally relieved us of that disagreeable task, I will not begrudge them in the slightest if they receive full credit for their diligence."

Senecio was impressed by his companion's faultless reasoning.

"So, what shall we do for the nonce?" he asked.

"I suggest we use our time profitably by locating something to eat before the others commandeer whatever food may be found in this place."

BEROSSUS STOMPED BACK TO Adulis ninety minutes later, where he was confronted by a huddle of about 30 townspeople of varying ages, including a few women, half-halfheartedly guarded by eight apathetic Romans. Some the conscripts were past middle age, others little more than children.

Berossus glared at one of the legionnaires. "These scrawny wretches are the best you could find? Why do you not bring me *men*?"

"The townspeople told us that all their men are at sea, aboard other vessels."

"A transparent lie. The barbarians said this with your knife to their throats?"

The legionnaire shook his head. “There was no need. They freely volunteered it.” He gestured toward the frightened, confused herd of townspeople. “Besides, had we begun to randomly kill the barbarians, there would be none left to assemble here.”

“Scour this *cloaca* for two complete crews and do not be duped by the savages' claim that all their menfolk are absent. And what of viands? What have you managed to locate, or did the barbarians swear a sacred oath that they live on air alone?

“The men continue to search for provisions even as we speak.”

“Neither you nor any of the squeamish weaklings of *Bestia* are worthy to be called 'Romans',” Berossus scowled. He unsheathed his sword and strode to the knot of people. “Which of you speaks Latin?” he bellowed.

No one responded.

Berossus clasped his sword tightly and swung it at the nearest Adulite, striking the woman across the side of her face with the flat of its blade. Shocked by the suddenness of the assault, she stumbled backward before tripping and stumbling to the ground. She sprawled, glassy-eyes, a welt on her cheek already developing.

Berossus coolly surveyed the terrified onlookers. “No one? My sword will taste blood with its next stroke unless one of you finds your tongue.”

An old man stepped forward. “I speak your language.”

Berossus looked back at the watching legionnaires. "Do you not find it remarkable how quickly even ignorant barbarians can be educated in Latin? One must simply employ tools appropriate to the task." He turned his attention to the collection of anxious Adulites who knelt around the dazed woman, who still lay on the ground.

Berossus sheathed his sword and glared at the old man. "Instruct them to leave her."

The man spoke a few words while motioning toward Berossus. The people slowly climbed to their feet and shuffled into small clusters. They continued to cast worried glances at the prostrate woman.

"How many of your people speak Latin?" Berossus barked at the old man, whom he automatically treated as the *de facto* spokesman for the entire town.

"As far as I know, I alone. I lived in Brundisium as a boy."

"Where are all of your young men?"

"Adulis is a maritime community. They serve on vessels that call here."

"None remain?"

The old man gestured wordlessly toward the townspeople gathered around him.

"There must be others, aside from old men, crones, and children," Berossus snarled.

"We were merely the first to be ensnared by your men. Do you fault us for their ineptitude in locating others? They will surely blunder into more."

"You mock me at your peril."

"Undoubtedly, but I am an old man. You can kill me but once."

Berossus studied his imperturbable prisoner through narrowed eyes. "When will your young men return?"

The old man shrugged. "Vessels call here when they will. Beyond that, you must ask the gods."

"We require food and provisions in addition to men. Where is it gathered?"

"We maintain no common storehouse. Your men will undoubtedly find everything they desire while ransacking our homes."

"Commander!" one of the guards blurted. "More approach."

Berossus turned to observe a collection of townspeople being herded in their direction by legionnaires. Several young men were among them. He glanced back at his informant.

"You told me that no suitable men remain in this place. I now see that you wish to deceive me."

"No," said the man. "I informed you that our young men serve on the vessels that call here. The gods know the literal truth of my words."

"The gods hate deceitful liars no less than those who profane them."

"As they do thieves and murderers."

Berossus smiled, coldly, and nodded. "Today, you swine are blessed, for with a single blow, I intend to educate all of you regarding the gods' disposition." He gestured toward a bent, old woman in the group. "Tell her to approach."

Reluctantly, the interpreter spoke a few words. In order to steady herself, the old lady clasped the forearm of a younger woman, perhaps her daughter, and they began to hobble forward in tandem.

"There." Berossus unsheathed his *gladius* and used it to gesture to a spot near him.

The old lady paused and looked with fear into the eyes of her helpmate, who smiled reassuringly and gently patted her hand. Together, they resumed their halting advance. Those near them stepped aside in apprehensive silence and allowed them to pass.

"*Subsisto*!" Berossus barked as they drew close. In alarm, the confused women halted. They look anxiously first at Berossus, then at the wizened interpreter.

"They have complied with your wishes. Do them no harm," implored the latter.

"The gods chastise only those who despise them," Berossus pontificated.

"These women, nor any of us, despise the gods."

"Indeed?" Berossus responded in mock surprise. "Where, then, are your young men? And provender sufficient for our voyage?"

The arrival of the second throng of captives interrupted their conversation. The new arrivals slumped to a halt before them. A legionnaire prodded one sullen prisoner, a male appearing to be in his late teens or early twenties, with a pike.

"Many attempted to hide or flee, including this one, Commander," he informed Berossus.

Berossus stepped to the offending captive. "What say you?" The man looked at him without comprehension but with unconcealed animus.

"He will do," Berossus stated. "How many more like him?"

"None yet, though we continue to search for others."

Berossus nodded with approval. "Place this one by himself in the interim. I do not wish the other barbarians to corrupt him with their seditious words."

"As you order, Commander," the legionnaire crisply acknowledged. "And the rest?"

Berossus surveyed the remaining prisoners, who averted their eyes. He pointed to a young girl, perhaps ten years old.

"I would fuck that one. Conduct her to a dwelling and confine her. Place all the others with these vermin and increase the guard. Inform the legion that they may take any of the women they please once a satisfactory crew has been assembled."

"As you order," the legionnaire dutifully repeated. He turned to a nearby soldier and parroted the instructions he'd just been given. The latter grabbed the terrified girl by one arm and dragged her, screaming and wailing, from the group.

Berossus turned back to the old man. "Again I ask, where are your young men?"

"They are absent, as I stated," the old man persisted. "Had we known of your coming, we would have gladly provided you both men and supplies."

"All of your young men are absent?" Berossus frowned. "What about that one?" With his *gladius*, he pointed to the young man who still stood, glowering, among the latest group of captured townspeople.

"I swear by the gods I did not know Meketra remained in Adulis," the old man avowed.

"That is his name? 'Meketra'?" The other man nodded. "How many more like him remain concealed, do you suppose?" Berossus taunted.

"Meketra has long done as he pleases. I promise you there are no others."

"Promise? You previously promised me there were none at all, though your memory appears to be failing," Berossus snapped. "Perhaps it will prove necessary to sharpen your wits."

The old man instinctively took a half-step backward. Now isolated, the two trembling women clung to one another. Still brandishing his gladius, Berossus turned and surveyed them in silence.

"Ask them their names," he finally ordered.

"They are 'Sarah' and 'Nofret'," the old man immediately responded.

Berossus distractedly nodded without taking his eyes from the women. "They are mother and daughter?"

"Sarah is aunt to Nofret."

"Where are her parents?"

"Long dead. Nofret was raised by Sarah."

Berossus turned from the women to fix a penetrating gaze on the old man. "Where are the hag's sons?"

“Sarah is a widow without issue. She was barren.”

“Oh? Then, she is not of much use to anyone.”

Berossus stepped toward the two women. Nofret immediately cast her eyes downward. The aged woman, however, raised her chin and looked directly at him with defiance.

Pursing his lips, he momentarily studied her before abruptly raising his *gladius* and thrusting its gleaming bronze point into the gaunt old woman's heart. Nofret emitted a panicked shriek and sought to shield her aunt as blood spurted from the wound. Berossus gritted his teeth as, using his *gladius*, he attempted to lift Sarah completely free of the ground. Quickly tiring of the effort, however, he dipped the point of his sword and allowed the old woman to slip to the earth. The younger woman collapsed next to Sarah's crumpled body, trembling and sobbing. The remaining captives witnessed the execution in stunned horror.

“Did you intend by that to endear us to the barbarians and render our task easier?” a bored legionnaire sensibly inquired.

Berossus wiped the blade of his *gladius* on the dead woman's clothing before restoring the weapon to its sheath. “You fret too much, Longinus. These wretches believe themselves too clever by half. I merely disabused them of their arrogance. They now understand that I am not to be trifled with.”

“That may be, yet we still remain without crews or provisions. By rashly killing the old crone, that is unlikely to change because the barbarians are now hardened against us."

Berossus scornfully laughed. "You do not think they were not already so? Only a fool would place any reliance on these simpletons. Though no better than dogs, even dogs can be trained to do our bidding through the vigorous application of a stick. So, too, these mindless brutes."

Berossus gestured for the interpreter to approach. He fearfully complied.

"Do you profess to be a Nazarene, old man?" Berossus asked him in a conversational tone.

"I so profess."

"Just as your god martyred himself for his followers, so that old hag sacrificed herself for you," Berossus said through a thin smile. "If you do not wish her death to have been in vain, tell me where your men are. Otherwise, more deaths will be forthcoming."

The old man gazed sadly at Sarah's broken body, over which Nofret continued to sob. He, too, began to cry.

"Our men will return with the merchant vessels on the next tide moon," he wept. "Do us no further harm, Roman."

Berossus turned to the other legionnaire. "As I said, even dogs can be trained to do one's bidding, provided one is not slow to employ the stick." He turned away. "Do not disturb me further, for I will be fucking."

FIFTEEN

LAIDLAW HADN'T BEEN TO BUKOBA for a few years simply because, until now, he had no reason to go there. However, in his new role as reluctant "Special Consultant to the Ministry of Wildlife", or "Overseer of Wildlife Refuges", or, more accurately, simple patsy, and having already visited the Selous refuge twice, he felt obligated to undertake the long drive to the Bukoba preserve. He had no idea whether the game rangers stationed there were participants in Mwanajuma's unconventional "look-the-other-way" conservation model but, when a dog breaks wind the stench does confine itself to a small area, but fills the entire room.

The bakkie being unlicensed for operation on public highways and suitable only for off-road driving, Laidlaw made the nearly five-hour drive to Bukoba in his old Jeep. He'd informed no one of his covert visit.

Because the isolated rhino refuge was actually located several miles outside the town itself, Laidlaw would have to use GPS to navigate his way on the network of dirt roads that crisscrossed the encompassing wilderness. Though Laidlaw had originally hoped to review the personnel files of the two game rangers assigned to Bukoba, he concluded that tendering such a request to Mwanajuma would accomplish nothing substantive while betraying a mission that he wanted to keep secret. Accordingly, Laidlaw had no choice but to simply play things by ear once he arrived at the refuge.

Traffic was heavy on the two-lane tarmacked highway. Notwithstanding that he hoped to arrive at Bukoba before sunset, Laidlaw was forced to drive well below the posted, optimistic speed limit because clusters of pedestrians and domestic livestock sauntered along the shoulder, and even down the middle, of the pot-holed thoroughfare.

Laidlaw shared the road with comparatively few passenger cars, the vast number of other vehicles being decrepit cross-country busses overloaded with passengers or lumbering trucks, of diverse sizes and configurations in varying states of disrepair, hauling freight: bales of hay or straw; burlap sacks of grain; large, dented sheets of tin; stacks of lumber; pallets of bricks; restive aggregations of goats, pigs, and cattle; mismatched furniture; boulders; heaps of raw vegetables; other human beings. All the trucks spewed polychromatic clouds of diesel smoke from their exhaust pipes, primarily black, but also white and gray of various hues. Aside from a forlorn bushbuck browsing on a dead shrub at the edge of the highway, Laidlaw saw no wildlife.

Throughout the 18th and 19th centuries, Africa's autochthonous peoples and magnificent, diverse wildlife were among the first casualties of Europe's mad scramble to control the African continent. Dutch, Portuguese, English, Italian, Belgian, French, German...all participated in campaigns of mindless slaughter. With regard to animals, their seemingly inexhaustible numbers were considered either an impediment to progress or simply a nuisance, usually both. In the 1890's, cattle infected with rinderpest were introduced into Eritrea during Italy's war with Somalia. The contagion rapidly swept south and the resulting epizootic decimated populations of indigenous hooved creatures...buffalo, giraffe, wart hog, every variety of antelope...in the incalculable millions. The loss of these animals caused widespread famine across sub-Saharan Africa. It is estimated that one-third of the human population of Ethiopia, and two-thirds of the Maasai people of Tanzania, starved to death during this period. By the time a rinderpest vaccine was developed, only isolated pockets of wildlife remained, though their travails were far from over. As late as the 1950's, even the surviving species remained heavily persecuted, often shot on sight by land owners who considered them competition for grazing and other resources needed for domestic cattle and sheep. Africa's nascent sugar industry in the 1960's accelerated the process of decimation because of the demand for additional land. Throughout the 1970's, Africa's beef ranchers, especially in Zimbabwe and South Africa, redoubled their efforts to extirpate the Cape buffalo, especially, because of hoof and mouth disease. The slain animals were either consumed by ranch hands or fed to dogs.

Though seemingly counter-intuitive, sport hunting was the salvation of Africa's large ungulates. Practical-minded politicians and hard-headed businessmen from across the continent finally undertook to study the precipitous decline in Africa's wildlife, ultimately concluding that hunters from around the world would be willing to pay substantial amounts of money for the privilege of hunting the storied game of Africa. Simply put, Africa's animals were worth more alive, than dead. As a result of this epiphany many, though certainly not all, African nations either initiated or revived policies officially sanctioning sport hunting.

A rising tide raises all boats. Aside from multiple licensing fees, taxes, and tariffs which flowed directly into government coffers, the ripple effect of Africa's audacious decision to establish a regulated hunting industry inevitably spawned, or strengthened, a panoply of derivative businesses: travel and booking agencies, outfitters, hotels, airlines, publishing companies, restaurants, taxi services, rental cars, taxidermists, clothiers, oil companies, retail merchants, sporting goods manufacturers, gunsmiths, trucking companies...the list was truly endless.

Africa had finally, after centuries of ruthless exploitation by outsiders, struck gold. Even so, the process of restoring and propagating its native wildlife proved arduous and costly. The solitary bushbuck along the side of the highway provided mute evidence that generations of collective extermination, mismanagement, and neglect are not easily reversed.

Laidlaw swerved to avoid a small herd of goats standing in the middle of the road. The front tire of his Jeep struck a pothole, causing the vehicle to bounce and shudder erratically before settling back into his lane.

He glanced at this watch. Another ninety minutes.

LAIDLAW FINALLY PULLED UP TO THE cinderblock headquarters of the Bukoba preserve late that afternoon. A puzzled game ranger hustled out to greet, and interrogate, his unexpected visitor .

“Hello,” he cautiously greeted. “You are lost?”

Laidlaw killed the Jeep's engine and stepped from the vehicle. “No, I think I'm in the right place. I'm Alex Laidlaw, from the ministry.” He smiled and extended his hand.

The black African ranger dubiously shook Laidlaw's hand. “I am Franklin Chalo. I know who you are, Mr. Laidlaw. Welcome to Bukoba. The ministry did not tell me you were coming.”

“That's because I didn't them them.” Laidlaw glanced around. “Your partner here?”

“I have no partner. I am the only ranger assigned to Bukoba.”

Notwithstanding that Bukoba was the smaller, by far, of the two rhino preserves, Franklin' revelation came as a surprisew to Laidlaw.

“Can you make room for me for a couple of days?” he asked.

“Of course. That is not a problem at all. I have plenty of room and welcome your company.“ Franklin spontaneously stepped around Laidlaw and leaned into the Jeep to retrieve the duffle bag containing latter's gear. “Follow me, please.”

Laidlaw lifted his rifle from its rack adjacent to the driver's seat. With Franklin leading, they headed for the steel building that served as both office and living quarters. He pushed its unpainted door open with his foot and motioned for Laidlaw to enter. “You are most welcome.”

Laidlaw entered the small structure and was immediately impressed by its tidiness. A simple cot, a striped wool blanket neatly folded atop it, lay along one wall. A collapsible wooden field desk on the opposite side of the room held the preserve's two-way radio. A gas hotplate, refrigerator, and various cooking pots and dishes occupied a spot along a third wall, while a thick wooden dowel , with a shelf above it, was mounted to the fourth wall and held Franklin' clothing. Two straight-backed wooden chairs completed the furnishings. As at the Selous, the privy was a separate outbuilding located in the back.

Franklin lowered Laidlaw's duffle bag onto the cot. "You may sleep here. I will take the floor."

"Nonsense. I have no intention of dispossessing you from your bed. I'll sleep on the floor."

"You are my guest," Chalo protested.

Laidlaw smiled. "That is true. And, as your guest, I prefer to sleep on on the floor."

Chalo was clearly perplexed. "Of course. As you wish," he acceded.

Laidlaw lifted his duffle bag from the cot and placed it on the floor in a corner of the room. He dragged one of the chairs across the room and sat.

"You haven't asked me why I'm here," he said.

Franklin sat on the cot opposite him. "There was no need. I knew you would tell me in your own time, though it is not hard to guess that the ministry wishes a first-hand report on the condition of its rhinos."

"You must be psychic," Laidlaw smiled.

"You may tell them the rhinos are well. I will take you to them whenever you are ready."

Laidlaw glanced at his watch. "There's about ninety minutes of daylight left. How far are they?"

"Not far...a half-hour, perhaps."

Laidlaw stood. "Let's go. We'll talk on the way."

LAIDLAW SAT IN THE PASSENGER'S SEAT of the Ministry of Wildlife bakkie as they bounced along a narrow dirt road toward the interior of the preserve. "How long have you been assigned to Bukoba?" Laidlaw shouted over the wind noise.

"Nearly two years."

"Do you like it?"

Franklin glanced over at Laidlaw. "I like the animals. It is a privilege to help save them."

"The rhinos?"

"All of them: rhinos, zebras, sable, waterbuck, elephants, wart hogs, leopards, roan. All of them," Franklin repeated.

"All of those species are here?"

"Those and many more besides."

Laidlaw thoughtfully nodded. "How bad is the poaching problem?"

Franklin looked askance at Laidlaw before responding. "Bukoba has experienced none of that."

"Really?" Laidlaw was unable to conceal his surprise. "I heard that Selous has a big problem with poachers."

"I have never been to the Selous. I do not know what happens there," Franklin responded, matter-of-factly.

"Do you know the rangers that are stationed at the Selous?"

Franklin abruptly yanked the bakkie's steering wheel hard left to avoid a chuckhole. "No, I do not know them."

Laidlaw turned his attention from Chalo to the surrounding landscape.

Layers of golden dust suspended in the warm, late afternoon air turned the drooping sun into an incandescent orange ball. As they drove, a small cluster of alarmed impalas burst from shrubbery along the roadway, where they'd been browsing . Franklin tapped the brakes to avoid striking any animals when the herd leapt in front of the bakkie.

"Beautiful," he murmured without taking his eyes from the road.

NIGHT DESCENDS QUICKLY IN AFRICA. In the rapidly diminishing light, Laidlaw and Chalo reclined in the bakkie's front seats, quietly watching a black rhino cow nose her way through some thorn bushes.

"How many total rhinos on the preserve?" Laidlaw asked in a low voice.

"Four cows and three bulls."

"And calves?"

"None yet, though I wait."

"And you've had no problem with poachers?" Laidlaw again queried.

"Sometimes men come here. I see their tyre tracks and campfires."

"Poachers?"

“If they are poachers, they are not very good at it,” the game ranger shrugged. “No rhinos have yet been killed at Bukoba.”

“What about the other species?”

Chalo turned to look at Laidlaw through the dimness. “My main duty is to protect the rhinos.”

“I'm aware of that. But you also told me that you try to protect other species, as well.”

“That is true,” Chalo conceded. “it is a privilege to do so.”

“So, what's their status? The other species, I mean.” The edge in Laidlaw's voice betrayed his growing frustration with the noncommittal ranger.

“It is much more difficult to monitor the other animals because they are more numerous and do not wear tracking collars.”

“Yeah, I know. But you must still have some idea of the extent to which they're being poached. It's pretty hard to hide a dead elephant.”

In the darkness, the other man chuckled but did not respond.

Laidlaw tried another tack. “You said that you've seen strange campfires, yes? Did you investigate them?”

“Of course.”

“And, other than tyre tracks, what did you find? Spent cartridge cases? Cooked animal remains? Trash? Did you hear any gunshots? Anything that could identify them?”

“Nothing. They left nothing behind.”

“'How many times have you seen them? Many?”

Chalo shook his head. “No, just a few times. I have not seen them for a while, though.” The rhino lumbered off into the darkness while they were talking. In the near distance, a lion chuffed.

In silence, Laidlaw pondered the game ranger's revelations. It seemed obvious the intruders were organized poachers, scoping out the preserve's fauna. The question was, were they independent operators or active participants in Mwanajuma's poaching racket?

“Well, let's head back. It's getting darker than the inside of a black cat,” he remarked. “Tomorrow morning, I want you to show me where you saw the intruders. I also want to see the the other rhinos.”

“Of course.” Chalo cranked the bakkie's engine to life and switched on the headlights. He turned the vehicle in a wide , bumpy, arc and headed back toward his compound.

The warm night air ruffled Laidlaw's hair as they drove.

JOCKO VANDERBEEKE DRAINED HIS BEER AND tossed the aluminum can into the campfire, where he watched it melt. He extended his legs and listened to the clamorous yipping and whimpering of a troop of hyenas in the darkness. "You salt those hides?” he finally asked without looking up from the dying flames.

“Yes, mabwana. Everything is good.”

Jocko nodded contemplatively. He continued to stare into the glowing embers. "I wanna check out giraffes tomorrow. They're a pain in the arse, but I got a buyer for some hides and tails."

"Of course." His lead tracker, Ali, paused. "Mabwana, my cousin told me that the ministry hired Alex Laidlaw." He sounded almost apologetic.

Jocko dragged a crumpled pack of cigarettes from his shirt pocket and stuck one in his mouth. Leaning forward, he pulled a stick from the fire and held its glowing tip to the end of the cigarette. "Laidlaw? What the fuck for?"

"You know him, mabwana?"

"Well, I ain't givin' him blow jobs, if that's what you're askin'." Jocko inhaled a deep lungful of smoke from his cigarette.

"No, mabwana. I just wondered."

"Yeah, I've crossed paths with Laidlaw. He's a washed-up old man living on the shards of whatever reputation he used to have."

"He and the minister are friends, I think."

"That why they hired him?"

"My cousin says he is supposed to protect rhinos."

"Your cousin the game ranger at Selous? He the one who told you that?"

"Yes, mabwana."

Jocko looked skeptically at Ali. "Tell me something. Is your 'cousin' really your cousin or do you just fuckin' call him that? Everybody you talk about is your bloody 'cousin.'"

"All males from the same tribe are cousins, mabwana."

"If you say so," Jocko muttered. "Anyway, your cousin told you that Laidlaw is working for the ministry?"

"Yes, mabwana."

"Yeah, well, good luck with that," Jocko laughed. "I hope the ministry got him at a discount."

"My cousin says that Laidlaw visited the Selous and is serious about protecting rhinos. He is very famous."

"Yeah, he's a bloody legend in his own mind. Just ask him," Jocko snorted. "But I ain't worried about Laidlaw. I'll just have to educate his arse if he becomes a problem, which he won't."

"Yes, mabwana. I just thought you should know." Ali paused before uneasily continuing. "Are we going to shoot rhinos?"

Jocko flicked his cigarette butt into the firepit. "If I feel like shooting a fucking rhino, I'll bloody-well shoot a fucking rhino. And Alex Laidlaw won't do shit about it. Hell, I may shoot one just for shits and giggles."

"There are not very many rhinos."

"'My arse! There's two fucking rhino preserves right here in-country. More rhinos than you can shake a stick at...we'll take our pick."

"We do not know which of them Alex Laidlaw will be at, mabwana."

"Who gives a shit? Fuck him. Bring me another beer."

Ali dutifully rose from the dented steel ice chest on which he'd been sitting. He bent and flipped open its lid. Removing another lager, he lowered the cooler's lid and popped the can's tab before carrying the beer over to Jocko's chair. Jocko automatically extended his hand without looking up.

Ali returned to the ice chest and plopped down. “So, what do we do now, mabwana?”

“*We*? Right now, *you're* gonna throw some more wood on the fire while I drink my beer,” Jocko replied as he settled into his chair and stretched his legs.

“No, mabwana, about Laidlaw.”

“We ain't gonna do shit. I just gotta figure out a buyer for the rhino we're gonna pop.”

IT REQUIRED A HALF-DOZEN ATTEMPTS over two days before Laidlaw's call to Paris finally went through. Fortunately, Dunn picked up immediately.

“I was wondering when I'd hear from you,” Dunn happily greeted him. “How's life on the Dark Continent?”

“Don't ask. I got roped into babysitting some rhinos.”

“Is that a good thing or a bad thing?”

“A bad thing. The wildlife minister volunteered me for the job. It was a case of either play ball or lose my PH license,” Laidlaw rued.

"Hold on...he actually threatened you with the loss of your license?"

"Don't be absurd. Of course not. What kind of government threatens its own citizens with the loss of their livelihood, or their lives, for noncompliance with its mandates?" Laidlaw dryly responded.

Dunn began laughing. "Only every government since the inception of governments!"

"Aside from those, I mean," Laidlaw clarified.

"So, what are you gonna do?"

"Babysit some rhinos. Unfortunately, it turns out there's more to it than that, but I don't want to get into it over the phone. But there *is* something I wanted to talk to you about."

"Okay, what?"

"Well, because of this rhino business, I'm not sure when I'll be able to get back to Paris, though I still want to continue looking into the knife I found. I was thinking that you might be able to poke around a bit, maybe talk to some other experts about it, until I'm able get back there."

"Absolutely. I planned on it."

"Great. I'll send you a secure email with the access code, so you can retrieve the knife from that storage place. Feel free to take it to whoever you think may know something about it...maybe somebody can provide an idea of what it's worth."

"When do you realistically think you'll be back?"

"I'm not sure. Hopefully, it won't be too long. I just have to sort through some stuff here."

"OK, send me the code and I'll resume working on the knife. Just keep me in the loop as to what's happening at your end. Harry's, and Anatole, miss you. Oh yeah, and Bonnie's been asking about you, too."

Laidlaw was hazy. "Who's 'Bonnie'?"

"You know, your British girlfriend from Harry's with the sick mum. Bonnie says she's counting the days until you two are reunited."

Laidlaw laughed. "Since they apparently don't have doctors in Liverpool, tell Bonnie to cart the old lady to Harley Street, in London. There's a million doctors there."

"I'll pass it along," Dunn chuckled. "Meantime, send me the code whenever you can."

"Will do. Shoot me a confirming email once you receive it. Glad we were able to touch base, Pierre."

"'Shoot' is an apt choice of words for a professional hunter," Dunn joked. "Take good care of yourself until next we meet, Alex."

Laidlaw terminated the call with a sense of foreboding. He wondered whether he'd ever see Harry's again.

In Primis Anno Regnantibus Imperator Caesar Titus Vespasianus (81 CE)

CRIXUS AND HIS SURVIVING COMPANIONS reentered the Nile well downriver of the Great Cataract. To their south, the faint roar of turbulent water was discernible as they slid their watercraft into the arcadian River of Paradise.

"Do you think we see the others again?" a legionnaire named Eraclius asked Crixus, referring to Eros and those who accompanied him.

"If they do not perish on the rocks of the Great Cataract. And, should they survive those, they must still avoid capture by the pirates that swarm the area. I fear that, should we encounter them in the future, it will be in the slave markets where Eros and our former comrades will be paraded about in chains."

"We will greet Eros in Rome if the gods decree it," Eraclius emphatically asserted.

"Perhaps, though it is not the gods who find themselves crowded into a small boat, attempting to navigate treacherous rapids in a river abounding with cutthroats."

Eraclius gazed wistfully at the vacant expanse of water upriver before stepping from shore. "I hope we see them again."

Harkuf interrupted his reverie.

"Come, Romans!" he ordered from his boat, already drifting toward the main channel of the Nile. "You will have abundant time to compare the sizes of your cocks once we have quitted this region."

The remaining men pushed off and began poling their watercraft into deeper water.

"Do you suppose we are now free of those perils that continually menace us?" a legionnaire asked Crixus.

"Ask the gods," the latter wearily replied.

CLOUDS OF BLACK FLIES AND mosquitoes clogged the muggy air, assailing the legionnaires and crawling into their noses and ears.

"By Hercules, I will be delighted when it begins to cool off," one of them complained as he slapped at the swarming hoard.

"Then you are destined to be disappointed, for it becomes hotter, still, the closer to Alexandria we draw," another informed him.

"And when can we look forward to that?" the other scowled.

"Two weeks, perhaps more."

The first man grimaced as he continued to swat the blood-sucking insects.

Their flotilla, though no longer worthy of the appellation, drifted northward on the languid, muddy Nile. Groves of date palms flanked the river and extended beyond it, into the barren, rocky desert that still characterizes the landscape of Upper Egypt. Numberless crocodiles basked along the shoreline, scrambling into the water in a frantic tumult when the Romans floated into view. In side-channels and deep pools, multitudes of irritable hippos congregated, only their nostrils, ears, and bulging eyes visible above the surface of the river. Other animals...vast flocks of doves and geese, gazelles, baboons, elephants...drank at the river's edge.

Once the sun began to descend behind the red sandstone cliffs lining the Nile's west bank, the men paddled to shore for the night. Heaving their boats onto dry ground, they gathered fallen palm fronds and brush in order to stoke cooking fires, which also served to deter nocturnal predators. Each morning, they dragged their boats back to the river and resumed their journey north.

Although they had yet to encounter an actual city, the voyagers passed a number of venerated sites scattered along the river: Philae, Abu Simbel, Djamet, Edfu, Nubt, Abdju. All were marked by cyclopean sandstone edifices, their surfaces bearing deeply carved rows of strange images and colorful representations of men, winged sun discs, vultures, and cobras. Clustered around these huge structures were modest buildings that housed workers, attendants, priests, as well as ordinary residents.

"By the gods, I have never seen such a prodigious accumulation of stone!" declared Junius as their boat glided on the Nile's ceaseless current.

"Look around," Crixus invited. "There are no trees. If the Egyptians wish to build, they have only stone with which to do it."

"What does their writing say?"

"No one may read it. The Egyptians will not allow their sacred writing to be profaned through decipherment."

Junius frowned. "Where do the rest of them live? Are there actual cities in this wasteland?"

"We should soon encounter Waset, a formidable city that was once Egypt's capital. After that, Mennefer, which the Egyptians call "The White Walls." Crixus dipped an oar into the water and guided their boat around a log protruding from the water.

"Are either near Alexandria?"

Crixus shook his head. "We remain far from there."

On the fourth day beyond the Great Cataract, the date groves gradually yielded to modest patches of cultivated earth displaying rows of cabbages, onions, radishes, and melons. So accustomed to seeing boats of every variety ply the river, the beleaguered peasants tilling these collective gardens scarcely paused at their ancient *shadoofs* to watch the Romans drift past. Small rafts of water lilies floated on the surface of the river, while thick clusters of papyrus reeds choked its banks. The ubiquitous flying insects increased in number and voraciousness

"At least we may eat something other than fish tonight," Junius remarked, gesturing toward the greenery on the eastern side of the river. He crushed an iridescent bottle fly between his thumb and forefinger and scrutinized its remains with interest.

"That would be a welcome change, though we have nothing with which to barter for edibles."

Junius laughed as he wiped the remnants of the insect on his fouled tunic. "Barter? You are a perfect fool, Crixus! What is to stop us from simply taking what we desire? A hodgepodge of impoverished farmers?"

"I do not think it right to rob others of their produce."

"Honesty is praised while it starves," Junius retorted. "The gods do not view with favor even a benighted savage's denial of food to travelers who have none. Besides, with whose welfare are you concerned? That of your own men or that of an alien people who cannot even read their own language? The gods have not preserved us this far only to abandon us to the whims of ignorant barbarians!"

Crixus nodded, thoughtfully. "You speak prudently, Junius, though I doubt the gods, assuming they even exist, will countenance flagrant theft. Yet, we may still be able to secure food without giving offense to either men or the gods. It may require nothing more than a simple request."

"Perhaps we should make a wager," Junius laughed. "Which do you suppose will prove most expedient? Sweet words directed at uncomprehending ears, or my proposal to simply take what we desire from peasants who lack the ability to prevent it?"

"Yes, we shall see," Crixus responded.

WHILE THEY AWAITED THE RETURN OF trading vessels to port, Berossus and most of the other legionnaires commandeered the homes of Adulis' unwilling citizens, where they took their ease and availed themselves of, not only food, but the domestic comforts of the wives, daughters, and sons of absent husbands. Neocles, Senecio, and a few others elected to sleep on the beach.

"You do not wish to rest in comfort indoors?" one of the legionnaires mocked them.

"On the contrary, I greatly desire it. But I am far from eager to have my throat slit by a vengeful wife while I sleep," Neocles replied.

"You are right," the other laughed. "Women outshine men in scheming."

"Do you suppose the blade would feel any less keen if, instead, it was wielded by her aggrieved husband?"

"I daresay their husbands posses no grounds for bitterness. Quite the reverse, they should be grateful to us for consoling the unsatisfied wives they stupidly abandoned!" the legionnaire chortled.

Neocles arched his eyebrows. "I look forward to learning the response of their husbands to such reasoning."

"I need not explain myself to those swine," the other man shrugged. "I invite them to kiss my ass, exactly as their wives have been doing with manifest pleasure during their absence."

CONSISTENT WITH THE OLD MAN'S ASSURANCES, merchant ships began to arrive in Adulis' harbor just over a week later. The customary assemblage of welcoming townspeople was not there to greet them, however. Arrayed on the wharf, instead, were armed Roman legionnaires. Puzzled crew members of the approaching vessels peered over the gunwales and looked at one another in consternation.

"What is the meaning of this?" one of them asked in alarm.

"What business have Romans here?" another muttered. "Where are our wives?"

From the pier, Berossus surveyed the approaching fleet. "Board each vessel as soon as it docks, disarm its crew, and seize all weapons you find aboard. Permit no one to leave the ships," he instructed his restive men. "Separate young from old. If any speak our language, assure them that their loved ones are safe and well but say nothing else. If any resist, cut their throats in front of the other men. From the youngest and fittest I will select suitable crews."

"We will require not just crews, but additional provisions, as well," one of the men remarked.

Berossus turned to him. "Do you not suppose that commercial vessels such as these are brimming with provisions?"

Each ship began to trim its sails preparatory to docking. The eclectic assemblage of merchant vessels spontaneously began to form a rough queue in the order of their arrival at Andulis, the laggards dropping anchor farther from port while awaiting their turn to unload their cargoes.

The crew of a cumbrous barge, fashioned of nothing more than thick bundles of dry papyrus reeds bound together, propelled their vessel by shoving long wooden poles into the muddy shallows. Once beyond the wharf, the men withdrew their poles and allowed the barge to drift toward the shore, its crew only using their poles to gently nudge it into position. The waiting Romans could see burlap sacks of grain arranged on its broad deck: lentils, barley, millet, spelt.

At least as least as far back as Herodotus, ancient texts, including the Bible, are replete with references to "corn." However, maize was completely unknown outside of the New World until Columbus introduced it into Spain in the 15th century. The "corn" spoken of by the classical writers was loosely intended to mean cereal crops collectively, including wheat, sorghum, oats, barley, and rye. Modern scholars estimate that such cereals provided no less than two-thirds of the daily caloric intake of the average Roman. A typical meal among the *hoi polloi*, for example, consisted of various grains baked into bread; olives; olive oil; and wine diluted with water. Occasionally, cheese, and rarely, meat or fish supplemented this sparse diet. Barley, especially, was a dietary staple of soldiers and gladiators, as it was believed to add a layer of fat to their bodies, thereby minimizing blood loss in the event of wounds. So, too, barley water, made by boiling barley grains in water, straining to remove the organic precipitate and, when available, sweetening the resulting distillate with honey.

Aboard the papyrus barge, a boy of about ten squatted and snubbed a length of flaxen rope around a wooden cleat projecting from the vessel's deck. He then stood and flung the remaining coil toward the wharf; it unspooled as it flew through the air. The rope splashed into the Great River short of its goal, where it undulated on the surface like a graceful serpent. None of the legionnaires moved to recover the rope. Puzzled by the Romans' obvious disinclination to provide assistance, the crew of the barge quickly resumed poling the craft toward the projecting jetty.

"Why do the soldiers ignore us?" one of them asked a companion through clenched teeth. They both strained against their wooden spars in order to guide the ponderous barge.

"I do not know, though it bodes ill."

"Perhaps we should make landfall elsewhere."

"And where would that be, Taa? There is no other place nearby to offload our goods. We are also out of food. And what of our families...shall we simply abandon them?"

"But if they rob us, what will be left to us?" Taa asked in consternation.

The other man looked directly at him. "Our lives," he stoically responded.

Aided by the current, the two continued to pole the papyrus barge into proximity of the wharf. The ship's boy launched another coil of rope landward, this time falling at the Romans' feet. One of them stooped to retrieve it and, hand-over-hand, laboriously began to haul the barge closer. Another grasped the rope to assist him.

"I hope the remaining vessels are more promising than this wreck," one of them muttered.

Once it was safe to do so, two legionnaires hopped the narrow gap between the pier and the barge. The two men guiding the craft dropped their wooden spars onto the deck and shrank from the Roman trespassers.

"Who speaks Latin?" one of the legionnaires barked. He pointed to a crewman. "You?" Totaling only three adult males plus the boy, they looked at one another in trepidation. The soldier turned to Berossus, who remained on the pier. "Commander! What are your wishes?"

"Those scrawny barbarians are not worth a jot," Berossus snapped. "Find whether they carry any weapons or provisions we can actually use. If not, push them away from the dock so the next vessel can approach. I do not intend to stand in the sun all day!"

"As you command."

While his associate kept a watchful eye on its attenuated crew, the legionnaire turned to the sacks of grain arranged along the barge's deck. Randomly piercing the side of one with his bronze dagger, a stream of yellow millet cascaded out. He sliced the sack immediately below it with the same result. He strode about the deck, randomly puncturing the burlap sacks and allowing their cereal contents to pour out. The helpless crewmen watched in silence, their frustration and anger mounting.

The legionnaire finally turned to the huddle of crewmen. "Where are your weapons?" he demanded. They glared at him without comprehending, prompting him to angrily display his dagger inches from their faces. "Your weapons, you stupid bastards!" Still, they failed to respond.

"They do not understand," the other soldier matter-of-factly observed.

"They understand well enough. They engage in such mummery in the hope of deceiving us."

"To what end? Do you suppose three old men and a boy hope, by their guile, to dupe the men whose captives they are?"

From the wharf, Berossus interrupted their debate. "Fools! Do you not see that other vessels, possibly laden with valuables, are prepared to dock? If the scow carries nothing worthwhile, shove it aside, for it is blocking the other ships!"

The legionnaire glared a final time at the four intimidated crew members. He ostentatiously sheathed his dagger. "There is nothing worth our while aboard this floating rubbish heap," he commented in a low voice. We must rid ourselves of it before Berossus suffers a fit of apoplexy." He bent to retrieve from the deck the two poles used by the crew to guide and propel the barge. "Push it back into the river," he said, handing one of the poles to the other legionnaire.

The two Romans sprang across the narrow gap separating them from *terra firma*. They turned, planted their poles into the side of the barge and, straining, shoved it away from the shoreline. The unwieldy watercraft slowly reentered the tranquil waters of the *Pontus Herculis* and began to float away, to the relief of its crew.

"Fucking Romans," one of them spat.

"Let us make landfall once we are out of their sight and steal our way back to Adulis, overland. I fear for my wife and children."

On the wharf near them, Berossus barked to another legionnaire. "Signal the next one." His subordinate complied by vigorously waving his arms in order to capture the attention of the ships remaining at anchor. He arbitrarily pointed to the closest vessel and, in a hopeful pantomime, directed it weigh anchor and make its way forward. Meanwhile, the two legionnaires previously aboard the papyrus barge joined the other men on the pier.

"I trust you two are well pleased with squandering time on your fool's errand?" Berossus chastised them. Neither responded.

One after another, the assembled vessels dutifully tacked their way toward the wharf in orderly fashion. Though nonplussed by the inexplicable presence of the Roman legionnaires, their crews initially hoped to quickly offload their cargoes and reunite with their families after weeks on the river. Their optimism turned to dismay, however, when they observed the untethered papyrus barge drift seaward, its deck still laden with sacks of grain.

"What do they want?" one of them asked aloud. No one answered.

THE AGGREGATE NUMBER OF SERVICEABLE items seized from the merchant vessels: five sacks of desiccated goat meat, some dried fish, and a dozen tarnished copper knives used to gut fish and cleave rope. To be sure, the ships bore much more...mountains of corn; live animals; animal skins; spices, herbs, and salt; textiles; glassware; incense and perfumes; amber; cheap jewelry...though none of it excited the interest of the practical Romans. Berossus surveyed the meager haul with disgust.

“I thought this pigsty was famed as a trading entrepot,” he grumbled. “A few additional slit throats would have produced far more agreeable results.”

“You saw for yourself the nature of the goods carried by the ships,” one of his men peevishly snapped. “These, alone, were worth the taking.”

After ransacking the vessels, in the process indiscriminately pushing most of the grain overboard and seizing whatever they desired of the remaining freight, the legionnaires ordered all vessels in Andulis' harbor to weigh anchor and depart at once. They had no intention of suffering violence at the hands of aggrieved husbands and brothers who felt themselves dishonored because, during their absence, the Romans had engaged in wanton rape.

“We depart two days hence,” Berossus announced. He'd requisitioned three ships, two to transport the legionnaires of *Bestia*, the third to carry supplies for the remainder of their journey northward to the *Mare Nostrum.* The three vessels were crewed with men dragooned into service from among the returning mariners. Berossus prudently kept their numbers at a minimum in order to minimize opportunities for intrigue or rebellion.

“If you hope to be reunited with your wives and children, serve us faithfully,” he cautioned the sullen crewmen. “Do not question what you are told. Obey and you will live to see your loved ones again. Defy us and death will be your reward.”

"The stupid bastards do not understand anything they are being told," Senecio muttered to Neocles.

"Though they may not understand Berossus' words, they comprehend well enough his meaning."

The wooden supply ship was moored to the pier, its deteriorating hull gently bumping against the wooden pilings. Berossus abruptly collared one of the luckless sailors and shoved him toward the hodgepodge of items seized from other vessels and now scattered on the wharf.

"Stow those."

The confused man looked anxiously at his fellow captives, most of whom cast their eyes downward.

"Why do you look at them, you dumb bastard?" Berossus snarled. "You will look at *me* when I talk to you!"

"He wants you to tote those things onto the ship, Sen," one of the mariners softly instructed.

Berossus spun toward the assembled crewmen. "Who spoke?"

The assembled crewmen awkwardly shuffled their feet without responding. Finally, a tall, youthful Nubian defiantly stepped forward. "Me."

Berossus, fully a head shorter, strode forward to confront him. He stood only inches away; the Nubian unconsciously took a half-step backward without taking his eyes off the Roman. Berossus was forced to tilt his head upward because of the disparity in their heights, not unmindful that the other legionnaires were watching attentively.

"You have a loose tongue but are a fool to exercise it," he said. The Nubian surveyed him in silence through narrowed eyes. Berossus turned to his subaltern. "This impudent fellow must be taught the consequences of speaking unbidden, else the others be tempted to mimic him. I leave it to you how best to educate him. Take care not render him a useless cripple by removing any of his fingers. Leave, also, his nose; I have no desire to look daily upon a deformed monster. You may otherwise deal with him as you believe most likely to impress upon him, and the others, the wisdom of remaining silent."

"As you order," his factotum crisply acknowledged. He motioned three other legionnaires to seize the unfortunate man, whose struggles came too late. "Put him on his knees and bend him forward, facing me."

With Berossus observing, a Roman kicked the Nubian's legs from beneath him. He tumbled to the wharf and the legionnaires lifted him to his knees. One grasped a handful of the man's hair and used it to yank his head downward while the other two legionnaires pinioned the thrashing man's arms.

The subaltern cast a surreptitious glance at Berossus to assure himself that his actions met with his commander's tacit approval. The latter making no effort to countermand him, the legionnaire unsheathed his bronze dagger.

"Hold him securely."

His comrade still clutching the prisoner's hair placed his free hand on the back of the man's skull and pushed down to further steady it.

Stepping closer to the immobile Nubian, the legionnaire placed the blade of his dagger behind the prisoner's left ear and sliced it from his head.

The squirming Nubian shrieked in pain. The severed ear plopped onto the wharf as blood streamed down the side of his face.

"He has no problem speaking. Perhaps his hearing may also benefit," Berrosus commented with approval.

AN EMERALD QUILT OF MELONS, CABBAGES, radishes, onions, and chickpeas crowded the Mother of Rivers and extended beyond her banks into the forbidding desert beyond. A complex network of irrigation canals and sluices, gleaming ribbons of water crisscrossing the fields, provided sanctuary for Nile catfish, perch, and bream. Geese and ducks nested in the papyrus stalks that grew in thick clusters along the banks while herons patiently stalked the shallows, spearing frogs with their rapier bills. Ferocious, bejeweled dragon flies poised delicately on reeds growing from the river and cliff swallows skimmed its placid surface, darting through the dense clouds of black flies and mosquitoes that clogged the stagnant air.

Crixus and the other men were as languid as the Nile, itself.

"Though it is green enough here, I could do without all the infernal bugs," Junius groused as he continuously slapped at the biting insects.

"I agree." An irritable Crixus scowled as he, too, vainly attempted to brush gnats away from his face. "The appealing scenery does not compensate for this vexation."

"Though it is early, we should beach our boats and stoke a fire. The smoke will drive the insects away."

Crixus reflected a moment. "Yes, we will do as you suggest. I weary of being confined to this cramped boat, anyway." He swiveled and signaled the other watercraft to head for shore.

"We should help ourselves to some of those vegetables," Junius hopefully suggested as he steered their boat landward.

"We will not steal from these people. Should they voluntarily offer us food, we will accept it with thanks."

"And if they do not?"

"That, also, we will accept."

Junius shook his head in bewilderment. "You are a most peculiar legionnaire, Crixus."

Crixus shrugged. "I do not know whether I should feel flattered or insulted. But, what is, is." He gestured toward the shore, where a body of inquisitive, ragged farmers had begun to gather. "Look."

Junius scarcely glanced at them. "I see none of them carrying food," he grumbled.

"No matter. Perhaps Harkuf speaks their tongue. If not, I will speak to them."

"How do you propose to do that? They sound like goats bleating when they talk."

"Some of them may speak Latin or Greek."

Largely because of television and movies, most people think that Latin was the primary, if not the exclusive, language of the Roman Empire. In fact, the *lingua franca* of ancient Rome was not Latin, but Greek. Similar to French, which is still utilized in modern diplomatic circles, the use of Greek as a bridge language by the educated elite was *de rigueur* throughout the Empire. On March 15, 44 BCE, as his blood from assassins' daggers pooled on the cold stone floor of the Roman senate, Julius Caesar uttered his dying words, not in Latin, but in Greek. And, although Jesus spoke Aramaic, the entire New Testament was written in Greek, Hebrew having long before ceased to be the quotidian language of the Jews. In practical terms, the ubiquity of cosmopolitan Greek made it possible for Rome to maintain hegemony over millions of disparate peoples who, otherwise speaking a plethora of indigenous languages, found themselves the reluctant subjects of Roman imperialism.

"If any of those bastards speaks either Latin *or* Greek, may the gods strike me dumb!" Junius laughed.

THE SMALL COLLECTION OF EGYPTIAN farmers remained some distance away as the Romans jumped into the thigh-deep river and dragged their watercraft to the riverbank. They glanced cautiously toward the intruders while quietly conversing among themselves. The legionnaires clustered around Crixus, though Harkuf stood some distance away and ignored them.

Crixus called to him. "Harkuf, do you speak these peoples' language?"

"No."

Crixus believed him to be lying, but was powerless to do anything about it.

"Well, do you intend to attempt communication, or shall I?" Junius pointedly inquired.

"And how will you accomplish that?" one of the other men scoffed. "I can barely understand you when *you* speak and I daresay you do not have the slightest idea what language they jabber." Junius simply glared at him.

"I would speak with them," Crixus said. "Remain here, that they will not be affrighted."

"I will give the rubbish something to be afraid of," Junius grinned, patting the *cultro* that hung at his side.

Crixus looked at him askance before turning to the small group of Egyptian farmers. Despite holding his arms at his sides with his palms outward, they eyed his approach with suspicion.

"Greetings," he called out to them in Latin with what he hoped was a disarming smile. The men glanced at one another but remained impassive. "Greek?" he probed in that language. They stared at him, dumbly.

Crixus suspended his advance about twenty feet from the group.

"How is your conversation progressing? We are unable to hear from this distance," Junius sniggered from behind him. Crixus ignored the jab.

"We are Romans," he continued in Latin. "We need food." Crixus pointed to his mouth, then to his stomach.

Toothless, relieved grins spontaneously animated the stony faces of the Egyptians.

"*Ta*," announced an old man to his companions.

"Yes, *'Ta'*," Crixus enthusiastically agreed, though he hadn't the slightest idea what that was. He again pointed to his mouth and stomach. "*Ta*."

The farmers huddled together and proceeded to converse in a tongue unknown to Crixus. Periodically, they looked up and glanced toward him. After a few minutes, two of the men detached themselves from the others and hastened across a low earthen berm that bisected a contiguous field. Crixus remained where he was, unsure what to do.

The old man, apparently the group's leader, spoke a few more words before stepping away from his ragged associates. He hobbled toward Crixus.

"Ta," he said when he drew near. He lifted a skeletal arm and vaguely motioned across the field in

the general direction the other two men had previously headed. Crixus nodded and pointed to his men, then to his own mouth and stomach. The old man nodded vigorously. *"Ta,"* he repeated as he patted Crixus' shoulder.

In Primis Anno Regnantibus Imperator Caesar Titus Vespasianus (81 CE)

"WHERE WE STAND AT THIS MOMENT," Junius pontificated, "Marcus Antonius rode in a golden chariot pulled by lions during the celebration of one of his many triumphs." The other legionnaires huddled around him on the *Via Imperiali* were duly impressed, both by his apparent knowledge of the city and by the splendors of Rome, itself. All of them hailing from the provinces, few had actually seen the capital of their Empire.

Overcrowded, squalid, and dangerous, certainly, but the multiplicity of stunning monuments in gleaming marble and polished granite reflected the boast of the Emperor Augustus that he found Rome brick and left it marble: the Forum and *Curia*, where the senate met to debate matters of state; the *Circus Maximus*; the *Theatrum Pompeii*; the *Basilica Iulia*; the Temple of *Hercules Olivarius*; the shrine of Jupiter the Thunderer; the Temple of Mars Ultor; the Temple of Apollo; the Temple of Portunus; the *Forum Boarium*; the Forum and Mausoleum of the Deified Augustus...their staggering magnificence was nearly overwhelming. But eclipsing them all was the city's newest crown jewel: the *Amphitheatrum Flavium*, known today as the Colosseum. Throughout the city, walls splashed with bright colors, as well as graphic posters affixed to every vertical surface, trumpeted that the official inauguration of the emperor's dazzling amphitheater would be marked by no less than 100 days of spectacular entertainment.

Notwithstanding the passage of more than two millennia, the Colosseum remains the largest extant amphitheater on earth. Even today, with two-thirds of the edifice gone, it is one of the most recognizable, and beautiful, structures ever built. Only one of many arenas scattered across the Roman Empire, the Colosseum is, in fact, structurally unique because, from its inception, it was designed to be entirely free-standing, supported only by a complex system of stone vaults and groins. Out of an abundance of caution, older amphitheaters were dug into hillsides in an effort to provide additional support for their superstructures.

Not the first, but inarguably the grandest in the Roman world, the *Amphitheatrum Flavium* measured 615 feet by 510 feet, its walls originally 160 feet high. Designed to accommodate 50,000 to 80,000 spectators, contemporary accounts report as many as 100,00 people packed into its aisles. By comparison, the average American football stadium has a seating capacity of around 70,000. Of its eighty entrances, seventy-six were open to the general public, while one was reserved for the emperor and another for the Vestal Virgins. The remaining two doors opened directly into the area, which measured 281 feet by 177 feet. One door was denominated the "Door of Life," through which a procession marched as a prelude to each event. The other was the "Door of Death," through which the bodies of slain men and animals were dragged to clear the arena before the next spectacle. The seventy-six public entrances were further segregated, a few being reserved for well-heeled patrons who splurged for the best seats. Food and gifts were regularly catapulted into the crowd between exhibitions, compliments of the emperor, and cooling, perfumed water sprayed over them from fountains and overhead pipes. An elaborate system of mechanical elevators, actuated by pulleys and counter-weights, raised animals to the floor of the arena, covered in sand to absorb blood, from a labyrinth of subterranean chambers. A sprawling zoo adjacent to the amphitheater enabled discerning *cognoscenti* to stroll among the caged, doomed creatures, admiring them before they were destroyed a few hours later.

At every venue across the Empire, animal extravagances were, without exception, scheduled for the morning sessions. Such contests matched exotic species from across the known world against each other: bulls and bears chained together; lions pitted against tigers pitted against leopards in a battle royal, the exhausted, bloody survivors immediately set upon by wolves; fights between flocks of birds; rhinos and elephants goaded into combat using flaming torches of twisted straw; chimpanzees clad in doublets and mounted on jackasses pursued by wild dogs; wolves battling hyenas. These amusements would typically be followed by contests between wild animals and *venatores* or *bestiarii*, experts trained, respectively, to either hunt beasts in the arena or fight them, hand-to-hand.

Similar to gladiators, both *venatores* and *bestiarii* specialized in different types of animals. Depending on the particular species, they might be lightly-clad and armed, as speed and dexterity were critical to avoid the teeth and claws of terrified, pain-maddened four-hundred-fifty-pound African lions. Alternatively, some wore full armor to absorb the charges of enraged bulls, while others carried shields, long spears, short swords, or heavy clubs studded with nails when battling wild boars and bears. Unlike *bestiarii*, *venatores* also rode horseback, using bows or spears to dispatch smaller creatures such as deer and antelope.

Like modern Las Vegas, the novelty of such entertainments quickly waned, spawning an unrelenting spiral of bigger-is-better one-upsmanship. Creative impresarios were forced to stage even more idiosyncratic spectacles in order to remain ahead of the curve and retain the interest of a jaded public: dwarfs dressed as satyrs, fauns, or gladiators used darts to attack storks, their wings clipped, and ostriches; slaves and prisoners of war scrambled up poles coated with animal fat in an effort to escape starving bears, where they would cling for as long as they could while the bears attempted to grab them from below; nude women...wives, sisters, and daughters of conquered enemies...armed with small shields and spears portrayed amazons as they frantically attempted to avoid being gored or trampled by wild bulls. Those that succeeded were bound before being serially raped by specially-trained dogs, apes, horses, or camels, to the delight of the aroused crowd. The bulls were finally dispatched by piercing them with arrows, their bodies then dragged from the arena through the Gate of Death and fresh sand rapidly spread over the bloody trail.

Wild animals were also widely utilized to stage recreations of popular legends: the impregnation of Olympias, Alexander the Great's mother by a serpent; Zeus's seduction of Europa in the guise of a white bull; Theseus in the lair of the Minotaur. Prisoners of war, for instance, were forced to mimic Rome's celebrated founders, Romulus and Remus, by suckling at a pregnant she-wolf before being torn to pieces by the remainder of the starved pack.

By mid-day the audience, restive, hungry, or simply bored, vacated the stands to empty their bowels; purchase food at one of the many vendors that lined the amphitheater's passageways; get a haircut; have a tooth pulled; or retain the services of one of the scores of prostitutes, male and female, that plied their trade in the structure's unlit coves. There was no lull in the activities during this period, though they were of a more pedestrian nature. Acrobats, tumblers, mimes, jugglers, and musicians performed while fans drifted back and forth to their seats. Prominent orators or poets sometimes declaimed at length.

The execution of ordinary criminals, deserters, fugitives, and those convicted of treason also took place during this *caesura*, sometimes via wild animals (*ad bestius*), sometimes by simple crucifixion, sometimes by being burned alive (*ad flammas*). In executions *ad gladius*, two condemned criminals were shoved into the arena, one of whom was given a sword and ordered to kill his unfortunate companion who, sensibly, took to his heels. After a chase, accompanied by the cheers, hoots, and encouragement of spectators, the armed man inevitably caught up with his unarmed quarry and killed him. Having done so, another criminal was immediately introduced into the area, the sword transferred from the previous victor to the new arrival, and the game began anew with the recent hunter transformed into the hunted. The last survivor was beaten to death by a slave wearing leather gloves studded with tacks, who was thereafter dispatched by strangulation.

Lighter fare, short comedic skits or absurd burlesques, were also introduced during the mid-day interlude: dwarfs astride sheep, or riding men on all-fours, brandished staves and engaged in proto-jousts; naked blindfolded dwarfs and young girls, also nude and blindfolded, battled each other with blunted wooden swords.

By universal accord, however, the afternoon clashes of gladiators unquestionably stoked the crowd's excitement to a fever pitch.

Like much else in the Western world, the guiding dictum in modern prize fighting, “styles make fights,” has its origins in ancient Rome. Among the multiple variants of gladiators, a *murmillo* might be pitted against a Thracian or a *hoplomachus*, a *thraex* against a *murmillo* or a *hoplomachus*, a *retiarius* against a *secutor*, a *cestus* against a *dimachaerus*. There are even surviving accounts of a handful of female gladiators. Although gladiators were officially scorned as nothing more than expendable human rubbish, many were, in fact, admired and esteemed by the masses, the rock stars of their day. And, like their modern counterparts, partisans of particular gladiators or fighting styles argued vociferously and endlessly, and wagered vast sums, deriding those who took issue with their expertise and discerning analysis.

Gladiators who boasted multiple victories in the arena enjoyed passionate fan bases and were widely credited with possessing extraordinary sexual potency. Exceptionally popular or successful gladiators might be awarded the *rudis*, a symbolic wooden sword, and awarded their freedom. These few retired to lives of fame, ease, and wealth, though such fortunates represented an infinitesimal minority of gladiators. Not many of their compatriots survived even into middle-age, ultimately succumbing to wounds or disease. Remarkably, rare surviving tombstones attest to gladiators who were married with families...loved ones to mourn, and recall the passing of, expendable human rubbish who died violent deaths on bloody sand in faraway arenas for the entertainment of the idle masses.

And so it went, day after day, week after week, month after month, year after year, for centuries.

On February 27, 380 CE, the Roman Emperor, Theodosius the Great, issued a formal decree establishing Christianity as the exclusive religion of the Empire, abolishing all others and authorizing the persecution of non-Christians: "foolish madmen that shall be branded with the ignominious name of heretics."

Tolerant and generous in matters of religion, "heresy" was a concept unknown in pagan Rome. Jesus was condemned to death, and his followers persecuted, not because of Rome's intrinsic religious hostility, but because they were considered a threat to the *political* stability of the state. Simply put, Christians were adjudged dangerous seditionists. Jesus suffered the penalty traditionally meted out to all such insurrectionists: death by cruxifixion. The Romans devoted little thought to the matter at the time because of the routine nature of the entire affair.

As the new creed gained ascendancy in the waning days of the Empire, the Church Fathers were emboldened to denounce the sanguinary pleasures of the arena, many of their incendiary polemics and tracts surviving to the present day. Ironically, their condemnation of the arena's bloody violence was not prompted by compassion for the millions of its victims, human and animal, nor to ordinary squeamishness. Rather, the Church opposed the exhibitions because of the unabashed enjoyment members of their Christian flocks derived from watching them, and the coarsening effect exercised on their sensibilities. No thought was given to the countless numbers who suffered unimaginable cruelty and pain in amphitheaters spanning the Empire, anonymous sacrifices to Roman *virtus*.

Aside from the Church's meddlesome censure, in practical terms the newly-Christianized Romans were also running out of Jews, criminals, prisoners of war, slaves, and pagans to kill following Theodosius' 380 CE edict. Gladiators had, by that time, ceased to be highly trained professionals, having deteriorated into mere simulacra of their illustrious predecessors. All the gladiatorial schools officially closed in 399 CE for lack of pupils. Even chariot races had become a farce and large, impressive wild animals were becoming increasingly scarce, Europe, Asia Minor, and North Africa having been largely denuded of them.

In a word, the impractical spectacles had simply become too expensive. They were finally jettisoned altogether, their passing unlamented except by a few old-timers who pretended to mourn Rome's glory days.

THE FINAL STAGES OF THEIR JOURNEY to Rome turned out to be surprisingly uneventful. Having arrived at the capital, however, Crixus was not entirely sure what he and his men were supposed to do, given that Romo and Eros, his original escorts, had fallen by the wayside during their journey to the capital. He finally decided to allow the remaining legionnaires in his charge to site-see while he hastened to the Forum, the seat of government for the Empire, where he would announce himself to whatever bureaucrats he might encounter there, though he hadn't the slightest idea how he might actually accomplish that. It was essential, however, that confirmation of his arrival in Rome be conveyed to *Legio XVI Bestia*, that Aulus and Neocles suffer no harm.

"What does that say?" one of the legionnaires importuned Junius who, alone among them, was marginally literate. He pointed to a garishly-painted sign.

Junius frowned as he struggled to read it. "It says that the opening of the emperor's amphitheater will be marked by 100 days of games and that not less than 9,000 beasts will be killed."

"And that one?" asked another.

Junius turned his head and studied the billboard. "A gladiator named 'Drax' will fight three others, hand-to-hand, though not all at once."

"Do you think we will be here long enough to see these things?"

Junius reflected a moment. "I hope not."

THE FORUM WAS THE EPICENTER, the *umbilicus urbis*, of the Roman Empire's entire political identity. There, the senate, a bubbling cauldron of wealth, power, privilege, pretense, intrigue, and deceit, conducted state business in the *Curia*, a building still largely intact. The Forum was also the site of dozens of other civic, religious, legal, and commercial edifices: the *Tabularium*, the Temple of Concord, the Temple of Vesta, the Temple of Castor and Pollux, the *rostra veteran*, multiple stalls of bankers, money changers, food vendors, and others. Paved with white travertine polished to a sheen by generations of foot traffic, the Forum, like all such places, also proved an irresistible lure for the flotsam and jetsam of Roman society: beggars, waifs, orphans, thieves, peddlers, touts, muscle-for-hire, prostitutes.

The *Basilica Iulia*, on the south side of the Forum, was home to the Roman law courts, though it was not uncommon for trials, invariably more theater than the pursuit of justice, to be held outdoors. Members of the public, many having a vested interest in the outcome, as well as bevies of professional claqueurs, avidly followed these performances. Pliny the Younger characterized their presence as "audience participation." Trials were conducted by such eloquent lectors as Marcus Tullius Cicero, Pacuvius Labeo, Lucius Lucinius Crassus, Marcus Porcius Cato Lucinianus, Lucius Plotius Pegasus, and a host of lesser lights, as well. Patrician males, for whom oratorical skill was absolutely *de rigueur* if they aspired to a career in politics, emulated these esteemed rhetoricians. Accordingly, the viewing stands were always full of ambitious youths eager to ingratiate themselves with such icons. It was one of these whom Crixus decided to approach.

"I am acquainted with Sempronius Niger," the adolescent, not more than sixteen years old, loftily assured him.

"The senator?"

"The same. I will speak of you to him."

"How soon?" Crixus pressed.

The youth eyed him, superciliously. "At my leisure."

"My friends' lives are at risk."

"I daresay they should have been more prudent than to hazard their lives on the whims of others."

"What is done cannot be undone."

"That much is true," the youth conceded. "Only if the gods will it."

"I do not have recourse to the gods...only to you."

"That is also true." Crixus' interlocutor looked pensive. "I will call on Niger this evening. Return here two days hence."

"WE ARE ALREADY AWARE THAT OUR dear friend and brother, Marcus Berossus, is in Rome," Niger dismissively remarked. "What survives of *Legio Bestia* arrived several days ago, though not before enduring frightful travails en route."

The youth appeared puzzled. “It is not Berossus of whom I speak, but a legionnaire named 'Crixus'.”

Niger nodded, knowingly. “Our dear friend advises us that a splinter-group of renegade legionnaires may already be in the capital, this 'Crixus' among them. We intend to bring the matter before the emperor and senate.”

“The emperor and senate? Why do they concern themselves with such trifles?”

Niger lowered his voice and adopted a conspiratorial mien. “The eruption of Vesuvio, the late fire in the capital, the current plague burning through the provinces...all of these, with their dreadful loss of life, clearly manifest the displeasure of the inscrutable gods. Titus is anxious to mollify their anger, and that of the plebeians, by presenting a spectacle without parallel in the history of the world. To that end, we will urge the pitiless destruction of the entire treacherous legion in the emperor's new amphitheater. No such sacrifice has ever before been witnessed, nor is likely ever to be bested! A more fitting tribute to the venal gods is beyond imagining!”

The young man was puzzled. “If you believe this 'Crixus' to be one of the disloyal, would it not prove wiser to punish the guilty legionnaires rather than destroy an entire legion?”

Niger shook his head, dismissively. “Berossus, alone, is *Bestia's* only trustworthy element. His fidelity cannot be questioned.”

“Still, would it not be more prudent to simply banish it, or dissolve it altogether and reassign its cohorts, as has been done with other disgraced legions?"

"Only the unhesitating sacrifice of one of the emperor's most valued legions will suffice to appease the gods. If the gods are to be placated, it cannot be done by halves."

The boy arched his eyebrow. "I was not aware that such an insignificant legion enjoyed Titus' particular esteem."

"Please, do not make me laugh, my young friend," Niger chuckled. "*Bestia* is less than nothing to Titus, but neither the gods nor the plebeians need know that. When will you next see this 'Crixus'?"

"I assured him I would speak with you today and meet him again in the forum in two days."

"Excellent!" Niger exclaimed. "The *cohortes praetoriae* will accompany you to seize the rascal. A little judicious torture will swiftly loosen his tongue regarding the whereabouts of his traitorous associates."

HINDSIGHT BEING 20/20, IT WAS NOW painfully obvious to anyone with eyes to see, argued the august senator, Sempronius Niger, that *Legio XVI Bestia* had been a mistake from its inception: costly to maintain and woefully unproductive, an unpardonable drain on the state purse. Worse, *Bestia's* acting commander, Berossus, an incontestably brave soldier and faithful friend of the senate, had grudgingly revealed that his predecessor, Pompeius Cornelius Corvo, was addicted to drink and had allowed all of the legionnaires under his command to sink into irredeemable indolence and debauchery, an outrageous affront to the senate, itself.

Notwithstanding Niger's oratory, a dismaying number of his senate colleagues, notably his political enemies, expressed skepticism.

"Aside from your bold assurances, Sempronius, I know nothing of this 'Berossus' of whom you speak, and still less about *Legio XVI Bestia*," snorted Sextus Marcellus Memmius Fabianus. "And I have little doubt that many of my distinguished brothers in this chamber," he swept his arm across the room, evidencing his apparent embrace of the entire senate, "share my reservations regarding Berossus' asserted declarations."

Enthusiastic "ayes" and a smattering of applause rippled through the *Curia*.

"I decline to pass judgment on the fate of any of our redoubtable legions based on the private disclosures of a single individual, regarding whom none of of us boasts the slightest knowledge," Memmius concluded.

"Memmius' thoughts are a reflection of my own," quickly asserted Servius Dolabella.

"And mine," added Publius Clodius Peatus, to the vigorus assent of his friends lounging on the polished marble benches around him.

While nonplused, Niger remained undeterred. He gathered his *toga praetexta* around his corpulent frame and again rose to his feet in order to address his peers.

"Gentlemen," he began with equanimity, "your reservations are merely the product of an ignorance to which you readily confess. Our steadfast friend, Berossus, remains at the disposal of this noble body to disabuse the skeptics among you of your misapprehensions."

"Pray, how will it profit us to oblige the fancies of one who is clearly your intimate?" Valerius Sabinus, who loathed Niger, retorted. "A lie twice parroted remains no less a lie, irrespective of its hearers." A smattering of laughter greeted his droll observation.

Niger smiled, indulgently. "Berossus is not alone in his condemation, for *Bestia's* appalling condition is hardly unknown to those who have troubled to inform themselves of its failings." He paused as he surveyed the assembled senators with a frown. "It is apparent, however, that many of my esteemed brothers, though charged with the profound duty to ensure the safety and integrity of the Roman state, have far more pressing matters they must attend to. Given such demands on their time, we should be unsparing in our gratitude for Berossus' display of initiative and selfless integrity in bringing forward this matter of utmost gravity."

Niger's majestic response notwithstanding, the senators remained largely unmoved.

"If, as you profess, *Bestia's* disarray is an open secret, by all means produce all those who possess knowledge of it!" invited Sextus Memmius. "Allow the senate to assess the merits of your words before passing judgment. Not even the condign punishment of a criminal or slave can be justified by reliance on the uncorroborated accusations of a single individual! Does an entire Roman legion stand convicted on less?"

"As you wish," sighed Niger. He struggled to conceal his annoyance at his colleagues' recalcitrance. "If my brothers of the senate please, an independant witness to all that I have avowed will appear in this chamber in two days time. Having heard his testimony from his own lips, I trust this distinguished body will put aside its squeamishness and fully embrace its duty to the emperor and people of Rome."

LIKE ALL ROMANS, TITUS WAS HIGHLY superstitious. Wary of the fickleness of the tempermental gods, he yet remained at a loss to account for the train of disasters that had lately befallen the Empire he inherited from his father, Vespasian: the catastrophic eruption of Mt. Vesuvio, fires, plagues, and earthquakes, to say nothing of the inevitable problems arising from the imminent inaguration of his late father's amphitheater. His anxieties were further exacerbated by the inability of the augurs and haruspices attached to his court to divine the reason for the gods' displeasure. It was clear, however, that something must be done to assuage their fury, and quickly.

Learning of Titus' distress and eager to ingratiate himself with the emperor, the enterprising senator Sempronius Niger hastened to the Palatine to volunteer a solution. The gods were clearly vexed, he conceded, stating the obvious, the cause of their pique eluding human understanding. Despite this, men are not without power to ameliorate the gods' displeasure. The Roman people still enjoyed the patronage of Fortuna, who was sympathetic to their plight. Indeed, the senator confided, the goddess had just delivered into his hands multiple deserters from *Legio XVI Bestia* who had lately slunk into the capital. Excellent use could be made of these criminals.

Indeed, how so? inquired the intrigued emperor.

The mass execution of ordinary criminals in the arena was a commonplace, Niger reminded him. The faithless legionnaires of *Legio XVI Bestia* were no different than the thieves and arsonists who routinely suffered public deaths. As part of the amphitheater's inaugural festivities, a hecatomb comprised of these traitorous, expendable soldiers would represent unequivocal proof of Rome's devotion and obeisance to the gods, thereby tempering their anger. As a bonus, such a display would provide inestimable entertainment to spectators and a simultaneous warning to Rome's enemies that disloyalty will neither go unnoticed nor unpunished.

A former soldier himself, Titus was resistent to the suggestion that an entire legion should be summarily extirpated.

"*Legio XVI Bestia* is a legion in name only," Niger officiously tut-tutted. "Maladministration and neglect have left it a cesspool of knaves, layabouts, and criminals. Having eliminated such trash, it will be a simple matter to restore *Bestia* to its former glories by filling its ranks with rock-ribbed legionnaires whose honor is above reproach."

Upon reflection, a reluctant Titus finally yielded to the senator's arguments.

"Inform the senate," he instructed Niger. "The decision shall be its, not mine."

NIGER SPENT THE WHOLE OF THAT EVENING on the Palatine, announcing himself at the palatial residences of preeminent senators.

"I have discussed the matter with the emperor, who is in agreement that *Legio XVI Bestia*, or what little remains of it must, for the good of the state, be cleansed of the corrupt elements that presently degrade it. He instructs you accordingly."

Where the ambitious senator was met with skepticism, invocation of the emperor's name and assertion of his purported imprimatur, combined with the deft application of blandishments, cajolery, open-handed bribery, and promises of future favors, rapidly surmounted such resistence. In the end, all came to agree that the welfare of the Roman people hinged on the sacrifice of *Legio XVI Bestia*.

JUNIUS INSISTED ON ACCOMPANYING Crixus to his second rendezvous with the young patrician. Entering the forum on the agreed day, they patiently awaited the latter's arrival. Instead, an armed contingent of the Praetorian Guard swarmed from the crowd and immediately surrounded the two men. They were quickly bustled away at the point of a sword.

"What is the meaning of this? I am a legionnaire!" Junius protested as he was roughly prodded forward.

"Orders from the senate," a praetorian grunted.

They were taken to the Mamertine Prison and thrown into a lightless pit.

"What have we done?" Junius fearfully whispered in the dark.

"I daresay we shall soon find out," Crixus stoically responded.

THE FOLLOWING MORNING, THEY WERE shoved, chained, into the *Curia.* Berossus, too, was in attendence. Resplendent in fitted armor of polished bronze, he was seated in the gallery and basked in the senate's applause when introduced.

Niger immediately began questioning the prisoners, quickly establishing that both were legionnaires in *Legio XVI Bestia.* How is it, then, the senator queried, that the men found themselves in Rome when their legion was stationed in sub-Saharan Africa? And where were their remaining comrades and their commander, Pompeius Corvo?

Overawed and intimidated, Junius was cowed into silence. When Crixus tried to respond to Niger's interrogation, Berossus began hurling derisive imprecations from the gallery.

It was preposterous, Berossus hooted, that, with his dying breath, a Roman would surrender command of his legion to his own prisoner! Where was Eros, Romo's immediate subordinate? Crixus and his friends obviously conspired to murder both Romo and Eros. Having successfully eliminated them, as well as the beasts they were charged with safeguarding, they slunk their way to Rome, their hands dripping with blood, where they were confident their crimes would elude detection. But *Fortuna*, determined that the innocent deaths of Romo and Eros would not go unavenged, revealed their whereabouts in the capital and exposed the entire despicable plot. One simply had to look at the prisoners to know the truth of Berossus' words...when have innocent men ever been compelled to appear before the senate *in chains*?

Crixus' attempted reply was greeted with shouts and jeers from the senators, completely drowning him out.

To Niger's eminent satisfaction, at the conclusion of the truncated proceeding the senators unanimously concurred there existed no need for additional tedious debate. That noble body summarily voted to dissolve *Legio XVI Bestia* forthwith and create an entirely new legion manned with fresh conscripts. The legion would be stationed in Syria and commanded by Berossus, his abrupt elevation in rank reflecting the esteem with which the grateful senate now viewed him. Because the senators could think of nothing else to do with them, *Bestia's* few surviving legionnaires would be consigned to the arena as a special gift to the people of Rome.

Crixus and Junius were led from the *Curia* and returned to the Mamertine pit. Crixus was thereafter tortured, though he steadfastly refused to divulge the number or whereabouts of his *Bestia* companions. Junius evidently proved less resolute, however, for Crixus never saw him again.

The swift round-up of the surviving legionnaires followed.

CRIXUS' TINY BAND OF MEN WAS shackled in a cluster on the stone floor just inside the Gate of Life, though they were not alone. Confined with them were the frightened remnants of *Legio XVI Bestia* that had arrived separately in Rome with Berossus, including

Neocles and Senecio. All were lost in contemplative silence. The thunderous pandemonium emanating from the spectators outside was deafening, nearly unbearable. Adding to the clamor were the roars of lions, leopards, and bears caged nearby.

RATHER THAN BEING THROWN TOGETHER WITH the common criminals, the execution of the legionnaires was scheduled to occur following the mid-day lull, immediately prior to the start of the gladiatorial contests.

Earlier, the heavily-pregnant consort of a loathed Sythian king had, accompanied by the crowd's ecstatic applause, been forced to give unassisted birth on a small earthen island in the center of a specially-constructed artificial lagoon. While the newborn suckled at her mother's breast, a number of Nile crocodiles were prodded into the arena, where they raced toward the perceived safety of the lagoon. Unwisely, the new mother shrieked in horror. Cradling her mewling infant, she struggled to her feet and looked frantically about for refuge. For nothing.

A ten-foot crocodile splashed through the shallow water of the lagoon and, angling its head, slammed its jaws shut around her ankle.

With a howl, she dropped her child and instinctively attempted to free her leg from the creature's grip. The shrill cries of the infant, combined with her mother's fruitless struggle, succeeded only in attracting additional crocodiles. Two smaller reptiles grasped the child on either side and began to tug in opposite directions, tearing her body into two pieces. Other animals converged on the woman and dragged her into the water, where they began to feast. Audience members in the first few ranks of seats were gratified to hear, even above the din of the excitable crowd, the hollow thump of the crocodiles' jaws as they gulped down chunks of meat. While the reptiles were thus preoccupied, slaves armed with long spears entered the area through the Gate of Life and began to slaughter the animals by stabbing them repeatedly, to the wild applause of appreciative spectators.

Crixus dragged himself across the floor and pressed his face against a narrow crack between the wooden slats. Romans from across the Empire, giddy with excitement, filled to bursting the *Amphitheatrum Flamium.* They would undoubtedly boast to their grandchildren of their personal attendence at its inagural games, where they were privileged to personally witness the execution of the traitorous legionaires of *Legio XVI Bestia*, one of Rome's most storied legions.

Attempting to peer into the arena, he was able to discern only a milky sliver of light. His recent beating had broken the orbits of both eyes, rendering him nearly sightless.

“What do you see?” Neocles nervously whispered from behind him.

“Nothing.”

A slave warder had informed the legionnaires that their mass execution would follow the exhibition currently taking place in the arena, where a wooden post had been driven into the sand. The condemned, a murderer, was led out in fetters and a small hole punched into his stomach. A length of his intestines was threaded through the hole and nailed to the post. Four cages, each containing a starved leopard, their necks encircled by a hammered gold collar attached to a length of chain, were then conveyed into the arena. The animals were tethered equidistant around the post before being released, their restraints enabling them to approach the post within three feet. By straining and extending their paws, they could nearly touch it.

A leopard immediately charged the fettered man. He instinctively sprang to the opposite side of the post, a glistening rope of his intestines trailing, where another animal lunged at him. He darted away, tugging more entrails from the puncture wound in his stomach. Round-and-round the prisoner ran in a hopeless attempt to elude the enraged leopards, his intestines encircling the wooden post like a maypole. Viewers in the stands were nearly delirious with excitement, watching the pinioned victim run to-and-fro, wagering on which leopard would be the one to finally seize him.

“Do you know how we are to be killed?” Neocles quietly asked above the din.

Crixus turned away from the light. “No.”

Neocles paused. “I do not know how to die.”

“I do not think it requires knowledge and the pain will be fleeting,” Crixus responded, though not even he believed the latter.

“You have been a true and faithful friend,” Neocles said, his voice trembling.

Crixus placed his hand on the other man's shoulder. “And you, no less.”

SIXTEEN

"HOW FAR AWAY IS THE HERD?" Jocko inquired.

"A mile, maybe more," Ali indifferently informed him.

The two men slumped in collapsible field-chairs, staring moodily into the campfire. The remainder of their crew, drunk on home-brewed *waregi,* snored in bedrolls just beyond the fire light. A log popped, sending a sparkling stream of sparks into the night air.

"Any of 'em worth a shit?"

"A couple of juvenile bulls and some cows. Some nice hides."

Jocko nodded, absently. "We'll pop 'em in the morning."

Ali slid farther down in his chair. He struggled to remain awake. "You have buyers, mabwana?"

"Always buyers for good hides. But I'd like a few sets of bloody horns, too. It'll stoke a bidding war between the Chinks and the bar-stool sportsmen in Dar."

"That is not a problem," Ali shrugged. "I will get you horns."

Jocko swiveled his head and looked directly at his tracker. "While we're on the subject, what's the story with your bloody cousin? Is he just gonna continue to talk rubbish, or is he finally gonna come through with some fucking rhino horns? That's where the money is...not this nickle-and-dime bullshit."

"He is afraid of Alex Laidlaw, mabwana."

"Jesus fucking Christ!" Jocko exploded. "I told you before! Fuck him. The only reason I haven't shot the rhinos, myself, is because you told me your cousin would save me the trouble...zoop, zoop. Now you're telling me that he's getting cold feet. Fuck your cousin *and* Laidlaw."

Ali didn't respond.

"Find out from your cousin when Laidlaw's supposed to be at the preserve," Jocko ordered. "I don't want to have to fuck with him."

"My cousin said that no one knows when he will be there because he tells no one."

Jocko reflected a moment. "No matter. That makes it all the easier. We'll bag the bloody rhinos whenever we feel like it."

"What will you do about Laidlaw?"

"I'll fucking deal with him when the time comes."

BECAUSE HE HAD NO CLIENTS SCHEDULED, Laidlaw decided to go through the motions of checking in on Owusu and Okubuna. Under the circumstances, he figured it didn't make a hill of beans difference, one way or the other, whether they, or Mwanajuma, or the man in the moon, were informed of his intended visit. Accordingly, he telephoned the minister before departing for the Selous preserve.

"Anything in particular I should know before I leave?" he asked Mwanajuma.

"I don't understand."

"That makes two of us. I'm asking whether there are any other little surprises you'd like to share with me so I'm not made a fool again."

"The latest information I have is that the rhinos at both preserves are prospering. I know nothing beyond that."

"You mean the rhinos that you haven't already earmarked as perks for the hired help."

"There is no need to be snarky, Alex. Given a choice, only a fool would forego half-a-loaf for no loaf at all. You, of all people, should know that, since your livelihood depends on having an adequate supply of huntable game."

"The operative word being 'huntable'. Not slaughtering zoo animals like cows in a pasture."

"It is pointless to dispute semantics. It is enough that our rhino program holds great promise."

"'Promise' for who?"

"For everyone."

"Yep, it's good business. I'll give you that." Laidlaw dryly remarked.

"Don't be so naive, Alex. In life, compromises must be made. We do what is necessary."

"Seems to me the only things being compromised are the rhinos. Everybody else is getting rich off them."

"My game rangers are hardly 'rich'."

"Okay, let me restate it: *some* people are getting rich off of the rhinos. Kinda like *Animal Farm*, I guess...everybody's equal, but some are more equal than others."

"Men 'have dominion over the fish of the sea, and over the fowl of the air, and over the cattle, and over all the earth, and over every creeping thing that creepeth upon the earth'."

"Correct me if I'm wrong, but didn't God also order that non-virgins should be stoned to death? And that children who criticize their parents should be killed? And we can't forget that He also ordered that slaves should happily submit to their masters. Just so I'm clear, that's the God we're talking about, right? So, tell me, Robert: do you cherry-pick the Bible verses you like and just ignore the rest, or is it an all-or-nothing packaged deal?"

Mwanajuma deflected Laidlaw's question. "You're full of surprises, Alex," he chuckled, unperturbed. "I had no idea that you're also a Bible scholar."

"Far from it. But I *do* know that sketchy people a try to rationalize all the shit they pull by cloaking it in religion. They figure that if God green lights everything, it must be okay...witch burnings, for example."

"I have never burned any witches, but that is neither here nor there. It appears that we will simply have to agree to disagree," Mwanajuma amiably observed.

"I can be pretty disagreeable."

"I have no doubt, though I'm hopeful you will ultimately come 'round to a more realistic way of thinking."

THE SHORT FLIGHT TO THE INTERIOR OF THE SELOUS was uneventful. Jahi, rather than Israel, was slouched against the bakkie when the Cessna touched down on the dusty airstrip.

"The minister radio you that I was coming?" Laidlaw asked as the airplane roared skyward after depositing him. He tossed his bag into the rear of the vehicle.

Jahi ground-out his cigarette and climbed into the driver's seat. "He said you would come...here or Bukoba."

"Where's Israel?"

"Camp." Jahi depressed the clutch and started the engine. He shoved the transmission into gear.

"Everything *status quo*?"

Jahi looked quizzically at him. "Why would it not be? What did the minister tell you?"

"Not a damned thing. I was hoping you would."

"I'll tell you whatever you wish." Jahi eased-off the clutch and the bakkie lurched forward.

"The minister doesn't have a problem with your talking to me?" Laidlaw responded with surprise.

Jahi slowed as they approached a washout in the middle of the roadway. "I am obliged to follow the minister's orders as they pertain to the care of the rhinos. He does not control who I talk to." Once clear of the impediment, he depressed the accelerator and the bakkie spurted onward.

"And Israel?"

Jahi answered without looking at Laidlaw. "Israel speaks for himself."

"A BOER?"

"From South Africa. There may be others, though I know only of the Boer and his trackers."

Laidlaw and Jahi sat at a rickety table outside the latter's cinder-block headquarters, drinking cold bottles of local beer. Israel was, according to Jahi, in the field, checking on the rhinos.

"Mwanajuma told me game rangers are permitted to supplement their income by shooting animals, including rhinos, and selling their parts."

Jahi shook his head vigorously. "That is a lie. We are charged with protecting the animals, not shooting them. We would be fired if we did that. Only the Boer is allowed to hunt on the preserve."

"You've actually seen him?" Laidlaw asked, incredulously. "The Boer, hunting here on the preserve, I mean."

"Many times, though he has not shot any rhinos. Only black-faced impala, kudu, sable, roan, eland, wart hog, I think. No buffalo or elephant because they are too dangerous," he scoffed.

"Why don't you and Israel stop him?"

Jahi shrugged. "The minister instructed us not to interfere with the Boer. I have a wife and children."

"Does he also hunt in Bukoba?"

"I don't know, though there is more game here in the Selous.

"Do you know the Boer's name or whether he lives in Dar?"

"No."

Laidlaw's beer had grown warm. He tossed the half-empty bottle into the burn-barrel and popped the cap off a fresh bottle. He leaned back in his chair to think. Assuming Jahi was telling the truth, Mwanajuma and at least one hunter, an unidentified Boer, were full-blown partners in the poaching biz. Further, the minister was attempting to deflect any suspicion of malfeasance away from himself, onto the game rangers in the field...plausible deniability.

"Why are you telling me this *now*?" he finally asked.

"Are you not supposed to protect the animals?"

"Just as you are."

"You do not have a wife and children that you are responsible for."

"That's true, but why tell me all this now? Why not the first time I was here?"

"You were from the ministry. I did not know you."

"But now you do?"

Jahi grinned. "I asked around. "Everyone says Alex Laidlaw is incorruptible."

"Whoever told you that obviously doesn't know me very well. No one is incorruptible."

"You're right," Jahi concurred. "But, deserved or not, that is your reputation. Maybe the minister just hasn't yet offered you an adequate bribe yet."

"Yeah, maybe. But, aren't you worried that I'll report this conversation to him?"

"I am not worried for myself, but for my family."

"So, why confide in me at all?"

Jahi drained his beer and looked directly at Laidlaw. "If not you, who? If not now, when?"

Laidlaw nodded thoughtfully before responding. "When was the Boer last here?"

Jahi looked absently into the distance while he thought. "Three weeks, maybe one month."

"Does the ministry give you a heads up when he's coming?"

"No. We only know he is here because we see him and his trackers out in the field."

"So, he could show up at any time?" Jahi nodded. "He drives to the preserve in a bakkie?"

Though remote, the interior of the Selous is accessible via a handful of rutted dirt roads, known and utilized exclusively by hunters.

Jahi nodded again.

"Have you talked to the Bakoba ranger lately? Has the Boer been up there?"

"I do not talk to him."

Laidlaw audibly sighed. Exactly the shit storm he wanted no part of.

THE INDOLENT LION DOZED ON HIS SIDE in the shade of a mopani tree, oblivious of the men monitoring him from 300 yards away. His ears flicked, and the tuft of black hair on the tip his tail twitched, as he slept.

"He is not yet fully grown, mabwana...maybe 170 kilograms."

Jocko squinted through binoculars, his elbows propped on the hood of the bakkie. "Yeah, he'll do," he muttered. "Where's the rest of the pride?"

"He has no pride yet because he is still a juvenile. He will get his own pride when he gets bigger."

"How's his mane?"

Ali continued to survey the insouciant animal through his own binoculars before replying. "Thin."

Jocko lowered his binoculars. "Well, it may bloody-well be thin, but my pocketbook is getting thinner by the day."

"We will find better lions, mabwana."

"Fuck that. I got buyers waitin' in line for a lion. I'm banging him."

Jocko stepped to the rear of the bakkie and grabbed his Kalashnikov from the back seat.

"That will not do, mabwana," Ali cautioned. "He is too far away."

"Then, get me fucking closer."

"The lion will wake if we try to drive closer and he will run."

"So, what the bloody hell am I supposed to do?" Jocko scowled.

"The other rifle is better."

Jocko stomped to the rear of the bakkie, where he switched his AR for an antiquated .303 British Enfield. He slightly retracted its bolt and looked to confirm the presence of a cartridge in the chamber.

He returned to the front of the vehicle and squinted in the direction of the mopani tree. "He still there?"

"Still sleeping, mabwana," Ali murmured without lowering his binoculars.

"He'll be sleepin' permanently in about two seconds."

Jocko propped the Enfield against the side of the bakkie before climbing into its passenger's seat. Lifting the rifle by its muzzle, he settled into the seat and laid the Enfield's barrel across the top of the bakkie's windshield in order to steady his aim.

"Fucker," he said under his breath as he drew a bead on the lion and flicked the safety off.

The recoil from the first booming shot caused the Enfield to bounce from the windshield. The 215 grain steel-clad bullet zipped directly over Ali's head and plowed into the earth three feet short of the sleeping lion.

"Low," Ali laconically advised, still looking through his binoculars.

Jocko realigned his rifle, ejected the spent cartridge, and settled in for a second shot. "Fucker," he said again through gritted teeth as he took aim. The lion continued to doze without care.

Jocko's second shot struck the animal squarely in the stomach. Instantly awake, the animal leapt to its feet with a roar before swapping ends and racing away.

"Son of a bitch!" Jocko snarled. "That shot should have put him down!"

Ali lowered his binoculars and turned to look at Jocko. "He is gut-shot. We will now have to track him," he said with disgust.

The other man nonchalantly ejected the second cartridge case. "That's why I pay you."

LAIDLAW NEEDED SOME TIME ALONE. He'd appropriated one of the bakkies from the the rangers' compound and was driving aimlessly around the preserve when he heard the shots. He slammed on the brakes and stared in the direction from which they came, listening intently. Although regulated sport hunting was permitted in certain sections of the greater Selous Reserve, it was strictly prohibited within the confines of the rhino preserve itself.

Based on nothing more than the sound, Laidlaw was certain that both shots emanated from a medium-caliber rifle discharged nearby, probably less than a quarter-mile away. The shots couldn't have been fired by either Jahi or Israel because, as far as Laidlaw knew, both men remained back at the compound, more than six miles away. The trespasser was undoubtedly a poacher.

Laidlaw reached into the rear of the vehicle and lifted his .375 to the front. It was only then that he realized his palms were damp and his heart was starting to pound. He was a professional hunter of animals, not people.

Despite his apprehensions, Laidlaw cranked the steering wheel in the direction of the rifle shots and released the bakkie's clutch. If not him, who? If not now, when?

ALI STRAIGHTENED AFTER examining the earth where the lion had been lying. "There's not much blood here, mabwana. He will be difficult to track if he leaves no blood trail."

"Well, I guess you better bloody well get crackin'," Jocko replied. "If you lose that fuckin' lion, it's gonna come out of your hide."

Ali looked about the area and pointed. "He ran in that direction. We should wait for his wound to stiffen before we begin to track him. He will have no more fight left in him and will try to hide."

"Whatever you say, mate," Jocko shrugged. "You're the expert. I don't care what the fuck you do as long as you don't lose him." He turned and strode to the bakkie, parked nearby. Ali trailed him in silence.

FROM BEHIND A TOWERING TERMITE MOUND, Laidlaw keenly watched the two men through binoculars, one of whom he immediately recognized as Jocko Vanderbeeke, his garrulous tablemate from the rhino symposium. Though Vanderbeeke's black companion was unknown to him, it was obvious the two men were responsible for discharging the rifle, the report of which Laidlaw heard a short time before. It was equally apparent they were searching for an animal they'd just poached but, for whatever reason, failed to recover. Laidlaw had no idea whether Vanderbeeke was the "Boer" spoken of the previous afternoon by Jahi, though it seemed probable. The immediate question was, what now?

Laidlaw could request the aid of the two game rangers by radioing them from the bakkie, but what would be the point? According to Jahi, the Boer enjoyed *carte blanche* to poach with impunity anywhere on the preserve. If true, neither ranger was likely to intervene. Laidlaw was, in fact, far from confident the rangers would even bother to acknowledge his request for assistance.

It appeared that Laidlaw was on his own. He returned to his vehicle, ill at ease.

VANDERBEEKE AND ALI WERE SITTING were sitting in their bakkie, drinking canned beer. They were shocked to see Laidlaw emerge from the bush and stroll toward them. He'd parked out of sight 75 yards away and carried his .375 in the crook of his arm.

"You boys doin' some shooting?" he casually greeted them. "I guess you didn't know this is a wildlife preserve. Shooting and hunting is prohibited."

Ali frowned at Vanderbeeke, who maintained his sangfroid.

“Well, fuck me runnin',” the latter grinned. “If it ain't Alex Laidlaw! Who'da guessed we'd run into you out here in the bush! You're a long way from home, mate.”

Laidlaw halted 100 feet away and transferred his rifle to his other arm.

“I was in the neighborhood and heard shots. Figured I'd see what was up.”

"Yeah, damned if we didn't hear 'em, too. Didn't we, Ali?"

The tracker didn't respond.

Jocko gestured with his beer toward Laidlaw's rifle and smiled, coldly. “Thought you said there was no shooting here, mate.”

“I wasn't shooting. You were.”

“We didn't know there was no shooting allowed here,” Ali quickly interjected. “We will leave.”

“Yeah, we were just shootin' at some cans,” Vanderbeeke added, holding his beer aloft. “See? No need to be such a hard-ass, mate.” He smiled again.

“Doesn't matter,” Laidlaw said. “You both hafta leave.”

Vanderbeeke turned to Ali. “He must think we been bagging tuskers! Show him what we been up to.” He tilted his head to indicate the spot where the lion had been sleeping.

Ali flung his empty beer can over his shoulder and it clanked into the rear of the bakkie. He hopped out and looked expectantly at Laidlaw.

“Over here,” he mumbled.

Laidlaw glanced quizzically at Jocko, who popped open another beer and reclined in the bakkie's passenger seat. He displayed no apparent intention of moving.

Laidlaw shifted the weight of his rifle and began to trail Ali, unsure of what he was being shown. After taking some twenty steps, he heard a sound behind him, stopped, and instinctively turned.

Jocko stood on the bakkie's floorboard holding his AR. It was pointed at Laidlaw.

“"You son of a bitch!" Laidlaw snarled. He began to raise his rifle.

"I wouldn't do that, mate. I've got the drop on you, as you Yanks say in your cowboy movies." Jocko tipped his head to one side. “Move away from him,” he ordered Ali.

After a moment of confused hesitation, the tracker complied.

“Do not do this, mabwana,” he implored. Vanderbeeke ignored him.

Jocko looked icily at Laidlaw. “Ya know, mate, I figured you for an arsehole the first time I laid eyes on you. But arseholes I can handle 'cause most of me mates is arseholes. That ain't the problem. The problem is *meddling* arseholes, which is what *you* are. But it ain't nuthin' personal...I actually kinda like you. It's just business, mate.”

In a flash, Laidlaw realized he had two choices: shoot it out with Jocko or dive for cover. Because it would require a minumum of two or three seconds to shoulder and aim his rifle, shooting it out seemed a bad idea. While he was fumbling, all Jocko had to do was pull the trigger on his AR and Laidlaw would instantly be dead. Even if, by some miracle, he managed to kill Jocko before the latter shot him, Ali remained a wild card with which Laidlaw would still have to contend. Under the circumstances, diving for cover seemed Laidlaw's only realistic option.

He flung himself into the brush and rolled the instant Jocko squeezed the trigger of his AR, releasing a stream of steel-cored bullets. Ali, too, leapt aside, mindful of Jocko's dubious marksmanship.

Laidlaw pressed his body to the ground, a searing pain blazing down his left leg. Though he still clutched his rifle, he lay atop it and dared not lift himself upward to free it, as doing so would expose him to Jocko. He had no idea where Ali was.

Laidlaw struggled to slow his panicked breathing. His heart pounded in his chest and sweat poured from his body. He cautiously shifted his head to peek through the bushes toward Jocko.

Jocko still stood in the bakkie, peering about. Laidlaw laid his head on the earth and, with agonizing slowness, slid his hand down to his left leg. His trousers were wet and sticky and his leg was beginning to throb.

One of Jocko's errant bullets had apparently managaged to hit Laidlaw as he dove for cover, though he had no idea how badly he was hurt. Even if it merely nicked his femoral artery, however, Laidlaw would bleed out in only a few minutes. Though the adrenaline that surged through his body had so far managed to supress most of the pain, that salubrious effect wouldn't last long, depending on the location and severity of his wound.

Laidlaw glanced slowly downward, toward his injured leg. His trousers and the ground were both soaked with blood.

Shit.

He inched his head upward a millimeter and looked in Jocko's direction again, unsure what to do. As quickly as he did so, he instinctively ducked as the South African began shooting indiscriminately into the bushes. Bullets sounding like angry hornets ripped through the brush and plowed into the earth near Laidlaw; twigs and fragments of leaves cascaded downward.

"I know you're hit, mate," Jocko called out. "I ain't coming in there after you but there ain't no sense bein' a martyr. I got plenty of beer and can wait here all day. Hell, why don't you come out and join me for a cold one? Ali, get your black ass out here!" He released another torrent of gunfire from his AK. The bullets flung dirt onto Laidlaw's prostrate body as they thudded into the ground near him.

Laidlaw's breathing had slowed somewhat but the burning in his leg was intensifying by the second. He was also becoming lightheaded.

His life was quickly ebbing away and he knew it.

If he could snap-off a quick shot, he might be able to kill Jocko before the bastard mowed him down with his AK. But he had to do it now, before he passed out from blood loss.

Notwithstanding that he could no longer feel his legs, Laidlaw gritted his teeth and floundered to his knees as he simultaneously attempted to shoulder his rifle. But his mangled leg refused to support his body weight and he immediately crashed to the ground.

Jocko didn't hesitate. He squeezed the AR's trigger and sent a torrent of slugs into Laidlaw. Powerless to evade them, the bullets sliced through Laidlaw's body as he struggled to again raise himself from the earth.

"Problem solved." Jocko leaned over and placed the AR on the driver's seat before plopping back down. Ali emerged from the brush and looked on in stunned horror.

"What do we do now, mabwana?" he quietly asked.

"He's got a nice rifle. Bring it to me then drag him into the bushes. The hyenas and buzzards will take care of him."

"What about the rangers?"

"What about 'em? They take their marching order from Mwanajuma. They ain't gonna do shit."

ISRAEL AND JAHI DID NOT UNDERTAKE to locate Laidlaw for more than 24 hours, assuming he was simply fly-camping somewhere in the preserve. It was only when Laidlaw failed, after multiple attempts, to respond to the two-way radio in his bakkie that they halfheartedly decided to look for him. Locating Laidlaw's vehicle would be a simple matter because it contained a GPS unit; hopefully, he was camped somewhere nearby.

The two game rangers resented having to babysit Laidlaw because they had work to do. *He* was supposed to be the world-famous, hotshot outdoorsman; they were just nameless functionaries tasked with cleaning up rhino shit out in the middle of nowhere.

They climbed into the remaining bakkie, confirmed Laidlaw's coordinates, and headed into the field. According to the GPS, he was less than ten miles away.

"Did he tell you he was going to camp overnight?" Israel asked Jahi as they pulled from the compound. Jahi merely shook his head...he didn't bring up his earlier conversation with Laidlaw.

The men chatted amiably as the bakkie bounced along the rutted dirt road, leaving a cloud of dusk in its wake. Guinea fowl scattered from beneath its tyres and a small herd of prehistoric-looking black wildebeest idly watched from 200 yards away.

The GPS tracker enabled them to locate Laidlaw's abandoned vehicle in less than three quarters of an hour. As they approached, Jahi drew his partner's attention to the column of vultures that soared in the thermal updraft directly overhead.

Israel hopped from the bakkie before it was completely stopped and looked around. Seeing no one in the immediate vicinity, he shouted Laidlaw's name.

No response. Jahi switched the bakkie's engine off and stepped to the ground.

"Someone else was here," Israel announced as Jahi approached him.

The latter squatted to examine tyre prints in the loose soil. He looked up at Israel.

"Yesterday."

"How many?"

Jahi stood and slowly crisscrossed the area, scrutinizing the earth as he walked.

"Two," he finally said.

Israel returned to Laidlaw's bakkie. Someone had obviously rummaged through it. Aside from Laidlaw's rifle, the vehicle's tool box, extra petrol can, spare tyre, and CB radio were missing. Nor was there any camping gear. He looked at Jahi.

"He's dead."

"ARE YOU CERTAIN? ABSOLUTELY no doubt?" Mwanajuma spoke into the speaker of his office telephone. Leo was on the other end, having just relayed news of Laidlaw's death. "Call Abe Najama and arrange a press conference. Tell him only that professional hunter and world-famous conservationist, Alexander Laidlaw, was apparently ambushed by poachers in the Selous. The Ministry of Wildlife is sickened by this horrifying news and will issue a formal statement as soon as more information becomes available. In the meantime, the ministry will not rest until the villains responsible for the monstrous crime have been apprehended and punished."

He silently nodded as he listened to his factotum's response. "Yes, yes, good. Keep me in the loop and say nothing of this to anyone other than Najama."

Mwanajuma punched the illuminated button on the face of the telephone, terminating the call, and leaned back in his chair. He was perplexed.

Notwithstanding Leo's call, he could scarcely believe that Laidlaw was, in fact, dead. Even if true, he was frustrated because, at least so far, he knew absolutely nothing of the circumstances: accident? murder? At the end of the day, though, the minister was a realist...it is impossible to survive in politics and not be a realist.

Laidlaw's holier-than-thou attitude toward the entire rhino project, and his unwilling, tepid participation in it, were problematical from the get-go and getting worse. His boorish moral crusading was insufferable and it was probably only a matter of time before Laidlaw unilaterally decided to make donors privy to the inner workings of the rhino project, irredeemably damaging its reputation and undoing all the good work it was accomplishing. Such temerity could not be allowed to happen.

Mwanajuma unconsciously smiled. Perhaps things have a way of working themselves out after all.

SEVENTEEN

AFTER HURRIEDLY VOTING TO DISBAND *Legio XVI Bestia*, the senate reconsidered its rushed decision and authorized the creation of another African legion: *Legio XX Libya*, conveniently garrisoned in what was once Carthage, denominated "Carthago" since its final destruction by the Romans in 146 BCE. The *Amphitheatrum Flavium* and hundreds of other arenas, big and small, spread across the Empire still required a steady supply of exotic animals, and Africa remained the most productive source for them.

The new legion formed at the urging of Berossus, *Legio II Syria Palaestina*, departed Rome for *Caesarea Maritima,* the capital of Roman *Judaea*, in the spring. While the legionnaires would be forced to march overland nearly 3,000 miles to their destination, their commander, the recently promoted and retitled

Marcus Berossus Magnus, chose to travel in greater comfort and leisure via the *Mare Nostrum.* At roughly the same time as *Legio II Syria Palaestina* left Rome for the East, *Legio XX Libya* boarded ships at Ostia for the relatively short voyage to its new home on the northern shore of Africa.

DUNN HADN'T HEARD FROM LAIDLAW in more than a week and was feeling antsy. Because his friend had previously provided him the security code to the vault where it was stored, Dunn decided to retrieve Laidlaw's dagger and continue researching its provenance while he awaited contact from Africa.

He looked forward to surprising Laidlaw with fresh revelations about the dagger when next they met.

The End

TERMS OF USE

WF Waldrip and his licensors do not warrant or guarantee that the functions contained in the work will meet your requirements or that its operation will be uninterrupted or error free. Neither WF Waldrip nor his licensors shall be liable to you or anyone else for any inaccuracy, error or omission, regardless of cause, in the work or for any damages resulting therefrom. WF

Waldrip has no responsibility for the content of any information accessed through the work. Under no circumstances shall WF Waldrip and/or his licensors be liable for any indirect, incidental, special, punitive, consequential or similar damages that result from the use of or inability to use the work, even if any of them has been advised of the possibility of such damages. This limitation of liability shall apply to any claim or cause whatsoever whether such claim or cause arises in contract, tort or otherwise.

The author gratefully acknowledges the copyrighted or trademarked status and trademark owners of the following mentioned in this work of fiction:

Airbus, Air France, Beefeater Gin, Biblioteque Nationale, British Museum, Cellini Moonphase, Cessna, Citroen, Cointreau, Coke, Coleman, Crocodile Hunter, CZ, Diet Coke, Enfield, Ford, Four Seasons, Green Chartreuse, Grimbergen, Harry's New York Bar, Hilton, Hugo Boss, Jeep, Jet Bridge, Jungle Jim, La Aroma de Cuba Reserva Pomposa, Leica, Mauser, Nissan, Paddington Bear, Pornhub, Ramon Allones Superiores LCDH, Red Bull, Remington, Rigby, Savoy Cocktail Book, Serengeti Lager, Stefano Ricci, Styrofoam, Swarovski, Tiffany, Uhuru Lager, Weatherby Mark V, XHamster

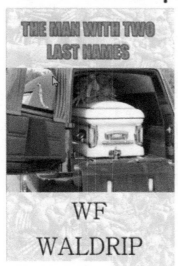

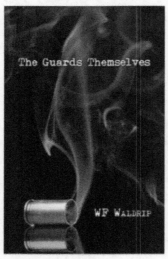

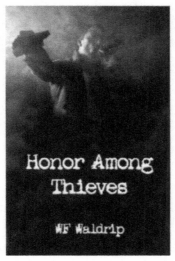

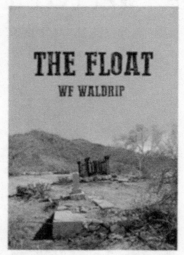